NEW YORK MINUTE

www.bobmayer.com

This is a work of fiction. Names, characters, places, and incidents either are the product of the author's imagination or are used fictitiously, and any resemblance to actual persons living or dead, business establishments, events, or locales is entirely coincidental.

New York Minute by Bob Mayer
COPYRIGHT © 2019 by Bob Mayer

ISBN: 9781621253358

NEW YORK MINUTE

By

BOB MAYER

Dedication:

**To Jimmy Breslin and Pete Hamill;
for so many years the voice of the people of New
York City.**

Sample Praise for Bob Mayer's thrillers:

Eyes of the Hammer (Green Berets)
Stephen Coonts: "A scorcher of a novel. Mayer had me hooked from the very first page."
WEB Griffin: "Exciting and authentic. Author Mayer, a Green Beret himself, gave me a vivid look at the world of the Army's Special Forces. Don't miss this one."

The Line (Shadow Warriors)
Publishers Weekly: "Mayer has crafted a thriller in the tradition of John Grisham's *The Firm*."

Dragon Sim-13 (Green Berets)
Kirkus Reviews: "Fascinating, imaginative and nerve-wracking. Mayer's tough, businesslike soldiers again include a tough, businesslike female."
Publisher's Weekly. "A pulsing technothriller. A nail-biter in the best tradition of adventure fiction."
Journal of US Special Operations: "This is one book you can trust."

Synbat (Green Berets)
Kirkus Reviews: "Action packed entertainment."
Assembly Magazine (Association of Graduates, West Point): "Mayer has stretched the limits of the military action novel as this is also a gripping detective story. Mayer brings an accurate depiction of military life to this book which greatly enhances its credibility."

Lost Girls (The Cellar)
Publishers Weekly: "Excellent writing and well-drawn, appealing characters help make this another taut, crackling read from Mayer."

Eternity Base (Green Berets)
Midwest Book Review: "Unlike most military stories this will appeal to general audiences as a fine thriller. Highly recommended, indeed."

Cut Out (Green Berets)
Kirkus Reviews: "Sinewy writing enhances this already potent action fix."
Southern Book Trade: "Clancy, Coonts and Brown might have the market cornered when it comes to hardware, but Mayer knows what

all Infantry types will tell you: it's the soldier who makes all the difference."

Bodyguard of Lies (The Cellar)
"Heart-racing, non-stop action that is difficult to put down."—Mystery News
"Thelma and Louise go clandestine."—Kirkus Reviews

The Rock
Kirkus: "A crackling science thriller in the vein of Crichton."
Publishers Weekly: "The best combination of science fiction and technothriller this year."

Hello from the gutters of N.Y.C. which are filled with dog manure, vomit,
stale wine, urine and blood.
Hello from the sewers of N.Y.C. which swallow up these delicacies when
they are washed away by the sweeper trucks.
Hello from the cracks in the sidewalks of N.Y.C. and from the ants that
dwell in these cracks and feed in the dried blood of the dead that has settled
into the cracks.
Son of Sam letter to Jimmy Breslin, May 1977

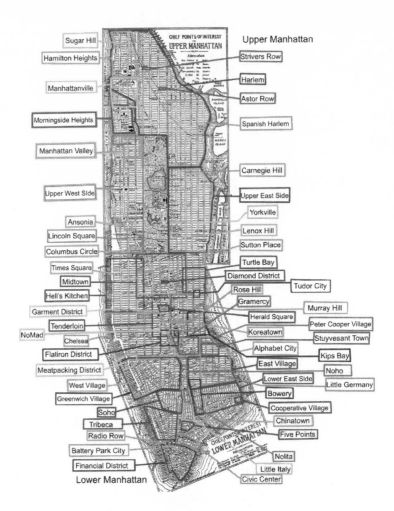

Thursday Night, 7 July 1977

WEST VILLAGE, MANHATTAN

On the far side of a lot cluttered with rotting garbage, dumped furniture and torched cars, the abandoned, elevated West Side Highway loomed like a curtain about to go down on New York City. Beyond, on the Hudson River waterfront, squatted the Christopher Street Pier, once the berth for classic ocean liners and cargo ships, but now dark, derelict and a haven for both furtive and brazen figures meeting to do what they dared not elsewhere. Most of Manhattan was brightly lit, but the waterfront was darkness, with the lights of New Jersey farther away than the width of the river.

William Kane waited on a slice, extra pepperoni, when he spotted a wraith he pegged as trouble approach from the darkness underneath the West Side Highway. The pizza joint was tiny, dirty and Kane wasn't optimistic about what was warming up in the oven, but he'd been following Alfonso Delgado all evening, it was almost midnight, and this was the only available food west of Washington Street.

Kane sat at one of two sticky surfaced Formica tables crowded along the wall, leaving barely enough room for someone to slide past to the counter. One of the long fluorescent lights was out, tilting the light in the joint. It was hot and oppressively humid. The absentee owner wasn't going to waste money on air-conditioning with two ovens going full blast and a single employee slaving away in the midst of a sweltering New York City July. Kane's chair was angled toward the propped open door, back to the wall.

The junkie entered reeking of sweat, desperation and the aforementioned trouble. Not just because he was strung out, a person couldn't swing one of the dead rats by the piers without running into the like, but also by the tense hitch in his shoulders and the one hand in the pocket of the stained olive drab Army field jacket. He was dirty white with filthy long hair of indeterminate color, scraggly beard, tall and thin in his worn-out, done with life, mid-thirties. A muscle on the left side of his face danced to the dark beat of his subconscious.

The stained field jacket presented history a former soldier like Kane could interpret via the subdued patches: the winged dagger of the 173rd Airborne on the right shoulder and Screaming Eagle of the 101st on the left. These indicated combat and current assignments, although both were in this guy's past. The standard embroidered US Army tag above the right pocket. The man earned a smart point for removing the nametag above the left pocket given the not-as-dirty-strip of exposed jacket along with the outline where the name and a combat infantry badge and jump wings had recently resided.

Kane hoped the youngster behind the counter wasn't willing to die for minimum wage and paltry tips.

The junkie eyed Kane and shifted to the pizza maker. "The cash. Now. On the counter."

Kane was only slightly better dressed than the junkie, but he was cleaner. Jungle fatigue pants dyed black with pockets on the thighs. The cuffs were banded over the tops of faded green canvas uppers and worn black leather jungle boots. He wore a gray t-shirt, covered by a slightly too long unbuttoned, blue denim shirt, with the sleeves rolled up as far as they would go. A rust-stained, green canvas map case rested on the Formica table.

Kane was six feet, lean, with an angular face smeared by two days of not shaving and topped with thick, black hair, poorly cut and not recently combed. Thirty-two hard years had sprinkled some gray in the hair and chiseled lines in his face. His eyes were green, a gift from his father's side of the family.

"Oh, come on," the pizza maker said. "Gimme a break. Second time this month and it's only the seventh."

The junkie pulled a small nickel-plated revolver out of the pocket and jabbed it around. "The cash." He checked Kane once more. "Don't get any ideas."

Kane had his hands flat on the map case. "I've run out of them today, sarge. I just want my slice. Got places to go. People to see."

"Yeah, don't we all," the junkie said. The revolver was crap; one of those cheap .22 caliber pieces the press titled 'Saturday Night Specials'. Their more realistic moniker was 'suicide specials'.

The pizza maker opened the register and slapped an anemic cluster of greasy bills on the counter. "That's all."

"The change."

"Oh, come on," the pizza maker said, displaying a limited verbal range of outrage. He grabbed a paper cup and clattered it with coins from the register's tray.

The junkie stuffed the bills in a pocket. Picked up the cup of change with his free hand. He turned toward Kane. Glanced at the map case. Kane looked him in the eyes, his face passive, and waited for the junkie's dancing pupils to focus.

The junkie evaluated through jumbled synapses. Trickles of sweat slid down his face. Kane arched an eyebrow and leaned forward slightly, enough to let the denim shirt fall to the side and display the rough grip for a .45 automatic in an un-topped holster on his left hip. "How you doing, Sky Soldier?"

The junkie's face twitched, but he gave a slight nod at the moniker for the paratroopers of the 173rd Airborne Brigade. "I've had better days."

"You probably want a few more," Kane said. "I've seen people kill with a twenty-two but they were experts and knew exactly where to shoot and were closer than you and I. With a forty-five, it's like depth charges and nuclear bombs, I only gotta get a piece of you and the rest is going with it."

"Yeah," the junkie said, still evaluating. He squinted. "That blood on the map case?"

"Old blood. Second of the five-oh-third."

"Fourth of the five-oh-third," the junkie automatically responded with his 173rd battalion designation. He pondered the course and length of the rest of his life for another moment, desired it to be a bit longer, and departed, gun in one hand, change in the other, still drawing air.

"What da' fuck," the pizza maker said to Kane. "You got a gun?"

Kane stood and looped the strap for the map case over his left shoulder to hang on his right hip, opposite the .45. "You think I'm gonna pull a gun on a guy over this?" Kane's accent was remnant Bronx, muted by over a decade and a half away from the city.

"He took everything from the register."

"The money's your problem," Kane said. "I'm talking about my slice."

"What da' fuck you carry a gun for if you ain't gonna use it?"

Kane frowned. "Habit? The frown twisted the end of a knotted sliver of scar tissue stretching from under the thick hair on the right side of his head. "My slice is done; I don't like it hot."

"The money ain't mine. It's my boss's."

"Not your problem then."

"He's gonna dock my pay," the pizza maker complained. "And why didn't he take your wallet? Or your bag?"

"He's not that far gone," Kane said. "He wasn't going to shoot and he didn't want to die. How much did he get?"

"Eight-two dollars. And the change. Maybe another five."

Kane pulled out a money clip, extracted six twenties. "He didn't take your tips," Kane noted, as he stuffed the bills into the coffee can that held lonely singles and loose change, mostly pennies. "That's the problem with being high. You miss things." He nodded toward the oven. "My slice?"

Muttering, the pizza maker removed the slice with his peel, slid it on a thin paper plate, which was immediately soaked with greasy oil. Kane picked it up with his right hand and folded in half. Took a bite while avoiding the run off.

It was crappy as expected but it was pizza and this was New York City.

He exited Dino's, as proclaimed by a muted neon sign, and vaguely vowed never to return. He drew the .45 with his left hand and flicked off the custom ambidextrous safety with his thumb. He stepped to the darkness at the side of the door to avoid being silhouetted against the lights. No sign of the junkie.

Kane took another bite. His boss, Toni Marcelle, called this R&D. Research and development. Except it never went beyond the research phase for him; the developing was her expertise. This was where he'd followed Alfonso Delgado, traveling alone, from a mob hangout, the Triangle Social Club on Sullivan Street in Tribeca. It was a good news, bad news situation. Good for Toni in her development of the divorce case that Delgado ended up here, but not so great on the research end for Kane. The norm.

Even though Kane lived eight blocks away, he hadn't been on or inside any of the piers in years. He had vague memories of his father driving the family down from the Bronx to see Grandma, his father's mother, off on a stately ocean liner to visit the 'old country'. The ocean liner days were long past, a casualty of LaGuardia and Kennedy Airports, another part of New York City's history overtaken by technology and time.

The West Side Highway, formerly the main car route along the west edge of the island of Manhattan, had been closed for four years from 23rd Street to the southern end. Ever since an overloaded northbound dump truck dropped through the roadway not far from here and it was reluctantly decided by the city that the road might be unsafe. New York was not a car friendly city, not just because of the terrible condition of the roads but the vertical density of the population. To keep a car in Manhattan was an expensive proposition.

The extensive subway network was the arteries that moved the people, but wasn't in much better shape than the West Side Highway. Subway cars were lathered in graffiti making it impossible to see out the windows. The PA system announcement for upcoming stations was a garbled crackle of static that seemed a taunt by burnt out conductors rather than an attempt at conveying location. Crime was rampant and the transit police traveled in pairs. Nevertheless, native New Yorkers made it the most traveled train system in the country.

Kane's right hand was slippery with oil when he finished the slice. He wiped it on his pants, staining the black darker. He walked underneath the West Side Highway, between rusting iron stanchions holding up the remains of the roadway, moving from city light to abandoned darkness. Kane paused on the far side a few moments. Checked if his presence spooked anything. He looked up, but the glow from the city behind him, diffused by the humid air and smog, hid the stars from view.

The pier extended into the polluted Hudson. It consisted of a long row of attached buildings and warehouses merging into one. Some had been passenger areas, others for freight. Now it was a maze of rotting wood and rusting metal sprawled on top of concrete slabs perched on pilings pounded into the river bottom.

Kane reached into the map case and retrieved night vision goggles. Turned them on, waited for the battery to boot, then slipped them over his head. He tightened the rubber straps as he did a survey. Everything on the interior screen was outlined in two-dimensional shades of green and the light was enhanced. The lack of depth perception was a drawback, but a worthwhile trade in order to see into the dark corners where the lions and tigers and bears preferred to hide.

The standard New York cacophony was behind him: sirens, traffic, car horns, the never-ending rumble of the City That Never Sleeps but was currently slumbering uneasily from fear of a gunman dubbed Son of Sam. Ahead was relatively quiet. Kane hefted the .45, finger resting on the outside edge of the trigger guard. The hammer was back and there was a round in the chamber and a full magazine in the grip, not approved for amateurs, which Kane was anything but.

The concrete floor was littered with debris so Kane slid his feet along, the way he'd done at night on patrol in the Central Highlands and on recon over the border in Cambodia, every nerve alert for a tripwire, expecting a burst of AK fire to shred his chest with 7.62mm.

Kane paused and took a few breaths.

There were different noises when he entered the largest building on the Christopher Street Pier and the sounds of the city dimmed. Below, the Hudson River gurgled and slapped against the pilings. Ahead there were grunts and murmurs and gasps in the darkness. The rhythmic smack of flesh against flesh.

The smell was rotting wood, salt water, pollution, urine, sweat and sex.

Fuck Alfonso Delgado for making him come to this place. Kane briefly played with the idea of killing him, but he could more realistically imagine Toni giving him shit: *what the hell, Kane? A dead guy can't pay alimony.*

This was New York, not Vietnam, and Kane had made a vow about ever killing. Again.

A flashing light from a beacon on the Jersey side of the Hudson cast abrupt shadows through the broken windows and fractured walls into the interior every ten seconds. It momentarily flared out the goggles each time. Kane waited through four iterations until he had the rhythm of the troublesome light.

Fuck New Jersey too.

Hushed conversations murmured, but it was mainly animal/human noises: raw, uninhibited sex. Two men were fucking to his left, one bent over the waist, the other standing behind holding a leash attached to a collar around the first man's neck. They wore only boots and leather caps. Two more, similarly undressed, waited in line, stroking their cocks in anticipation. He saw them and three seconds later they saw him in the strobe of light. They ignored and he returned the favor since none were Delgado.

Kane went deeper into the illicit abyss. A light flared in the distant darkness, a blaze in the goggles, someone lighting up a cig or joint. Kane thought of a sniper waiting in the dark for that brief illumination and squeezing off a bullet directly into the spot, putting an exclamation point on the Surgeon General's warning.

An odd, snapping sound caught his attention. There was a glow coming through a gap in the interior wall. Kane turned the NVG's off and pushed them up on his head. Through the hole he saw several candles flickering in a circle. In the center, a naked man was tiptoed on a two-foot high wood crate. A rope was cinched around his neck and went over a ceiling strut, terminating at a small winch that was snap-linked to one of the metal supports. The man's hands were on the rope, grasping it above his head, keeping himself steady. His legs were shaking on his precarious perch. Blood and sweat dripped down bare skin and his cock was erect. Another man, wearing black leather pants and vest, head covered with a black leather hood stood behind him, whip in hand. A half-dozen silhouettes surrounded the spectacle in rapt audience. None wore suits and unfortunately the naked man wasn't Delgado.

Kane slipped through the gap and gave the group a wide berth.

There was movement to the right, along the outer wall, partially hidden by a stanchion.

The whip struck flesh.

A suit had his back against the outer wall, pants down, two people kneeling in front of him. Kane slid the .45 into the holster and retrieved the camera from the map case. Oriented the camera toward the subjects and squeezed his eyes shut.

The flash went off, then once more.

"Motherfucker!" Alfonso Delgado screamed as he scrambled to pull up trousers.

Kane opened his eyes. He shoved the camera in the bag, drew the .45, and retraced his steps, surer of the way, avoiding the whipping and other debauchery. He removed the goggles as he left the pier, walked underneath the Highway, and re-entered what passed for civilization in lower Manhattan. He skirted the hulk of a burnt-out car sitting on blocks in a vacant lot. Kane holstered the pistol, levering the safety into its slot on the modified slide as he did so.

He proceeded along West 10th. Few people were about this late. He paused on the corner of Washington, which ran north-south. To his right, rising above the brownstones, vacant lots filled with debris and the run-down tenements and businesses of Greenwich Village, were the brilliantly lit, shiny, twin pillars of the World Trade Center. The ground had been broken for them the year Kane graduated West Point, 1966, and both towers had topped out in 1970. Four years of construction mirroring the four years of deconstruction in Kane's life. From proud West Point graduate parading on the Plain to abject military prisoner. Red aircraft warning lights were flashing on what had been the world's tallest buildings until three years ago when the Sears Tower in Chicago bested them, another chunk of pride bitten out of the Big Apple.

Kane felt the ghost of something, combat past or threat present or dismal future, tingle his spine.

He peered at his back trail but the street was clear.

Headlights cut the darkness as a bulky yellow cab rumbled by on cobblestones.

He remained still, waiting. Nothing.

Kane proceeded north on Washington, a main artery of Greenwich Village. A scattering of pedestrians, wary of each other, some crossing the street to avoid close passage. It wasn't just the usual native caution; there was the specter of Son of Sam, still out there almost a year since his first attack. Kane continually checked for anyone following, zigzagging the street four times, with the occasional pause.

When he reached Jane Street he cornered right, remaining on the south side until mid-block. The street was cobblestone with trees arcing overhead along both sidewalks. A few streetlights struggled against the night.

Kane crossed over. Swung open the gate in a waist-high black wrought iron fence leading to the lowest level of an old three-story brownstone. The oiled hinges were silent. After shutting the gate, he knelt on the steps and faced back the way he'd come, hand hovering over the .45. No one on the street. Waited twenty heartbeats. Rose and took the four steps. The entrance for the basement apartment was to the left, underneath the steps leading to the main floor. There was a small arched alcove in front of the door.

Kane checked the matchstick stuck in the door jamb a foot above the ground insuring it was undisturbed, then unlocked and entered, putting the matchstick on the small table inside. Turned the light on. Out the entry, he was in a small sitting area with a horizontal, narrow, street-level window under the low ceiling. Down the short hall was a bedroom with no window, bathroom to the left side crammed beneath the upstairs hallway and finally a tiny kitchen and a door leading to steps to the small courtyard in back where the owner kept a struggling garden surrounded by buildings fore and aft and wood fences left and right.

The furniture was cheap second-hand, suitable to an equally inexpensive rental from the owner residing on the top two floors. The walls were lined with cinderblocks supporting bowed boards loaded with books. Hardcovers and paperbacks were stacked upright, sideways, there seemed to be no pattern to the placement. Above the door frame leading to the bathroom was a four-foot-long board with holes every three inches in it. Two long pegs were inserted. The bathroom doubled as a field expedient dark room and Kane carried the camera inside, then stepped back to the frame, gave a slight jump, grabbing a peg in each hand. He did several pullups, then moved the left peg one hole further out, a few more pullups, extended another hole and several more. When his arms were vibrating from effort, he dropped and got to work developing the film.

Propped against any available wall space not covered by books were framed prints of maps, primarily of New York City in various phases of its evolution from the Cortelyou Map of New Amsterdam in 1660 through a Michelin map from 1962, Kane's senior year in high school. The glass and frames were covered in dust. None had been hung.

As Kane mixed chemicals in the old sink to develop the film, he reflected on another shit job completed and nobody dead. A decent evening. Especially given the last and most significant time Kane was involved in a killing it ended up on the cover of Life Magazine.

Perhaps that wasn't the best thought for Kane to have. With the photos hanging and developing, he dragged his poncho liner and sleeping pad under the kitchen table and settled down. As he drifted off, crossing the threshold of his tight conscious control, the junkie in the pizza joint wormed out of his subconscious.

The 173rd and Ted had been the last thing he needed to be reminded of.

Monday, 24 October 1966

AUXILIARY FIELD SEVEN, EGLIN AIR FORCE BASE RESERVATION, FLORIDA

"Previous class said he's crazy," Ted Marcelle whispers to Kane as they ride in the open back of a deuce and a half truck through the flat Florida panhandle wasteland. Endless scrub, palmettos, stinking water, gators, mud and, of course, snakes, await.

According to the scuttlebutt from the last Ranger class to pass through, there is worse in human form.

Ted looks like hell. The left side of his face is blistered and swollen from poison ivy brushed against in the mountains of Georgia. It's covered in white Calamine lotion, but the medicine hasn't been helping.

"Doolittle trained his crews for the Tokyo mission here." Kane points at the cracking and weed infested long stretch of concrete: Auxiliary Field Seven.

Ted doesn't care about history. He's looking ahead. Literally. *"You don't think he killed them?"* Ted asks, indicating the bodies.

Fires flicker in barrels. An old truck burns. Soldiers wearing American uniforms are strewn about. The trucks carrying Ted, Kane and the rest of their Ranger Class roll through the ambush. A man wearing black pajamas stands in the far treeline, an AK-47 in his hands. As quickly as he's seen, he disappears into the scrub.

The Ranger students have all lost weight over the past six weeks of training at Fort Benning and in the mountains around Dahlonega, Georgia.

They're battered, bruised, exhausted and despite a brief 24 hours respite before this phase, starving. Six weeks of one c-ration a day takes everyone down a step on the evolutionary scale. Many are regretting the steaks they'd gorged on during that short break, as it reignited the hunger. They'd reached the point by the end of the mountain phase where hunger is such a constant it's the norm. A partly deranged Ranger student trying to put imaginary coins into a tree believing it's a vending machine is viewed with little notice.

The same with exhaustion. They're surviving at the first, base level of Maslow's hierarchy of needs: lacking food, water, warmth, rest, and shelter. Ranger School is breaking them down to see how they act and react under stress. War is chaos, war is confusion, war is exhaustion, war is man at his most primitive. Ranger School is the Army's attempt to get as close to that as possible without killing them, although students occasionally do die in the swamps, usually from hypothermia.

Kane had not been able to see his newly born son during the abbreviated break before this phase, because Taryn had gone to her parents in New York, rather than sit alone with Joseph in a squalid apartment in Columbus, Georgia for two months amongst all the rednecks. He'd talked briefly with her on the phone. Listened to Lil' Joe cry in the background. Felt the distance. The absence.

With a squeal of brakes, the truck abruptly stops. The Ranger students tumble in the cargo bay. It's deliberate, as the other trucks halt the same way.

"Get out!" A Ranger Instructor, RI, screams. "Get out!"

The students don't wait for the cargo strap in the back to be unhooked or the gate dropped. They've been in this situation before. They pour over the sides of the trucks, falling to the ground with their gear.

Kane hits hard, his rucksack twisting his back, his rifle almost impaling him. He scrambles to his feet. Ted is upright, weapon at the ready.

"Fall in!" the RI orders.

The Ranger Students assemble. Their numbers are less than the 212 who started six weeks ago. Injury has taken the unlucky, although most will be recycled, once they heal, and go through it again. Some have quit, an unthinkable and career-ending decision for an Infantry officer. Kane and Ted had watched a couple of classmates they'd thought competent simply give up.

This isn't West Point. This is finishing school for Infantry officers and the training for enlisted who are members of elite Ranger units. The newly installed commander of this phase, Charlie Beckwith has taken it to another level: this is preparation for the real war raging on the other side of the globe; no longer just a career ticket punch.

"Ground your rucks."

They shrug off their rucksacks and deposit them at their feet.

"In the bleachers!"

The students rush the bleachers. Nothing is done at a walk.

One small blessing is the decent weather. Not the brutal heat of the Florida summer. Not the chilling, wet cold of the winter to come where graduates sewed their tab on with white thread ever after. They are in the sweet spot for Florida Ranger.

The hard, wooden bleachers are uncomfortable. Kane barely notices. He's in a timeless zone inside his head.

There's a faux tombstone propped against a tree:

Here lies the bones

Of Ranger Jones

A graduate of this institution.

He died last night

In his first fire fight

Using the school solution

Be flexible!

It's counter to the West Point culture of tradition. Indeed, contrary to the US Army's attitude toward warfare. A fact that is causing turmoil as a regular army fights an irregular enemy on the other side of the world in a place few have ever heard of. The Army is trying to unlearn the lessons of World War II and Korea and relearn what their own predecessors had successfully implemented against the British two hundred years ago. It isn't going well.

"I think the n in Ranger stands for knowledge," Ted whispers to Kane.

Unlike many around him, the burst of automatic weapon firing from the swamp doesn't startle Kane.

"Listen carefully!" An RI dramatically holds a hand to his ear.

Another burst.

"That," the RI intones, "is the weapon of choice of your enemy. The AK-47. It sounds different than an M-14 or M-16. Get to know the sound. You WILL hear it again. We're going to make sure it isn't the last sound you ever hear."

The man in black pajamas appears out of the swamp. He's covered in mud. As is the AK in his hands. He fires a burst, a testament to the Russian weapon's functionality. The students duck. The crack of the rounds going overhead is the first time most have experienced bullets coming their way.

"Listen up, you fucking pussies!" Major 'Charging' Charlie Beckwith strides forward, owning the ground and their minds and bodies for the next three weeks. Commander of this, the final phase of Ranger School. They'd lucked out with the weather, but that luck hadn't held with running into Beckwith's taking over here a few months ago. He'd transformed this phase from tough, but regular army under the previous commander, into his version of hell on Earth and the reality of unconventional warfare.

"Your enemy wants you dead." Beckwith's voice is a southern growl. Born in Atlanta he'd played for the Georgia Bulldogs and been drafted by the Green Bay Packers. He'd turned down the pro contract in favor of the Army and the Korean War.

"They tried killing me," Beckwith informs them. He rips the mud encrusted black shirt open, revealing a nasty scar running diagonally across his torso from pelvis to clavicle. This is the result of a large .51 caliber bullet hitting Beckwith while he was riding in a helicopter over Vietnam. He should have died and before the next weeks will be over, everyone in the bleachers will wish he had.

The scar gets everyone's attention.

"They will kill you!" Beckwith is at the bleachers, stalking back and forth, staring students in the eye. "Each one of you. Every one of you. Unless you kill him first. We're going to teach you how to do that. If you listen to us, if you learn, if you get the shit out of your ears, and all the useless bullshit you've brought with you, your mother won't get a telegram saying your son died because he was fucking stupid! It will just say your son died."

*****

Three weeks later, on 12 November, it's over. A surprise cold snap added unexpected misery to the ordeal, producing hypothermia casualties and wiping away the 'fortune' of arriving between summer and winter Ranger. But Kane and Ted and most of the others endure.

The last mission, a seaborne assault in small rubber boats across a stretch of the Gulf of Mexico to the objective on Santa Rosa Island is a success, culminating after midnight. The head RI for the exercise actually congratulates the students, ordering them onto deuce-and-a-halves to ride back to Field Seven for graduation at 10 am later that day. He promises a warm, full breakfast, as appealing as the black and gold Ranger tab to the starved students.

"We did it," Ted whispers to Kane, as if afraid being overheard will puncture this bubble of success. "We did it."

"We did," Kane agrees, also not quite believing it. He extends his hand to his friend. "Ranger Marcelle."

"Ranger Kane." Ted pulls Kane to him and they exchange a rancid, exhausted, proud hug.

Ted's face is a disaster, the poison ivy much worse. His left eye is swollen shut. He's fought the RI's who want to medically recycle him, insisting he can do the mission.

And he has.

It's as satisfying a moment as tossing their hats into the air a few months earlier at West Point. But Ted isn't the same and it isn't just the Ranger School regime. A shadow hangs over him. Eight days earlier during a mission he cracked one smart-ass comment too many. The leader of the ambushers, a staff sergeant RI, had not been impressed, and ordered his men to take Ted prisoner.

Ted was gone for 24 hours before returning to the patrol. He refused to tell Kane what had happened. But he was different, withdrawn, his sense of humor gone. He just muttered something about 'these motherfuckers'.

But that was all in the past now.

Kane and Ted, along with the other students, collapse in the beds of the trucks, bodies piling on top of each other. Fall into what an observer might consider sleep, but is the unconsciousness of utter exhaustion. A tangle of sweaty, dirty, muddy bodies, rucksacks and weapons. The trucks roll through the darkness toward food and graduation.

Not long after, the slamming of brakes shifts the bodies, but most do not rise to consciousness.

RIs go down the line of trucks, banging on the metal sides with pipes. "Everyone out! Get your asses out of the trucks. ASAP! Move it! Move it!"

"You gotta be shitting me," Ted mutters. "These motherfuckers."

Kane sits up.

A flashlight is dancing about as an RI drops the gate and shines it into the cargo bay. He grabs the closest student's LBE and pulls him out. "Form up!"

Ted sits. "This isn't Field Seven."

"Maybe they brought chow to us?" one student wonders.

"Ha!" Ted snaps.

Kane pushes along the metal floor toward the edge. Slides to the ground before he can be pulled out. Ted tumbles next to him. Grumbling, cursing, the survivors of the Ranger Class form ranks in a gravel parking lit by a single, sputtering light high on a telephone pole. Crickets chirp. No one has a clue where they are, except it's not where they were told they were going. There's no smell of cooking food or hot coffee. Just the chill dampness of a dark Panhandle night.

A jeep skids to a halt in front of the scraggly formation. Beckwith jumps on the hood as several RIs direct their flashlights at him. He hovers otherworldly in the halo of light.

"Men! Listen up! Field Seven might be attacked unless we get there first. We've got one more march to make. I give you my word. Just one more." He points to his left, along the dark stretch of road. "We only have to get there. That's all. We don't have to be tactical. We'll take the road. That's easy enough."

"Why not take the fucking trucks then?" Ted mutters, but no one laughs. Curses of despair and rage ripple through the ranks, but Beckwith seems not to hear.

"I'm going with you men," Beckwith says.

"Lucky us," Ted says to Kane.

"Gut it out minute," Kane replies to his Beast roommate.

"I don't think Field Seven is a minute away," Ted notes.

The class begins to move. Two columns, one on either side of the road. No one knows how far they have to go except Beckwith and the RIs.

As he staggers along Kane hears someone crying in the darkness. Others are cursing repeatedly, a mantra of hate toward Beckwith.

There's a clatter as a student throws away his rifle and falls to his knees. "I can't. I just can't." He curls into a ball, sobbing.

The columns leave him behind. Occasionally a civilian car rolls past, wide eyes staring at the line of dirty zombies staggering on either side of the road. Beckwith is everywhere, exhorting, cajoling, threatening, praising, cursing them to keep moving.

Eventually, after seven miles, they cross the bridge from Santa Rosa to the mainland and that gives them a rough idea how far they are from Field Seven.

Ten more miles.

Another man collapses at this realization. Beckwith pulls him to his feet and pushes him stumbling in the right direction.

They lose track of time except when BMNT tinges the eastern horizon.

"Will?" Ted says.

Kane hears his friend with some distant part of his mind. He focuses on the minute. That's all he has to do. He passes it and focuses on the next minute.

"Will?"

"Yeah?"

"I can't go any farther."

Kane glances at Ted. He looks like a ghoul. Face drawn, good eye bulging, the other swollen shut, drool on the sides of his mouth. Dried snot under his nose. Caked sweat. The left side of his face a mass of blisters and sores.

"Bullshit," Kane says. "You can do it."

"I can't. These people are crazy. You got no idea."

"Gut it out for a minute, Ted," Kane says. He holds up his wrist, peels back the Velcro covering on the Army-issue watch, the same camouflage band as the one on Ted's wrist, which they'd bought at Ranger Joe's on Victory Drive outside Fort Benning just before signing in to Ranger School. "I'll time it. You can quit after a minute. Okay? Just a minute."

"Just a minute? You promise?"

"Just a minute. I promise."

They stagger along.

"That's gotta have been a minute," Ted finally says.

"You're right. How about just one more? Then I'll quit with you."

They continue on. Each 'gut it out minute' gets longer and longer, until it's almost ten minutes before Ted asks. And each time Kane promises he'll give up with his friend after just another minute.

Finally, Ted says: "Fucking New York minutes, Will. You're using New York minutes."

"Yeah, Ted. Another New York minute."

"You're an asshole," Ted says, but he gives a small laugh and Kane knows his friend will make it.

Beckwith suddenly appears in front of Ted. "You going to make it, Ranger?" His eyes widen as he sees Ted's face. "You're the one! I heard about you. You're one tough son-of-a-bitch, Ranger. I'd serve with you anywhere."

"Fuck you, Beckwith," Ted mutters.

Beckwith moves to Kane. "Going to make it, Ranger?" He goes to the center of the road. "Oh yeah, boys. You want to run? Why don't we run this last part?"

And Kane realizes Beckwith is telling the truth, it is the last part. Because there are the bleachers and there's Field Seven and here's the smell of hot chow in the air.

"Come on, Ted." Kane breaks into an accelerated stagger, a mockery of a run. Ted automatically follows.

Beckwith howls something almost inarticulate at the students as they cross the final line.

Kane finally understands as Beckwith howls it again.

"You're Rangers now!"

A New York Minute:
The smallest measurable time in the universe. Approximately equal to the time a traffic light turns green and the cab driver behind you starts honking his horn.
Urban Dictionary.

Friday Morning, 8 July 1977

MEATPACKING DISTRICT, MANHATTAN

Kane put the five spot on the edge of the table. The corner booth in Vic's Diner was across from the swinging door to the kitchen and through there an exterior kitchen door. To the rear were the bathrooms, with no exit or windows. With his back to the wall, Kane faced the rest of the diner, one end of the u-shaped counter anchored just past a pay phone on the wall between kitchen door and counter. There were six booths along Washington Street. Six more on the other side of the counter along Gansevoort Street. Cheap linoleum tables, sagging and slashed red vinyl booths, faded black and white tile floor all bore witness that Vic hadn't been big on upkeep. On the flip side, the floor, the counter and the windows were spotless.

The ceiling was made of tin tiles, artistic for those who were into old things and bothered to look up. The diner was air-conditioned, but the old industrial unit was having a hard time with the heat and humidity. While it seemed a tad chilly to Kane, everyone else was teetering on the verge of comfortable, leaning toward barely tolerable. Kane had clear fields of fire and a quick escape available through the kitchen.

The corner diner had two customer doors, one facing each street that formed the intersection of Gansevoort and Washington in the Meatpacking District on the northern edge of Greenwich Village. A faded sign above the diner's windows on each street proclaimed and promised:

VIC'S DINER!
GOOD FOOD!

It was BMNT in military and nautical terms: begin morning nautical twilight, when the sun is just below the eastern horizon and the eye has difficulty discerning shapes. When the French and Indians attacked and vampires returned to their coffins and the city hovered between the denizens of the night and the workers of the day.

This area in southwest Manhattan confused even some native New Yorkers who were used to the regular grid system of streets, numbered south to north and east to west that constituted most of the island. That pattern had been dictated by the city master plan in 1811, displayed on one of the prints leaning against the wall in Kane's apartment. By then the area that became Greenwich Village and lower Manhattan had been settled for almost two hundred years, businesses and houses established, and the irregular pattern of streets retained many of their Dutch names. Similar to the piers, the meatpacking element of the neighborhood was in steep decline, overtaken by the widespread use of refrigerated trucks and frozen foods.

The diner was on the southeast corner. Angled across the intersection was the stub end of an elevated rail-line, the High Line. It had originally run all the way south to the Battery, as indicated on another of Kane's maps, but as its use declined with the rise of the Interstates and truck usage, it had been amputated bit by bit, much like the industries it supported.

The waitress put a cup of coffee and a glass of tap water bobbing two cubes of ice in front of Kane along with a folded order ticket. Her nametag block lettered MORTICIA and that was bolstered by her long ebony hair with a single streak of white in it, pale face, and tight, ankle length black dress. Slender and a smidge under six feet tall, she was a presence. She'd first appeared on the job thirty-three days ago. She'd taken Kane's specific instructions reference coffee and water and cubes without comment that first morning and never asked again.

She was too old to have been named after the character on the TV show from only a decade earlier and either she'd modeled herself after the Addams Family matriarch and changed her name or she'd been christened with it by parents who valued the obscure. She was gone as abruptly and silently as she'd appeared, tending to another booth. She moved in a beguiling manner, taking short, smooth steps underneath that long dress so she appeared to glide over the floor.

The handful of customers in the diner represented the end
of the night shift in a rough part of town and well before the 9
to 5 breakfast crowd. A quartet of truck drivers sat at the
counter, finished with their nightly runs to the outer boroughs
delivering fresh meat to local butchers. A trio of creatures of the
night, two female, one transvestite, were wearily exchanging
miseries of the trade in a booth. There was a scattering of others,
all worn out, ready to sleep after imbibing some food. Kane was
none of the above, sometimes starting his day here or ending it;
the morning stop in the diner a ritual anchor in his wandering
days and nights.

Kane wrapped his callused hands around the mug, absorbing
the warmth. He spooned the two cubes out of the water and into
the coffee. Watched them slowly dissolve. When the last trace
was gone, he took a sip. He unfolded the ticket. Three blocks of
five letters in the first line and two in the second, all in
unintelligible sequences, unless one had the Special Forces
trigraph memorized, which an experienced commo man or a
savant could do. Thao, the cook, had been the first years ago and
had always been the second. Kane retrieved the moleskin
notepad from his shirt pocket and used the trigraph with their
personal one-time pad, which was the diner's sign. He quickly
decoded the message.

TONIA TELEV ENXXX

CALLF ARRAH

Kane struck a match from the book next to the ashtray and
burned the ticket, stirring the remnants to dust in the tray.

The Kid bounced in through the Washington Street door,
checking out everyone, a grin at the ready. He had a newspaper
tucked under one arm. He wore old jeans, both knees shredded,
brown work boots that had never seen a construction site, and a
red and black checked lumberjack shirt, the sleeves cut off at the
shoulders revealing string-muscled arms. The shirt was
unbuttoned to the navel exposing a smooth chest. He was five-
ten, too skinny, and his face was struggling against acne. A street-
hardened teenager with long sandy hair freshly combed. He blew
a kiss at Morticia, walked directly to Kane's booth, tossed the

New York Times too close to the coffee and had the fiver in his pocket in one smooth movement.

"It's gonna be a sunny day," the Kid said. His accent was tinged southern trying hard to sound New York. He was most likely a refugee from some small town where his high school classmates flew rebel flags on their pickups and had guns in rear window racks.

"Hot," Kane said. "And humid."

"But sunny."

"Hold on," Kane said as the boy turned to go.

The Kid turned. "Yeah?" He was smiling yet his body was tense, ready to flee, but that was a learned trait of his lifestyle.

"Were you at the piers last night?"

"Nah. The piers tend to rough trade. I only go there with a buddy I trust or a safe hook up. I was around Washington Square most of the night. Why?"

"You know a junkie who hangs out on the waterfront, white, scruffy, thirties, veteran who wears a fatigue jacket with a screaming eagle patch on the left shoulder, winged dagger on the right, both with Airborne scrolled above them?"

The Kid laughed. "I don't do junkies and they aren't interested in me. They like their stuff better. Plus, people don't score at the piers. Very frowned upon. No one wants the cops coming by. It's one place they leave us alone."

"This junkie knocked over Dino's last night."

The Kid shrugged. "That place gets ripped off every week. The night guy has to slip any cash over twenty into a safe he can't open. Everyone knows that. And the pizza sucks, not enough cheese, but where else can you go that late?"

Kane removed a brown manila envelope from the map case. Put a picture on the table. "Ever meet this guy?"

The Kid glanced at the picture of Delgado in flagrante delicto. "Nope." He walked away.

"Hey Kid—" Kane began.

The Kid turned. "Yeah?"

"Nothing."

The Kid was gone via the left door, not looking back. Kane put the photo in the envelope and into the map case.

Morticia set a plate in front of him. "I don't know what it is."

Kane eyed the concoction he hadn't ordered. Rice, vegetables, and a brown sauce. "Thao knows I don't like peppers."

"I don't think he cares what you don't like," Morticia said.

Kane glanced at the high bar behind the counter dividing that area from the kitchen. Thao was short, even for a Montagnard, barely topping five feet, which was the height of the bar. At that moment just a pair of brown hands snatching an order ticket from the carousel.

"You want me to take it back?" Morticia asked, crossing her arms across her chest.

"Funny," Kane said. "I did that once. A long time ago in a faraway place. Big mistake." With his left he surreptitiously drew the .45 and rested weapon on thigh, under the table. "Send my regards to Chef Thao."

"Your regards to the chef. Sure." Morticia slid away to serve another customer.

Kane picked up the fork right handed and, with Morticia out of hearing, thumbed off the safety.

Alfonso Delgado came in the door the Kid had gone out of. Two men accompanied him. One, a muscle-bound weightlifter, bald, Cro-Magnon forehead, stayed by the door. The other, a tall, slim knife of a man dressed in white pants, red shirt and white linen jacket, flanked Delgado, eyes hidden behind aviator glasses. His face was narrow with flawless pale skin, but there was an odd triangular section of skin, an inch tall and half an inch wide just below the right lens that was scarred reddish black. He sported black, pointed boots. His thick red hair was styled straight to the rear. Kane spotted a glimpse of dark metal under the jacket on the guy's right hip, not enough to determine specifics.

Delgado wore a rumpled gray well-cut suit, no tie, collar open. His dark hair was disheveled and there were deep pockets under his eyes, above his thick black mustache. There was a bulge under his left shoulder, the sign of an amateur because it was a long way from the shooting hand's resting position; a man could be perforated several times before he made the reach up and across his body.

Delgado stopped at the booth. "You're a hard man to find."

"Not really," Kane replied. "You found me. Can't be that difficult."

"Funny guy. I was told you was a funny guy."

"You have the wrong person then." Kane was looking at Delgado, but watching the red head.

"I talked to your uncle earlier this morning," Delgado said.

"Which one? I've got a bunch of uncles."

"The one that gives up where you go to breakfast every morning with just a phone call," Delgado said.

Kane shrugged. His fork was still hovering over the plate. Around his right wrist was a brass bracelet. "Like I said. I got several uncles." He shifted his obvious attention to the other guy. "I'm Kane."

The guy nodded. "I know. That's why we're here."

Kane noted the slight accent. "You're not from around here. Australian?" he deliberately wrongly guessed.

"Doesn't matter where I'm from," the man answered. "I'm here now."

Kane pointed the fork at Delgado. "Him, I know. We met last night, actually earlier this morning. And you might be?"

"*I'm* talking to you," Delgado said.

"I'm nobody important." The guy smiled joylessly and sat across from Kane, his hands out of sight. Kane slid his finger from alongside the trigger guard, inside, tenderly feeling the sliver of metal, for the first time considering how the top of the table would affect the trajectory of a round.

Delgado was out of the loop. He thumped a fist on the table. "I want the fucking camera."

"Have a rough night, Alfonso?" Kane asked.

"Only my friends call me by my first name," Delgado said, his face red. "You ain't my friend. Unless you want to be my enemy, I want the fucking camera."

Kane put the fork down, reached across his body, and drew the envelope out of the map case. "Here."

Delgado blinked. Snatched the envelope. "What's this?"

"The pictures."

"Where the fuck did you get them developed?" Delgado demanded.

"Did it myself. Aren't you going to look at 'em?" Kane asked.

"If these ain't the pictures," Delgado said, "you'll regret it."

"I'm already regretting a lot of things," Kane said.

"The negatives?" the guy across the way said.

Kane pulled out a smaller envelope and handed it to Delgado. "You got it all."

Delgado peeked in that envelope. He smiled. "I heard you couldn't make it in the Army, Kane. They booted you out. Think of that," he said to the man across the table. "This guy got booted out of an army that lost a war and had to draft people. That's pretty fucking sad. Isn't it Kane?"

Kane was staring at the enforcer across the table. The aviator glasses were dark, no way to see behind them. Kane briefly wondered how he got that red hair to stay in place.

Delgado thumped the table again. "I heard you've had a sad life, Kane. I heard your ex and your kid—"

The enforcer held up his left hand, interrupting Delgado. The fact Delgado heeled indicated who held the real power.

Kane was focused on the man's moving right hand, indicating he was re-holstering whatever he'd drawn when he sat down. Kane returned his trigger finger alongside the guard and the situation de-escalated from mutual suicide.

The enforcer was quiet, but firm. "Time for us to be going, Mister Delgado." He exited the booth. "We have what we came for. A successful morning all around, wasn't it, Mister Kane? No hard feelings?"

"Depends on your definition of success," Kane said.

"Excuse me, gentlemen," Morticia said. She eased between the two men and put another plate in front of Kane, next to the first. "Chef Thao apologized for the peppers."

"Come on," the enforcer said, taking Delgado's elbow with his left hand.

Delgado ripped his arm out of the grip. "I go when I want to go."

The enforcer removed his sunglasses and stared into Delgado's eyes. That ticked the clock to 'want to' and Delgado bee-lined for the door. The enforcer looked back at Kane.

Dead brown eyes. The enforcer waited a few heartbeats, nodded at Morticia while still fixed on Kane. "Ma'am. Mister Kane." Then he followed.

"A step to the left, please," Kane quietly said to Morticia.

She slid out of his line of fire.

The weightlifter opened the door and they were gone.

"What was that?" Morticia demanded.

"Lately I'm having problems getting food without being interrupted," Kane said. "Tell Thao thanks."

Thao was watching over the bar, standing a crate. Kane nodded and Thao nodded back, a smile briefly splitting his dark brown face, revealing a single gold tooth among the white, then he hopped down, out of sight.

Morticia watched the exchange. She placed her hands on her narrow hips. "You can put your gun away, Kane."

"Yes, ma'am." Kane clicked the safety in place and re-holstered.

"You're messing with the mob," Morticia didn't phrase it as a question. "That's not smart."

"I'm not known for my smarts," Kane said, picking up a pepper from the first plate with his fork, still using the right hand. "Or my sense of humor." He turned the pepper to and fro, examining it. "Ever wonder who was the first person desperate enough to eat one of these?" His hand was shaking ever so slightly.

"Oh, screw you." Morticia said it casually, not really caring.

"I don't like condiments," Kane said.

"Peppers aren't condiments."

"I put them in the same category," Kane said. "Ever see the sunglass guy before?"

"Nope. A flashy dresser and he gets a good haircut. A stylist. Sounded like he was from down under."

"Kiwi," Kane said. "New Zealand."

She indicated Kane's hand. "At least they made both of us nervous."

Kane noticed. "That's not nervous." The hand became steady.

Morticia turned away, but then stopped. "What's with the Times every day?"

"Old habit from school." Kane bit into the pepper, producing tears. "The thing that really puzzles me, is who ate a pepper the second time?" He put the remains on the plate and pushed it away.

"Catholic school?" Morticia asked.

"What?"

"The paper?"

Kane shook his head as he forced a swallow. He took a deep drink of water and cleared his throat. "We got the NY Times every day at Hudson High. Delivered to our doors."

Morticia frowned. "'Hudson High'."

"My Rockbound Highland Home," Kane said.

"Speak English."

"West Point."

"Bull," Morticia said. "You went to West Point?"

"Even graduated."

"By who?" Morticia asked.

"By who what?"

"Who delivered the Times to your door every day?"

"The plebes. The freshmen," he clarified. "But we never called them freshmen. Plebes."

"Sounds screwed up."

"It was. For some. Some loved it."

"You ain't the kind that loved it," Morticia said with authority. "What's his name?"

"Whose name?"

"The young man who brings you the paper?"

"The Kid."

"I know *you* call him that." Morticia persisted. "His name?"

"I don't know."

"You give him five bucks for a twenty-cent paper every day and you don't know his name?"

"Ten on Sunday. He wants me to know, he'll tell me."

Morticia shook her head. "You're a piece of work, Kane. And I don't mean that in a good way." She glided away.

CIVIC CENTER, MANHATTAN

"I don't get to go inside and sit in the comfy chair?" Kane asked the secretary.

"Not if Ms. Marcelle isn't in the office." Mrs. Ruiz kept typing as she spoke, an earpiece whispering dictation from a microcassette recorder she controlled via foot pedal. "No one goes in there alone."

"I bet you do," Kane said.

Ruiz, a heavyset, dark-skinned, older woman, replied by putting an extra pop in her typing.

Kane leaned back in the hard-plastic chair those made to wait had to endure, stretching his legs out, heels on the marble floor. On the opposite wall portraits of old, white, distinguished men in suits stared back with implicit disapproval. He was outside Toni's office at *Marcelle, van Dyck, Feinstein & Marcelle.* Her father's name led the way and Toni was the last and most recent addition to the firm, bookending the descendant of the old blue blood New York City family, and the Jewish attorney every New York law firm seemed required to have.

Each of the partners had a corner office on the uppermost floor of the 18-story Broadway-Chambers Building. The center of the top floor held the boardroom and law library. The firm occupied the uppermost three floors. The 16th and 17th floors were abuzz with associates, paralegals, and clients coming and going. Here, things were quieter and the deals were bigger. Clients that made it to the top floor didn't have to wait in the chairs; summoned employees were another story.

The building was on the corner of Broadway and Chambers, designed before the turn of the 20th century. The same architect had gone on to design the Woolworth Building and the United States Supreme Court, which was a factor in Thomas Marcelle headquartering his firm here. It was within walking distance of the US District Court, the Court of Appeals Second Circuit, the County Clerk of New York, and the New York City Criminal

Court. It looked down on City Hall. Chinatown was to the north, Tribeca to the west, the Financial District to the south, and the East River where it's named. Thus, it was at the center of the legal structure of the city and north of the financial hub of Wall Street, so designated because it had been the line of the original defensive wall built by the first Dutch settlers, one the many pieces of trivia that Kane loved about his home town. The fortification was delineated on his framed 1660 survey of New Amsterdam.

Kane had the map case on his lap, ounces lighter than when he'd left his apartment this morning. He was still sweating from his jog east across the Brooklyn Bridge, workout at Gleason's Gym, and fast walk back across the East River to Manhattan. The air conditioning was a bit extreme. His arms and legs burned from sparring and the heavy bag, a satisfying feeling.

The elevator dinged. Thomas, never Tom, Marcelle, lord and master of this domain and beyond, exited, his daughter at his side. Thomas Marcelle had been Assistant U.S Attorney for the Southern District of New York before Toni reached her teen years and everyone who was anybody had assumed the District's top job was his in a few years and eventually a good shot at Attorney General with the correct administration. Fate had intervened and Thomas Marcelle had ditched that life for these more lucrative trappings via the other side of the courtroom. He was one of the top defense attorneys in the City with clientele ranging from upstanding, wealthy citizens in need to the rich, darker side of society always requiring a legal shield. He was bald, swarthy, barrel-chested and wore an expensive, tailored suit the way Kane had worn his full dress as a cadet and nothing since.

Antonia Marcelle never went by her full first name, except for her mother, and she'd eviscerate anyone who tried. In her late-thirties, Toni turned heads when she walked into a place. She had lustrous, thick black hair that cascaded to her shoulders and an angular face. Her nose had originally been eagle-like in a Roman patrician manner but sometime during Kane's time away had gone under the knife and was thinner and less pronounced. Kane didn't like the change.

She was 4 inches shorter than Kane, her body intriguingly out of proportion with long, athletic legs. She wore a gray pants suit that emphasized the legs, and a white blouse under the sharply cut jacket. Her outfit was completed with a gray scarf that cost more than Kane's entire ensemble minus the custom-modified .45 on his hip, not that he'd bought it.

Father and daughter had been arguing but quieted when they came out of the elevator. They faced each other and Marcelle said something to his daughter in a low insistent tone. Then he spotted Kane and his face went from stone to steel. He said something else and she glanced over her shoulder. She shot a quick, tense smile, then returned attention to the man who commanded it.

Kane stood and waited. Thomas Marcelle was the first to turn away, marching toward his office, thus dismissing his daughter.

"Mrs. Ruiz has never seen *Monty Python*," Kane said as Toni approached, loud enough for the secretary to hear. Ruiz typed away.

Toni didn't respond, opening the door, ushering Kane in and shutting it behind him. He headed for his usual corner chair angled toward the door, the desk and the windows beyond, with a wall behind him as she went behind the desk, taking off her jacket. There was a hint of black bra visible through the thin white blouse.

She had the least favorable office of the four corners. Behind her, northwest, toward Duane Street, was primarily a display of taller, newer buildings. Her wood desk was antique, the front facing engraved with blindfolded Lady Justice holding the scales in one hand and a sword in the other. The surface was crowded with files and papers, one framed photo facing her, and a phone. The walls were unadorned with several empty hooks where the previous occupant had dangled his pedigree and she hadn't placed her own. Four steel filing cabinets lined the wall, combination dial on the front of each drawer.

"Your father doesn't like me," Kane said.

"You came back," Toni said as she sat down with a sigh. "Ted didn't."

There was nothing he could say to that. There was a reason he didn't like small talk.

A red, white and blue *New York City Needs Bella Abzug* button was on her desk, half covered by some papers.

"What does your father think of you backing Bella?" Kane asked, at a loss for something else to say. According to the Times, Abzug currently topped the polls for the Democratic nomination to this fall's mayoral election, which meant she led the polls for mayor. The run off was the deciding factor, not the actual election, with the Democratic candidate a shoe-in for years.

Toni tossed the button in a drawer. "He doesn't know. There's nothing for him to think about. And just because I have a button doesn't mean I'm for her."

"Right," Kane said.

"Are you sweating?"

"I was at Gleason's. I didn't run back, I walked. But it's hot out. Sunny though," he added.

"Ever hear of a shower, Will?"

"You wanted me here at eleven unless Thao got the message wrong, and Thao doesn't make mistakes. Hey, do you guys *have* a shower?"

"The executive lounge next to the boardroom," Toni said, "and you are not getting a key."

"Do you have one?"

Toni stared at him for a few seconds. "You know there's a gym right around the corner."

"Yeah. I've done some sparring there. But then I wouldn't get my run in. I like going across the Bridge. Thinking about the men who built it. You know the city used to rent out some of the open space in the anchorages to store wine? Always exactly sixty degrees."

"Fascinating."

"Plus, Gleason's has an aura. You know who—" Kane halted as Toni held up a hand.

"What did you get on Delgado?" She indicated the map case.

"I *had* pictures of Alfonso Delgado getting blown by two male hookers in the Christopher Street pier."

"I don't like that past tense," Toni said.

"Delgado showed up at Vic's this morning. Now he has the pictures."

Toni frowned. "You gave him the negatives too?"

"They were requested. It did not seem a fortuitous time to argue the request, given I was in a lose-lose situation with his help."

Toni looked at the ceiling of her office. "Lord, give me patience."

"He ain't listening, Toni," Kane said. "You need to go to mass more often."

She snorted. "Coming from you? What do you mean lose-lose?"

"His associate and I had guns drawn on each other in the booth. No instant kill shot that low on the body and I doubt I could get an accurate one through the top of the table. If one of us fired, the other would too and we'd be shooting each other for a while, a second or two at least. It wouldn't have been pretty."

"A second or two is a while?"

"When you're pulling a trigger, it is. Everything okay here?" Kane asked, nodding his head toward the door.

"Father's wound a little tight lately," Toni said, "which means all of us are wound a little tight. It'll pass."

"I don't think anything just passes around here," Kane said.

"You said Delgado had help? The guy in the lose-lose?"

"He's the one who remembered to ask for the negatives," Kane said. "Tall, about six-four. Thin. Red hair combed straight back. Dressed in a white suit of some weird material. Black pointy boots. New Zealander. Who is he?"

Toni slumped back in the chair. "That's Quinn. You were right to give it up. He's Cappucci's right hand man."

"The Cappucci of the Cappucci family? The old man?"

"Not the old, old man," Toni said. "After a nasty go around in Queens with the Rosado's, the eldest Cappucci was forced by the Five Families to relinquish his position and retire a few weeks ago. He's gone to molt in Phoenix, but it's a lucky mobster who makes it to his age so he shouldn't complain. Actually, did him a favor. Maybe he'll die in his bed. This is his son, old enough, somewhere in his fifties. He inherited Quinn from his dad. Quinn's the family's enforcer."

"You say 'Five Families' like it's a religion," Kane said. "Up there with the Holy Ghost and the Twelve Apostles and the Stations of the Cross."

"To them it is a religion," Toni said. "They burn a picture of the Virgin Mary as part of their ceremony to be a made man."

"You might not know this, but in my previous life I was an altar boy," Kane said. "That ceremony sounds a bit sacrilegious, you know, given the—"

Toni cut in. "Best to treat it like a religion because they do. There's been a lot of turmoil in the mob since Carlos Gambino's heart attack last year. Power plays."

"Why would Cappucci send his enforcer with Delgado over some pictures?" Kane asked. "And why does Cappucci have a foreigner as his muscle?"

"What did I tell you about Delgado?"

"You don't remember?"

"I've got a lot on my mind, Will."

"You told me to get dirt on Delgado. Said he was a capo in one of the families. You didn't even tell me which of the 'Five Families'," he said, mimicking her tone, "other than he hangs out at the Triangle Social Club, which is actually run by Vincent 'the Chin' Gigante, a progeny of the Genovese family, so that might have confused me a tad. You said it was normal, routine surveillance to find cause for divorce. Found that, just don't have the evidence anymore."

Toni held up her hands defensively. Jewelry glittered on several fingers. "Yeah, yeah, yeah. Sorry. You're right. Delgado is married to Boss Cappucci's daughter."

"Gee, that helps. And?"

"She came to me."

"For?"

"Same thing every woman who comes through my door wants. A divorce. That's why father gave me this swanky office. I handle the women of means who desire to terminate their marital relationship."

"That sounds very formal and professional," Kane said. "So Cappucci's daughter wants to divorce Delgado. Who is Cappucci siding with? Daughter or son-in-law?"

"Do I have to give you a lecture on how the mob works?"

"In the Bronx, where I was growing up naïve and innocent, the mafia meant old, fat guys in wife-beaters at the corner social club making book and playing cards outside when the weather was nice."

"The Bronx is the dark side of the moon," Toni said. "Even mobsters are afraid to go there."

"Not the entire Bronx," Kane hedged. "I'll admit even cops are afraid of the South Bronx. And it's hell for FDNY. My Uncle Liam is stationed at the firehouse on 138th and—" he stopped upon seeing the look on her face. "Okay. That's the extent of my mob knowledge. I was in the Army a while in case you forget."

Toni's eyes went to the lone picture on her desk, now that her ex-husbands was deep-sixed. "I remember very well that you were in the Army, Will."

Kane didn't have to see to know what was inside the frame: Taken in front of Battle Monument on Trophy Point at West Point. Toni in the center wearing a knee length green dress. Kane to her right, her younger brother, Ted, to her left, both in full dress gray, 'tar buckets' on their heads. It had been snapped right after graduation parade. The two cadets held their sabers over her head, the tips crossing, her knights who'd sworn that day to protect her forever after she'd spent the four years the two men had attended the Academy being the older, wiser sister to both of them. She'd written letters, sent 'boodle' packages of food via the mail, and answered when one or the other, sometimes both, crowded together in a phone booth, called. She'd been their desperately needed lifeline to the outside and 'real' world. But it had turned out that she couldn't protect either of them, nor could they save each other.

"Sorry, Toni," Kane said. "It was a long night."

They were quiet for some moments.

Toni waded out first. "I shouldn't be snapping at you, Will. First my fucking dad, now the fucking mob. And then there's the fucking campaign that has everyone up in arms."

"That's a lot of fucking," Kane said and Toni laughed.

"It is," Toni said. "My father wouldn't like my choice of Bella if he knew. Thus, he doesn't know. Yet." There was a slight slur to her words and Kane finally realized lunch with father included liquid refreshment.

"Who's he for?"

"Cuomo, but he's keeping quiet publicly," Toni said. "Ultimately he'll be for whoever wins once it's over. That's the way to do business in this town. Don't burn any bridges."

"That's not building any bridges either, though."

"Father's already got his bridges," Toni said. "He doesn't go to others, they come to him. I know who he *isn't* for. And Bella Abzug is number one on his list."

"Is that why you're for her?"

"No." Nothing more was forthcoming.

"Why is your father against Abzug?"

"Lots of reasons, but primarily because she opposes Westway, the replacement for the West Side Highway. She got Congress to change the requirements for the Federal infrastructure funds that the city needs so that it can be spent on Westway *or* mass transit. So that fight is ongoing. Westway or the subway. The election will swing the decision."

"I'm assuming you father doesn't take the subway."

"It's about money, Will. There's no money in the subway."

"That's why they're so lousy."

"You don't understand. I mean there aren't big construction contracts, which means there's no money for those who skim their percentage off those contracts. The subway is a clean-up, modernize endeavor and the companies who make trains and track are specialized and come from outside the city. The Westway means city contracts, especially concrete, which the mob totally controls. The city has already spent forty million on it."

"Doesn't look like they've spent a penny from what I saw last night. Where's the money going?"

"Planning."

"Hell, I could plan it for a fraction of that. Blow up the elevated roadway and pave over what's underneath. Done deal.

I know some demo guys from Tenth Group up at Fort Devens who'd do it just for fun."

Toni shook her head. "Westway is a big plan, Will. They're going to completely redo the lower west side. A landfill along the shore replacing the piers, with a tunnel for the highway. Parks and shops and other buildings on top. We're talking billions. It's the biggest project in the city since Central Park."

"1857," Kane said.

"What?"

"That's when construction for Central Park began based on the Viele Map of 1855. It wasn't in the original 1811 plan for Manhattan so they carved that rectangle out of the city and evicted everyone in the way. Poor people, of course. Did you know they used more gunpowder clearing the area for Central Park than was fired at Gettysburg?"

"Fascinating," Toni said dryly. "Your Jesuit at the Mount give you that one?"

"Some days Father Benedict was the only reason I got on the subway to go to high school."

"You went because you didn't want to be home."

"Ouch," Kane said. "But Father Benedict was a great teacher. Last I heard he's still up there in the Bronx."

Toni picked up a letter opener, a replica of a West Point saber, and idly turned it in her hands. "Even after a year, father still hasn't forgiven me for the divorce. He liked Robert. He not only lost a son-in-law, he lost a partner at the firm."

"Yeah, but you got your name back, this swanky office, and your dad gained a better partner at the firm to handle future rich divorcees. And you got rid of an asshole."

"Robert wasn't an asshole," Toni said, but there was no fight to rote defense.

Kane let it go.

Toni looked at the letter opener, realized what it was and dropped it. "I thought I'd told you what was going on. I didn't think it would turn bad."

"Not a problem," Kane said. "No harm, no foul. Listen, it ain't like Delgado is suddenly gonna become a virgin or lop his dick off. I follow him, he'll stick it somewhere he isn't supposed to. Just a matter of time."

"Yeah," Toni said. "You really didn't make copies?"

"My plan for the day, before I was so rudely interrupted, was to come here as you requested after Vic's and my run and Gleason's. I didn't plan on getting jacked."

Toni smiled, the skin around her eyes wrinkling. "I know. But, geez, pictures of him with his dick in some guy's mouth. Not only do we get adultery, we get leverage. And he's a guy I could use some leverage on."

"Two guys," Kane said. "I doubt they were of legal age so there's also statutory, but we'd never get testimony. Cappucci sending Quinn means the boss doesn't want you to have leverage. I think you can assume the divorce is going to be contested."

"It was going to be, sooner or later. I always prefer later."

"The thing I wonder," Kane said, "is how did Delgado know it was me? He couldn't have seen me in the pier. The flash blinded him. Does he know his bride came here?"

"Sofia says he has no clue," Toni said. "But going to a lawyer is like going to confession. People tend to lie a lot. What you should be wondering is how did he know you were in Vic's?"

"My uncle told him."

"Conner?"

"Yeah. Who else?"

"Your fucking family, Will. You deserve better."

"They'd disagree."

"Exactly."

"The other thing is that Delgado knew who I was," Kane said. "I mean my past. He knew about the Army."

Toni frowned. "Did your uncle tell him?"

"Doubtful," Kane said, "but I'll ask. Delgado also hinted he knew about Taryn and Joseph and *that* is something even Uncle Conner wouldn't blab about."

"You—" She paused as there was a rap on the door. Mrs. Ruiz came in with a sheaf of legal papers. Slid them in front of Toni, pointed where to sign, flipped a page, and the pattern was repeated a dozen times. She left without a glance at Kane.

"What did I do to her?" he wondered after the door shut.

"She's never watched *Monty Python* and she doesn't have much of a sense of humor," Toni said.

"I don't have much of a sense of humor," Kane said. "But I say hi, at least."

"You run hot and cold on that," Toni pointed out. "Ted used to say going to West Point was akin to getting a social lobotomy. If you had any social skills when you showed up there, and I doubt *you* did given your family, by the time you graduated they were long gone. I watched it happen to Ted. He retrograded."

"True enough. Hudson High. Two centuries of tradition untouched by progress."

"And *Monty Python*? That's been off the air for a few years, Will."

"It was the only thing in English playing overseas at the time. I think I have every skit memorized. Some of it was actually funny."

"Overseas where? That aired what? Seventy to seventy-four? Where did you go for those years after the accident, Will?"

The intercom buzzed. Toni pressed a button.

Mrs. Ruiz sounded pleased. "Ms. Marcelle, Mr. Marcelle needs you in the boardroom. Right away."

Toni stood abruptly, grabbing her jacket and slipping it on. Kane looped the map case over his shoulder and walked her to the door. He paused before opening it and picked something out her thick hair. A piece of glitter.

"Party?"

"Oh. Last night. I was out late."

"Someone's birthday?" Kane asked.

Toni turned to face him. They were close, inside the space that Kane carried around him like a flak jacket. He could smell her, a mixture of perfume, expensive booze, hairspray and Toni.

"A new club," Toni said. She was staring into his eyes and didn't step back. "Studio 54. Opened a few months ago. They scatter glitter over the dance floor."

"You danced?"

Toni smiled. "Yes, Will. I danced. I didn't get that social lobotomy at Columbia. We also had fun."

"You also protested against the war at Colombia."

"I didn't protest you. I did it in memory of Ted."

"Gotta be careful at night," Kane said. "That crazy Sam guy is out there."

"You worried for me?"

"Of course." Kane sensed she'd moved a little closer, but he wasn't sure.

"I was safe," Toni said. "Frank limo'd me there and back and stood watch." She was referring to another hired hand at the firm, more bodyguard and driver than investigator.

"Right." Kane didn't know what else to say.

Toni looked down, then met his gaze again. "Can I ask you something, Will?"

"Sure."

She ran the edge of his open denim shirt between forefinger and thumb. "This past year we've been working together, since you came back, and I got divorced, how come—well, you know?"

Kane blinked and answered without thinking. "I like you."

It was Toni's turn to be surprised and she removed her hand. "What does that mean?"

Kane retreated half a step, his back touching the wall. "It's complicated."

"Is it about Taryn?"

"Some of it," Kane said. "I don't know, Toni. You know my head's kind of fucked up." He tried to lighten the conversation, pointing at the scar. "Hell, I got shot in it. On it. Whatever."

Toni flushed, her olive skin turning a prettier shade. "I'm sorry. I didn't mean to put you on the spot. I miss Taryn, too."

"You've never heard from her?" Kane asked.

Toni shook her head. "Nothing since the accident."

"None of the checks were returned here?"

"Not yet. None have been cashed?"

"Not as of the last statement."

"Geez," Toni said. "Eight years." She reached past him, her hand brushing his as she grabbed the knob and opened the door. They walked out together. "Stay on Delgado when you can. But be careful out there."

"Right."

Kane watched her walk away while Mrs. Ruiz glared at him. Looking past Toni, he spotted Thomas Marcelle escorting an older gentleman, short and fat, dressed in a well-tailored dark suit with a green and red striped tie as if it were Christmas, not July. He had strands of hair slicked back like dark threads on a liver-spotted cue ball. He sported thick, dark glasses. Like the junkie the other night, Kane knew the guy was trouble, just of a different sort. He looked vaguely familiar but Kane couldn't dredge up a name.

Toni saw the man at the same time and missed a step. She muttered under her breath: "Fuck!" She glanced over her shoulder at Kane, as if seeking succor, but resumed her dutiful march toward the two men.

The old man's dark glasses turned in Kane's direction and he leaned close to Marcelle, whispering. Marcelle glanced past his daughter at Kane and said something back. They disappeared into the boardroom and Toni followed.

Kane looked at Mrs. Ruiz. She was upright in her chair, arms folded across her large chest, glaring past him. Apparently, there was someone she hated more than Kane.

"Who was that?" Kane asked.

Mrs. Ruiz shook her head and resumed furious typing.

"Gonna break it," Kane said.

She ignored him.

Kane took the fire stairs down the eighteen flights and entered the lobby. He paused inside the front doors. A gold stretch Mercedes with dark windows was illegally parked in front of the building on Broadway. Three old men stood next to it. Despite the heat they were dressed in black slacks and black turtlenecks. Bulges at the waist indicated they were carrying and not being subtle about it.

More trouble but not Kane's. Nevertheless, he turned around and exited the building by the service door as discretion was the better part of no trouble.

*****

A headlight makes a unique popping sound when it shatters. Kane heard the first one as he walked toward Trimble Place, off of Duane, a block and a half away from *Marcelle, van Dyck, Feinstein & Marcelle*. He heard, and saw, the second one on his old Jeep get broken.

The weightlifter from this morning's visit at Vic's Diner had just done a swing and a hit, not that it's hard to miss an inert object. He wore sweat pants and a skintight workout shirt with thin straps over his massive shoulders.

"Yo, Reggie," Kane called.

The weightlifter turned. "My name ain't Reggie."

"I was guessing, you know, because you swing like Reggie Jackson. Powerful. Smooth." Kane angled his walk to put the hood of the Jeep between himself and the bat with the muscles. Trimble was one block long, more an alley between Duane and Thomas. There was nobody on Trimble, but pedestrians were hurrying by on both the end streets. Being New Yorkers, they were aware of, but pointedly ignoring the brewing confrontation.

"Reggie Jackson is a punk," weightlifter said. "He should shut the fuck up and listen to Billy. Always gotta to listen to the coach."

"Technically, in baseball, I believe Billy Martin is called a manager." Kane halted on the driver's side. "You're a Yankees fan?"

"Of course." He frowned. "Ain't you? Not the fucking Mets, are ya?"

"Neither. Baseball has never done much for me," Kane admitted. "People get all excited if there's a no hitter, but doesn't that mean nothing happened? What's your name?"

"Cibosky."

"That doesn't sound Italian."

Cibosky choked up on the bat, bringing it up for a swing. "I'm Italian. My mother was pure and my father half and half. It was my father's father who—"

"I don't want your family history," Kane said. "I was trying to be polite. I was recently told my social skills are lacking. Now we're done with that. Why are you beating up my Jeep?"

"Alfonso Delgado is sending you a message."

"What? He doesn't like classic jeeps?" It was old, 1965, the first year the engine got an upgrade with the six-cylinder option, spray painted flat black, windshield folded down, with the original Army canvas seats on metal springs, no top, no doors, four tires, an engine, a locked footlocker chained down in the cargo space, and now, two busted headlights. Classic was a stretch. "You didn't break my taillights, did you?"

"Not yet."

"How about not ever?"

Cibosky began to come around the front of the Jeep.

Kane drew the .45. "It'll hurt you more than me."

Cibosky spit. "Coward gotta hide behind a gun."

"You have a bat."

Cibosky tossed the bat aside and showed off, rolling every muscle in his upper body like an anaconda on steroids spotting a deer with a broken leg and preparing to swallow it whole. He frowned when he saw that Kane hadn't lowered the .45.

"I got rid of the bat."

"I didn't ask you to."

"Chicken-shit," Cibosky said. "Mister Delgado was right when he said you wasn't much of a man. Fucking Army failure."

"But he didn't say I was stupid," Kane pointed out. "How did he know I was in the Army?"

"You gonna shoot me?" Cibosky wanted to know. "An unarmed guy in broad daylight? There's a firehouse around the corner. They'll come running."

"Yep," Kane agreed. "Ladder One, Battalion One. Got an uncle on the job up in the Bronx. I don't think they'd turn me in. Probably help me."

Cibosky ignored him, relishing his inspiration. "You'll end up in Rikers. We got people on the inside. We got guards on the take. You'll get shivved." He sounded enthused about the prospect.

"I've been in jail before," Kane said. "You're right. It sucks." He slid the .45 back in the holster inside his denim shirt and drew a smaller pistol with a longer and thicker barrel out of the map case.

"What the fuck?"

"When you go to the hospital after I shoot you," Kane said, "you can tell your friends who come see you, if you have friends, don't want to presume, that you were shot by a classic."

"What?" Cibosky had his hands up, sort of pugilistic, more wrestling, but he wasn't moving forward any longer. Despite the gun, they were still 'invisible' to people hustling by on the side streets. Even more so because of the gun.

Kane waggled the pistol. "This is a suppressed High Standard .22. Nobody outside of you or me is going to hear it when it puts a hole in you. Wild Bill Donovan demonstrated one in the Oval Office for President Roosevelt during World War II and the Secret Service outside the doors didn't hear. The round is small but it's a special bullet, made by a friend of mine, and if I put it through your eyeball, your brain will get turned to mush, if it isn't already, and you *will* die. Trust me on that. But for today? What do you think two headlights are worth? Thigh? Nah. You need to walk to the emergency room. See? I'm considerate, despite what some people say about me. You've got big biceps. Left or right handed?"

"Fuck you."

"Is that what you and Delgado do? Admire each other's muscles? You know what was on those photos, right?"

Cibosky glared. "I don't give a shit."

"Does Quinn know you're here?"

The bravado flaked at the edges. "None of his business."

"How did Delgado know I was in the Army?"

Cibosky shrugged. "He and Quinn was talking about it when I drove them to the diner."

"How did he know about my ex?"

"Same thing. Delgado was asking Quinn."

Kane pondered that for a moment. "How did you guys know it was me at the pier taking the pictures?"

Cibosky shrugged, burning calories to move that much muscle mass. "I just drive."

"Back up a bit," Kane ordered.

Cibosky was confused.

"Step back. I shoot you at this range, the bullet will really fuck up your muscle. Let's give it some distance. You can probably start lifting again six weeks after they dig the slug out. Sadly, the muscle will never be the same, as tissue will be torn up. Trust me on that. You were holding the bat in your right hand. That leaves me with a decision."

"You ain't gonna shoot me." But Cibosky took two steps back.

"Eeny, meeny, miny, moe," Kane recited, aiming the High Standard from one arm to the other.

Kane took one step forward and Cibosky reverse mirrored him.

"Catch a tiger by the toe."

"Oh, come on, man!"

"If he hollers, let him go." Kane slid onto the driver's seat, resting the suppressor on top of the steering wheel, clear shot over the folded windshield. "What was the message?"

Cibosky frowned. "Huh?"

"You said Delgado was sending a message by having you beat up my Jeep. What was I supposed to make of that?"

"Stay the fuck away from him."

Kane shook his head. "I thought we had an understanding this morning. This will be on him from here on out. Tell him that."

A frown appeared on Cibosky's face as he tried to understand.

"You going to holler?" Kane asked.

"Huh?"

Kane sighed. "'Never underestimate the power of human stupidity'."

"Huh?"

Kane depressed the clutch, turned the switch and the Jeep's engine belied the outer appearance, turning over with a throaty roar. The tall gearshift lever poking up from the floor was already in first. Kane kept the High Standard aimed at Cibosky as he released the clutch while using his right hand to twist the wheel hard left. He rolled past Cibosky, left hand aiming the gun across his body. Clear of the muscles saturated with steroids and stupidity, Kane tossed the gun on the passenger seat and leaned over, snatching the bat off the ground. He chucked it in the passenger seat well.

Exiting Trimble, he hooked left on Thomas to loop around the one-way street toward the entrance to the FDR Drive underneath the Brooklyn Bridge. On Barclay, short of the Drive, and across from City Hall, he pulled over to a pay phone, enraging cab and truck drivers who swerved around. He engaged the parking brake, left the engine running and slid the High Standard back in the map case. Looped the bag over his shoulder. He went to the phone, dropped a dime and dialed.

It was answered on the second ring. "Ms. Marcelle's office."

"Mrs. Ruiz, it's Will Kane." Disapproval crackled through the phone line. "I know she's in a meeting but you have to give her a message. You ready?"

"I am always ready, Mister Kane. Proceed."

"Right. Tell her she needs to check on our mutual client. That Delgado sent someone after me. That it isn't sanctioned by Cappucci. Delgado is off the leash. She'll understand."

"I'm sure she will."

"Thank you." He waited a heartbeat. Then another. Just silence. "All right, then." He hung up. Spent two more dimes, first calling his eldest uncle on his mother's side, then the youngest, ignoring the horns blaring. He got back in the Jeep. Drove underneath the Brooklyn Bridge onto the FDR to travel north to the Bronx along the east side of Manhattan.

THE BRONX

Friday Afternoon, 8 July 1977

COUNTRY CLUB, THE BRONX

"Does anybody here own a yacht?" Kane asked.

"Does anybody in here look like they could own a yacht?" Conner Riley replied. "We're drinking nickel draft, Will."

"The place is called the Pelham Bay Yacht Club," Kane pointed out.

They were seated at an old wooden bar, the surface scarred by generations of drinking. The view out the row of propped open windows was Long Island Sound between the Bronx and City Island. Sunlight danced on small waves. Directly across the water was Rodman's Neck, where the NYPD ran a firing range. To the left, along this side, was Pelham Bay Park, and on the far end of that, next to Coop City, in an accurate barometer of the condition of the city, was a massive ten story high toxic dump that the Sanitation Department was adding to on a daily basis with an unending convoy of garbage trucks. At one time a previous mayor, Lindsay, had suggested it could be made into a ski slope after it was closed. There were many reasons he wasn't mayor anymore and his presidential ambitions had sputtered to vapor, but that bright idea hadn't helped.

"Every place gotta be called something," Conner reasoned. "It's on the water. It's a club. Got to be a member."

"Is that expensive?"

"Not if you're a cop." Conner drained the mug and leaned over the bar, filling it from the unmanned tap. He was a blocky man, once strong, now booze flabby. His face was red and mapped with broken blood vessels that pointed to a bad ending. Thinning brown hair kept baldness at bay for the time being. He wore a cheap suit, the tie pulled loose and the top shirt button open. The possibility of it ever being closed was remote, perhaps impossible. A snub-nose .38 was on his belt, right front, a silver badge on the left front, indicating plainclothes, not the gold of detective, but the step up from wearing the blue uniform of patrol.

"You pay as you go or you have a tab?" Kane asked, his own already empty.

"I'm keeping count." Conner gave Kane a questioning look but grabbed his glass and topped it off.

"Right," Kane said.

A couple of tables were occupied by folks like Conner; fat, older white guys who were either retired or marking time to retire, who served themselves as needed, all doing the tap. The well drinks were for later. The building was two stories, faded white, on the eastern edge of the Bronx. There was a yardarm in front from which the club's flag hung, occasionally energized by a breeze; a white ship's wheel with spokes against a blue background and the white letters PBYC, not exactly on a level with a Union Jack pennant or Stars and Bars.

"What's so important you call me off the job?" Conner asked. "You seen your mom lately?"

"Nice try, Uncle Conner. Did someone call you this morning asking about me?"

Conner looked out the old, open windows at the water. "I think in the old days there might have been yachts. Big boats at least. Used to tie up to the dock before it fell apart. Fancy people with money. Back when the north Bronx still had some farms. I remember when your folks moved up to their place from the apartment on 148th Street. Guy dressed in white delivered milk door to door in a box out front of each house from a local dairy, fresh that morning."

"Yeah, the good old days," Kane said. He had faint, black and white memories of that. And of an old man walking next to a mule pulling a wagon rattling along on the cobblestone street, calling out in a strong foreign accent for housewives to bring their knives and scissors out to be sharpened.

His tone got his uncle's attention.

"Someone called me," Conner admitted. "Had my home phone number which ain't listed. Woke me up, which is never good. Woke the lil' missus up which is worse."

Conner's wife, Aileen, was indeed little, barely over five feet, and scrawny, but she ruled him with a sharp tongue and hair-trigger Irish temper. He counteracted that with copious amounts of alcohol, which pissed her off even more and they made a fine Irish cyclone together.

Conner continued. "Said they had a friend outside my house. I went to the window and there was someone sitting in a Caddy, just down the street, engine running. One of those nice guinea caddies, not a nigga pimp-mobile. Ugly white guy staring ugly at the house. I took them serious. All they wanted to know was where they could find you. I didn't give 'em your apartment."

"You told them I stop at Vic's every morning."

"I had to give them something. They had someone sitting outside the house."

"You're a cop."

"I got kids in the house," Conner snapped. "Got to protect my kids." It was out before he could grab it. "Sorry, Will."

Kane waved that off.

Conner pressed his case. "Did you get hurt? You look okay. The guy said they just wanted to talk to you about something you was up to with that lawyer you work with."

"You're a cop," Kane repeated, more for himself.

"Yeah? And?"

"Do you know who you gave me up to?"

"Oh, come on." Conner mustered some fake outrage. "It's not a state secret where you eat breakfast. It's a public place."

"You dropped a dime on me."

"*They* called *me*. I'd never drop a dime on family."

Kane spoke slowly, enunciating every word distinctly. "Do. You. Know. Who. Called?"

Conner pretended to be interested in the seagulls once more. "No."

"Bullshit." Kane drained the glass of beer. Leaned over and drew himself another. "That's on your tab. A fucking nickel."

"What's wrong?" Conner said, frowning at the refill. "Why you so upset and drinking? You look okay."

"I got threatened," Kane said. "Twice. Once indirectly, then directly. Busted up my Jeep."

"That old clunker, why—"

"No, Uncle Conner. Don't do that. I had to pull my gun."

That fixed Conner's attention. "Did you shoot?"

"No. But I really hate doing that because it escalates a situation into possibilities I don't like."

"But no shooting. Okay. No harm then. Right?"

Kane closed his eyes, taking some deep breaths.

Conner spoke into the silence as he stared out at the Sound. "When we was growing up on 148th, my father, you don't remember him well do you, he used to take Nathan up here. Across the way, over there to Rodman's. They'd take the Six to the end of the line and walk through the park and over the Hutch bridge to the range. To shoot. And I used to get so jealous. The old man never took me. It pissed me off."

The breeze shifted and the stink from the landfill wafted this way, sliding in the open windows that had been trying to catch some cool off the water. There were muttered curses from a few of the club members.

"What are you trying to say?" Kane asked. "That's the reason Nathan turned out to be the cop he is and you're you?"

"Hey, I'm a good cop! I'm a collar man."

"What does *that* mean?" Kane asked.

"It means I lock guys up." Conner's face was redder. "Guys who rob, rape, hurt people. Nathan thinks he can make the world a better place. Take down the big shots. The crooks who steal millions, but with a smile and a suit and a handshake behind closed doors. You can't stop *those* people. They own Nathan even though he doesn't know it. They own me. They own *you*. They own the world. What the fuck you think Vietnam was? What was that all about? You think those gooks were gonna come over the ocean and invade us?" He gestured at the scar mostly hidden under Kane's hair. "Why'd you get wounded twice and then go back *again* and get totally screwed over? You were a good soldier, wasn't you?"

Kane stared at his uncle. "I admired both of you. I remember you in your new uniform coming to the house with Uncle Nathan, also in his blues. And Liam in his FDNY dress uniform. Nathan was bursting with pride that his youngest brother was on the job with him. That was the party my mom hosted after you graduated the Academy and got your badge. She was so proud of you. I was just a kid."

"Hey, fuck you." Conner's face flushed, the interstate of veins scarlet. He poked Kane in the chest. "This is *your* problem that got dumped on me. Not mine on you. I don't know what you're doing with that dyke guinea lawyer. Probably something shady, so don't come crying to me when your shit blows over me. *You're* the one who should be apologizing for getting *me* involved."

Conner tried to do another poke to make the last point, but Kane reflexively grabbed the hand, twisted it, causing Conner to stagger off the bar stool and go to his knees. Standing over his uncle, Kane muscle-memory flowed the move, bending the hand back at the wrist and Conner cursed in pain. Kane's other hand was drawn back, open-palmed, angled to slam the nose upward, into the brain.

Kane immediately let go. "I'm sorry, Uncle Conner."

Seven semi-mid-day-drunks were staring at them. Then they went back to their primary concern.

Kane reached out to help Conner, but he slapped the hand aside. He got to his feet, grunting in pain and embarrassment.

"It was someone from Cappucci's crew that called you," Kane said.

Conner sat down, drank half his glass. He was staring straight ahead.

Kane pushed. "You heard of a guy named Quinn?"

"Nah." Now Conner had found something interesting in the bottom of his glass. "Nathan knows all those mobbed up guys from his time on the Organized Crime Task Force. Ask him. We don't get many of those mafia mobsters in the Bronx. We got the bullshit spic and nigga and guinea street gangs that wear colors and fight over corners and drugs."

"Did you tell whoever called about my past? The Army?"

"I just told them you were in the diner every morning. That's all that was asked." Conner decided to drown whatever had held his attention in the bottom of the glass by filling it from the tap. He sat on the stool and faced Kane. "Yeah, I knew it was someone mobbed up. That was clear from the caddy outside and the way the guy talked. But I don't know what you're into, Will. It *could* have been about your business, some contact you wanted to make. How the fuck am I supposed to know? Nobody in the family really knows what you do. Not your mother or father. You sure don't fill anyone in on nothing. That's the Kane family thing. Don't say shit to nobody is your father's fucking way. Like just breathing is a secret in that fucking house you grew up in. The last time you were in 'Nam we all had to learn about what happened to you on the news. We still don't know where you were the years after the, well, you know." Conner stumbled to a halt.

"Like the Riley's are a font of information?" Kane countered. "How's Liam doing? Still cut off for marrying a Puerto Rican and then getting divorced? Double damned? How's his kid? Dave, right? How is he? Seventeen now?"

"Shit, Liam hardly gets to see the kid," Conner said. "Fucking spic bitch."

"My dad is over there where that smell is coming from," Kane said, indicating the north with his glass. "Doing his job. At least he knows his garbage. When he was a sandman on the trucks, the house always smelled of it. No matter how many times Mom washed his uniform. Hung it out there on the clothesline. I think it permeated him and the house." The glass was empty so he refilled. "He doesn't care what I'm doing. Once I was out of the Army, especially the way it happened, I was dead to him."

"That ain't true," Conner protested. "He was so proud of you at the Point and then in the Army. It hurt him when you left the military. He had visions of you as a general. He was always boasting about you."

"It hurt *him*? I didn't leave, Conner. They got rid of me. And I never heard any boasts."

Conner squirmed on the stool. "Well, I don't know much about all that."

"You know enough about me to send a mob nutjob to my breakfast this morning."

Conner faced him. "I'm sorry. Okay? And they didn't know where *you* lived, but they sure as hell knew where *I* did!"

Kane subsided. "Yeah, all right. You got a point. They would have shown up at the diner sooner or later anyway."

"And don't knock your dad's job," Conner said. "Sanitation Department goes on strike; the city notices right away. Takes longer when the cops go off the job."

"Yeah, he's the garbage master."

"He's a fucking superintendent now," Conner said. "Been a long time since he's had to toss a can. He runs a lot of guys and trucks. He's got good years in. He took care of my sister and you kids. Put all of you through Catholic school and that ain't cheap, especially when he was on the ass end of the truck. He was always doing overtime to pay the bills. He did for your mother even though he never converted like the priest wanted."

"Lucky us," Kane muttered. "The nuns were a blast."

"Let me tell you something," Conner said. "A couple years ago, when you was off wherever you was off to, we were all shitting we'd lost everything. Sanitation, police, fire. Banks wouldn't cash city checks and then the checks were delayed. We thought all those years of work was out the window. Our fucking retirement gone. Fucking Abe Beame and his heeb shysters nearly had the city bankrupt."

Kane walked around the bar and refilled both their glasses, tired of discussing his father or the state of city civil servants. At the end of the bar was a large jar with *For The Widows And Orphans* written in bold letters on cardboard taped to the front. It had several bills stuffed in it. "What's that?"

Conner was also glad to change the subject. "What it says. Money for the ones in the Old Country."

"What ones?"

"The families of those the Brits kill or throw in jail on trumped up charges." Conner's eyes shifted past Kane to the front door. "Fuck. You called him too?"

Kane turned. Nathan was six years older than Conner's forty-seven, but looked ten years healthier. Fit, slender and wearing an off the rack, buy-two-get-three, suit from the loud mouth guy who advertised on TV all the time, with the cuffs a fraction too long. He sported a head full of thick, silver hair. Nathan walked across the room to the bar with the confidence Conner had never tasted. A gold badge glittered on his belt. His gun was out of sight.

Nathan extended his hand. "William. Good to see you."

"Uncle Nathan."

Conner took a step away. "I'm still on the clock at the precinct."

"Hold on, Conner," Nathan said to his youngest brother. "They're adding people, a lot of people, to the Omega Task Force. You want, I can put a word in with the Inspector."

Conner snorted. "No, thanks. I just wanna do my thirty."

"Could mean a gold badge," Nathan dangled.

Conner shook his head. "I don't *want* a gold badge. I'm too old and too tired. Plus, only if they catch that Son of Sam bastard. He keeps killing, heads are going to roll from that Task Force." Conner downed the rest of the glass.

"We'll catch him," Nathan said.

"Yeah. Sure. I gotta go catch some of the *other* bad guys." Conner beat a hasty retreat.

Nathan assumed his brother's seat. Pushed away the empty glass, glanced at Kane's but didn't say anything. "How you doing, William? What happened to your Jeep? Saw it outside. Still making friends everywhere?"

Kane gave a quick synopsis of events at Vic's Diner and in the alley. He left out the law firm segment.

Nathan's face was lined with wrinkles that could be called crevices. He called them the 'price of the job' and in Kane's cloudy memory they'd always been there.

Nathan cut to the chase. "You can't blame Conner for telling someone where you eat breakfast."

"I understand," Kane said. "Do you know this Quinn guy?"

Nathan nodded toward a rear door. "Let's take a walk."

Kane followed as Nathan led the way down wood steps to a narrow spit of hardscrabble sand awash with seaweed and low-tide stranded trash that the club called a beach. Several tires were partly buried. Fifty yards to the south was the burnt out, rusted remains of a Chevy Nova.

They had the beach to themselves, because there was no reason for anyone to be there. The greenish-black water looked particularly uninviting. The breeze had shifted and for the moment they had slightly cooler salt air from Long Island Sound.

"Hot ain't it?" Nathan said, the normal family dialogue. "They keep saying it ain't the heat, it's the humidity, like that makes a difference."

"Sunny though," Kane replied.

Nathan gave him an odd look. The older man reached down and picked up a small stone. He tossed it, skipping a few times until it disappeared into the murky water. "Quinn is the guy Cappucci taps when he wanted someone taught a lesson, permanent or less than. Of course, the old man is out west now, but his son, the new boss, inherited him.

"Complete psycho but smart. If I remember rightly, he's only been on the scene a few years. Came here with a tough street rep via Boston. He worked his way into the family by making his bones fast and furious. He's never gotten arrested which means he's good at what he does. Also means they don't completely trust him either, though. Which is the screwed-up logic of the mob. Like it's a badge of honor to have been behind bars instead of a sign someone fucked up. Don't mess with him."

"I don't plan on it. But I don't understand why Cappucci would send him with Delgado to threaten me."

"You know how it would reflect on Cappucci if people find out his son-in-law is a fag?"

Kane shrugged. "I guess. But Delgado dispatching *his* muscle guy after me with a message bothers me. I don't think Quinn was aware Delgado sent a guy from his crew after our breakfast meeting which means the left hand and the right don't know what they're doing. That's a recipe for trouble. I don't think Delgado's going to stop."

"So *you* stop," Nathan said.

"It's my job."

Nathan turned to face Kane. "What's your job? Digging divorce dirt for those shysters?"

"Toni is my friend."

Nathan put a hand up. "I know, I know. I've always liked her. She seems solid. She looked after you and Ted while you guys were at the Point."

"You looked after me too," Kane said. "Remember? You came and got me for plebe Christmas leave. Drove me home. First time out of that place since reporting to Beast in July other than a few hours for Army-Navy. Six long months there as a plebe, sucking shit, I finally get let out, and my dad couldn't take a single day off work to get me. It wasn't like the date my leave started was a surprise. Hell, we literally counted the days down to it as part of the shit they used to haze us with."

Nathan cocked his head and gave him a strange look. "That was Conner who got you that first Christmas, cause our sister asked. I picked you up at the end of plebe year the next summer."

Kane frowned. "Conner?"

"Yeah. I'd have done it but I was on duty and he was off. Not a big deal for either of us. It's a nice drive up the river. And it was years ago."

"I thought it was a big deal at the time, and at the end of plebe year when you did it, and still do."

Nathan nodded, flushing slightly. "Yeah. All right. And it was nice of Toni to give you a job when you finally came back to the city. But her father? Thomas Marcelle? The other people there? Bad news, William. I remember when Marcelle was with the US Attorney's. He was solid and a bulldog going after people. People called him the Hammer. Then he switched sides. And now she's a partner. That means she's going to be involved in some dirty stuff."

"It's a law firm," Kane said. "Don't lawyers only deal in dirty stuff? Just like cops?"

Nathan chuckled. "You got me there, nephew. Yeah, not like I spend all my time chatting with upstanding citizens and the law-abiding."

"And as you say, Marcelle was on your side for a long time," Kane added. "He only went private after Ted died. He cared about Ted more than anything."

"Yeah, sure," Nathan allowed. He shifted topics. "If you met Quinn, you know what he is. Stone cold killer. I'm sure you saw worse in Vietnam. Speaking of which, I was wondering if I could pick your brain a bit?"

"For what?"

"The Son of Sam Task Force."

"The one you wanted Uncle Conner on?"

"I don't blame him for not signing on," Nathan admitted. "There're a number of experienced guys, top detectives, who've declined to join Omega. Afraid it'll damage their career however it turns out. The notes that bastard leaves are bothering us more than we publicly let on.

"Then we got other guys, ones with daughters, beating down the door to join. Scared for their kids. The city is going nuts." Nathan sighed. "We've had all sorts of experts come in. Shrinks, handwriting analysis guys to go over his letters, even, and don't tell anyone this, some psychics who claimed they had what they call insights. Bunch of bullshit. Nobody has given us anything solid."

"I always thought if a psychic were real, they'd be living off their lottery winnings or bets at the track," Kane said. "Like priests. Promising shit they can't deliver on."

"Hey. Watch that stuff, especially around your mother."

"*Mea culpa.*"

"Anyway," Nathan continued, "that's how little we have. The shrinks say he's what they call a paranoid schizophrenic. Like someone walks around with a blinking sign on their chest with that. They say he's been rejected by women; hell, ain't that every man? A lot of mumbo jumbo that doesn't get us any closer to putting cuffs on someone."

"Okay," Kane said. "What do you want from me? I was a soldier, now I'm a two-bit private investigator working for a shyster law firm, according to my uncle the detective."

"Nice try, William. You weren't just a soldier," Nathan said. "You were Special Forces. A Green Beret. You were around killers, right? Maybe you'd have some insight into this guy? What makes him tick? Why is he doing this?"

"That was war," Kane said. "Not New York City."

"I know," Nathan said. "But we're desperate. Women are getting their hair cut and dying it blonde since he seems to favor longhaired brunettes. The clubs are empty at night and going out of business. The city is locking up once it gets dark. People are scared like I've never seen and I've seen a lot over the years on the job. I thought if you took a look at what we have, you might come up with something, no matter how small. You'd bring a fresh set of eyes with a different perspective. Cops tend to think alike. We could use your expertise."

It was Kane's turn to pick up a stone, slide it through his fingers, touching the smoothness of thousands of years of surf. He nodded toward the north. "Over there. The Hutchison River Parkway. Know who it's named for?"

Nathan shrugged. "Nah."

"A woman. Anne Hutchinson. A Puritan who got kicked out of Boston in the 1600's for preaching. She had fifteen kids and settled somewhere around here. Then they got massacred by Indians. One daughter survived because she hid in Split Rock." Kane looked at him. "It's a big rock broken in half between the off ramp to the firing range and the Hutch. Thousands of people drive right by every day and don't know anything about it or that it's even there or the people who died."

"Okay. And?"

"There's things I know, like that. And lots more I don't know."

"Like what?"

"I don't know what I'm doing, Uncle Nathan."

"I don't get it. What do you mean? What's that got to do with Indians? And a massacre?"

"Randomness." Kane shrugged. "That's my life. I follow people around. As you say. Dig up dirt for divorces. Check into businesses to see who's skimming to pay some broad they have stashed in an apartment or hiding money in their secret overseas account. Do background checks. Other jobs as Toni needs. Research is what she calls it. Then she takes it and does whatever it is she does with the other side's lawyer. It never makes a courtroom, but gets settled. I don't even know how most of it turns out.

"Lately I've been doing some bodyguard gigs when she asks. But it's, I don't know, just shit. Still, what was I going to do? No one would hire me with the dishonorable discharge." He looked at his uncle. "Not the cops. Not the Feds, not that I'd work for those fuckers. My skill set isn't exactly applicable to many jobs in the civilian world."

"You need money?" Nathan asked.

"Nah, I got money," Kane said. "That's not the issue."

"What's the issue then?"

Kane shook his head in frustration. "I don't know."

"You got an engineering degree from West Point," Nathan noted.

Kane snorted. "You know what they call a West Point degree? A fifty grand education shoved up your ass a nickel at a time. Spec and dump is what we did. Memorize, pass the test, and move on. I didn't do any engineering in Vietnam or since. If I show someone my work history, they see the dishonorable discharge and that's that. Plus, there are the missing years. I'm screwed either way."

"But that's where you might be able to help the Task Force," Nathan said. "You've seen things other people haven't. I can get you some money as a consultant. We've been paying these worthless bums. But you're the real deal. It could open up a new line of work for you if things break right."

"Is working for cops that much different than lawyers?" Kane asked.

Nathan tapped the badge on his belt. "We uphold the law. Lawyers twist it whatever way they get paid to twist it."

"I saw lawyers in action during the trial," Kane said. "I also saw the cops, the military cops. Some were good and doing their job, and some were doing it because they liked having power over people. I ran into some shit MPs who were sadists. Conner says he's a collar man. That he does real police work, getting bad guys off the street."

Nathan looked away. "Conner is a collar man and we need those. But here's the thing, William. Don't be too hard on Conner. Even with Serpico's shitstorm and the Knapp Commission, being an honest beat cop is hard. Guys don't trust you if you're one hundred percent straight. They don't trust you enough, they might not back you up when things get bad. That's what happened to Serpico. He got shot in the face and the other cops with him wouldn't 10-13."

"Who you talking about?"

"10-13 is officer needs assistance. Serpico got shot during a drug bust. Some think it might have been a set up to get him. His fellow cops on the call left him on the floor to bleed. Conner has to do things to get along with the other cops in his precinct so he can trust they got his back."

"Did you? Do things to make sure your back is covered?"

Nathan faced him. "Yeah, when I was on patrol. Not anymore. Not in a long time. But never anything to hurt civilians. Only the bad guys. Like take a touch of cash when busting a drug deal. That's true with Conner too." He reached out, putting a hand on Kane's shoulder. "One of the vics in the last Son of Sam shooting went your old grammar school. She survived but others haven't been so lucky."

"You're grasping now," Kane said.

"I told you we're desperate. *I'm* desperate, William. What more do you want? Want me to beg?"

Kane was taken aback. "What do you need?"

"Come to our headquarters on the Island," Nathan said. "We're in the one-oh-nine precinct, second floor, in Flushing. A couple of blocks from Shea."

"When?"

"Tomorrow good?"

"Tomorrow's Saturday."

"Son of Sam doesn't know it's the weekend, William. We have to catch him before he kills someone else."

"I know the killer doesn't care it's the weekend."

Nathan realized the Saturday issue. "You still go there every Saturday at the same time?"

"Since I've been back."

"It's been years, William."

"Three-hundred-and-fifty-three weeks."

"Jesus, Mary and Joseph," Nathan whispered. He regrouped. "Is eleven late enough?"

"I'll be there."

Nathan forced enthusiasm into his voice. "I'll show you around, then lunch is on me. I'll buy you a couple of hot dogs from the guy around the corner from the precinct. You don't even have to put condiments on 'em."

Kane smiled. "Sounds good, Uncle Nathan."

"What the hell was that all about anyway?" Nathan asked. "I never could figure it out, just saw you guys fighting about it."

"Dad used to take me to that hot dog vendor he liked on Bruckner when I was a kid," Kane explained. "I always took mine plain which pissed him off, because he figured it was the same price when putting everything on it, like sauerkraut and other crap. He used to pile everything on his. Kane kids aren't supposed to waste money."

Nathan shook his head. "My sister is a saint to put up with him." They headed back toward the 'yacht club'.

"One thing bothers me," Kane said as they climbed the stairs.

"What's that?"

"How did Delgado know it was me that took his picture last night? He couldn't have seen me. He must know his wife went to Marcelle's firm and that I'm on the case. But Toni says he shouldn't know about the pending divorce. He hasn't been served."

"Toni's naive," Nathan said. "Someone at the firm talked out of house. I'm sure Cappucci would pay to find out his daughter walked in about a divorce. You can't trust anybody at that place."

"Quinn also knew about my past. The Army. Taryn. He told Delgado about it."

Nathan frowned. "How did Quinn know that?"

"Another mystery," Kane said.

"Again," Nathan said, "must be someone at Marcelle's firm. They all know what happened to Ted and then to you."

"I guess."

They went through the bar.

"Hey, let me ask you something," Kane said. "Conner said grandpa, your father, used to take you shooting at Rodham's and never took him. He sounded real bitter about it."

Nathan laughed. "I hated shooting with pop. The old man would give me grief about everything I did. How I held the gun. My stance. It was a nightmare every time. Conner had nothing to be jealous about. Geez. He's still bitching about that?"

"Yep."

"I don't think he remembers clearly," Nathan said. "Our mom died before Conner or Liam were old enough for pop to take them shooting. Once mom was gone, pop had no interest in doing anything with any of us. He never shot again. He dove into the bottle. If it wasn't for our older sister, your mother, God bless her, we'd have starved in that apartment. She raised Liam, Conner and me after mom passed." Nathan glanced sideways at Kane. "What do you remember about your grandfather?"

Kane shrugged. "I don't know. Not much. He smelled funny."

"The booze," Nathan said.

"I guess."

They were through and down the front steps. Nathan's unmarked Plymouth Fury with its black-wall tires was next to Kane's Jeep with busted headlights.

"Now go see my sister," Nathan said. "She's always worried about you. Make her feel better. She's a saint, she is."

*****

Kane passed on visiting the saint and chose damnation. He pulled the moleskin notebook out of his breast pocket and found the number. He needed not only the digits but to remind himself of the names of the other pertinents. He dialed, leaning against the fractured and graffitied Plexiglas in a phone booth on Bruckner Boulevard. The Jeep was double-parked, horns were blasting and middle fingers extended by drivers going around, accentuated with screamed profanities.

The phone was answered on the third ring. She sounded drowsy. "Hello?"

"Hey, Farrah, it's Will. Will Kane. Got your message at the diner. Didn't wake you, did I?"

"Howdy, stranger. It's been a while. No, I was getting up anyway. You beat the alarm by a minute."

"Yeah."

A few seconds of silence ticked off.

Farrah stepped into it. "What are you doing, Will?"

"I'm up in the Bronx. Talked to my uncles."

"You visit your folks?"

"No."

"Going to visit them?"

"I don't have the energy today."

"Probably for the best. You know. Family."

"Yeah."

"Are you all right?"

"Been a rough day."

"I'm sorry to hear that."

"What's going on?" Kane asked. "Why'd you call the diner?"

"Oh, nothing much," Farrah said. "Just thought it would be nice to talk with you." A few seconds of silence. "How long would it take you to get downtown?"

Kane glanced across the boulevard to the Expressway. "Traffic is bad. It's Friday afternoon. Probably forty-five minutes or an hour taking the FDR unless there's an accident. That too long? I know you've got, you know . . . " he trailed off.

"I'll see you in an hour, Will." It was not a question.

"An hour."

"I can't wait."

Kane hung up. He leaned forward, resting his forehead on the pay phone, the Act of Contrition beating on his conscience. He could smell the beer on his breath and was light-headed from drinking on an empty stomach and a long time since he'd last imbibed.

A horn blasted. "Hey fuckwad! Move that piece of shit!"

GRAMERCY, MANHATTAN

An old woman walking a tiny, yappy dog with a sparkly collar along Gramercy Park West stared at Kane and the Jeep with the combination of disgust and trepidation the Romans must have felt looking over Hadrian's Wall at the Picts painted in blue. It was likely she had a key to the gate into the actual Gramercy Park across the street, the only private park on the island of Manhattan, which summed up the neighborhood.

The black doorman wore a coat that would work outside Buckingham Palace. He looked like he was part of the building; solid, old and distinguished in his uniform and despite the heat, not sweating. He surprised the old lady by indicating for Kane to park the Jeep in the loading zone.

He shocked the old bitch when he opened the door to the lobby and gestured for Kane to enter the exclusive domain of 7 Gramercy Park West and greeted him with a smile: "William."

Kane nodded. "James. Thank you. How's Malcolm?"

James grimaced. "Taking too many pills. I try to talk to him, but what can I say? I don't know what he's feeling. What he's been through."

Kane nodded. "It's tough."

"Yeah," James said, "it is. Maybe you can help him?"

Kane's regret at damnation deepened. "Right. I'll talk with him."

"Thank you."

Kane walked to the elevator. It dinged open and an older couple, dressed for dinner, gave him the once over, then the wife pointedly looked away. The man appeared ready to say something but Kane was hot and tired and damned for all eternity so he didn't give the guy a chance, abruptly pushing past into the elevator.

The operator, the doorman's son, was in a wheelchair, both legs missing from mid-thigh. The empty pants legs of the uniform were neatly folded and safety pinned with a blanket, the material the same as the uniform. "Will."

"Malcolm." Kane shook his hand. "How you doing?"

Malcolm shoved the lever shutting the doors. Waited until they were closed before talking. "VA giving me a hard time about the meds."

"Fuck the VA," Kane said.

"Amen to that," Malcolm said as he pushed the other lever for the desired floor. "You look like shit."

"I feel like shit." Kane noted that Malcolm's hand was shaking on the lever.

Malcolm laughed. "You'll feel better soon."

Kane's face went red under the dark scruff.

"Hey man," Malcolm said. "Farrah is all right people. And you did right by her. And my dad and me by running that punk off. No need to feel weird."

"I was raised Catholic," Kane said.

"Hey, we're all going to hell," Malcolm said. "This is the least of your worries. Might as well go smiling. You still practice the faith?"

"Nah." Kane laughed. "Besides, I got plenty of things I'm already going to hell for including marrying outside the faith."

"I didn't know you was married," Malcolm said.

"Not any longer."

"Fucking bitches. All of 'em."

The elevator stopped at the sixth floor. Malcolm opened the door.

Kane stepped out, but paused with one foot still in the elevator. "Do you believe that?"

"What? Bitches?"

"Hell."

"Hell?" Malcolm shook his head. "We've already been there. You and I. We go to hell again, we'll waste that Satan motherfucker together." He made a gesture of firing a machinegun. "See how he'd like some seven-six-two up his ass. Go down fighting."

"Yeah. On your shield or with it."

Malcolm frowned. "What's that mean?"

"It's what the Spartan women used to say to their men when they marched off to war. Either come back with your shield in hand or being carried on it. Coming back without the shield meant you threw it away and ran."

"Fuck that." Malcolm laughed bitterly. "I can't run, but I can fight."

"Roger that." Kane removed his foot.

The door slid shut.

*****

"Am I keeping you from something?" Kane asked as Farrah opened the door to the apartment.

"Told you," Farrah said. "I always have time for you."

Young, blond, slender, and wearing a sparkly, white dress with wide cleavage. Her breasts, which were small and crowned with eraser nipples, were exposed when she turned. The back was bare to right above the buttocks. Her skin was pale and flawless. She sported a silver disco-mesh necklace two inches thick. Farrah had big, blonde hair, modeled after her chosen namesake, the most popular *Charlie's Angel* and current record-breaking poster girl.

"Come on, Will." Farrah led him along the hall and opened the door to the left. They entered a bedroom with a cozy queen-sized bed. The comforter was covered with pillows and stuffed animals. "Get comfortable."

Kane put the map case on a chair. Took the shirt off. He slid the A7A cargo strap he used as a belt out of the loops, making sure not to cut his fingers on the steel wire garrote fixed on the inside by a handful of threads. He put the holster and .45 on top of the map case. Removing the belt also released the sheath holding the shortened Fairbairn-Sykes fighting knife in the middle of his back and he placed it next to the gun.

"How do you sit with that thing?" Farrah asked. She made no move to undress.

"Carefully." Kane pulled the t-shirt over his head, revealing a crater of scar tissue on his lower left abdomen and a linear, thin pale scar across the top of his chest. A small ring, a miniature of Kane's original West Point ring, hung on a steel chain around his neck along with two dog tags wrapped with black electrical tape.

He paused, but Farrah was behind him. She ran her fingers down his chest, avoiding the ring and tags, across his stomach, and deftly unbuttoned the jungle fatigue pants.

He was already hard which bothered him.

She pressed up against him, still dressed, but he could feel her nipples through the material. She chuckled against his back. "The boots, Will. You always forget the boots."

"Sorry." He leaned over, removed the boot bands and unbloused the pant legs. He pulled out the double knot at the top of the jungle boots, then awkwardly jerked the laces, removing them from the top holes. He shoved them off along with the socks.

Farrah pushed his pants down. "Why don't you wear underwear?" she asked as he stepped out and she guided him toward the bed.

"Jungle rot," Kane said. "Got used to not wearing any."

"Real sexy foreplay, Will. I have heard better."

She turned him toward her. Smiled. Pushed him gently to fall back on the bed. His feet were still on the floor as she got on the mattress. She pushed aside a pillow and knelt beside him. She leaned forward and kissed his neck. "'Jungle rot'? That doesn't sound good at all."

"It's not fun," Kane said.

"Relax," Farrah murmured. Her left hand slid up his thigh, cupping his balls. She looked into his eyes. "Relax, Will. You're safe." Her right hand encircled him, coated with something warm and slippery as she stroked him. "You're safe here."

Kane closed his eyes. He reached up and placed his hand on her back, fingers gently running along her smooth skin. His other hand went to his chest, covering the miniature ring and dog tags.

"You're safe," Farrah breathed as she continued her ministrations.

The muscles in Kane's stomach were ridged as he tensed. His entire body was vibrating. Farrah continued to play him, each time pulling back right before he came.

"There's no hurry. You're safe."

Kane exploded with a deep groan and she continued to stroke him for several moments, until he was done. A wave of shame and guilt tsunamied over him. A stern internal voice vowed never to come back.

"Stay here," she said.

Kane nodded weakly, eyes still closed, sinking into the soft bed and depression. He reluctantly removed his hand from her back.

She went to the bathroom. Ran hot water and soaked a washcloth. Came back and cleaned him off with gentle wipes.

Kane finally opened his eyes. "Thank you."

Farrah laughed. "You are something, Will Kane. You're the only guy who just wants a handjob."

Kane frowned. "What do you mean? Is it weird?"

"No," Farrah hurriedly said. "Not at all. I like it. I like feeling you in my hands."

"What do most guys want?" Kane sat up.

Farrah had been drying him off with a towel but stopped. "I'm not going there."

"Sorry," Kane said.

Farrah put a hand on his shoulder. "Hey. I like doing this with you, Will." She got off the bed. Washcloth in one hand, towel in the other. "I'd like to do more with you." She smiled. "A lot more."

Kane shook his head. "I'm sorry, Farrah." He went to the chair holding his clothes and weapons. "I just can't. Nothing to do with you."

"Your ex?"

Kane pulled on his jungle fatigue pants. He buttoned them. "I don't know. I don't think so. It wouldn't feel right. Not because of you," he hurriedly explained. "Nothing to do with you, Farrah. I'm fucked up. I shouldn't be doing this."

"I don't think you're fucked up." Farrah got off the bed and walked to him. She kissed him lightly on the lips, which was a first and surprised him. "At least not that much. Comparatively speaking."

"You know—" Kane began.

"What?"

"You're the only person I've touched like that since I got back to the States this time and . . ." He stumbled into silence.

"You're joking?" Farrah was shocked. "But you only touch my back."

Kane didn't say anything as he sat and put on his boots.

She turned away and put the towel and washcloth into a bin but Kane caught the grimace on her face. "Hey!"

Farrah was startled at the abrupt change in Kane. She spun about. "What?"

"You're in pain. What happened?" He went to her.

Farrah put a hand on his chest, pushing him away. "Easy. Something got a little out of hand a few days ago. But it's okay now."

"Is that why you called me?"

"I just wanted to see you," she lied.

"Bull. I told you to call me if something got out of hand. And you mean *someone* got out of hand."

Farrah smiled sadly. "Will, if I called you every time someone got a little freaky, you'd have to move in. It's the life."

"What did he do?"

"No. We're not going there."

"You only get one of those," Kane said. "What happened?"

She indicated the necklace. "He got a little rough. Left marks. No one is supposed to do that."

"Let me see."

Farrah removed the necklace, revealing bruises, thumb on one side of her narrow neck, two fingers on the other.

"Did you black out?" Kane examined them.

"No. It was just a little too hard." She replaced the necklace.

"Who was it?" Kane pulled his t-shirt on. Then carefully began rethreading the A7A strap, looping it through the holster, which was Army issue, well-worn leather, mink oiled to suppleness, the flap cut off. A loop of parachute cord was woven around the lower part making it snug enough to keep the gun from falling out, but easy to draw. He passed the belt through the knife sheath in the middle of his back.

"Just a guy."

"You seeing him again?"

"If it's the job."

"Let me know if he hurts you again," Kane said, pulling the cargo strap belt tight. "I'll straighten him out." He slid the .45 into the holster.

"I can't have you straightening out the high rollers, Will. There's this thin line."

Kane paused, denim shirt in hand. "What line?"

Farrah looked toward the windows overseeing the green rectangle of Gramercy Park. "I don't want to do this forever. I've been saving money. Most girls say that, but they're snorting it or wasting it on clothes or shoes or have a pimp taking it or some bullshit. I been saving. I want enough to go someplace that isn't the city and settle down. Have a good life."

"Where's home?" Kane asked,

"Oh no," Farrah said, putting a finger on his lips. "You don't go there. *This* is my home. Here and now and that's all that matters. And I have to work that line. He was real sorry. Real sorry. I made an extra five hundred."

"Does *he* know where the line is?" Kane asked.

"Don't worry about it. The bruises will heal."

"What if he does something that doesn't heal?"

Farrah nudged him, pushing him toward the door. "I do have to be somewhere, Will."

"Do you carry a purse?"

Farrah nodded.

Kane reached down and drew a very short, double-edged knife from inside his left jungle boot.

"I'm not going to ask how you walk with that in your boot," Farrah said.

He removed the sheath, unthreading it from inside the canvas upper of the boot. "Will this fit inside your purse?"

"Yes, but—"

He extended it. "I insist. I'll rest easier knowing you have it."

"It's pretty small." Farrah laughed. "Those are three words I'm never, ever supposed to say."

"Three-inch blade," Kane said, "but it's razor sharp. Knives, even a small one, can be very effective. You don't stab. Too many bones in the body unless you know exactly what you're doing and where to do it. You slash. People, especially cowards, don't like getting cut. Slash and then run. If you're cornered, slash at the eyes. No one likes a knife coming toward their eyes."

"How do you know he's a coward?"

"Only a coward would hurt a woman."

"You have some peculiar notions." Farrah reluctantly accepted the knife. "Don't worry. I can take care of myself." She led him to the door. "But I love when you visit. It's my favorite time."

"Really? Nah."

Farrah smiled, revealing perfect white teeth. "Really. You know when I tell you to relax?"

Kane nodded.

"When you're here, that's what *I* can do."

"What about when you're alone?" Kane asked. "Aren't you relaxed?"

"Take care of yourself, Will."

*****

"She okay?" Kane asked Malcolm as the elevator rattled toward street level.

"I don't know," Malcolm said. "I don't care for those guys that visit. You're the only one who comes around that I like."

"Who hurt her?"

"I didn't know she got hurt," Malcolm said.

"Someone choked her. Left marks on her neck."

"We all got scars," Malcolm said. "She's just fighting a different war than we did."

"Your dad is worried you're taking too many pills," Kane said.

"That was smooth, honkie," Malcolm said. "Jump right into my personal shit with no preamble?"

Kane had no response.

The elevator halted with a slight jar. "You can't save everyone, Kane."

"I'm not trying to," Kane said. "I don't even want to."

Malcolm pulled the lever and opened the doors. "Fuck the VA, man."

"Yeah. Fuck the VA," Kane agreed. He walked into the lobby, the elevator shutting behind him. "I am *not* heartily sorry," he muttered to himself, just before James opened the lobby door.

GREENWICH VILLAGE, MANHATTAN

Kane drew the .45, thumbing off the safety as it cleared the holster. The matchstick lay on the concrete in front of the doorjamb to his apartment. It was dusk and there was just enough light in the dark entryway for him to see the tell. He retreated and glanced up. The front bay window on the main floor of the brownstone glowed. Kane holstered the gun and climbed the main stairs. Knocked.

"Come in," his landlord called out in an English accent. "Door's open."

Kane entered the main floor of the brownstone. He paused in the entry hall. "Hello?"

"In the kitchen," Pope announced.

Kane passed through the sitting room and the hallway to the kitchen. The thin, old man sat in a comfortable armchair, facing a round wooden table. It was covered with newspapers and books, some open, others paged with index cards. The room had the pleasant aroma of pipe smoke that filtered the light from the reading lamp behind Pope. A teacup rested next to the book in front of him. Pope wore khaki shorts and a short sleeve, colorful Hawaiian shirt. He sported a white straw hat with a black band on his balding head, completing the image of a refugee from a bad thirties movie supposedly set in the tropics. He had a pair of reading glasses perched on his nose. He raised the pipe slightly toward Kane, who acknowledged it with a finger to his right eyebrow.

"Evening, William."

"Evening, Mister Pope."

"I've told you, young man, just Pope. Everyone at the paper called me that. All my friends and all my enemies and all the unwashed masses in between." His British accent was unmuted by three decades in the city.

Kane took a position where he half-faced Pope and the back door, with the old fridge flanking him toward the front of the building. "I'm wondering if you went into my apartment today?"

"Not that I recall and I hope I am not yet at that stage of forgetfulness."

"Did you see anyone go in?"

"I did not, but I was wandering the stacks most of the afternoon. You Colonists are savages in many respects, but the bastion of knowledge guarded by Patience and Fortitude is a wonderful exception."

"I don't quite recall which is which," Kane said. "Is Patience on the left as you go up the stairs?"

Pope smiled. "Ah, you show your knowledge of your birth city. You have me stumped on that one, William. Why do you ask if I entered your apartment?"

"Someone opened my door."

"Were you robbed?"

"I haven't gone in yet."

"Then how do you know someone was in there?"

Kane explained the matchstick.

"*De omnibus dubitandum*," Pope said.

"I tend to be," Kane said.

Pope was surprised. "You know Latin?"

"I was an altar boy. Went to Catholic school for twelve years."

"Ah, one of those wonderful parochial schools grandly titled Our Lady of Perpetual Agony or some such." Pope peered at Kane over his glasses and under the brim of the straw hat. "I don't see the altar boy in you."

"He wandered away a long time ago."

Pope nodded. "I remember the exact moment I lost God. Rather, I should say, He lost me. After all, He is the all-powerful Being, not I, thus it would seem logical He has all the responsibility in the relationship."

"You'll have to tell me some day," Kane said, "but right now I've got to see if I have a guest. I recommend you stay here. If you hear shots, call the cops."

Pope removed the reading glasses. "And an ambulance?"

"If I shoot call a hearse." As soon as he said the words, Kane regretted them. Not because they were a boast, but because they portended a possibility he'd vowed never to visit again.

Kane exited and stood just outside Pope's front door on the high stoop. He scanned left and right. A couple walked down Jane Street to the east, heading away, but otherwise the sidewalks were empty. None of the parked cars appeared suspicious. Kane went down Pope's steps. Drew the .45. He opened the gate and took the steps slowly. That familiar dread stirred.

Lions and tigers and bears, oh my.

The door was locked which could mean several different things. Kane unlocked and pushed the door open, staying out of the line of fire. Waited twenty heartbeats.

He entered fast, as he'd been trained, crouching low, gun high, eyes following the barrel as he swept the sitting room, finger light on the trigger. No one. He moved on to the bedroom and bath and then kitchen, muzzle of the gun leading. No one. The back door was locked.

Kane stopped at the small kitchen table he used as a desk. Someone *had* been in here.

Kane swung about, bringing up the .45 as he heard noise from the sitting room.

"Everything all right?"

"I asked you to stay upstairs," Kane said, holstering the gun.

"You are not only suspicious of all," Pope said, "you are prepared to deal with all."

"I'm a real Boy Scout," Kane said.

"Anything stolen?"

"Not that I can see."

Pope was looking around. "None of the furnishings. Not that I packed the place flush with objects d'art. I appreciate your maps. One can literally see the history of the city in their flow." He frowned as he saw the bed. "That's exactly the way I make my bed."

"It's the way you made this one," Kane said.

"That was a year ago," Pope said. "Do you perchance sleep in a coffin? Should I pinch some garlic from the garden to protect myself?"

Kane pointed at the closet. A thin sleeping pad and camouflage poncho liner were underneath a hanging row of similar denim shirts and black jungle fatigue pants. A brown leather jacket bookended the wardrobe on one side. A heavy winter coat on the other.

"Do you have an aversion to beds?" Pope asked. "A phobia? I've heard of more esoteric fears. We all have foibles."

"A bed is where someone expects you to be," Kane said.

"Ah." Pope nodded as if he understood, or was humoring Kane. "You're also not very diverse when it comes to wardrobe."

"One less decision to make every day."

Pope smiled. "I've never been a fashion mogul." He spotted the pegs and board above the bathroom. "That's new."

Kane went to it, jumped and grabbed the pegs. He pulled one out and reached across, inserting it another hole. Did the same with the other. A couple of pull-ups. Let go and dropped. "A decent upper body workout. I'll fix the drill holes when I leave."

"Intriguing," Pope said. He turned back to the bedroom. "Perhaps a false alarm? Your matchstick slipped?"

Kane shook his head. "I don't think so."

Pope pointed up. "Would you like some tea? Good for the nerves."

"I thought that was booze," Kane said as he followed him.

"Ah, son, you must learn my lexicon."

They re-entered Pope's kitchen and he turned on the overhead fluorescent, pushing the darkness away. The room was neat and orderly, other than the reading material on the table, much like the man. He reached into a cupboard, retrieving a bottle of scotch. Poured a jolt into his teacup. "Tea for calming the nerves."

"No, thanks," Kane said as Pope made to pour into another cup. "I gave up on hard liquor a long time ago." He took the cup and poured some tap water into it.

Pope sat down. "Who would break into your apartment yet take nothing?"

"Apologies. I misspoke," Kane said. "Something was taken. An envelope I hadn't mailed yet."

"Was it important?"

"To some people." Kane apparently changed the subject. "Did you cover the mafia when you were at the Post?"

"I was on the city beat," Pope said. "In New York that necessitates covering the current iteration of La Cosa Nostra. More accurately known as the Five Families beginning in 1931. Thus, I know a little but would not qualify myself as an expert compared to those who are."

"What do you know about the Cappucci family?"

"That's a broad topic," Pope said. "Do you desire something specific?"

"Why did the Families make the eldest Cappucci leave town?"

Pope thought for a moment. "Technically it wasn't the Families who ordered that, it was the Commission. That's the top of the food chain for the mafia in the United States. However, I do believe there is a trans-nation organization, a supermob if you will, of which the mafia is only an obvious and rather blunt part, but that my friend, would have to be a discussion for another day and require considerable patience on your part and is, as I note, only a theory. I've often thought of writing a book on it but never had the time."

"What's the Commission?" Kane asked.

"Did you not see *The Godfather*? Or *Part Two*?"

"They came out while I was overseas. I usually do books."

"A man after my own heart. However, if you get a chance, partake and savor. Both were well done. There *is* a book the first one was based on. I have it around here. I'll lend it to you, although I have specific rules about lending books. Given the number of volumes in your abode, I'm surprised you don't possess it."

"I'm still working on my to be read pile."

"As we both will be until the day we pass on," Pope said. "The Commission consists of not just the Five Families from New York, but also the Outfit in Chicago, which runs LA, plus the families in Buffalo, Philadelphia and Detroit. The Commission was formed to keep internecine fighting between the different factions to a minimum so they could focus on the profit margin. Cappucci ignored their warning about a specific issue and had one of his enforcers kill someone in the Rosado family."

"Which enforcer?"

"A fellow named Quinn."

"Why wasn't Quinn punished?"

"How do you know he wasn't?"

"He joined me for breakfast this morning. He looked healthy."

"Interesting. So, this is relevant. I was wondering about the change in topic."

"Why did Quinn kill whoever it was?"

"The hearsay is this Quinn chap was acting on Cappucci's orders when he did the murderous task so the blame was not technically his. He *allegedly* committed the act, to properly legalese, as he was not arrested and no proof has been uncovered. Thus, the eldest Cappucci was banished and his son took over as Don. It's still a Don Cappucci running things, just a generation younger. Their territory is a slice of Brooklyn and some pieces here and there in Manhattan. The mafia treats the city as a smorgasbord, with each family taking profitable portions."

"Anything else on Quinn?"

"Not in my frontal lobe at the moment. What happened at breakfast?" Pope asked.

"Cappucci's son-in-law Alfonso Delgado, wanted something from me."

"Did you give it?"

"Yes."

"What was it?"

"Photos I took when I was surveilling him."

"If you don't mind, why were you following this Alfonso Delgado?"

"His wife wants a divorce. I was looking for grounds."

"Did you?" Pope asked. "Until '67, adultery was the only legal cause for divorce in New York State. I believe it's expanded since then, not that I've participated in the sacrament or the unraveling of."

"Found exactly that and took a photo. A copy was in the envelope that was stolen."

"Interesting. I could find out more about Delgado and Quinn?"

"If it's not much trouble," Kane said.

"I still have friends at the Post. One of them knows considerably more about the mafia than I. I'll ask around."

"Thanks."

Pope had been forcibly retired from the New York Post two months ago when an Australian, Rupert Murdoch, bought the venerable New York City newspaper. Murdoch immediately cleaned house and was shifting the New York institution, founded by Alexander Hamilton in 1801, from serious newspaper to sensational tabloid in a bid to increase circulation.

Pope took a sip from his teacup and took advantage of Kane's silence. "What do you make of this Son of Sam tragedy?"

"Why?"

Pope was slightly taken aback by Kane's reaction. "It's the topic everyone in the city is discussing. Those I know at the Post are being roasted by Mister Murdoch to come up with something, anything, factual or not. The paper is doing an abysmal job of legitimate coverage, sensationalizing it for sales. Of course, that's sadly working in terms of circulation. Thus the ignorant reward their exploiters. But the press should answer to a higher calling."

Kane nodded in apology. "It's just strange you should mention it. I saw my uncle, who's a detective on the case, today. He invited me to the Omega Task Force HQ tomorrow."

Pope leaned forward, forgetting his 'tea' for the moment. "Really? I'd love to chat with you afterward."

"I can't speak out of house," Kane said.

"Off the record, of course." Pope said. "I wouldn't give those gangaroos Murdoch flew in anything."

"'Gangaroos'?"

"The Australian reporters he brought with him. All they know how to do with expertise is drink to excess. They believe they can understand a city by simply getting off a plane. It takes decades to imbibe the essence of New York City."

"How long have you been here, Pope?" Kane asked.

"You'd think after thirty-two years I'd be saying boids and toitles from da Bronx zoo."

Kane chuckled. "My sisters talk like that. I don't think my Bronx is that bad. Thirty-two years?" He did the math. "Right after World War II? Did you serve?"

"In a manner of speaking. His Majesty's forces wouldn't take me as I was a tad young when the war broke out so I became a reporter to do my bit. Seems no one wanted my references or cared about my age for that job, just that I was willing to travel and could string together a coherent sentence. I accompanied His Majesty's forces around the world. North Africa. A stint in Italy. Even Yugoslavia for a few months. Then France and across the Rhine with the boys. The end of the Thousand Year Reich."

"You probably saw more combat than most soldiers," Kane said.

Pope looked out the back window into the darkness for a moment. "Possibly. And I wish never to see any more."

"Amen to that." Kane raised his cup and Pope lightly touched it. They both took a sip.

"That still doesn't explain why you came to the US," Kane said. "Unless you don't want to talk about it."

"I was present when a camp in Poland was liberated," Pope said. "Between that and having nothing holding me in England, Europe was done for me. I wanted a fresh start. All your exuberant GIs indicated this might be the place. A different spirit than a war-weary continent. My home island was exhausted after two World Wars and the Empire was experiencing death throes; not a pleasant spectacle."

"Did you get one? A fresh start?"

Pope quaffed the rest of the Scotch. "Best I can do is arise each morning and get through the day making the most of it I can. The human condition. I had my job and that consumed me. Now, I have the library, my books and the garden." He poured into his cup. "I find it intriguing that Alexander Hamilton died nearby. One of the reasons I gravitated to this abode years ago." He pointed with the teacup in his hand toward the front door. "Directly across the street. The original house is long gone, but there's a little plaque commemorating his passing. Few passersby's notice."

"Thought he died in Jersey," Kane said. He'd looked for and found that sign the first day he moved in. "Where everyone is already dead."

Pope chuckled at the weak joke. "No. He and Burr scurried over to New Jersey to assuage their manhood because dueling was outlawed in New York. The stories of how the duel unfolded are varied; a case of differing witnesses with after the fact agendas to skew their account. What is of no doubt is that Hamilton was gravely wounded. His friends rowed back across the Hudson while he was still clinging to this mortal coil. Carried him to a house across the street where he expired the next day."

"Dueling seems kind of stupid," Kane said.

"There was a pretense of honor about the entire affair, but it's like war. When two sides go too far and then neither has the courage to back down."

Kane raised the cup. "Truth."

Saturday Morning, 9 July 1977

MEATPACKING DISTRICT, MANHATTAN

Kane put the five spot on the edge of the table. Three meat drivers held quiet court in a booth. A guy in a cheap security guard outfit sat at the counter, reading a comic book. He had a pair of handcuffs and a short billy club hanging from his belt. Enough stuff to get him hurt. An old beyond her years hooker with a tan raincoat draped over her slumped shoulders sat at the counter and chatted wearily with Thao.

Morticia placed the cup of coffee and glass of water with two ice cubes in front of Kane. Then she broke routine and sat across from him.

She indicated the diner. "Most of the vampires have crawled off to their coffins. We won't see the weekend crowd for a bit."

Kane cradled the mug, feeling the warmth. "Right."

"That's called making conversation."

"Right."

"I'm told you been coming here for a while," Morticia said. "I asked Thao about you."

"What did he say?"

"You know Thao better than me, don't you? What do you think he said?"

"Not much."

"'Not much'," Morticia agreed. "He called you *dai yu*. What's that mean? It didn't sound like he was cursing you out. You know, like someone would say asshole in another language."

"That's Vietnamese for captain." Kane glanced toward the counter where Thao was pouring the hooker a refill and passing her some meds in a brown paper bag.

"Was he in the South Vietnamese army?"

"Not exactly. He's a Montagnard. They live in Vietnam, but they're a separate tribe."

"What's the difference?"

"He's one of the mountain people." Kane lifted the cubes and plunked them into the coffee.

"Now I know more about him from you, than you from him," Morticia said.

"Why do you want to know anything?" Kane asked.

"I'm bored," Morticia said. She leaned back in the booth. "Got no one else to serve at the moment and Thao has the counter. You know he gives some people medicine?"

"Yes."

"Okay. So, you're all I have for conversation."

"Lucky me."

"Unlucky me," Morticia said. "What was with the peppers yesterday?"

Thao looked over, smiled, poured the security guy a refill, and disappeared into the kitchen.

"Ask Thao."

"I did. He just shrugged."

"You're awfully curious this morning."

"I'm concerned for my welfare," Morticia said. "Those guys were bad news. But you're bad news too, Kane. You had your gun out. The other guy had a gun. What were you going to do if the conversation turned ugly? Turn this place into the O.K. Corral?"

"You're not really bored," Kane said. "What did his gun look like?"

"Comparing sizes?"

Kane sighed.

"What's that?" Morticia indicated the bracelet on his right wrist. "Thao has one. They're pretty."

"It's a Montagnard bracelet," Kane said. "Hand-made from the brass of expended shell casings. Thao's people gave it to me."

"Why?"

"It was part of a ceremony in their village to accept me as one of them."

She expressed mock surprise. "They liked you?"

"We fought together. That's stronger than like." He frowned. "But yeah, I guess."

"Thao's always here," Morticia said. "He's the only cook I've worked with. Does he take any days off?"

"Ask him," Kane said.

"I did. He just smiled. It's like he lives here."

"He does." Kane pointed. "On the roof."

"'On the roof?" Morticia was puzzled. "What do you mean?"

"He built himself a place on the roof," Kane said. "Reminds him a little bit of home. You know. Concrete jungle. Looks like a hut but it's pretty cozy."

Morticia shook her head. "He might be as crazy as you. Speaking of which. What do you do? I thought maybe you were a cop when I first saw you, but you're definitely not a cop."

"I'm a part-time investigator for a law firm."

"Thao did say you got him out of Vietnam when it fell. Brought him here to the States. That he owes you his life."

"I owed him my life," Kane said. "So, we're even."

"What about his family?"

"They didn't make it. What's with the inquisition?"

Morticia pointed with a long, pale finger. "What happened to your head?"

"I got shot."

"In a diner? Just checking."

"No. Vietnam. The end of my first tour." He glanced at the kitchen. "That's when Thao saved my life. He found me after I'd been shot. Kept me alive."

"Didn't you have other Army guys around to tend to you?" Morticia asked.

"Most of the Army guys around me were dead or dying."

"Oh." Morticia was silent for a few moments. "Thao sent those peppers as a warning," she finally said, not a question. "He saw those guys coming down the street. He's got that little window in the door on the side of the kitchen. He can spot any car coming by on Gansevoort since it's one way toward the river or down Washington, which is also one-way coming from uptown. He's got a mirror angled on the far wall of the kitchen so he can see that way. Pretty neat."

"Very observant," Kane said. "Makes this a nice place, doesn't it?"

"For what? A last stand?" Morticia continued. "And he's got a wood crossbow in the kitchen. He hides it, but the kitchen isn't that big. Specially to hide a crossbow. He had it out when I went back there after the visitors yesterday. He was covering you, wasn't he?"

"Sounds like it."

"A crossbow? That big machete he has isn't for cooking. Living on the roof?" Morticia put both hands on the table, long, pale fingers spread, no rings. "Here's the thing, Kane. I've been asking you all these questions, but you've never asked me a single thing. All the times you come in here, every morning. You wouldn't know my name if it wasn't on my nametag, would you?"

"I'm not good with names. Is that your real name?"

An upward twitch of her thin pale lips. "That was honest. And no. It's not my real name. It's a persona."

"A what?"

She lifted her hands and indicated the diner. "I work the early shift at a diner in Greenwich Village. Do you expect Peggy-Sue from the farm in a joint like this?"

"Are you Peggy-Sue from the farm?"

"No."

"Who are you then?"

"In here? Morticia. That wasn't much of a question."

Kane sighed once more in exasperation. "Okay. How old are you?"

"Jesus Christ, Kane. That's the *last* question you ever ask a woman."

"I just come in for my paper and a cup of coffee."

"I was twenty-two at Woodstock."

"Oh. Peace, love and revolution?"

Morticia smiled. "There was some of that."

"Did you have a good time?"

"Second best moment of my life. Did you do the math? You know when Woodstock was?"

"Summer '69." Kane calculated years by where he was. "I was in LBJ."

"'LBJ'?"

"Long Binh Jail. Vietnam."

"You were a bad boy?"

"I was accused of murder."

Morticia stared at him. "Murder in Vietnam? Is that possible?"

Kane nodded. "*That* was my problem with it."

"Did you kill a fellow American?"

"I killed the enemy. Allegedly."

"I thought that was the concept of war, although the whole thing is pretty insane." She returned to the present. "Can I ask you something?"

"It would obviously be better than the reverse although I did try."

"You work for a lawyer, right?"

"Just told you that."

"I've got a friend who needs some legal help," Morticia said. "She—" she paused as the Gansevoort door opened. "They're back. Every Saturday morning like clockwork."

Two Chinese men entered. They were dark haired, identical in every way, including their black silk suits with white shirts and thin black ties. They were stocky, five and a half feet tall, and their fingers were crowded with gold rings. They wore wraparound black sunglasses. They walked to Kane's booth, bowed in concert, several gold chains around their necks dangling. Kane bowed his head in reply. They executed an about face and marched into the kitchen.

"Who the hell are they?" Morticia asked.

"Van Van."

"What?"

"Ting Van and Tong Van, but we called them Van Van."

"Is that a joke?"

"No, that's what they go by. You talk to one, you're talking to both of them. I've never seen them apart."

"Still not telling me why they come in here every Saturday and bow to you, then go talk to Thao."

"They're Nung," Kane said.

Morticia waited for more of an explanation, but when none was forthcoming, she looped back. "Okay, I've got a friend—"

She was interrupted as the Kid entered. He was dressed in tight, short shorts, a tie-dyed t-shirt, and flip-flops. He looked achingly young to be living his persona. He had a big smile and was bopping in his head and singing to himself.

He paused seeing Morticia in the booth with Kane, then plowed forward, tossed the paper and took the money. He nodded hello to Morticia. "Morning, lovely lady."

"Good morning, sweetie," Morticia said.

"Gonna be another sunny day," the Kid said.

"You ever work on cars?" Kane asked.

"What do you mean work on?"

"I'm not asking you to rebuild an engine. Do you think you could replace the headlights on my Jeep?" Kane peeled two twenties from his money clip. "You know where it's parked?"

"The old garage around the block from the Stonewall. With the big padlock."

"There are replacements in a cardboard box to the right as you enter." Kane removed the key for the steering wheel lock and a spare for the garage and handed them to the Kid. "Bring the keys back to Thao when you're done."

"When do you need it?" The Kid pocketed the money and keys.

"I'm taking my motorcycle today," Kane said. "Any time before tomorrow is good."

"That 125 Kawasaki dirt bike? Better not get on a highway with it. Does that thing even hit fifty?"

"Downhill with a good wind behind you," Kane said. "But where can you hit fifty in the city?"

"A valid point." The Kid smiled. "I'll do it after the movie."

"What movie?" Morticia asked.

"*Star Wars*," the Kid was bouncing on his feet, anxious to be going.

"You told me you already saw it," Morticia said.

"I've seen it four times. Today will be five."

"I've heard good things," Morticia said.

"It's like nothing you've ever seen," the Kid insisted. He made a swooshing noise as he pirouetted, pretending to have a sword and slashing through the air.

"What's that?" Kane asked.

"Light saber."

"'Light saber'?"

"Luke Skywalker has to learn to master the Force," the Kid said. "So he can defeat the bad guys with his light saber. It's like a laser sword."

"They don't have guns?" Kane asked.

"Yeah," the Kid said. "They got guns, but real warriors, the Jedi, use light sabers. And the bad guy does too. Darth Vader. He's a really bad cat. But Luke is part of the Force. The good Force. He's a Jedi. And Vader is the bad Force. He works for the evil Emperor. Darth Vader dresses all in black. Black helmet covering his whole head. His voice is freaky."

"Do the good guys win?" Kane asked.

"Of course," the Kid said. "Except Vader gets away." He was abashed. "Sorry. Shouldn't have told you that. Now I messed it up for when you see it." He waved a hand in front of his face. "Poof! Forget I said anything!"

"Done." Morticia turned to Kane. "What was the last movie you went to?"

"I don't remember," Kane said.

"Oh, you *have* to go!" the Kid insisted. "Fucking far out, man. Really." A stray synapse connected. "Oh, yeah, that junkie who ripped off Dino's?"

"Yes?" Kane waited.

"His street name is Wiley. You know, like the cartoon. Always chasing the smack. If you want to find him, he lives on the West Side Highway, the other side of the plywood." He jerked a thumb over his shoulder. "Close to where the hole is."

"'On' the West Side Highway?" Morticia asked.

"He means the closed section," Kane surmised.

"You're not going to mess him up, are you?" the Kid worried.

"He served in my old unit," Kane said. "I'd never mess up a fellow Sky Soldier."

The frown disappeared from the Kid's face in a flash and he was back with the Force. "Cool." He checked the clock above the counter. "I gotta run to catch the first showing."

"Enjoy," Morticia said.

"May the Force be with you!" The Kid bounced away.

"Hey, Kid!" Kane called out before he got to the door.

The Kid looked over his shoulder. "Yeah?"

"Be careful out there."

As the Kid opened the door, he stepped back and waved Toni Marcelle in with a flourish. She gave a terse smile in appreciation.

As Toni approached, Morticia slid out. She met Toni halfway. "Coffee?"

Toni nodded. "Thank you. Black." She was dressed for an evening out, not breakfast in Vic's. A short black leather skirt that displayed her legs to great advantage and a red blouse. A small purse was tucked under her arm.

Kane stuffed the Times into his map case as Toni sat across from him.

"What's wrong?" Kane asked.

"What's right?" Toni said. "I got your message yesterday. There've been some developments. Delgado is losing his shit. Cappucci received your photos."

"That's not good."

Toni was staring at him. "They were delivered to Cappucci by courier late yesterday. The same service we use at the firm. And the firm was on the return address with attention my name. You told me you didn't have the negatives or make copies, Will."

"How do you know Cappucci got them?"

"Because Alfonso Delgado confronted me outside Studio 54 earlier this morning. He said he still has the pictures and negatives you gave him. Said you lied. He was pissed to say the least. Frank and the bouncers had to protect me. I left by the back." She recited it like a summation in court.

Kane considered this development. Out of the corner of his eye, through the kitchen door window, he spotted Van Van as they departed via the side door.

Toni tapped the Formica with a long, red fingernail. "How did photos that only Delgado had get couriered to the last person he'd want to see them?" She gave Kane only a second to ponder. "You lied to me, Will. You made copies. Did you send them?"

"Why would I do that? Someone broke into my apartment yesterday and stole them."

"You lied to me."

"You already said that."

"Fuck," Toni muttered. "If I can't trust you, Will, who can I trust?"

"I was covering my ass," Kane said. "You cover your ass, don't you?"

"Do you keep copies of everything?"

Kane leaned forward. "We burned the interrogation transcript of the double agent in Vietnam. That was before we knew we were going to get charged with his murder. We destroyed a key piece of evidence in our favor. His confession. Pretty stupid. I learn from my mistakes."

"You don't trust me," Toni said.

"Of course, I trust you," Kane said. "This has nothing to do with that. I don't trust the world, Toni. Don't take it personal."

"What else was stolen from your apartment? You've done a lot of work for the firm."

"For you," Kane said. "Just the photos. I don't keep anything sensitive there. I was mailing them to my cut out."

"Your what?"

"A person who keeps my stuff safe. He's a cut out, because I don't know where he hides it. That makes it secure."

"It's not *your* stuff, Will. It's our stuff. My stuff. Who did this?"

"Someone from your firm?"

"Good thing you didn't become a lawyer. Let me follow your logic. Someone from my firm broke into your apartment and stole photos, which I didn't believe you had, but needed for my case, and sent them to Cappucci?"

"Okay. Who would want to shit on Delgado? His wife? Does she know *I'm* on the case?"

"She knows I have someone following her husband, but same questions. No way she'd know where you live and that you had copies."

"Maybe they weren't my copies," Kane said.

"You just said they were stolen from your apartment." She tapped the table. "This is my job, Will. I'm a lawyer. I follow logic."

"All right."

"Let's stick with facts. You did have copies, correct?"

Kane nodded.

"They were stolen from your apartment?"

"Yes."

"Cappucci got a set. The only other set we know of was in Delgado's hands along with the negatives. He's the last person in the world to want Cappucci to see them."

"Maybe someone took them from him? Or stole them from him and made another set?"

"No," Toni said. "Delgado said he still has the photos and the negatives. These were the ones stolen from your apartment. By the way, Delgado is pissed at you too. Says you lied to him. Like you lied to me."

"Hey—" Kane started, but tamped it down.

Toni continued her logic train. "Which brings up the question of how did someone know where you live? And who would break in?"

"Fuck me," Kane said. "He was there."

"Who? Where?"

"Quinn. The other night at the pier. He must have been following Delgado. He saw me snap the pictures. He followed me home."

"If he saw you take the pictures, he could have stopped you."

"He could have tried," Kane allowed.

"But he didn't."

This logic was more Kane's expertise. "Quinn was following Delgado, like I was. Except I never spotted him. I was focused on Delgado. Then he tracked me home. I should have picked up on that. Another mistake."

"And you made copies," Toni threw in. "That's three."

"Could you please stop tapping the table," Kane asked.

Toni rolled her fingernails in a staccato. "Does it bother you, Will?"

"Maybe we can find a blackboard?"

Toni stopped finger-nailing. "Why would Quinn do this?" She didn't give him a chance to answer. "He wants leverage. The leverage we should have had. I don't think there's any love lost between Quinn and Delgado. The way things stand, if Cappucci dies with no son, and it isn't likely his wife is going to produce one at her age, Delgado might be the next Don, or more likely his wife, Sofia Delgado, the Don's daughter, will run it from the shadows through him. Quinn wants to own Delgado as he's the anointed one."

"But he wouldn't send them to Cappucci," Kane pointed out. "He'd keep them. Hold over Delgado's head."

"Maybe. Our immediate problem is Delgado thinks I sent the photos," Toni said. "He was foaming at the mouth."

"Why would Quinn set you up as the source?"

"I'm Mrs. Delgado's lawyer."

"Where is Delgado now?"

"No idea. But some muscle-bound freak was standing outside my apartment when I tried to go home, so I had Frank drive me around for a couple of hours. Then drop me here."

"That's Cibosky," Kane said. "Delgado's pet. Wanna-be Jeep mechanic."

"Great."

"Why not go to the cops?"

Toni gave him the stink eye.

Morticia floated up. "Can I get you anything?"

Kane shook his head.

"Some orange juice?" Toni asked.

"Sure thing, darling." Morticia looked at Kane. "I think Thao is cooking you something with peppers." She glided away.

"Did I interrupt the two of you when I came in?" Toni asked in a lower voice, indicating Morticia.

"Nope. We were chatting about jewelry. The usual. Why didn't you call your dad?"

"There's stuff going on," Toni said, "at the firm. Father wants to bring me further in, but there's a lot I don't know."

"Further or deeper?" Kane asked, watching both doors.

"What does that mean?"

"I'm just the guy that digs dirt," Kane said. "How deep the hole is? No clue. Apparently, you don't either. But that doesn't explain why you didn't call your father. He's got a lot of pull in the city. He could have Delgado locked up with one call. And he's got investigators who are willing to do more than I am. Like Frank."

"I solve my own problems."

Kane arched an eyebrow.

"Oh, fuck you," Toni said. "This is your screw up and your problem too."

"He's across the street," Kane said, as if he were asking for the ketchup.

"What? Who?" Toni looked over her shoulder. Cibosky was in the shadowed space underneath the stub of the High Line, arms folded across his large chest, glaring into the diner.

"Since you didn't go home, Delgado probably told Cibosky to come here and ask me about the pictures." Kane was looking past her. "Train still runs on the High Line a couple times a week. Used to go all the way to the Battery, before they started dismantling it. You know why they elevated it?"

Toni turned from watching Cibosky. "What?"

"The High Line," Kane repeated. "The tracks used to run along Tenth Avenue. But it ended up being called *death avenue* because the trains would hit trucks and cars and pedestrians. Even though they had guys on horses, West Side Cowboys, riding in front of each train waving red flags and warning people. Seems some people don't take warnings seriously. So they elevated it."

"Fascinating," Toni said. "What are we going to do about the knuckle-dragger across the street?"

"'We'?" Kane sighed. "You want to know where I went after the accident, Toni? The years I disappeared? Besides watch Monty Python in black and white?"

"Father thinks you went in a hole somewhere and stayed drunk," Toni said.

"I tried that for a while and it didn't work. I tried a lot of things that didn't work. I also learned some things."

"Do I want to know what you learned?" Toni asked.

"Got no choice now. Watch my map case, please." He exited the booth and headed for the Gansevoort door.

"Kane?" Morticia said, a pot of coffee in her hand, three fingers looped through the handles of cups in the other, pausing on her way to a trio of streetwalkers who'd wandered in via Washington. "What are you doing?"

He ignored her. Pushed the door open. Walked diagonally across the street into the dimness under the High Line. "Hey, big fellow."

"The man with the guns."

This early there wasn't much traffic or many pedestrians.

Kane pointed further into the shadows, toward the brick wall of a warehouse built beneath the tracks. "Over there."

Cibosky frowned. "So you can shoot me with your little gun?"

"I left that inside the diner."

"Your big gun?"

Kane walked past him, out of arm's reach. He put the .45 on a wood crate and turned about to face the muscles. Cibosky cautiously followed.

Kane held his hands out wide and empty.

Cibosky grinned and stepped forward, raising his arms.

Kane struck three times so fast that Cibosky didn't lose the grin until the third blow: a sharp right-hand jab in the solar plexus, a strike in the throat with the left, and a flat palm from the first hand straight into the nose as Kane closed the distance between them. The crunching of the nose breaking matched the disappearance of the grin.

Cibosky would have screamed in pain, but the first two blows had taken his wind and bruised his throat respectively. He made a sick, gurgling noise as he doubled over, trying to get his breath back, blood pouring from the nose.

Kane took advantage of that position by cupping his right hand over his left fist to double the power to his left elbow. He rose up on his toes to deliver the blow downward. The elbow hit the back of Cibosky's skull with a dull thud.

Cibosky crumbled face down onto the garbage strewn ground.

Kane rolled the big man over. Checked his pulse. Opened his mouth and inspected the airway as he tilted the head back. Then turned the head to the side so Cibosky wouldn't choke on his own blood.

"What the fuck?" Toni said.

Morticia and Toni were casting long shadows in the early morning sunlight angled down Gansevoort. Morticia still had the coffee pot and mugs in hand.

"He'll be all right," Kane said. "He'll have trouble talking for a few days. But he had nothing important to say anyway. He'll have to get the nose set. Or not."

He recovered the .45 and walked back toward the diner, the two women following. Thao was standing in the doorway to the kitchen, his wood crossbow in hand, a bolt loaded. Seeing that Kane was all right, the Montagnard went back in. There were several pedestrians who'd observed, but being New Yorkers, they quickly went on about their business. The three hookers at a table booth had seen but avoided Kane's eyes as he returned. They talked quietly among themselves.

Kane reclaimed his spot.

"Told you to watch the bag," Kane admonished Toni as she sat across from him. Morticia was completing her original task delivering coffee to the hookers.

"What was that?" Toni asked.

"That's what I did most of the time I was gone," Kane said. "I studied some things. What do you think I do at Gleason's? Move weights about and stare at myself in the mirror?"

"And what now?"

"I dealt with the immediate problem," Kane said. "What subsequent problems are going to arise from this temporary solution I don't know. But Delgado sent me a message yesterday.

I just replied. I doubt he'll take it to heart." He pointed. "You've got glitter in your hair again."

Toni stared at him.

Kane nodded toward the door. "You can get a taxi easier on Hudson."

Toni walked out.

Kane checked his watch.

Morticia was hovering nearby. "A crossbow, Kane?"

"It's their traditional weapon. Thao is good with it. He's also very dangerous with that machete."

She shook her head. "The two of you are a piece of work."

WEST SIDE HIGHWAY, MANHATTAN

Kane skirted the street level barriers that would block a car and drove the Kawasaki up the closed northbound ramp on 19th then turned south on the West Side Highway toward the original closure. Grass and weeds and a scattering of small bushes grew along the gutters of the elevated highway and from long-standing mud puddles in the roadway in both directions, making the road a burgeoning wilderness. He wove the dirt bike around the large clumps and avoided the places where the roadway had fallen through or looked close to that fate. The center divider splitting the three northbound and southbound lanes was a raised concrete curb. Evenly spaced along the divider were cast iron lampposts, with dual masts, a light hanging over each side. The light posts had a solid concrete base and when the road had been open, had claimed many an inattentive or drunk driver with an abrupt and deadly stop.

An uneven and incomplete wall of warped and rotting plywood marked the edge of the northward creeping death of the West Side Highway. Several thick railroad ties were scattered in front of the plywood as a deterrent against vehicle traffic even though the road was closed farther north. The dump truck had gone through the roadway on the northbound side of the Highway in December '73 approximately where Gansevoort ran under it a block west of Vic's. This section north to 26th was slated for demolition later in the year. But for now, what remained was an elevated refuge for the city's lost and forgotten.

The word CLOSED was barely visible in faded yellow spray paint on the plywood. All three northbound lanes where the dump truck had gone through were gone. Kane found a break in the southbound barrier and killed the engine. He kickstanded the bike, dismounted, and eased through the opening.

A scattering of shacks made from a wide range of material dotted the road as far as he could see. A small tendril of smoke was on the northbound side, past the missing section. Kane walked toward it, stepping over the center barrier. An old man sat on a wood milk crate, carefully tending a #10 can hanging on a precarious tripod over a small fire. He had a worn and faded cap on his head, a dirty white beard, and wore second-hand clothing.

Kane raised a hand in greeting. "Morning."

The old man watched his approach with apathetic concern. He got to the heart of the matter quickly. "What do you want? You got money?"

Kane had a five spot ready. He held it out. "I'm looking for a veteran. Goes by Wiley."

"Wile-dash-E." The old man corrected him. "Like the coyote in the cartoon. Wile-E."

"Right," Kane said. "We served in the same unit."

The old man spit. "Vietnam. You lost. I was in the Big One. We won."

"What outfit?" Kane asked.

"Marines. The Pacific."

"Once and always," Kane said.

"Got that right, kid." He held out his hand, palm up.

Kane surrendered the bill. "My dad was a Marine too, same theater."

The old man could care less. He pointed, bill crumpled in hand. "There."

Kane followed the direction of the black fingernail. A piece of corrugated metal was propped against the west edge of the highway, forming a lean-to.

"Thanks."

The old man was once more intrigued by whatever was in the can, Kane already a lost memory.

Kane knelt at one end of the lean-to. Wile-E was asleep, the field jacket an expedient pillow. The smell was atrocious, a combination of rotting food, dirty human, unwashed clothes, all baked by the heat. Wile-E was stirring in his unconsciousness, legs twitching, the tic on the side his face doing a dance.

"Sarge." Kane tapped the man on the shoulder. "Sarge."

Wile-E snapped awake, hands scrambling for the gun in the pocket of the field jacket, but Kane snatched that as soon as his head lifted.

Wile-E blinked, seeing only a dark silhouette. "Give me my jacket."

Kane stepped back.

"Who the fuck are you?" Wile-E asked. "Give me my jacket."

Kane checked the pockets, carefully. The same cheap gun. A kit rolled in aluminum foil. Some cigarettes. He kept the gun and tossed the jacket back. "I got a proposition for you."

Wile-E patted the pockets. "Give me my gun." He crawled out of the lean-to, squinting in the sunlight. "You were at Dino's the other night."

"I made a call," Kane said. "Guy I know works at the Soldiers and Sailors Club. You know where that is?"

Wile-E stood up, eyes bleary. "What?"

"Lexington Avenue," Kane said. "Between 36th and 37th."

Wile-E blinked at Kane, not following.

"Soldiers and Sailors Club on Lexington. You go there. Tell the guy at the desk that Kane sent you. He'll give you a room for tonight and tomorrow night. You can shower. Wash your clothes. Lexington Avenue. Between 36th and 37th. Got it, sarge?"

Wile-E shook his head. "I can't pay for—"

"They'll give you a room," Kane said. "Just tell them Kane sent you."

"Kane. With a C or K?"

"K."

"Yeah, okay, whatever."

"You going to do it?"

Wile-E's eyes narrowed. "Why do you care?"

Kane pointed at the winged dagger on the right shoulder of the jacket. "That's why." He turned and walked away. He didn't look back.

"Hey. My gun!"

Kane left the Saturday Night Special on the concrete base of a lamp post as he crossed over.

BAYCHESTER, THE BRONX

Kane bounced over the curb onto the cracked sidewalk and used his left toe to shift the Kawasaki dirt bike into neutral. He stood with the motorcycle balanced between his legs. The intersection of East Gun Hill and Eastchester Roads. Holy Rosary Church was a block away, north on Eastchester, where his mother and older sister Our Fathered every morning. Where he'd been an altar boy. The other surrounding blocks contained parks.

In the park in the southern quadrant he'd fallen off the monkey bars and had the wind knocked out of him, feeling the panic that he'd never be able to breathe again. To the west, where a bunch of white teenagers hanging in the shade of an anemic tree next to a basketball court, were passing a joint, he'd been chased away by the cops when he'd drunk his first beer that a more enterprising classmate from eighth grade had gotten someone older to buy for them. Beyond the monkey bar park, on Arnow Avenue, was the six-story brick building housing Holy Rosary elementary school, where he'd spent eight years of his life getting whacked on the back of his hand by nuns with rulers who tried to force him to write right handed. That capricious discipline had been of some use years later when shooting off-hand and in boxing and martial arts.

Kane could never have imagined that the most important moment in his life would occur here, where these two roads met, when he wasn't around. He turned the engine off. Looked at his watch.

10:07.

The police report listed 10:12 as the time of the accident, but Uncle Nathan had told him that was an estimate. A couple of minutes either way was possible, but all that mattered was the instant.

The truck had t-boned Taryn's car on the passenger side. Where Joseph was sitting. In a car that predated the law passed the previous year requiring seat belts in all sitting positions.

Joseph never had a chance.

Kane had entered Ranger School at Fort Benning on 12 September 1966 on a rushed set of orders, typical Army fashion, giving him only 24 hours to drive all night from Fort Hood, Texas, his short-term duty assignment after graduation to prepare him for Vietnam. Taryn had stayed behind and packed all their worldly possessions into a trailer. She was halfway to Benning when her contractions began. She gave birth on the 13th of September, frightened and alone, and unable to contact Kane, in a clinic in a small redneck town in southwest Louisiana.

Kane didn't see his son until after graduation from Ranger School two months later.

He'd missed his son's death by a few hours as he was flying back from Vietnam in late 1969.

Bookended by the two Vietnam tours, with a stint in the hospital and the Special Forces Qualification Course between the birth and death, Kane had been present for under a year of Joseph's abbreviated three years and nine weeks of life.

The accident happened when Taryn had been driving with Joseph to Kennedy Airport to meet Kane upon his return from Vietnam. He'd finally been released after the prosecution against him and seven of his Green Beret brethren for murder had been abruptly dropped by the Secretary of the Army.

Kane's mind raced down a familiar rut of regret. If that trial had not occurred, if the killing that precipitated it had never happened, if Kane had never been in Special Forces, if Kane had never been in the Army, if he had never gone to West Point, if they'd never gotten married, if his older sister had never set him up with Taryn, the list of ifs was as long as his life, and somewhere in there, Joseph would never have died.

A pack of teenagers rumbled along Gun Hill Road, passing paper bags with quart bottles of beer. One of them carried a boom box on his shoulder, blasting a heavy beat. Kane didn't recognize the song. They were a collection of Puerto Ricans and blacks. Five years earlier it would have been an unusual racial mixture given some were wearing the colors of the Black Spades on their denim jackets with no sleeves, but the gangs in the Bronx were in turmoil just like the city and the neighborhoods. Territory and hard times was making allies of previous enemies.

They spotted him on the bike.

It was easy to discern the leader. He wasn't the biggest, he wasn't the loudest, he was the opposite. The quietest, wearing a red pork-pie hat, precariously perched on a mid-sized Afro. His ebony skin glistened with a light sheen of sweat and he wore only the vest, no shirt. Someone nudged him, pointing at Kane.

Kane put the kickstand down, swung his leg over the bike and stood. He stared at the leader as they came closer. They made eye contact and Kane maintained it. The leader slashed his hand, quieting the yammering guy and gave an abrupt shake of his head. He gave a nod of acknowledgement to Kane along with a smile that said 'not today'. The gang angled away through the park.

Across the way the whites in the basketball park had grown silent. Most wore the colors of the Golden Guineas. The Black Spades saw them and Kane was no longer a factor as glares were exchanged between the groups.

Out of the corner of his eye, Kane spotted a blue and white Plymouth Fury rolling up Eastchester. The police cruiser paused at the curb next to Kane, ignoring the gangs. The driver's window scrolled down and a red-faced young cop squinted at Kane. The older cop in the passenger seat appeared to be sleeping.

"What ya doing? Get that motorcycle off the sidewalk."

Kane looked at his watch. 10:11. His heart was racing, but cold, hard fingers were wrapping around it, squeezing.

The older cop stirred, blinking. He leaned forward and looked to the left. "Keep rolling, rook. Leave him alone. He's here every Saturday."

The rookie was confused. "What?"

"Shut the fuck up and drive." The older cop nodded to Kane.

Kane nodded back.

The cops drove away.

Kane checked his watch. 10:13.

Kane spread his left hand over his chest, gasping for breath, disconcerted and disoriented. It took a few moments for him to regain his composure.

The Black Spades swaggered down Gun Hill Road, toward the subway station. The Golden Guineas returned to smoking dope. The cops drove away, ignoring both. No harm, no foul. Another day in the Bronx.

A short, lean kid was coming from the subway, headed directly toward the Black Spades. He was dark-skinned and wasn't wearing colors, only jeans and a dark t-shirt. He didn't cross the street to get out of the way of the oncoming gang but possessed a confidence that wasn't a swagger. He walked through, some looks exchanged, but nothing more. He didn't look back once he was past, but headed directly toward Kane.

"Mister Kane?" he said as he halted a few feet away.

"Yeah."

"I'm Dave."

Kane waited for more information.

"Dave Riley."

Kane put the kickstand down and stuck his hand out. "How you doing, kid?" He noted the white hoodlums across the street were watching.

Riley shook it with a firm grip. "My dad said I could find you here."

"How is Liam?" Kane asked.

The kid avoided the question. "I asked him about you."

"When did you see him last?" Kane asked, trying to get the lay of the land and not get roped into family drama.

"I went to his station house last week. He's okay. On the job. You know."

"What can I do for you?" Kane asked.

"I'm going to enlist and wanted to ask your advice."

Kane waited, not sure he had any worthwhile advice on that topic for a seventeen year-old.

Dave plunged on. "I'm considering Marines. My dad was. Your dad. Your older brother is, aint he?"

"Right."

"But." Dave hesitated, trying to not possibly offend. "Seems like once you get in the Marines you're a grunt and that's it. I want to do more."

"What kind of more?"

Dave shrugged. "Just more. I don't know. Be the best. You were in the Green Berets."

"Special Forces," Kane said. "Girl Scouts wear green berets." Kane backed off. "Yeah. Green Berets. Why don't you go for something that could teach you a skill you can use in the real world?"

"I think I want to go Special Forces eventually," Riley said. "Like you."

Kane had some memories of seeing Riley as a very young child, but not after West Point, since Liam and Dave Riley's mother had split up. "You don't want to be like me."

Dave spread his hands, indicating the place. "I don't want to be this. I know those guys across the street are watching. That's every day. I aint all Irish, I aint all Puerto Rican and I don't want to be part of any gang. That's a dead end. My dad thinks I should be on the job like him or maybe the cops like his brothers, but I want to get out of the city. I want to be part of something better. Are you telling me Special Forces isn't better?"

"The Army's fucked up," Kane said. "The war did that."

"This isn't fucked up here?"

Kane didn't answer the obvious.

"Even Special Forces is messed up?" Riley asked.

"There's good people in it," Kane admitted. "But it's not the place to be to have a career and make rank. The rest of the army thinks SF are bastards with no home." Kane thought about it. "We aren't at war. And you can go places. Do things. A lot of interesting training. But you have to do an Infantry tour first. Enlist eleven-bravo. Then pass the Q-Course."

"Eleven-bravo. I'll do that."

Kane stared into his young cousin's eyes, seeing the determination that must have been in his and Ted's at the same age. The desire to do something, anything, but what was laid out in front of them. "You seem pretty certain."

Dave shoved his hands in his pockets, shifting his eyes. "I'm real sorry about what happened here. With your kid. When my dad told me, he cried. I'd never seen him cry. Before or after, even when my mom left."

Kane felt the surge in his chest, the pressure behind his own eyes. He took a deep breath to settle down. "Your dad's a good man."

"I guess. My mom doesn't like me talking to him. But I call him at the firehouse. Sometimes. From pay phones."

Kane tried to think of an alternative to the Army for young Riley. "Special Forces has good people," he finally said.

Riley nodded. "I want to be with the best."

Kane pulled out his notepad, wrote the number for the diner on a page. Thumbed through, found another number and name. He tore it out and handed it to his young cousin. "The top number is where you can leave a message for me with a guy named Thao. The other is a buddy living outside Bragg. When you get to the Q-Course, he should still be there. He's retired. Call him. He's was in Group, Special Forces, a long time and can help out."

"Thank you. Thanks a lot." Dave stood there awkwardly for a moment. "I'm sorry if I interrupted anything."

"Nah," Kane said. "I was getting ready to leave."

Dave Riley walked away with a bounce in his step and Kane watched until he was out of sight on Gun Hill Road.

Kane started the bike and rolled the throttle. He headed for the post office on the corner of Gun Hill and Arnow but abruptly changed direction. He pulled in front of the wide, concrete stairs that ascended to the front doors of Holy Rosary Church. Killed the engine.

Kane walked up the steps. Four sets of wood doors. He pulled on a handle. Then another. They were all locked. Once upon a time, Kane had had the set of keys for all the locks in the church and the combination for the safe in the sacristy. Kane stepped back and looked at the tall steeple.

"Have I offended thee?" he whispered.

He remounted the motorcycle. Drove to the post office and paused at the box on the corner. Retrieved the two envelopes from the breast pocket of his shirt. Pulled the handle back and tossed them in. One held a check, the other cash.

Same as every Saturday for the past year. When he was overseas, he'd consolidated and sent a monthly check and cash, given the delivery was less certain.

Not a single check was cashed. Nevertheless, Kane deducted them from his original checking account he'd had since he was a plebe at West Point as if they had been.

Because not a single one had ever been sent back to the return address, which was the Marcelle Law Firm. The cash didn't have a return address so he assumed it was used by the receiver.

He headed for the Hutchinson River Parkway to take the Bronx-Whitestone Bridge to the Island.

FLUSHING MEADOWS, QUEENS

The 109 Precinct was housed in a quiet, two story brick building not far from Shea Stadium where the Mets played. Their fans were still mutinying after the trade of Tom Seaver to the Cincinnati Reds a month ago, as if the event evaporated the last tendrils of the feel-good 1969 World Champion 'Miracle Mets'. Attendance at Shea was breaking records in terms of empty seats. For many the loss of Seaver was indicative of the loss of hope in the City. Pete Hamill had written in the *Daily News* the previous month that *'this is not simply a sports story, it is a New York story . . . A city struggling for survival can't lose a single hero.'*

Kane considered that a bit over the top, because the problems in New York went much deeper than baseball.

The Yankees had also made Shea their home field for the last couple of years while their hallowed Stadium underwent renovation in Kane's home borough. But now the pinstripe boys were back in the Bronx. Fans were thronging to the Mecca of baseball and cheered for the team while pitted against each other in the Billy Martin-Reggie Jackson feud, which was more apropos of the state of the city. Trailing the Red Sox for the pennant, the almost brawl at Fenway Park at the end of June between Jackson and Martin had made national news. The Yankees even made winning a clusterfuck and fought each other harder than their Boston rivals.

Kane parked the Kawasaki a block away from the 109, chaining it to a light pole. He walked in the front door of the precinct and was confronted by a young uniform.

"You a reporter?"

"I'm here to see Detective Riley," Kane said. "He asked me to come."

The cop stepped aside and pointed. "Upstairs."

Kane opened the door at the top of the stairs. A large room buzzed with activity. Phones were ringing nonstop, blurring into a continuous noise. There were over forty men in the room. Most worked at desks, others stood along the walls, which were covered with maps and crime scene photos. Kane didn't see Nathan so he studied the closest corkboard to the right, which didn't have anyone attending to it.

Crime scene photos surrounded a map of the City. A red thread was thumbtacked between each cluster of photos to a spot. There were five threads. The photos were of what used to be women. Young women as best Kane could tell through their mutilation. Two white, two black and one brown. It was hard to discern much about them because they'd been beheaded and the heads placed on their stomachs. The faces were unrecognizable; seared red meat and blackened bone, all the skin and hair burned off. The naked bodies were staked down, arms and legs akimbo.

A bold Irish brogue cut across the room, which quieted it for the moment. "Now who do you be, laddie?" The speaker was tall, dressed in a smooth tan suit. Steel rimmed glasses framed blue eyes. His gray hair was neatly combed. He strode across the room toward Kane. Behind him, Nathan stood up from a desk where he'd had his back to the door.

"I'm Will Kane."

"You're not one of my detectives," the Irishman said. He looked Kane up and down. "You're not one of my plainclothes and you're not in uniform. Are you a Fed?"

Nathan interceded. "He's my nephew, Inspector." He nodded at Kane. "William, meet Inspector McDonald. He runs the Task Force. Sir, this is the Vietnam veteran I talked to you about."

"On with it then," he brusquely said to Nathan and walked away.

"Heavy on the brogue," Kane said to his uncle once McDonald was out of earshot and the noise level in the room amped back to frustrated frenzy.

"He was born in the old country," Nathan said. "County Kerry. His folks didn't come over until he was in his teens. He's been on the force since 1940 so he's got a lot of experience. A bit bookish and a stickler for details, but we're going to need details to crack this. Scuttlebutt is that he was the third choice to lead the task force. First two said no."

"So Uncle Conner isn't stupid."

Nathan gave a wry smile. "No, he's not stupid."

Kane pointed at the map and photos he'd been studying. "This isn't Son of Sam."

"No," Nathan said. He indicated the four clusters. "These are current unsolved multiple killings. We're checking for connections, just in case."

"'Multiple killings'?"

"Same perp, more than one vic, over a period of time. Same MO in each cluster."

Kane was surprised. "We have that many multiple killers in the City?"

"We average five homicides a day, William," Nathan said. "Most involve drugs, robbery, alcohol, or are husbands, boyfriends, or gang related. But some, yeah, they're multiples."

"Why?" Kane pointed at the images. "Why would someone do this?"

It was Nathan's turn to be surprised. "'Why'? Who the fuck knows? That's the thing with Son of Sam. Why is he shooting people? Why does he target girls with long brown hair? If we knew why these people acted the way they did, we could catch them. That's what we're trying to figure out with Son of Sam."

Kane indicated the wall of multiples. "Why aren't these headlines?"

"Three of these four multiples kill prostitutes. Most are runaways." Nathan pointed at the decapitated cluster and the next two. "We've got three different patterns in multiple hooker killings with five, three and four vics respectively. At least that's the number of bodies that have been found and connected." He pointed at the last grouping. "The fourth multiple is someone killing homeless using a nail gun. Can you believe that? Five vics from that nutjob now that we know of. A nail gun. Honestly? No one gives a damn about these. You know how many hookers and homeless are in New York? Welcome to Fear City. We're on track for a record year in homicides." He tapped Kane on the arm. "Come here."

The Fear City comment was in reference to the campaign waged by the police union, the Police Benevolent Association (PBA), a few years ago after the mayor laid off some police. The newly unemployed and pissed off former cops picketed Kennedy Airport, Grand Central Terminal and the Port Authority handing out brochures with those words along with an image of the grim reaper on the cover and suggestions on how to survive the city. Those included not riding the subway and never go out at night. In essence, don't come.

Nathan led Kane to the far wall, which was crowded with photos. In the center was a map of the entire city. More crime scenes and red strings pointed to the Bronx, Brooklyn and Queens.

"This is our guy," Nathan said. "Seven attacks so far. Six dead. Based on his last letter, we're worried he's ramping up for the anniversary of the first attack, on the 29th." He tapped the picture of a young girl with a line stretching to a spot in Bayside, Queens. "She's the one from your old neighborhood and school. Hit in the head, shoulder and neck."

"Surprised she survived."

"He fired through the windshield so the bullet fragmented."

Kane scanned the photos, the timeline and the map. "He's all over the city, except Manhattan."

"He doesn't take the ferry or the Verrazano out to Staten Island either," Nathan noted.

"Who does?" Kane noted the picture of a gun. "Revolver, so you don't get any casings."

"Which means no fingerprints," Nathan said. He indicated the cacophony of phones. "We're receiving over a thousand calls a day. Most are wack jobs, but you never know. We're getting more detectives, plainclothes and patrol in to help. Dressing officers as women and putting decoys in unmarked cars at popular make out spots and disco club parking lots."

"You said the city has five homicides a day. This asshole has killed five over a year. Why is everyone going nuts over him?"

"His attacks are random but not random," Nathan said. "And he's made it very public in the letters taunting us. The media's run with it and once you get something in people's heads it bounces around in there until there's a resolution. When people get afraid, they focus on it."

Kane turned to his uncle. "You got hundreds of years of homicide experience in this room. I don't see how I can help."

Nathan faced the board. "It goes back to what I was talking to you about. We know the nuts and bolts of how to work a case. We've had the shrinks in here, giving us their mumbo jumbo. But even they don't really know the *why*. They have theories. We're lacking what's between their theories and our nuts and bolts."

"How can I help there?"

"You've killed people, haven't you, William?"

Kane went perfectly still. There was a rushing noise in his ears, the sounds of the phones ringing and multiple conversations faded, and he stopped breathing for several long moments.

"Listen," Nathan hurriedly said. "We don't have to do this. It's just that we're desperate and the anniversary is coming and Son of Sam specifically mentioned the date in his letter to Jimmy Breslin."

Kane took a breath. Nodded. "Yeah. I've killed people. But that was war, not something I conjured up on my own."

"Even the double-agent?"

"You think I pulled the trigger?" Kane stared hard at his uncle. "He got our people killed. Our friends. He was the enemy. Worse than the enemy. He betrayed us."

"But what does it feel like?" Nathan asked.

Some of the nearby detectives pretended to work, but listened. Across the room, Inspector McDonald watched.

"It doesn't feel like anything. When you make contact, you do what you're trained. You fight for your friends, your teammates. You've got combat vets on the force. Ask them." He pointed at the map and photos. "This? This isn't war. This is crazy. Loco. He's not fighting for anyone else. He's fucked up. Okay? Do you think I'm crazy? Is that why you're asking me?"

Nathan put his hands up. "Take it easy, William."

Kane walked out. Nathan caught up to him on the stairs.

Kane paused. "You better tighten security. If I could get in this easy, a reporter will be taking pictures before you know it."

"I'll talk to the desk sergeant," Nathan promised. "Come on. Let's get some hot dogs."

"I'm not hungry."

"You don't even have to use condiments or get sauerkraut," Nathan tried.

"Bringing up my dad being an asshole doesn't help."

"I talked to my sister. You didn't stop by home yesterday after you left the club."

"Fuck you." Kane walked out of the 109th.

GREENWICH VILLAGE, MANHATTAN

Pope was perched on the stairs outside the brownstone, reading the *NY Post* in the fading light from the sun over New Jersey. He held the paper as if it were hemlock yet he had to taste. A small thermos rested on the step next to him. His straw hat was canted to shade his face.

"Waiting for me?" Kane asked. He'd parked the Kawasaki in the derelict garage next to the newly headlighted Jeep, a few blocks away.

"Enjoying the warmth and the sunlight. Even after all these years, I do not pine for the English weather."

"A bit hot isn't it, though?"

"A tad." Pope folded the paper, grabbed the thermos and stood. "Care to join me for a spot of tea?"

"I'd appreciate some water."

Kane followed his landlord into the main floor.

Pope dashed some 'tea' into his cup from the thermos. He eyeballed the interior, retrieved the bottle and topped off, screwed the lid and slid it inside his leather satchel. Kane went to the sink and got some tepid water.

"You look none-too-happy," Pope observed as he settled into his chair. "Did your meeting with your uncle not go well?"

Kane took a chair facing the back door. "Not particularly."

"Ah. I'm afraid I'll be adding to your woes then."

"How so?" Kane asked.

"One of those chaps you wanted me to investigate. Quinn."

"What have you learned?"

"In a former life he was New Zealand military. Special Air Service."

"Fuck me," Kane muttered.

"Of course you would know of the SAS and their capabilities."

"How did Quinn go from SAS to the Cappucci family?"

"An intriguing story that was not easy to acquire and has missing pieces," Pope said. "I called transatlantic and contacted an old mate in London who has ties to dark places. He's former SIS, more popularly known as MI-6. It was rather late his time, but he came through for me with as much as he was willing or could. I ran up quite a long-distance bill."

Kane reached for his money clip, but Pope waved that off. "I tellied from a line at the Post. That piker Murdoch will pay for the call. And understand that nothing I tell you will be attested to by myself or my source. Her Majesty is rather touchy regarding the actions of the SAS."

"Understood, but you said New Zealand SAS, not UK."

"Her Majesty is possessive of her colonials," Pope said. "If Quinn had been British SAS, I doubt my source would have whispered a word, but there is a little bit of daylight, or in this case, night light, between the two islands."

"There were New Zealand SAS in Vietnam," Kane said.

"Indeed," Pope said. "As well as Australian troopers."

"I didn't work with any directly," Kane said, "but heard good things."

"Quinn was seconded to the British SAS," Pope said, "which is why my source knew of him. Not in Vietnam though. He got caught up in the dust-up in Oman in July of '72. Are you aware of the Dhofar Rebellion?"

Kane nodded. "Yeah. Between that and what the SAS did in Malaysia, the few times in modern history an insurgency was defeated."

"You may know more about it than I," Pope said. "The entire affair was very hush-hush."

"I have the broad outline," Kane said. "A communist insurgency in Oman was defeated by the government's troops with the aid of the SAS. Not much more."

"Communist guerillas were rebelling," Pope began. "In the old days, who'd give a bum-fuck about Oman, eh? But oil? Righto. The Empire had been propping up the old Sultan for far too long. A slimy, selfish bastard who was a rallying point for the commies to direct the people against. We sponsored a coup and put his son in power. Who was younger but as much a despot. Thus, there was still unrest among the people, since little changed for them. Whitehall sent the SAS on the sly to assist the regime's military. Of course, assist turned out to be fight the red bastards themselves."

"That's the way it goes," Kane said. "You can't lead your allies from the rear. Have to be out in front."

Pope leaned forward slightly and lowered his voice, a slight slur in his words. "An element of SAS was garrisoned at a small fort that was a key position in protecting the capital and, more importantly, the Strait of Hormuz. Through which most of the world's oil passes. There were nine SAS men with some native troops. Place called Mirbat. They were attacked by over five hundred communist guerrillas."

Kane had the cup halfway to his mouth, but paused. "I heard something of the battle but not details. Run those numbers again?"

"Five hundred against nine."

"That's not good," Kane said.

"Of course, they had a contingent of government troops they were technically supporting."

"Go on."

"It was a bloody mess, but the troopers acquitted themselves admirably. Except there were ten SAS there, not nine. Quinn was the tenth, but since he was New Zealand, he wasn't officially counted. Post-battle, he was put in for a VC for gallantry but that was withdrawn when the Omani government made formal charges against him. It seems in the course of the battle he threatened the Sultan's troops to get into the fight. Threatened them rather aggressively."

"How aggressively?"

"He killed one to motivate the others."

"That can work," Kane acknowledged. "I can also see why the Sultan wouldn't be happy."

"The fighting had been intense for years," Pope said, his words muddy from tea. "It was a rather brutal campaign. This Quinn killed one of the government's soldiers to motivate the others to fight. It worked. The fort might have been overrun otherwise."

Kane nodded for the old reporter to continue.

"That battle broke the back of the rebellion. The Sultan wanted Quinn to be turned over to pay for his crime, despite the fact he and his mates saved the regime. There was no way the SAS would give up one of their own, even a colonial, so they got him out of country. This was the end of '72. Apparently the SAS didn't mourn his departure because he was considered a bit of a loose cannon prior to this event.

"The New Zealand government cashiered him from the service and denied him re-entry. A few months later Quinn surfaced in Boston doing nefarious deeds and making a name for himself in the underworld. Made his way here in '73. Worked his way up the ranks in the Cappucci organization rather quickly given his special skills and willingness to wield them. I would assume he's a rather bitter man." Done, Pope sipped his 'tea'.

"That's a pretty big change," Kane said. "From SAS to mob enforcer."

"Indeed," Pope said, peering red-eyed at Kane over the reading glasses perched on his nose.

"Yeah, I see it," Kane acknowledged.

"I'm not saying your current occupation at *Marcelle* is the same," Pope said.

"Quinn's been a step ahead of me," Kane said. "More than a step. What about Alfonso Delgado?"

Pope waved his hand dismissively. "A captain in the Cappucci family. Which he wouldn't be except he married the boss's daughter. A bit of a dim bulb. Quinn is the one to worry about." He put the cup down a bit too hard. "Have you perchance been wandering about trying to catch that Son of Sam fellow? You've had many the late night out."

"No idea where to find him," Kane said. "The cops have plenty of manpower on the job."

"One of my mates at the *Post* told me there's an interesting take on the Son of Sam name," Pope said. "There's a theory it means son of Uncle Sam. A Vietnam vet. The killer wore a fatigue jacket at one of the killings according to a witness."

"Anything's possible."

"You carry a gun, I understand."

Kane pushed aside his denim shirt. "Forty-five caliber, M1911. Semi-automatic pistol, not a revolver. Son of Sam uses a revolver. A special one."

"You fancy guns?" Pope asked. His eyes were half-lidded, a long day of drinking and the heat taking a toll.

"They're tools."

"Why use that particular gun?"

"It's personal for everyone. I'm used to the forty-five. I like that the magazine is in-line, not staggered. I prefer the larger round. After all, you don't throw a gun at a person; it's the bullet that does the damage. 1911 is the year it was invented. It's still around which I view as a positive endorsement."

"What about Son of Sam's gun?" Pope leaned forward, intrigued. "I've read that he uses a .44 caliber bullet but nothing about it being special other than that. Pray tell, lad?"

"Off the record?" Kane asked. "No going to your friends at the Post?"

Pope closed his eyes and was silent for a few seconds and for a moment Kane thought he'd fallen asleep. The eyes flickered open. "Hamilton is spinning in his grave. All right. Off the record unless someone else verifies it. How does that sound?"

"Son of Sam uses a .44-caliber Charter Arms revolver," Kane said. "Five round cylinder, single or double action and—"

Pope cut in. "What does that mean?"

"Means you can pull the trigger with the hammer forward, cocking it and firing with the trigger action. That's double. Single is the hammer is already back and pulling the trigger fires. First way is less accurate. My .45 is single action. I need to have the hammer back to fire, thus it has a safety. Revolvers don't have safeties. A smart person keeps the chamber under the hammer empty to avoid accidental discharge."

Pope nodded, waiting.

Kane continued. "Some of the cops have latched on to the fact it's the gun used by air marshals. They think that means it isn't as powerful, because air marshals have to make sure their rounds don't penetrate the skin of the aircraft. Depressurization." Kane paused, memories of counter-terrorism training intruding. "But that's because of the special bullets the marshals use. Put a hot load in a .44, it will punch through a car window or the door. But Son of Sam is using regular rounds. In his last outing he shot a girl that had gone to my old elementary school in the Bronx. She was sitting in car with a guy outside a club. Only reason the two of them are alive is he fired through the windshield. Bullets fragmented."

"The Bayside shooting. You knew her?"

"Nah. It's one of those weird connections in a city this big."

"The city isn't that big, William," Pope said. "Trust me, lad. I learned that and if you haven't yet, you will. Stories run deep here and often have strange ties. I asked my friend at the Post for the latest. One of Murdoch's bloody gangaroos had a song, Jimi Hendrix's *Purple Haze*, analyzed by some sort of audio expert. Claims there's a hidden track repeating 'help me Son of Sam'. Utter rubbish but, of course, they printed it. They're making things up, considering Hendrix has been dead for years and the song was recorded a decade ago. Anything to sell papers."

"Even the cops are grasping at straws," Kane said.

"How so?"

"They invited me to help," Kane said. "That's pretty desperate."

"You underestimate yourself." Pope reached across the table and briefly patted Kane on the arm. "Never do that. Leave that job to the many others waiting in line who are more than willing to do it for you."

Kane didn't respond.

"Anything else you care to share?" Pope finally asked.

"I wasn't there long. My meeting didn't go well. Mind if I ask you about something else?"

"Fire away, my friend. All I have is time and knowledge."

"Do you know Thomas Marcelle?"

"Thomas 'the Hammer' Marcelle? The fire-breathing US Attorney? Or the revised Thomas Marcelle who walked away and hung his placard out to the highest bidder?"

"Same guy."

"No, no, not the same," Pope slurred. "No, no, no, lad. Marcelle was a power for good when he worked for the government."

"And now?"

"And now he is a force for his clients," Pope said. "Whoever they happen to be, which means whoever can pay the most."

"His son's death affected him," Kane said.

"Perhaps," Pope agreed. "Certainly, it was a factor."

"'A factor'? What else happened?"

"I'd have to dig a bit," Pope said. "While I remember much, not every facet is readily available in my frontal lobe. But there was a political angle to it, I believe. Some sort of stink at the time. I fear you are in deep waters, lad."

"I've been there before," Kane said.

Pope slumped back in his chair. Kane waited a minute, but the former reporter began to snore.

Kane walked around the table. The old man wasn't heavy. He carried him to the master bedroom on the top floor facing Jane Street. Gingerly laid him down. Pulled his shoes off. Turned on the fan in the window.

Kane started to leave, then returned to the bed. He took Pope's spectacles off, folded them, and placed them on the nightstand.

As he headed for the stairs he spotted a manual typewriter perched on a folding dinner tray with a stool underneath. In the dim light Kane glanced at the piece of paper inserted in the carriage.

It was blank, awaiting the first touch of finger to key.

Blood and Family
Darkness and Death
Absolute Depravity
.44
Return address on Son of Sam's letter to Jimmy Breslin,
April 1977

Monday, 21 July 1969

LONG BINH, SOUTH VIETNAM

Captain William Kane, United State Army Special Forces, takes shuffling, shackled steps into prison. As he and his comrades are processed, the eight Green Berets will not be the only prisoners in Long Binh Jail accused of murder. There are men here who've fragged their officers or NCOs. Those who've killed for reasons other than the war, such as robbery, rape, hate, revenge, and some because there was a weapon handy when they were drunk, or high and angry.

In essence, the rule is Uncle Sam brought them to Vietnam to kill, but only who and where and when Uncle Sam authorizes.

The Green Berets, however, will be the only ones held in LBJ whose crimes are classified.

Long Binh is the largest American base in Vietnam with over 60,000 personnel, essentially one out of every ten Americans in country. What those who are in the jungle, boots on the ground, call REMFs: rear echelon motherfuckers.

The prison is a collection of gray, cement buildings with tin roofs, surrounded by a cyclone fence topped with razor wire occupying a corner of the sprawling military complex. Guard towers with MPs manning machineguns dot the perimeter. Facing inward. Toward fellow Americans in a war zone. During the Tet Offensive earlier in the year, the VC and NVA were able to penetrate into Long Binh and cause a spectacular explosion at the ammo dump, but they didn't attack the prison.

In a bare room, the Green Berets are ordered to take off their belts and shoelaces by a hard-faced Sergeant. Their small shaving kits are inspected as if they contain weapons. Two MPs have M-3 greaseguns at the ready as the Sergeant goes through the gear.

Someone in the next room begins whistling. A lively melody they've all heard and the irony is not lost.

The Sergeant is disconcerted for a moment. "Grab your stuff," he orders.

They gather the meager supplies they're authorized.

"Get in line." The Sergeant enjoys ordering officers around. He points at the Colonel, the Fifth Special Forces Group commander, then to another sergeant waiting at a door. "You go with him."

The Colonel pauses. "Stand for each other, men."

The Colonel is pushed through the door. One by one, the others are taken away to solitary confinement. Kane is the last. The Sergeant appears nervous. He indicates the door through which the whistling is drifting. "There."

Kane walks into an interrogation room.

A man sits on a small gray metal table. There are no chairs. Three Nung mercenaries in civilian clothes talk quietly among themselves in a corner.

The man wears unmarked khakis and black, blocky glasses with thick lenses. His face is red, whether from the sun, heat or drink? He smokes and the room reeks of it. A half-dozen cigarette stubs are mashed on the tabletop.

"Did you recognize the tune I was whistling, Captain Kane?"

"Bridge On The River Kwai."

"It's actually called Colonel Bogey's March," the man says.

"Who are you?"

"Name's Trent."

The door shuts behind Kane with a solid thud. The walls are lined with soundproofing.

"Technically you command the A-Team stationed at camp 8414," Trent says. "You're not part of Gamma."

"You're CIA," Kane says.

The three Nungs cease talking and greedily watch.

"Why are they here?" Kane asks. Special Forces often employs Nungs, ethnic Chinese in Vietnam, who are willing to work for the highest bidder. The CIA also does that. As do the South Vietnamese, the Viet Cong and the NVA.

"Oh, don't worry about them," Trent says. "They don't understand English. They serve other purposes. Here's the way I see your situation. You were in the wrong place at the wrong time and helped out your Green Beret brethren. Bad luck, really. It should never have gone this far."

"I agree with that last bit," Kane says. He's uncomfortable in jungle fatigues, no belt, his boots de-laced. His pants are loose, as he's lost weight over the months of this tour of duty. It's the first time in country he's not armed.

"Do you know what Gamma does?" Trent asks. He chains another cigarette from the remains.

"Not my place to say."

"You're in here on murder charges, Captain," Trent says. "You need to think about your place."

"It's classified," Kane says.

"That's right," Trent agrees. "But you know what they do or else you'd never gotten involved. Your camp isn't that large."

Kane doesn't reply.

"Of course, your team, separate from Gamma, has done its own covert missions. You're part of MACV-SOG. Studies and Observation Group. So innocent sounding."

Trent waits for something, but Kane doesn't respond

"Still being honorable?" Trent wonders aloud. "Really? Got that West Point ethos? Duty, honor, country, etcetera?" He pauses a moment. Then continues. "Gamma is running recon into Cambodia. So we can bomb the fucking gooks coming down through what they view as a sanctuary. Hell, Kane, from your camp you can hear the bombs when they go off. Nothing like an Arc Light. B-52s are flying so high the gooks can't see or hear them. First notice anyone gets of hell on earth is when things start going boom. I understand it sucks the air out of the lungs from those on the fringe. Obliterates those inside."

"'Crack the sky and shake the earth'," Kane mutters.

"What was that?"

"What someone told me it was like," Kane says. "We're not supposed to be bombing Cambodia."

"No shit." Trent smiles, revealing yellowing teeth. *"General Abrams is one of the few with the clearance to know. I know. You know. Your fellow Green Berets in Gamma know. The pilots. Not many more. An illegal order straight from the fucking White House. Tricky Dick himself. Expanding the war without authorization. You see the problem?"*

"I see your problem," Kane says.

"Look around, Kane. This is much more your problem. This needs to go away. Who was the shooter? Give me the name, everyone else gets out of here today, and this never happened."

"You don't have that authority," Kane says. *"This is an Army matter."*

"True," Trent admits. *"You and your buddies are in here because General Abrams has a bug up his ass about Special Forces. Hates you fuckers. Regular army through and through. Which is why he's losing this war."* Trent waits. Continues. *"That movie,* Bridge on the River Kwai. *Remember it?"*

"British commander in charge of POWs builds a railroad bridge for the Japanese," Kane says. *"It's blown up."*

"A concise summary," Trent says. *"But think what it represents? Regular Army officer, in the name of honor and professionalism, does something unbelievably stupid, almost treasonous. Sort of like arresting one's own men for killing the enemy. The last time I was at General Abrams HQ I heard singing coming from his hooch, and a mighty fine hooch it is. Air-conditioning and a wet bar. He had staff officers in there. Singing a spiritual.* 'He's Got The Whole World In His Hands'. *For entertainment. What does that tell you?"* Trent twirls a finger next to head. *"Nut job living in a different time, fighting the last war. But it's the only one he has. So that's a reality."*

Trent lights another cigarette from the remains. *"You green beanies, you're getting it. War has different. Hearts and minds. And bullets in the head. I am assuming it was a bullet to the head for Ngo. Right?"*

Kane doesn't respond.

"Here's another funny thing about that movie," Trent goes on. *"The guy who won the Academy Award for writing it? Didn't write it. Two fucking commies on the blacklist wrote it. And here we are fighting commies. Is that called irony?"* He indicates the room. *"This is the real world, Captain Kane. We own you. Lots can happen in here. There are race riots on a regular basis. Someone gets killed, they go on the daily casualty report*

coming out of country. KIA. The family weeps. Things move on." Trent *takes a deep drag on the cigarette. "Oh, I'm sorry." He holds out the pack.* *"Want one?"*

Kane *doesn't answer.*

"Concerned for your health? Thought green beanies were tough." Trent *flicks ash onto the floor and contemplates* Kane. *"I'm trying to help you, Captain. Help the country. Hell, even bail out Abrams, because this is going to bite him in the ass. It's going to bite a lot of people in the ass."*

"Including the CIA," Kane *says.*

Trent *laughs. "Oh no. Not us. Nothing touches us. You're* the guys *in here."*

Kane *takes the bait. "What do you want?"*

"Who was the shooter? One scapegoat and we can get Abrams to drop this mess. We'll make it a personal thing, not double-agent bullshit for a unit doing a mission that isn't supposed to exist. Hell, Kane, give me a name. Doesn't even have to be the real shooter. And here's the thing? Whoever it is won't even serve time. A dog and pony show for Abrams, then it all goes away."

Silence.

Trent *rubs his forehead, as if forestalling a headache. "We have the helicopter pilots' testimony. We know you got on that chopper with Ngo. We know you came back without him."*

"We made contact after insertion," Kane *says. "He was KIA and we couldn't get to his body. We had to call in a Prairie Fire. Emergency exfiltrate."*

"Weak cover story," Trent *says. "The thing is you weren't the only one on the chopper. We know who was. They're in here with you. We know where you and the others got off the helicopter in Cambodia. How close to the LZ is Ngo's body?"*

"The LZ is in a country off limits to Americans," Kane *points out. "But feel free to fly over and take a look."*

"Maybe you were the shooter, Kane. I don't give a shit. Hell, you had a Yard on the bird. Finger him. He seems to have disappeared. Who gives a fuck about the natives? Give me a name and we'll sort this shit out and everyone can go back to the war."

Kane *is silent.*

Trent shakes his head. "We only get so many choices in life, Captain. And only so much time to make those choices. This was your first chance. You blew it." He looks at the three Nungs. "Di."

They came at Kane with the experience of having beaten many prisoners. Trent resumes whistling as the fists and boots strike.

Sunday Morning, 10 July 1977

VAN CORTLANDT PARK, BRONX

Kane charged up Cemetery Hill, legs churning, white leather running shoes with a red Puma stripe on the side detonating small puffs of dirt with each foot strike. The ridge was named thusly because it had been the burial ground for the Van Cortlandt family, which settled the land before 1700. The grave markers had been moved after they were vandalized in the 1960s. The adjacent golf course had its own unique set of New York City rules. A player could do a drop if their ball was against one of several derelict cars or the abandoned boat on the course. Golfers disdained the traditional foursome and went in larger packs to deter muggers.

Kane was in his own pack, a line of runners stretching up the hill. The leaders were already over the crest. He was in the midst of the New York Road Runners Sunday 'fun run'. They'd already looped once around the Flats, gone through the Back-hills, around the Flats again, up the Cowpath and now it was over Cemetery and back to the Flats.

He reached the top and pushed on, avoiding the rocks and roots of the worn-out cross-country course in the Northwest Bronx. He'd competed on these paths in high school and returned a year ago, enjoying the run through the woods, an enclave of nature in the City. He'd reluctantly begun to participate in the Sunday runs, not for the comradeship, after all it's the loneliness of the long-distance runner, but for the regimen. They met at the same time every Sunday morning and it provided structure.

Kane came down the backside of Cemetery running hard. A bridge straight ahead led to the Back-hills and he considered another loop, but the other runners were acknowledging the heat and cutting back this weekend. He went with the flow and turned left, sprinting downhill with the Henry Hudson Parkway to his right. Coming out of the hills, he reached the Flats, a large former parade ground for the National Guard. A cinder path cut through weed-infested grass parallel to Broadway.

With the finish in sight, Kane picked up the pace, passing other runners. He crossed the finish line, where those who'd been ahead had halted. Out of the corner of his eye he saw Uncle Conner.

Kane kept going, peeled back the Velcro on the wristband and checked the second hand on Ted's Army issue watch. He ran hard for another minute, legs pumping as fast as he could push them. When the second hand completed a revolution, he stopped. He bent over to catch his breath, lungs burning. His sweat dripped into cinder. He glanced to the right. He was fifteen feet past the small stone he'd left as a marker on the edge of the cinder path last week. He retrieved the stone and pushed it down in the grass on the side of the path for next Sunday's run.

"What was that? Trying to show the other runners up?" Uncle Conner was panting after the walk from the finish line to catch up to him. He looked worse than usual, hung-over, face red, sweat forming dribbles on his face.

Kane was puzzled. "Why would I want to show them up?"

"You didn't stop," Conner noted. "Or was it you saw me and didn't want to talk?"

"When I was in Beast Barracks," Kane said, "my first detail squad leader always made us continue for an extra minute on every run or forced march after everyone else stopped. He called it the gut it out minute."

"Sounds like an asshole."

"He was and he wasn't," Kane said.

"You see the Yankee game last night?" Conner asked. "Fucking Martinez choked. They better make up for it today."

"You betting on the games?" Kane asked.

Conner gave a bitter laugh. "A man has to have some excitement."

"What brings you here in your Sunday best?"

Conner wore his work 'uniform' of cheap suit and loosened tie. His battered red Chevy Nova was illegally parked on the sidewalk off Broadway.

"Nathan called me." Conner wiped his forehead with a handkerchief. "We got to talk, Will."

"Okay, let's talk."

Conner shook his head. "Not here. I need you to come with me."

"You need me to or you'd like me to?" Kane asked. His t-shirt was sopping.

"Both," Conner said. "Where's your stuff?"

Kane pointed. "Back of the Jeep."

"Let's get it."

"What's going on?" Kane walked toward the Jeep, Conner at his side.

"There's been a homicide."

"Uncle Nathan says there are a lot of them."

"Nathan called me to get you. He's at the crime scene. He wants you there."

"Who died?"

"He wouldn't tell me."

Kane put his foot on the back bumper and untied one of his running shoes, removing the key from the lace. He swung open the back gate and unlocked the footlocker, pushed up the lid and retrieved jungle fatigue pants and a dry shirt from the top tray, uncovering his pistol. He pulled the pants over the shorts. Tossed the wet shirt over the passenger seat and put on the dry one. It immediately sported dark spots from sweat. He sat on edge of the small cargo bay. Replaced the soaked socks and running shoes with dry socks and jungle boots. Put on a clean denim shirt and rolled the sleeves.

He retrieved the .45, slid it into the holster.

"Fuck him," Kane said.

Conner was startled. "What?"

"He asked me to help on his task force. He thought I could give him insight into Son of Sam. I went out to the one-oh-nine yesterday. He tried messing with my head as if I was just like this fucking Son of Sam nutjob. I told him I wanted no part. I'm not going to one of his task force crime scenes. There's nothing I can help him with." He looked at Conner. "We agree on that, don't we?"

Conner shook his head. "You don't understand, Will. This isn't Son of Sam. Why do you think I'm here? We have to go to the crime scene because Nathan told me you're a suspect."

MEATPACKING DISTRICT, MANHATTAN

Kane followed Conner's car along the Henry Hudson Parkway, crossing from the Bronx to Manhattan on the bridge also named after the first European explorer of the river. They drove along the remaining West Side Highway until the roadway was blocked and they had to take the last southbound exit at 23rd. Then they negotiated the narrow streets until they arrived at Gansevoort.

Two cops sat in their patrol car in front of Vic's, windows up, engine running, air conditioning blowing. There'd been a great hub-bub about the city buying patrol cars with air conditioning since it meant the cops would be driving around with their windows up and couldn't hear the cries for help from civilians.

They got the air conditioning.

Across the street from the diner a single strip of yellow crime scene tape drooped between two High Line stanchions. An unmarked cop car was parked near the tape. Nathan was standing on the other side of the tape in the shadow of the rail line, arms folded.

Kane looked at Vic's, saw Morticia staring out through the clean windows and his shoulders relaxed. Kane parked the Jeep and headed to Nathan, arriving the same time as Conner.

Nathan lifted the tape without a greeting, allowing them through. The body was covered by a tarp. Nathan stopped next to it but didn't remove the covering.

The detective took a notebook out of his suit pocket. Despite the burgeoning heat, his tie was cinched. "Found this morning. Called in anonymously. First unit was on scene at six-forty." He looked at Kane. "Don't you eat breakfast every morning in the diner?"

"Not this morning. And good morning to you too."

"Why not this morning?"

"I go to Van Cortlandt every Sunday to run," Kane said. "I used to stop by early on Sundays to get my paper, but then Mary started calling the diner every Sunday morning, asking if I was going to mass with her and mom. It's the only way she knew how to get hold of me so she used it. Relentlessly. So now I come here after getting back from my run. And after mass is out."

Conner nodded. "Yeah, that's Mary. She can be persistent. You know it wouldn't kill you, and your mom would love it, if you went to church with her once in a while."

Nathan ignored his brother. "What time were you at Van Cortlandt?"

"Seven."

"Where were you before that?"

"Home."

"Still on Jane Street?" Nathan asked.

"Yep."

"Not far away."

"No. Not far."

"Were you alone?"

"Yes. Who is it?" Kane finally asked. Conner had told him he didn't know who the body was, just that Nathan had called him at home, told him to get his ass in gear, grab Kane and come here. And that it was connected to Kane.

During the drive down, as it became clear where they were going, Kane had worried possibilities. Someone from the diner? Morticia? Thao? A robbery? Just like Nathan to keep the most important piece from his own brother, and thus from him. Kane suspected Nathan had done that to get his reaction to the identification. Which pissed him off because it meant Nathan had doubt about Kane's innocence. But Morticia was watching and the body underneath was too big to be Thao.

Then it hit him: the Kid?

Kane knelt and grabbed the edge of the tarp.

"Whoa!" Nathan said. "Hold up."

Kane jerked it aside.

Cibosky's remaining eye was cloudy with death. The other eye socket was a black hole with a splatter of blood spread over his face. Even with his brain turned to mush, the heart had continued pumping for a little while longer, which meant the muscle had outlived the mind. An apropos end for Cibosky.

Kane stood.

"You know him?" Nathan asked.

"You know I know him," Kane said. "Else you wouldn't have ruined Conner's Sunday bringing me down here. Let's stop playing games, Uncle Nathan."

Nathan was out of patience. "I agree, William. Let's stop playing games. Tell me what's going on. We have statements from two people that you beat the crap out of this guy yesterday morning right here. It's obvious his nose was recently broken."

"I hit him four times," Kane said. "Solar plexus, throat, nose and then back of the head. He was breathing, but unconscious, when I left him. He didn't die from getting beat up."

"No, he died from a round through the left eye," Nathan said. "Damn good shooting."

"Helps if someone is really close," Kane said, earning hard looks from both cops.

"Nobody heard a shot," Nathan said. "But a nuke could go off and no one would say they heard a thing. What's weird is there's no exit wound. Usually a shot like that would blow out the back of the head. Especially since it entered through the eye socket. There should be brains all over."

"There's no blood on the ground," Conner interjected. "He was dumped here."

"Really, Conner?" Nathan sarcasm was obvious. "There're plenty of smarter places to dump a body, like a couple blocks west in the Hudson." He glanced at Kane. "What do you think?"

"He was part of Cappucci's crew. A mob hit."

"Why would the body be where you beat him up yesterday?" Nathan asked.

"No idea." Kane was staring at the wound. *Lions and tigers and bears, oh my.*

"I've got to open this crime scene to Manhattan South," Nathan said. "I was only able to grab the spot and keep it clear this long using my pull from the Task Force. McDonald is going to rip me a new one when he finds out I abused my authority for a family matter. I've put my neck on the chopping block here for you, William."

"You didn't need to," Kane said. "I didn't kill him."

Nathan and Conner exchanged a glance.

"You have no alibi," Nathan said. "You beat him up yesterday. Looks like he was killed by a pro. You're a pro."

"I'm not a 'pro'," Kane said with some heat. "I'm a guy who does leg work for a law firm."

"You were a Green Beret," Nathan said.

"Past tense. Years ago."

"You say you didn't kill him," Nathan said, "and Conner and I believe you, but things aren't looking good."

Kane faced Nathan. "*Do* you believe me?"

Nathan met the stare. "Yeah, I do. I think you're capable of killing, in fact, you told me yesterday that you've killed people, but that was war, right? And if you say you didn't, you didn't. I believe you."

Conner was nervously watching the two of them. "I might not be a detective, Nathan, but even I can see an obvious set up. It's over the top."

Nathan broke his stare with Kane. "Yeah. It is too much. Why did you beat him up, William?"

Kane gave his uncle a brief summary of the first confrontation at the diner and then the second.

"It's a good news, bad news situation," Nathan said when Kane was done. "The good news is the guy was mobbed up so it can be written up as an internal mob hit and that isn't a high priority unless the papers jump on it, but they only do that for the big names. The bad news is there's enough connecting you to Cibosky to cause the detective who gets the case to hesitate writing it off so easily. Depends who it is."

"Cibosky might have been waiting here for me," Kane said. "To pick up from where I left things yesterday or on orders from Alfonso Delgado. Someone came along and killed him."

"It's a possibility," Conner offered.

"Except he wasn't killed here as you noticed, Conner," Nathan said with a tinge of irritation.

"Can I get some breakfast now?" Kane asked.

Nathan looked at him as if he were crazy. Conner was shaking his head.

Another unmarked police car rolled up. The two cops who'd been half-asleep in the patrol car leapt out, putting their caps on and scrambling over to 'guard' the crime scene. A black man of average height but exceptionally broad shoulders and girth exited the car. He wasn't fat, he was a solid wall. His suit was one step up from Nathan's and out of Conner's league, gray with a white shirt buttoned to the top and dark red tie; tailor-made for his build. He shrugged on his jacket. He strolled across the street, looking all about. His hair was cut high and tight, military fashion. As he walked by, he glanced at Conner's Nova, Kane's Jeep, then Nathan's unmarked.

"Fuck," Conner whispered. "It's Strong."

"I can deal with him," Nathan said. "You don't say a word, Conner."

Strong stopped on the other side of yellow tape. His lips moved but they couldn't hear anything.

"He talking to himself?" Conner asked.

"Looks like it," Nathan said. He spoke to Kane. "He's an odd duck but don't underestimate him."

One of the patrolmen hurried over and raised the tape for Strong.

"Nathan Riley," Strong said as he arrived. "It's a long way from the Bronx for your brother."

"Omar Strong," Nathan said. He extended his hand. "Been a while."

Strong shook it, but studiously ignored Conner, who did not offer his hand.

"Who is this?" Strong indicated Kane.

"My nephew," Nathan said. "William Kane."

Kane put his hand out. Strong did not reciprocate. "Why is *he* in my crime scene?" he asked. "Of more import, why are the Riley brothers standing in a Manhattan South crime scene?"

"When I saw it come across," Nathan said, "I thought it might be related to the task force."

Strong looked at Cibosky. "How stupid do you think I am? That isn't a young girl with long brunette hair. That isn't a .44 slug in the head. And it's Sunday morning. How did you see it 'come across'?"

"We're working seven days a week on the Task Force," Nathan said. "Everyone's been authorized overtime."

"That explains why no one else can get any," Strong said. "Why'd you grab this?"

Nathan said nothing.

"All right." Strong looked at Kane. "It must have something to do with this fellow."

"Let me buy you a cup of coffee," Nathan said, indicating the diner, "and I'll fill you in."

"You're going to have to buy me breakfast," Strong said. "And it better be a good story." He continued to ignore Conner. "Can I trust your brother to maintain the integrity of the crime scene, Nathan?"

Conner took a step, face redder than normal, but Nathan chopped his hand and Conner heeled.

The two detectives walked across the street, leaving Kane alone with Conner.

"You guys don't seem happy to see Strong," Kane said.

"He's an all right detective," Conner grudgingly allowed, watching them. "We had a run in some years back."

"Great," Kane said.

"Hey!" Conner turned on him. "Nathan *has* put his shit on the line here. If he can't talk Strong out of calling McDonald, not only will he be kicked off the task force, he could lose his shield." Conner paused. "You really *didn't* kill this guy, did you, Will?"

"Who do you guys think I am?"

Conner was looking at the diner. "Why did Nathan really want you at the Task Force?"

"To pick the brain of a killer."

"No wonder you were pissed at him."

"I still am."

Conner turned to him and indicated the body. "Will, this is on you. Nathan is doing you a solid. Don't be a dick. You've gotten us both involved in your shit."

"Right."

"Right'?" Conner repeated. "They need to catch Son of Sam. Fast. Or more girls are going to get shot. They need Nathan on the task force. When Nathan gets on a case, he's like a bulldog, but he's got sharp elbows."

"What does that mean?"

"It means," Conner explained, "he doesn't think about, or particularly care, who he has to shove through to solve the case. Or who he has to knock down. In this case you felt those sharp elbows. I've felt them in the past too. You know, of course, that his offer to me yesterday at the Club was bullshit, right?"

Kane couldn't see the two detectives through the windows. "What?"

"He would have shit if I'd said yes," Conner said. "He knows me and he knew I'd say no. I get it now. He was playing me in front of you to play you. He's good at what he does. Take his lead when you talk to Strong."

"Roger that."

Conner indicated Cibosky. "And how about staying away from the mob? Nothing good can come of it. Guys like this, they're fucking nut-jobs."

"Cibosky wasn't crazy," Kane said, "just dumb. Whoever killed him is the crazy one."

"I'll tell you one person who ain't gonna be happy about this," Conner said.

"Who?" Kane asked.

"Delgado. This guy was his right-hand man, wasn't he?"

"I hope he's a leftie, because Cibosky wasn't much of a hand."

"I heard you were in the Bronx yesterday," Conner said.

"I'm in the Bronx every Saturday," Kane said. "And Sunday," he pointedly added.

"I'm going home and enjoying the rest of my day off," Conner said as he started to walk away. "That's if the Yankees don't choke again in Baltimore. Fucking Reggie." He paused and looked over his shoulder. "Why don't you go to the fucking cemetery like a normal person, Will? He *is* buried in a cemetery isn't he or do they do something different in his religion?" He was shaking his head as he got in his car and drove off.

A crime scene car pulled up and two bored techs reluctantly left the comfort of the air conditioning.

"Hey, Will!" Nathan waved from the door to the diner.

Kane crossed the street. Strong sat in Kane's booth, in his spot, facing the door. He filled most of that side of the table. Nathan led the way and Kane sat next to his uncle across from the detective. The thick Sunday New York Times was pushed against the wall next to the condiments.

"Your uncle has briefly filled me in," Strong said, checking his notebook, a mechanical pencil in one hand. The handwriting was precisely lettered. "I have some questions though." Strong looked up. "Your story is that Cibosky was here twice. Once inside, the other time across the street. Friday morning, he waited by the door and was in the company of a known organized crime figure, Alfonso Delgado of the Cappucci family. You had no contact with Cibosky. Yesterday he was across the street alone, approximately where his body currently resides, and you left here to confront him without any provocation."

"His presence was a provocation," Kane said. "That was actually the third time I met him." He related how Cibosky busted the Jeep headlights on Friday afternoon.

Strong made a few notes. Then he tapped the pencil for several moments. "You nervous? You keep looking over your shoulder."

"I don't like having my back to the door."

Morticia floated to the table. She put a cup in front of Kane along with his glass of water with two cubes. She filled it from the pot. "Refill?" she asked Strong. He nodded and she topped him off. Same with Nathan's cup.

"Thank you, ma'am," Strong said.

Morticia smiled welcome and moved away. Not very far.

"How are you involved with Delgado?" Strong asked Kane.

Kane explained following the mobster Thursday night and the photos.

"Who hired you to do that?" Strong asked. "Who is this woman, whose name you studiously avoid divulging, who you felt was threatened by Cibosky's presence across the street yesterday morning? For whom did you so gallantly sally forth to beat up a mobster?"

"Antonia Marcelle."

Strong's pencil stopped scratching across the page. He looked up. "Of *Marcelle, van Dyck, Feinstein and Jenkins*? Her father is Thomas Marcelle?"

"The last name in the firm has changed," Kane said. "Jenkins is gone. Antonia Marcelle is now a partner."

Strong closed the notebook. Tapped the pencil.

Kane couldn't stop from looking over his shoulder as he heard the door open. One of the techs came in. He went to Strong, leaned over and whispered in his ear. Strong nodded. He grabbed the guy's shoulder so he could whisper something back. The tech nodded and left.

Strong returned his attention to Kane. "Your uncle told me about you. West Point. Two tours in Vietnam. I was One-Nine Marines. 1967. You?"

"You were in the Walking Dead on the DMZ," Kane said. There was acknowledgement in Strong's eyes of the informal nickname for that unit. "First tour, I was 173rd Airborne in the Central Highlands in '67 and then 5th Special Forces in '69."

Strong nodded. "Special Forces. Bunch of wild men. In the mountains with the natives. Did you go native?" He indicated the bracelet on Kane's wrist.

Kane didn't say anything.

"I heard rumors you guys were doing other things," Strong said. "Hush-hush cross border stuff. Assassinations. Killing people up close."

Kane remained silent.

Strong spoke. "You don't look stupid. Are you stupid?"

"No."

"Stupid people don't know they're stupid," Strong said. "That's the problem in the world. They think they're as smart as everyone else. Your uncle says you boxed Golden Gloves in high school. Then you go out of your way to beat up our deceased. It's been written '*Only dumb guys fight*'."

"Written where?" Kane asked. "It's not the Bible."

"A poet. You've never heard of him. But I have to agree with Detective Riley that it would be more than stupid for you to shoot this guy and dump his body across from where you eat every day. It would—"

Nathan interrupted. "The body was dumped?"

Strong turned to him. "That eye wound bled but there's no blood around the body on the ground. Some other things. But you and I know that, Riley. Even your ignorant brother probably knows it. Don't play up to me. Word is you're a stand-up guy. That's the reason we're sitting in this booth chatting and I haven't dialed my captain to call your boss to let loose the world of hurt that would storm upon this circus you're presiding over."

He shifted his attention back to Kane. "As I was saying. It would be dumb for you to drop a body across the street from where you eat. It would be dumb for you to have the bat the vic used still in your Jeep if you killed him."

Kane looked outside. The tech lifted the bat out of the passenger well of the Jeep.

"That is the bat, correct?"

"Yeah. Forgot the taking the bat part of the story. Didn't think it was important."

"Details are always important," Strong said. "They determine the truth. And you say the deceased dropped the bat because you pulled a gun on him. You've got a .45 on your belt. Own any others?"

A familiar dread was seeping through Kane's body. He shifted uncomfortably on the vinyl seat.

"Do you own any other firearms?" Strong repeated. "You have the key for that locker in the back of your Jeep?"

"You have a warrant?" Kane asked.

"Hey, William," Nathan said. "We're trying to clear this up."

"I need to talk to my lawyer." He stared at Strong. "Unless you have cause to arrest me?"

"William!" Nathan pleaded.

"No, Mister Kane," Strong said. "No cause. Yet. Mind telling me where you live?"

"Yes, I do."

Strong leaned back in the booth. Folded his hands over the notebook. "You have some ID on you?"

"I do."

"I can legally ask for that. And I can arrest you if you don't show it."

"He's my nephew," Nathan said.

Kane retrieved his money clip, pulled the tattered New York State driver's license from the center and handed it over.

"What is this?" Strong demanded. The faded piece of paper was barely readable. Strong squinted at the writing. "How old is it? It's not even the current iteration of license."

"I got my license in 1961."

"It's 1977," Strong said.

"I was in the military," Kane said. He tried to defend his legal laziness. "According to New York state law we don't have to renew."

"You're not in the military anymore," Strong said. He tore it up and dropped it in the ashtray. "Now you can't drive that Jeep or I'll have you arrested. And it's illegally parked. Thus I'm having it towed." He pointed. "You're carrying a firearm. Which requires a city permit. Let me see it."

Kane slid the document out of his clip.

Strong checked it. "You know what the law says about gun permits? The city giveth and the city taketh." He slid the license into his notepad. "Your gun, please, Mister Kane."

Nathan looked like he was about to say something, but didn't.

Kane felt a rushing in his head, a lightness in his arms. As if he weren't here but watching it play out on a movie screen and he was in the audience. The script was written by someone else.

"I'm being polite," Strong said.

Kane pulled the .45 and laid it on the table, pointing toward the wall. "There's a round in the chamber. The trigger is twitchy if you're not used to it."

"Thank you," Strong said as he picked up the gun. "Ambidextrous safety, machined slide. That's unique. Serial number burned off. That's unique also and not good." He dropped the magazine, pulled the slide and ejected the bullet. It hit the table and rolled off.

Morticia caught the round before it hit the floor, maintaining the pot of coffee upright in her other hand. She held out the bullet. "Whom does this belong to?"

"I'll take it," Strong said.

She handed him the bullet. He tried to press it into the magazine.

"It's full," Kane said. "We always carried seven and one in the pipe."

Strong put the magazine into his jacket pocket along with the permit. The gun rested in front of him. He rolled the bullet across the table to Kane, who picked it up. "Who is 'we'? Where'd you get a sterile gun?"

"Anything else?" Kane put the bullet in his shirt pocket.

"You're not helping yourself," Strong said.

Morticia had not moved, observing the conversation from the edge of the booth.

"I know about helping myself," Kane said, "and sitting here with you isn't doing that. That I am certain about." Kane stood up, taking the Times. "Good day, gentlemen."

"William?" Nathan said.

Kane headed for the door. He noticed Thao standing on his crate, staring over the kitchen serving wall.

Morticia walked next to him. "You all right?" she whispered.

Kane lied. "Sure."

"Bullshit."

"Tell your friend who needs legal advice to talk to Toni Marcelle. She's in the book."

Kane exited into the stifling heat in time to see them loading Cibosky's body into the coroner's van. A patrolman stood next to his Jeep.

Kane walked south, toward the twin towers of the World Trade Center.

CIVIC CENTER, MANHATTAN

"There are three possibilities," Kane said, "and two of them are bad."

They were in Toni's office. She wore a nondescript blouse, Calvin Klein jeans and no makeup. Her hair was a tousled mess. Despite that, her skin was smooth and glowing, without any indication of perspiration. A yellow legal pad was in front of her, covered with notes from Kane's recital of events since the confrontation with Cibosky the previous morning. A steaming cup of freshly made coffee was next to it.

"Go on," Toni said.

"One," Kane said. "That my High Standard isn't in my footlocker and was used to kill Cibosky and will turn up somewhere and match ballistics. My prints are all over that gun and magazine and shell casings. Two. That the gun was stolen, used to kill Cibosky, and is back in the locker and Strong will get a warrant and open the locker and find it and match ballistics. Three. It's in there and wasn't used. Number three is not likely."

"Back up. How do you know Cibosky was killed by a .22?" Toni asked.

"I've seen that wound before," Kane said. "Suppressed .22 caliber pistol, fired at close range, straight into the eyeball. Easy entry through the socket. The round splinters as it traverses flesh. Churns the brain. It's low velocity in order to be subsonic and quiet coming out of the suppressor. That's why there was no exit wound. It was one of the weapons of choice for a liquidation technique employed in the Phoenix Program. I'm pretty sure it's my gun. It's not a weapon that is widely distributed. They were specially made for the CIA."

Toni let out a deep breath. "Jesus, Will. 'Liquidation' The 'CIA'?"

"Jesus is not going to help us."

"When you say 'liquidation' you mean kill, right? What the hell was this Phoenix Program?"

"Something the CIA ran. I wouldn't write that term down."

"The war is over," Toni said.

"Some parts will never be over."

They were alone on the top floor of the firm. The offices were quiet, only the hum of cool air being pushed out of the vents.

"How long will it take Strong to get a warrant for the footlocker?" Kane asked.

"You're lucky it's him," Toni said. "He's a straight arrow and will actually get one before he'd open it. Many detectives would have reported the lock broken and been in it already."

"I don't think having Strong on my case is lucky," Kane said. "He looks like he has his act together. And he's a veteran of the Walking Dead."

"The what?"

"1st Battalion, 9th Marines," Kane said. "He said 1967, which means he was on the DMZ. That battalion had the highest casualty of *any* Marine unit in *any* war, Toni. He's seen the shit."

"He's a competent cop and a fast rise in the Department," Toni said. "It's Sunday. There's one judge on call. I don't think Strong will bother him on the weekend, especially with your Uncle Nathan vouching for you and given who the victim is. But just in case, I'll ensure I get a call from the duty clerk if a warrant is pushed through today. But most likely it will be tomorrow. Hold on." She turned her chair and picked up a phone. Had a quiet conversation. Hung up. "I'll know the moment any warrant with your name on it is processed. Same goes if he wants to search your place."

"So I've got a little time," Kane said.

"Hopefully," Toni said. She looked at the notepad. "How did someone get your gun, if they did?"

"Broke into the place I park the Jeep and motorcycle. I lock the High Standard in the footlocker in the back of the Jeep when I'm not carrying it."

"You didn't see it this morning?"

"I only used the top tray this morning for my clothes and to secure the .45 when I went for my run. The .22 is in the lower part. You remember our West Point footlockers."

"Ted's was shipped back to us," Toni said. "Dad still has it in his office." She drummed her fingernails. "Okay. You didn't kill Cibosky. Who did?"

"Quinn," Kane said.

"You sound certain."

"Okay, most likely Quinn. Or someone else working for Cappucci. But my money is on Quinn."

"Why?"

"We need to know what Cappucci is doing about the pictures," Kane said. "Because this could be his first step against Delgado. Take out Delgado's muscle first. It's what I would do."

"Don't ever say that again."

Kane pressed on. "Or it could simply be a lesson. Cibosky told me Quinn didn't know that Delgado sent him to give me a message so Quinn had considered the matter settled at breakfast. Maybe Cibosky got killed for stepping out of school? Or Cappucci had Cibosky whacked to send Delgado a message."

Toni tapped her fingernails on the leather covering her desktop, not as annoying as the Formica at Vic's. "We still don't know who broke into your apartment and took the photos and sent them as if they were sent by me."

"Quinn," Kane once more accused. "Cibosky getting dumped across from Vic's sounds like him."

"Why?"

"To fuck with us," Kane said. "I'm not that concerned with the 'why' right now. The first priority is to get into my footlocker and see if the gun is there. That's a lot more leverage than the pictures and it's against me."

"Motive is always important," Toni said. "It's the key to everything."

"No," Kane said. "Politics and power are. You know that. As you said, Quinn is bad news. I've learned more about him and he's worse than you think."

"How so?"

"He was military," Kane said. "In a New Zealand unit that's the equivalent of Special Forces."

"Fuck," Toni said.

"Exactly. We need to bring your father in. I noticed that Strong blinked when I mentioned your firm. He recognized it. We need all the help we can get."

Toni stopped the fingernail drum roll. "My father doesn't know I'm representing Mrs. Delgado."

"You said she got referred to you since that's what you do here," Kane said.

Toni stood up. "You want some more coffee?"

"No, thanks."

She walked out of the office and to the machine in the lobby. Kane didn't follow. He was trying to mentally unravel this Gordian knot otherwise known as a clusterfuck.

Toni came back. "I'll make some calls. See what I can find out. Maybe I can get this squashed before Strong moves any further. You're right. The firm has a lot of connections. I am a partner here. We've made bigger problems disappear."

"What are you doing here?" Kane asked.

Toni was confused. "What do you mean? You called me."

Kane waved a hand. "This office? The firm? You were working for the public defender's office when I lef the country."

"I'm Ted's replacement," Toni said.

"What?"

"Father revised his plan for Ted once he made the decision to go to the Academy. Looked good on paper: West Point, Army, combat vet war hero and then law school. Come here, hang his shingle. Eventually take over. It was all planned."

"Plans go to shit once you make contact," Kane said.

"That's what happened, wasn't it?" Toni said, voice dripping with bitterness.

"That doesn't mean you have to take Ted's place," Kane said.

"Don't worry about me, Will," Toni said. "I've got my own plan and I'm pretty far along on it. Right now, you've got an immediate problem."

Kane stood. "I'm going to get into the footlocker."

"We'll fix this," Toni promised.

Kane shook his head. "It's going to get worse."

"You didn't kill Cibosky," Toni said. "It can't get worse."

"You don't understand," Kane said. "I've been here before. I think you need to bring your father in. I got a bad feeling about it."

"What are you talking about?"

"*'No one expects the Spanish Inquisition'*," Kane said without any attempt to imitate the accent of original Monty Python phrase.

"That's not funny. This isn't funny."

"No, it's not. But there's truth in humor. We should always expect the Spanish Inquisition.By the way, the waitress at Vic's, Morticia, has a friend who needs some legal advice. Told her to give you a call." Kane walked out.

IMPOUND LOT, LOWER MANHATTAN

Conner had given the location of the impound lot for the southern half of Manhattan with no questions asked. Much like he'd given up breakfast at Vic's, Kane thought as he surveilled the lot.

He felt naked without a gun on his hip even though he'd never fired any firearm outside of a range since coming back to the States. He didn't like the feeling, because it meant he was less than because of a piece of hardware.

Other than the chain link fence, topped with razor wire, all around it, the impound lot resembled many vacant lots in the city. Some vehicles inside were abandoned cars that had been picked up before they were completely stripped and most lacked tires. There were some intact newer ones, obviously moneymakers for the city's coffers when the owners came to claim them. Most likely picked up on alternate side of the street parking violations early in the morning. Some of the cars were evidence in various investigations. His Jeep was closer to the wrecks than the high-end cars.

There was one attendant in the lot, an old white guy in stained gray coveralls. He sat on a folding chair in the shade of a large umbrella near the open front gate. He supervised a clipboard hanging on a hook made from a coat hanger on the fence.

Kane watched a city wrecker bring in a red Volkswagen camper covered in poorly hand-painted rainbows. The attendant got up, talked to the wrecker driver, took down some information from him, then pointed. The tow truck pulled the camper next to the Jeep. The driver unhooked it, stored his chains, then drove out of the lot. The attendant resumed his seat in the shade. He had a small cooler next to him and he would reach in, pull a can out, take a slug, and return it to the safety of the cooler.

Kane looked up. It was late afternoon, but wouldn't be dark for several hours. He couldn't wait that long. Toni had no way to get a hold of him if a warrant was being processed. And there was more to do this evening.

There were a number of possible tactical options to get inside. Kane withdrew his money clip and peeled off a twenty. Kane had learned the art of the tight fold into the palm for the quick slip from another one of Toni's investigators, Dutch, a cop before he worked for *Marcelle*, who'd retired the previous year to Florida to play the pony's. He'd been appalled at Kane's lack of fixer skills and done his best to pass on decades of tricks and contacts during their overlap time.

Kane walked to the gate. The attendant looked up and waited.

"I need to get something from my Jeep."

"That old piece of junk yours, is it?"

"Yep."

Kane stuck his hand out as if to shake.

The attendant didn't reciprocate. He checked the clipboard. "Says it was illegally parked. Normally, for that, I could let you drive outta here for fifty. But it got a flag on it from a detective named Strong. No release unless he authorizes it."

"I need to check something in it."

"Check or take?"

"If it's there, take. If it's not there, it's just a check."

The attendant smiled, revealing a fine set of dentures. He shook Kane's hand, taking the bill. He unfolded it, negating Kane's suave and practiced effort. "Jackson. I need his twin."

Kane pulled another $20 off the clip and handed it over, unfolded. The attendant tucked both bills into the chest pocket of the coverall. "Five minutes. I don't wanna know what you do."

The Jeep's back gate was well-oiled and opened smoothly. The lock appeared intact. A chain was looped through two eyehole bolts Kane had drilled into the back of the locker and reinforced with a steel plate on the inside.

Kane slipped the key into the padlock on the battered, black footlocker. His name and serial number had once been stenciled on it but long ago spray-painted over. He'd signed for the locker on 2 July 1962. R-Day; Reception Day for Beast Barracks at West Point. He'd hauled this footlocker through four years of West Point. It had sat in its appointed place at the foot of his bunk in the barracks. Opened every Saturday morning for SAMI (Saturday AM Inspection), top tray pushed back and tipped up so that the lower half was partly exposed. It had been shipped to Fort Hood for his first assignment, then to Benning for Ranger School in 1966, then to his other duty assignments over the years. Then finally to New York City in the cargo hold of a civilian airliner.

Kane swung up the lid. Lifted the tray out. A towel was unwrapped in the left side of the bottom.

The High Standard was gone.

GREENWICH VILLAGE, MANHATTAN

Kane called the bad news to Toni via a payphone on his way home. She was still in the office and sounded distracted. She cursed a few times, informed him no warrants had been submitted, and that she'd meet him at Vic's tomorrow morning for breakfast and to plan.

Kane's hand instinctually went to his naked holster upon seeing the door to his apartment wide open. He paused at the top of the stairs. The intruder was whistling the Colonel Bogey March.

Kane sighed and walked down the stairs and in the open door. The sitting room was cloudy and reeked of cigarette smoke. Trent was inspecting the books, his sports jacket tossed on the couch. He was in his late fifties, portly, thinning black hair, flushed red face, and thick, slightly tinted glasses with black frames. He had a cigarette in his left hand, the ash precariously long.

He stopped whistling and turned. "Captain Kane."

"Been whistling long, Trent?"

Trent tapped his right ear, indicating the thin wire leading to an earpiece. "Ever since my security radioed you were approaching. Thought I'd make some noise and give a heads up rather than have you charging in." The ash fell off the cigarette onto the pockmarked wood floor.

"You need security?"

"History and recent developments suggest you're a dangerous man."

Kane turned a chair by the street level window to face the visitor, then sat down. He waited.

"No 'how you doing'? 'Long time no see'? 'Missed you'?" Trent spoke with a slight New England accent which Kane didn't recall from their previous meeting.

"No. More along the lines I hoped you were dead. Of something particularly nasty. Prostate or rectal cancer comes to mind as being appropriate but lung cancer is more likely."

"You never were funny." Trent sat down on the couch.

"I keep hearing that."

"You're well read," Trent said. "If you've read these books. They might have come with the place."

Kane didn't reply.

"What's with all the maps?"

"I like to know where I am."

"We'd like to know where you were," Trent said. "You were off the reservation for a few years."

Several seconds passed.

"How come you don't have that Life magazine cover framed?" Trent asked. "You guys were famous. Or should I say infamous. The Green Beret Affair. Do you keep up with the fellows?"

Kane remained silent.

"Phil King says hi." Trent was watching Kane. "He's doing well, if you're interested. Director of Covert Ops. Right under the Director of the Agency. Technically he reports, but Bush is

a politician, not a career man. He couldn't hold a candle to Wild
Bill. Of course, Truman screwed Donovan by not making him
the first director. Fucking politicians. We keep Bush out of the
loop on the things he doesn't need or want to know." He
chuckled. "Which is pretty much everything."

"We trace our lineage in Special Forces to the OSS and
Donovan," Kane said. "We uphold his tradition better."

Trent snorted. "Right. Fucking boy scouts. Or should I say
girl scouts with your pretty green berets."

Kane didn't rise to the bait.

"So King is DCO," Trent repeated. The cigarette was short,
barely enough to hold. He took another inhale. "It's actually the
most powerful position at the Agency. Odds are, once we get a
more aggressive President, he'll be the next Director."

Kane interlaced his fingers in his lap, pressing them tight.

Trent went on. "I'm doing pretty good myself, thanks for
asking. A little of this, a little of that. I happen to be doing some
work in New York City, which is why Phil called me earlier.
Asked me to send his greetings."

"We never met."

Trent gave what might be a smile, but appeared to be a
grimace, revealing yellowish, stained teeth. "That's why they call
Phil the Gray Ghost. He seems to be everywhere, but nowhere.
How many times did you guys show up, asking us to take that
gook off your hands? What to do? Geez, fucking amateurs. You
were right outside his door several times, but never saw him."

"I was never outside his door," Kane said.

"Oh yeah, that's right, you weren't part of Gamma."

"He didn't show at the trial, either," Kane said.

"Yeah. Like he's ever going to set foot in a courtroom."

"That was your job," Kane said. "And you lied your ass off."

"Truth is relative," Trent said.

"In your world."

"My world is the real world," Trent said. "I'd have thought
you learned that in LBJ." He lit another cigarette from the stub
and it joined the others in the ashtray. He held the pack out.

"No," Kane said.

"Scared?" Trent said. "Shit, Kane, you've got nine lives. You haven't used all of them, have you?"

"Why are you here?" Kane knew he'd yielded by asking the question that Trent wanted him to, but he was tired of sparring and it was going to come out sooner or later.

Trent wagged a thick finger at Trent. "You know, of the eight, I ended up having the most respect for you. You kept your mouth shut. Never said a thing. Not to me. Not to your lawyers, not in court. Nothing. But it cost you, didn't it? You're the only one with the dishonorable discharge. That's fucking irony since you were being honorable. Sticking to a code of honor got you shafted. Bet you didn't know at the time how much that would screw you over in the civilian world, did you? You were Army since you were seventeen and went into the Academy. Your West Point classmates, they're what now, majors? Lieutenant colonels?"

"Thirty are KIA."

"And to double down on the irony," Trent continued, "that pussy Carter pardoned the draft dodgers in January. Can you fucking believe that? Those cowards broke the law, ran away like chickenshits and now they're coming back and are citizens with all their rights just like you. Well, not like you, because you have a dishonorable discharge. They're actually better off than you."

"They had courage."

Trent evinced surprise. "You believe that?"

"They made a choice. Choices are hard, especially when they aren't popular. And that's the third time you've mentioned my discharge."

"I wasn't counting. You're not being very hospitable. You haven't offered me anything to drink, not that you have anything worth drinking. I checked. Seriously, Kane, you're not a drunk? Seems like you'd be a prime candidate for it."

"I have other outlets."

"I am sorry about your personal loss, though." Trent watched Kane carefully as he said that. "A real tragedy. Where did you go to grieve?"

"Not here."

"And the wife?"

"Not any more."

"Too bad." Trent shifted back. "Green Berets. You guys like to think you're strategists. Big picture guys. But you don't see it. You never saw it in Vietnam. You went into the mountains and became buddy-buddy with the Yards. Lived like you was one of 'em. Rolling around in the mud. Loved them little fuckers, didn't you? Except you have to remember that the Vietnamese were the ones in the cities driving scooters and cars and had TV's and the choice real estate and the best rice paddies and your guys were wearing loincloths and living in fucking huts on the sides of hills, chewing on roots. Think you made the right choice?"

"They're honest people."

Trent chuckled. "Fair enough. And where did that get them? Massacred. Re-education camps. The ones who survived are still living in huts."

"The South Vietnamese didn't do so good either with their scooters and cars and TV's and our weapons and *your* help."

"Another valid point," Trent allowed. "Fuckers deserved what happened to them."

"You forget it was your people who started funneling aid to the Montagnard and got them involved in a war they didn't have a side in," Kane said. "The South Vietnamese government hated them even more than the VC. We got stuck with what the CIA initiated."

Trent waved it away. "Everyone has their place. The Yards had theirs. Your Green Beret buddies have theirs. But what is yours now, Kane?"

"What are you doing here, Trent?"

"Your name came up today," Trent said.

"Came up where?"

He waved the cigarette. "Did you see that movie, *Three Days of the Condor*? With Robert Redford playing the Agency analyst? I mean Robert Redford as an analyst? Who believes that?"

"I read the book," Kane said. "It was six days. It's on the shelf there."

"What's it they say? The book is always better or is it the movie is always shorter?" Trent shook his head. He inhaled, blew smoke. "But someone talked out of school to the author.

Because we actually *have* places like that. Where bookish people get paid to sit and read and read and read. Everything. Communications between various agencies at all levels. Newspapers, magazines, books, all sorts of documents. They summarize key words and feed that to big computers. But none of them are Robert Redford."

More smoke.

"Personally, I don't like computers," Trent said. "You know why?"

Kane didn't respond.

"You're not a very good conversationalist," Trent said.

"I've got a long list of faults."

"I don't like computers for a very simple reason. They can't lie. Humans can lie. We can even believe our lies. That makes us superior."

"Computers will lie if you feed them false data," Kane said.

"Yeah, but that comes from a lying human, doesn't it?"

"Or one who has been deceived by someone else's lies and believes they're telling the truth."

"Anyway," Trent dismissed. "So the analysts are like little hamsters on their information wheels, spinning away. You and I know raw information is not intelligence. But the computer has a list of alerts it's programmed to and—oh, fuck it, I don't know how the damn computer works. But I assume lights go off, a bell rings, whatever."

"A bell rang and you came scurrying," Kane said. "Like a rat in a maze."

Trent sucked on the cigarette, the tip glowing, ash falling off onto his pants leg. He brushed it onto the floor. The fingers holding the cigarette were stained, the fingernails uneven.

"I was driven here," Trent said, "because your name is on that long list of alerts. The bell rang earlier today when one of those analysts scanned a request from the NYPD to the FBI's criminal database and entered the pertinent data."

"That was fast," Kane said.

"We're efficient. Didn't they teach you in the finishing school you went to at Bragg that timeliness is the most important aspect of intelligence gathering?"

"They did."

A spark of anger from Trent. "Then why did you dumb fucks take ten days to liquidate Ngo? You almost blew the whole fucking war apart."

"Would that have been bad?"

Trent calmed just as fast. "Anyway," he said. "Your name came up." He tsk-tsked. "Really. Murder, Kane? You should have left that behind in Vietnam."

"I didn't murder anyone in Vietnam. Or here."

"I eventually pegged you as the trigger man," Trent said. "That's the one thing none of you gave up. Who pulled the trigger? We were putting bets on it at the Center, but it never came out. Still hasn't. I wonder what happened to that pot?"

"Why does the CIA have me on an alert list?" Kane asked. "Why are you here?"

"I like New York City," Trent said. "The rest of the country thinks it's circling the drain, going under any day now. The city government might. But you've got the United Nations, all those embassies. Lots of foreigners. Lots of spies."

"That's the FBI's job."

"Boys in suits," Trent said, his tone indicating what he thought. "We like to keep our own eyes on things."

"The CIA can't operate domestically."

Trent mocked with an incredulous face. "Have you learned nothing? As I said. There's a lot going on. I keep my finger on the pulse. And it's not just the foreigners. Wall Street and the big banks are critical. Nothing happens without money. There are no freedom fighters, no terrorists, no covert ops, no wars, without money. In fact, wars are fought *over* money in one form or another." He briefly hummed the *Money* refrain from *Cabaret*, which was lost on Kane. Seeing this, Trent ceased and chained another cigarette. Then continued. "We keep your name on a list, because you have a unique skill set, Kane. An interesting background and breadth of experience. One you're pissing away."

"You want me to work for you?"

"I want you as my asset."

"No."

"I can make this NYPD thing go away."

"I didn't kill that guy."

"Yeah, that defense didn't turn out too well in Vietnam. There might be some money in it for you."

"No."

Trent sighed and got to his feet. "Think about it."

"I don't have to," Kane said. "You fucked me over once. Stupidity would be letting you do it again."

Trent wagged the hand holding the cigarette, scattering ash. "Oh, no, no, no, Captain Kane. *You* fucked yourself over. You did it all wrong, Kane. You and your buddies."

Trent waited. Tossed the remains of the cigarette in the ashtray without putting it out. "I'm gonna do you a favor, Kane. Give you a piece of advice you should've figured out by now. This world?" He twirled a finger. "It's a machine. We're all cogs in the machine. Didn't you ever think that standing on the Plain at West Point. That you were just one more automaton standing at attention among a thousand other pieces like you? Interchangeable parts? Think it through. The Long Gray Line? In its essence, what does that mean?

"The key, Kane, is where in the machine your part fits. It's either in a place that gets plenty of oil and serves a useful function or it's in a dark, rusty place that is unnecessary and eventually gets tossed out on the scrap heap or ground down to nothing. I'm giving you the chance to get back in the machine and be useful."

Kane remained silent.

Trent picked up his jacket and shrugged it on. Pulled a pen out of the breast pocket. Grabbed a paperback off the shelf. Scrawled something on the back, tossed it on the table.

"Call that number and ask for me after you've come to your senses. No rush. Unless you get arrested." He walked toward the front door. "The matchstick thing is cute. Tradecraft. Oh yeah, by the way, if things go well and you do what we ask, there's always the possibility of us reaching into records. Perhaps change that dishonorable discharge. It's just a mark on a piece of paper. They get changed all the time."

Trent began humming the theme song from the newly released Scorsese movie, *New York, New York*, as he departed into the growing darkness.

Sunday Night, 10 July 1977

GREENWICH VILLAGE, MANHATTAN

Kane had no clue what Trent had been humming when he left. He was still in the chair, watching the thin tendril of smoke rising from Trent's last cigarette, when Pope walked through the open door.

"You all right, lad? I saw that chap leave. Friend of yours?"

"No."

"Ah!" Pope said, as if he understood. "I just returned from the Post. Doing the research we discussed and a few other chores." He noted the overflowing ashtray and the smoke. "Your not-a-friend is messy. Would you like to join me upstairs for some tea while this place airs out? I have learned a thing or two that might be of use to you."

"Coffee for me," Kane said.

"I assume you mean that literally," Pope said, "and are not introducing me to a taste of your vernacular?"

"I have to work tonight."

"I believe I have some we can make," Pope said. "As long as instant suffices."

"I used to chew instant from c-rats on missions," Kane said.

"I assume that means yes." Pope led the way out.

Kane crushed the burning embers, and left the door to the place open since it seemed an ineffective deterrent against the company he was receiving.

Pope looked over his shoulder as they walked up the front steps. "If you don't mind me asking, who was that man? A rather large car pulled up for him with an unsavory chap opening the door."

"CIA."

"Interesting with all that is going on." Pope led him to the kitchen.

"You don't know all of it," Kane said.

"One never does, but we can strive for that grail." Pope searched through one of the cupboards. "I'm sure I have some instant. A lass from the Daily News I used to liaise with every so often desired it in the wee hours of the morning. Such was my effect on the fairer sex. Ah." He brought out a jar with a faded label. "The rest I will leave to you." He sat down and topped his teacup.

Kane put the kettle on the stove. He filled Pope in on the crime scene and Cibosky's murder with a brief overview of the previous encounters.

"Are you going to call this Trent fellow?" Pope asked.

"No. We have a history. He was the mouthpiece the CIA put on the stand in Vietnam. He testified that the Agency never authorized the killing, when, in fact, they suggested it."

"That's the past," Pope pointed out. "Right now, it sounds as if you might need some assistance. He offered."

"Like the devil in the desert," Kane said.

"Waxing biblical. What will you do?"

"You didn't ask if I killed Cibosky," Kane said.

"You said you didn't."

"You take my word for it?"

Pope sipped some scotch. "Son, I've met all sorts. Camp guards who snatched screaming babies from their mother's arms and tossed them into ovens. Soldiers executing POWs. Here, in the city, I've talked to murderers. Rapists. CEOs. Psychopaths. Wife killers. Children killers. You didn't kill Cibosky."

Pope paused as Kane turned off the stove and poured boiling water over the instant coffee. The stale granules struggled to dissolve. He carried it to the table and sat down.

"Nothing further on Quinn, I'm afraid," Pope said. "And I'm leery of pursuing it. Her Majesty's Secret Services don't like poking in certain areas and the SAS is one of them, even a colonial."

"That's all right," Kane said. He pulled out his notebook and checked. "Hey, what poet wrote '*Only dumb guys fight*'?"

"Langston Hughes," Pope said. "The Harlem Renaissance. I believe he passed away in the last decade. Intriguing fellow. Met him once. That came out of nowhere."

"Someone quoted it today. What did you find out about Thomas Marcelle?"

"That was less dicey," Pope said. "At least the surface facts. He was nicknamed 'The Hammer' as a prosecutor because he went after organized crime and political corruption with a vengeance. Made his bones on it, to borrow a phrase from those he investigated. You postulated the common theory that Marcelle changed after his son died in Vietnam."

Pope reached into the leather satchel and retrieved a composition notebook, stuffed with papers secured by two thick rubber bands. He removed the rubber bands, placing them around his wrist. Turned pages as he peered through the glasses on the edge of this nose. "Let's see that was--"

"22 June, 1967."

Pope looked over his glasses. "You are familiar with the event?"

"I was there. Close by," Kane amended.

"Connections clicking into place." He tapped the notebook. "Here's the interesting part. Early in 1967 Thomas Marcelle was put in charge of one of the Southern District's biggest cases. A notorious man named Sean Damon, head of the vestiges of Tammany Hall, was indicted on a number of charges. It was an attempt by the Federal Government to break that political machine once and for all and deal a powerful tangential blow to organized crime and corruption in the city."

"Damon," Kane said. "Dark glasses? Nice suit? Not much hair, slicked back?"

Pope raised an eyebrow underneath the brim of his hat. "The man to a T. He has a problem with his eyes that requires he wears the glasses all the time. At least that's the story, but I've met a number of good hands at poker who sport dark glasses to hide their eyes, which are the window into the soul, the bluff and the winning hand. You know him?"

"I saw him the other day. With Thomas Marcelle."

"*Curiouser and curiouser! Cried Alice*," Pope said.

Kane nodded. "Yeah, we're going down a rabbit hole. I thought Tammany Hall was done when LaGuardia was re-elected?"

"Almost," Pope replied. "Damon is a holdover and he maintains considerable ties across the city." Pope checked the notes. "Damon had, according to the charges, sold judgeships, steered municipal building, streetlight and parking meter contracts to companies with strong mafia ties while taking a percentage, and assorted other Federal charges, including tax evasion. Tens of millions of dollars were involved. The case was rock solid and it was expected Damon would be behind bars for the rest of his life."

Kane stirred the cooling coffee, swirling crystals in muddy water.

Pope went through the papers, found what he was looking for. "There is a flow to history and a flow to news. This was in early 1967. On 12 June Thomas Marcelle stunned everyone by cutting a deal with Damon's attorney. In exchange for a guilty plea, Damon received an eight-year term at a low security Federal prison, eligible for parole in three. All his assets and money were confiscated by the government."

"Who did Damon give up in exchange?" Kane asked.

"That was the shocking part," Pope said. "No one."

"Then what was the deal?" Kane drank the coffee, imbibing intact granules.

"That's what everyone wanted to know. The papers were signed before Marcelle's own boss, the U.S. Attorney for the Southern District, knew about it. Marcelle's resignation was on his desk the next day."

"Ten days before Ted died. Was Marcelle bribed?"

"Oh, that was most certainly looked into. The US Attorney and the Feds dogged Marcelle. Bank accounts, home, the entire financial spectrum. They investigated him for years. Nothing."

"Except his new law firm," Kane said.

"There is that," Pope agreed. "However, Thomas Marcelle's wife comes from old money. She funded the establishment of the firm and after that the revenue rolled in."

"What is Damon up to now?" Kane asked.

"He got out in late '70 after doing the minimum three years. Rebuilt his fiefdom. The biggest issue in the city at the moment is the election. Damon still has most of his old connections. He's a player."

"What would Damon want of Thomas Marcelle?"

"That is a mystery, but there are many possibilities, few of them good. I'll investigate further."

Kane washed out the coffee mug. "Thanks."

"You're welcome to bad instant coffee and a chat any time, my young friend."

"Not what I meant." Kane stood. "Thanks for believing me."

MIDTOWN MANHATTAN

Kane raced north on 8th Avenue with lights off, weaving in and out of traffic on the Kawasaki, earning him belated blasts of the horn from startled drivers who spotted him as a blur going by in the darkness and the glimpse as he crossed their headlights.

It was easy to follow Delgado's convoy of two black Cadillac's. Kane had stationed himself near the Triangle Social Club, on Sullivan Street, below Washington Square Park, after leaving Pope's. The Triangle was the first floor of a six-story tenement, with a dark door and two blacked out windows. Men with the same genetic code as Cibosky stood outside, making sure no one who wasn't supposed to enter stepped into the mob hangout.

While it was owned by Vincent Gigante of the Genovese family, this was the third time Kane had tracked Alfonso Delgado to it in the evenings when he'd followed the heir apparent to the Cappucci regime from his home in Brooklyn. This wasn't unusual as the various crime families shared many illegal interests and capos from various families passed through the Triangle.

This was the first time, though, that Delgado was traveling with some of his crew. As a capo in the Cappucci regime, Delgado had his soldiers who did the street work, mainly extortion and gambling.

The Cadillac's flashed their lights and raced up on bumpers, scaring other motorists out of their path on the one-way street uptown. They hit the green lights in perfect order, something drivers could do late at night, running the entire length of Manhattan without ever stopping as the lights changed in a ripple.

As they zipped past 31st Street, the large oval of Madison Square Garden was to the right, occupying two blocks on top of Penn Station. Hookers, hustlers, pimps and their furtive customers blurred by as the convoy, Kane trailing. Times Square approached to the right. The cars didn't slow as they went through the theater district above 42nd Street. There was a scattering of pedestrians enjoying their after-theater dinner and daring the muggers. Marquees advertised plays as diverse as *Annie* and *for colored girls who have considered suicide/when the rainbow is enuf.*

Kane slowed as the lead Cadillac signaled right. Both cars turned east onto 54th Street and their brake lights immediately lit up. Kane rolled past and saw the cause of the abrupt stop. The street was blocked by a festive and desperate mob. A black marquee on the south side of the street was lit with an angled 54.

Kane spun the bike about, bouncing onto the sidewalk on 8th Avenue. He chained it to a lamppost, then hustled back to 54th. The caddy's were inching their way through the crowd, following a line of limousines and high-end cars depositing their contents in a roped off area in front of the nightclub.

Kane walked down the far side of the street, skirting the wanna-get-ins outside the ropes. The ground was vibrating, the echoes of powerful base from Studio 54. There was a short man on a tall stool scanning the crowd, every so often pointing and directing someone from the mob into the sanctum. The doors to the club were blacked out and a doorman swung a center one open for the anointed.

None of these people seemed concerned about Son of Sam.

It took Delgado's car ten minutes to creep past the barriers. The gangster exited the passenger side. The man on the stool was yelling and gesturing, rallying his bouncers and directing them toward Delgado's gathering crew. The man hopped off the stool, disappearing behind the crowd.

Kane stepped up on the hood of a car for a better vantage. Delgado and five of his crew were faced by a dozen bouncers. The man from the stool pushed through, confronting the mobster. The two argued furiously. Kane didn't need to hear the gist given what Toni had told him occurred on Friday night.

It appeared the mafia held little sway here. With a flurry of obscene gestures, Delgado and his crew remounted their cars. Kane jumped down and melted into the shadows of a storefront entrance half a block away, pressing back against the metal barrier. Leaving was quicker than entering for the cars, but they didn't go far, double-parking on the corner of 54th and Broadway.

Delgado left a driver with each car and led the remaining five goons. Kane followed as they entered the alley behind the row of buildings on the south side of 54th. Kane checked his own trail, but the alley was empty to Broadway except for dumpsters overflowing with trash. Kane used those as concealment to follow the gangsters, none of whom were concerned about being shadowed, their focus on their leader.

A single bouncer stood outside a door. He was reaching for a walkie-talkie on his belt when one of Delgado's goons charged him, wrapped the man in a bear hug and slammed him against the building. Dropped him like a rag doll.

Delgado tried the door and cursed.

The wait wasn't long before a young man wearing only tight shorts and sneakers, naked torso wet with sweat and dotted with sparkle, opened the door, letting out a blast of music. He had a large bin in hand. He joined the bouncer with a clatter of empty bottles. Kane sprinted toward the door as the mobsters slipped inside, timing between arriving before it closed and not getting seen.

He didn't make it.

The door shut with a thud and clicked.

Kane stepped back. The building was vibrating from the music. Kane picked up the walkie-talkie. There was chatter on the net, undisciplined, people talking across each other in an almost unintelligible garble. The door clicked.

Another scantily dressed young man exited and froze at the sight of the two bodies in the alley. Kane shoved the radio at him. "I'll get help." Kane pushed into the club.

He headed toward the music via a corridor lined with overflowing trashcans and cases full of bottles. Through another room bustling with activity as waiters grabbed bottles, cases, and buckets of ice, hauling them out. They paid no attention to him or the threesome in the corner.

The music was deafening, a rhythmic thumping that rattled the teeth and shook the body. Kane entranced Studio 54 main, stage right. A DJ was on the center of the stage spinning discs. Lights were flashing, lasers reflecting off a large disco ball hanging from the high ceiling of the former television studio. The dance floor was a mass of sweaty, spinning, flickering bodies. There were balconies surrounding the main room. Around the dance floor were couches, tables and chairs. It was impossible to determine the exact layout with the lack of consistent lighting and the crowd. A layer of cigarette and marijuana smoke hung over it all like the club's own high-end smog.

Spotting Delgado, however, didn't take long. The mobster was bulling across the dance floor, his soldiers a phalanx of fat and muscle. Kane scanned along their vector.

Briefly highlighted by a flash of light were Toni Marcelle and Sofia Cappucci, aka Mrs. Delgado. They reclined on a couch in a somewhat discreet corner, a bottle of champagne in front of them. They were oblivious of the approaching testosterone rage, engaged in a deep and passionate kiss. They broke the kiss and Toni rested her head comfortably on Sofia's shoulder. Sofia Cappucci was Rubenesque, giving Toni a comfortable spot for her head.

Frank, the bodyguard from the firm, spotted the coming storm and stepped around the couch in a protective mode. Kane gave him a plus for facing the oncoming mobsters and moved to the edge of the stage to hop off into the dancers and slide through to assist, but before he committed to that, the bodyguard's position was bolstered as a cluster of bouncers pushed through the crowd and joined him. The man from the stool was with them, screaming at Delgado as the two groups collided. One of the bouncers held up a silver badge, also yelling, an off-duty cop, temporarily resuming the job.

The music and dancing continued unabated. Grace Jones' *I Need A Man* was thumping.

Kane backed into the shadows on the wing of the stage. He scanned the balconies. Difficult to see details. The lasers flashing off the disco ball, the strobing lights, the smoke, and the overall dimness obscuring the field of observation. A random laser beam reflected back from something on one of the balconies. Kane kept his focus there.

At the far edge of the dance floor, the confrontation shouted and threatened and then subsided as Delgado screamed futilely at his wife and Toni. He reluctantly turned and gestured for his men to follow. The two women didn't appear particularly upset as Sofia Delgado laughed and picked up the champagne bottle to top off their flutes.

Kane stared at the balcony from which the laser beam had been reflected. Quinn's tall, slender form was briefly silhouetted against a door opening to a hall behind the balcony, then he was gone.

Kane rapidly retraced his steps, out the back, where the two victims were being attended to. He ran to his motorcycle, unlocked, fired it up and drove around the block to a vantage point to observe the double-parked Cadillacs and the front of Studio 54.

Despite the oppressive humidity and heat he was barely sweating. His hands were steady, his mind centered. Sirens echoed in the distance, but that was standard for the city. It was doubtful the club owner would call the police; no one in the business needed that kind of attention.

Delgado was still venting as he stormed to his car. He cursed at the driver who opened the passenger door. Disappeared inside.

The convoy squealed away, turning south on Broadway.

Kane didn't think Delgado was heading to the piers with his entourage in tow. He killed the engine.

Quinn exited, smoothly palming one of the bouncers. Dutch wouldn't have had to teach him. Quinn slithered through the party mob of unanointed but pathetically hopeful for their fifteen minutes. Straight toward Kane. The absence of the .45 tilted Kane's tactical situation. Quinn wore a black silk suit and red shirt, but instead of boots, a pair of green, canvas sneakers, more like moccasins. And he wore his sunglasses at night. A camera was looped over one shoulder.

"Did you enjoy being on stage?" Quinn halted ten feet away, the perfect distance to keep an armed advantage over an unarmed man. "Nice motorcycle. Useful for the city traffic. Better than your Jeep, eh, mate? Got to have the right tools for the right job."

Kane didn't reply. The ground was vibrating from the music and the crowd was loud, but Quinn and Kane were in their own bubble.

Quinn pointed at the green sneakers on his own feet. "Used these in in the bush while tracking. Had to move quick. Make no noise. They wear out fast, a week maybe in the bush. A bit faster here in the city but I've got plenty. You were easier than you should have been. City life's made you soft."

"I have a long list of faults," Kane said. "Soft isn't one of them."

"Lost your edge then; whatever you want to believe, mate."

"We had an understanding," Kane said.

"We did," Quinn agreed. "Unfortunately, Alfonso Delgado is a complete muppet."

"Does that mean idiot in Kiwi?"

"You broke the deal, Kane. You shouldn't have sent those photos to Mister Cappucci."

"I didn't."

"Sure, you did. The ones Mister Cappucci received were taken and developed by your hand, were they not? And yet you said there were no copies. Thus, you breached the agreement before it had time to settle into place. Your photos, your fault."

"Your logic is a mess."

Quinn laughed. "We're both messes, are we not William Kane?" He pointed at the mark under the lens of his sunglasses. "Viper. Almost got my eye. Had to cut it deep, then grab a stick out of the fire and cauterize to stop the venom. Natives say if the viper don't kill you, you end up becoming one, or some such nonsense."

"Sounds like a pretty accurate legend."

"Why I always wear these glasses," Quinn said.

"Because you're afraid of snakes or are one?"

Quinn remained still for several moments.

Kane waited but when nothing was forthcoming, he filled the void. "Why did you kill Cibosky?"

"I believe you are the prime suspect in that," Quinn said. "Or are the NYPD completely incompetent?"

"I've discussed the matter with them."

"Yet here you are. Must help to have uncles on the force. Perhaps the police need more evidence?"

"I don't think they do."

"The understanding went two ways. You shouldn't be following Mister Delgado."

"The understanding was negated in all directions when you killed Cibosky."

"Ah, such an accusation. With absolutely no proof. The sign of a desperate man." Quinn held up a single finger. "Go home, William Kane. This matter is no longer your province."

"As long as I'm the prime suspect in a murder, it is."

"My speculation would be that if you went home and interfered no more, that will not be an issue. As it is, all the current evidence the police possess is highly circumstantial, is it not? As long as that remains so, you'll be fine."

"Why are you following and photographing Ms. Marcelle?"

"Ms. Marcelle? Perhaps the subject of my hobby is Mrs. Delgado? As the subject of yours was Mister Delgado?"

"What is Cappucci doing about the photographs from the pier?" Kane asked.

"No clue," Quinn said. He unfurled a second finger. "Go home." His right arm crooked ever so slightly, the hand closer the edge of his black jacket. "I'm graciously allowing you to depart. Don't waste the opportunity."

Kane was perfectly still for five seconds and met Quinn's cold gaze. Kane started the motorcycle's engine. Drove past Quinn who stepped to the side, staying out of arm's reach. Kane turned on the lights and rolled away. Rounded the corner on Ninth and drove south.

When he reached the bend where Ninth turned into Hudson Street, he braked, pulling over to the side of the street. The towers of the Trade Center were brilliantly lit above the tenements and brownstones of the Village, the lofts of Soho and Tribeca. Entire floors in the silver pair of buildings blazed with lights, others were sprinkled with them.

Kane sat there for several minutes. Then drove to the Village. Unlocked and stored the motorcycle in the old garage on West 4th, off Seventh Avenue. There was an empty space where the Jeep should be, a mirror to the lack of the .45 on his hip. He looked about the dark space. Kane unscrewed the handle of a broom. He tucked it tight to his left side as he exited, slid the door shut, and locked the warehouse. He took a deep breath, then dove to the left.

A bat thudded into the door where his head had just been. Kane continued the dive, tucking his chin in, rolling, letting the flat of his left upper back take the impact with the sidewalk. He used the momentum to go to his knees and swing the broomstick, hitting the goon who'd missed with the bat in the front of the left shin.

The batter screamed a curse and hopped back, his leg stinging. There were two of them armed with bats, weapon of choice by Delgado's soldiers. Both were big, dressed in the standard uniform of sweat pants and muscle shirts. One bald, the other with a crew cut. Baldie was still cursing, gingerly testing the leg. Lots of steroids and not Studio 54 material.

Kane got up, rising on the balls of his feet, right foot slightly forward, feet far enough apart for good balance and lateral movement. He had the broom handle in both hands, diagonally across his body, right side up.

"This is for Cibosky," Crew Cut said. He charged, bat held high.

Kane gave ground and snapped the broom handle into position, one end locked under his left armpit, the other end angled downward like a lance. Crew Cut's momentum rammed his testicles into the end of the stick. The bat, a few feet shorter than the broomstick, whiffed harmlessly in front of Kane as Crew Cut doubled over in agony.

Kane removed the end of the broom stick from his arm pit and spun it, rotating his hands and hit Crew Cut on the back of the head with a solid strike, knocking him to his knees. He blocked a swing from Baldie, the bat shattering the stick in the middle with home run force.

Kane's hands stung from blow, but now he had a three-foot stick in his hands, each with a sharp point on one end. He took a step, twirled both to get the feel.

Crew Cut was still on his knees moaning and shaking his head, his brains scrambled.

Baldie was pulling the bat back for another strike when Kane attacked with a flurry, sharp end of one stick jabbing with his right hand, the left battering at Baldie's head. Kane slid his feet forward, jabbing, hitting, as Baldie backed up. The bat dropped as Baldie raised both hands to protect his head from the blows, so Kane used his right hand to jab the stick hard into his solar plexus. Baldie gasped in agony. The jagged end of the stick came back red with blood.

To the left, Crew Cut was trying to get to his feet, reaching to his waist. Kane took advantage of Baldie's agony to pause the stick attack and lift his left leg, knee high, then strike straight out with a side kick, the heel of the jungle boot hitting Crew Cut in the forehead.

Crew Cut was out, crumbling to the dirty sidewalk.

Kane turned back to Baldie.

"Fuck you!" Baldie yelled as he charged, wildly swinging his fists.

Kane kept out of striking range and targeted Baldie's hands, bones audibly cracking as the sticks battered them. Baldie kept coming, a testament to whatever drugs he'd taken this evening or slow nerves. Kane dropped low and did a leg sweep. Baldie fell forward, instinctively putting his hands out to cushion his fall. That was a mistake as the already broken bones crumbled.

Baldie screamed, but it was squelched as Kane kicked him between the legs from behind, the toe of his boot smashing testicles. Baldie curled in a whimpering ball and Kane was on top of him, one stick raised high and aimed for the throat.

Baldie's face was covered with open wounds. He was trying to say something through his agony. Tears of pain mixed with the blood. The stick was vibrating in Kane's hand. He shifted focus from the throat to his own hand. The shaking stopped. Took several deep breaths. Put both sticks in his left hand and did a quick search with his right, pulling a snub nose .38 out of Baldie's waistband.

Kane went to Crew Cut. He frisked the unconscious mobster and found a similar .38. Kane stuck one in each cargo pocket of his pants. He returned his attention to Baldie. "Delgado sent you?"

The man nodded.

"Tell him I didn't kill Cibosky."

Baldie's head drooped, chin on chest.

"Did you hear me?" Kane demanded.

A nod.

"Because if I killed Cibosky, I'd kill both of you. Right now."

Baldie looked up, tear-streaked blood on his face, eyes wide.

"Get the fuck out of the city," Kane said. "After you give Delgado my message. Tell him to stay away from Toni Marcelle. Got it?"

Baldie nodded.

Kane walked away. He went directly home, checked that the matchstick was in place, then the piece of clear tape he'd added for redundancy at the top of the door.

He entered, locked the door and dead bolted it. Went into the bathroom and washed the blood off his hands. He didn't bother to get undressed. Dragged the sleeping pad into the kitchen, underneath the table. Crawled onto it and put the sticks to one side. He twisted, pulled his shortened Fairbarn-Sykes out of the sheath and rested that hand, with blade, on his chest. He considered the confiscated revolvers, but trusted the blade. He lay there, sweating, unable to sleep for an hour.

Finally, he rose. Taking the knife and both sticks, he went out the back door, among the plants in the garden. Found a corner of dirt by the back wall, hidden from view. He could smell the greenery, the dirt, the pungent odor of the city.

Kane settled into an uneasy slumber.

Monday, 2 JULY 1962

UNITED STATES MILITARY ACADEMY, WEST POINT, NEW YORK

"Sir, New Cadet Kane reports to the man in the red sash, as ordered."

"Drop your bag," the Man in the Red Sash commands. The cadre member wears gray trousers, a starched white shirt, a black nametag on the left chest with a polished set of jump wings above. A white cap with a shiny black bill shades his eyes. Gray epaulettes on the shoulders sport a black shield with Academy crest superimposed and three yellow stripes indicating he was a 'Firstie' and his rank. And, of course, a wide red sash around his waist.

New Cadet William Kane leans over and puts his bag on the hot pavement while making sure his toes are exactly on the line of tape two feet on front of the First Classman. He resumes a strict position of attention, as best he understands.

The Man in the Red Sash smiles and Kane swells with a sense of accomplishment. They stand in an area surrounded by gray-stone clad barracks on three sides. A row of five Men in Red Sashes have lines of newly arrived youngsters nervously waiting in front of them.

"Pick your bag up, please," the Man in the Red Sash says pleasantly. Kane, a bit confused, picks it up.

"DROP THE BAG, YOU DUMB SMACKHEAD!" the Man in the Red Sash screams, his face just inches from Kane's, spittle spraying.

Kane's hand responds while his mind tries to catch up, releasing the bag. It thuds onto the pavement. The Man in the Red Sash's face is beet red, a vein bulging in his temple.

"When I order you to do something, you do it instantly. Do you understand, smackhead?"

Kane thinks the man's array of insults seems limited. "Right, sir."

"NO!"

The Man in the Red Sash appears to be taking this overly personally.

He leans forward, his shaded eyes peer unblinking into Kane's. "Wrong answer, shit for brains. You have three answers and only three. I'm going to tell them to you. Once. They are: 'Yes, sir. No, sir. No excuse, sir'. Do you understand?"

"Yes, sir."

Kane gains reprieve as there is a commotion among the Men in the Red Sashes. A limousine has rolled up on the far side of Thayer Road and a young man is exiting. He stands and holds the door as an older, distinguished looking woman and a younger one with thick black hair, exit.

"EYES FRONT!" the Man in the Red Sash screams at Kane, but he and his comrades are smelling the scent of fresh meat. And more.

"Girlfriend?" a Man asks his fellow Men.

"Not for long," one replies. "She's too hot for a beanhead."

"Sister and mother," another says. "See the resemblance. The mom isn't bad either. I'd give her a six. The sister is definitely a nine; she loses one for that big nose."

Kane can't help but rotate his eyeballs. Sees hugs to the unsuspecting not yet New Cadet accompanied by tears from the two women. Farewells. Kane had said his ten minutes ago to a gruff father and his teary mother. The not yet New Cadet breaks away and walks across the street.

Kane can't believe it. The guy is carrying a bag in one hand and a tennis racket in the other. That is not on the list of what to bring. And, the guy is smiling.

More spittle sprays his face. "GET YOUR BEADY LITTLE EYEBALLS TO THE FRONT, CROT!"

Kane only hears Theodore Marcelle's welcome to the Corp of Cadets as he's greeted by a hell-fire cluster of cadre.

*****

Kane almost falls to his knees as he shuts the barracks room door and drops the load of clothing and gear. It is the first time he is out of range of a cadre member since reporting to the Man in the Red Sash four hours ago.

Kane has reported to the Man multiple times, each leading to orders to go to a new place as a list safety-pinned to his newly issued shorts is checked off. The old, musty gym where he's weighed, needled with shots, given the same confusing physical fitness test he'd had to pass to even be considered for entry consisting of pull-ups, push-ups, a shuttle run and throwing a basketball for distance while kneeling.

He imagines the last one might have something to do with throwing hand grenades? But why kneeling?

He's visited the barber and been scalped. The tailor and been measured. Photographed. Issued an identification card. Other places to collect an ever-growing, confusing array of uniforms, shoes, and other equipment until he can barely carry it all.

Finally, to receive this room assignment.

He is not alone. Another New Cadet is sitting on his bed, his accumulation at his feet. He's staring at a broken tennis racket.

"Did they do that?" Kane asks.

Surprisingly, the young man smiles. "Yeah. They don't have much of a sense of humor." He stands, extending his hand. "Ted Marcelle."

"Will Kane."

Ted has olive tinged skin, cropped hair, a hook nose, and black eyes. He's solidly built and possesses what can only be defined as presence.

"Where from in the city?" Ted asks. "I can hear it."

Kane nods. "The Bronx."

Ted laughs. "Da Bronx. Manhattan here."

The door bursts open and they're startled, but it's another victim of the Red Sash. A hulking, six foot two, New Cadet staggers in, followed by Cadre screams. A football recruit.

His face is smeared with tears.

Kane and Ted exchange a glance.

*****

"As was true for all of the 24,400 who have preceded you, this has been a day none of you will forget," General Richard Stilwell, the Commandant, informs the New Cadets dressed in freshly issued uniforms. They are formed on the Plain, their ranks amazingly straight given they'd been civilians when they woke this morning. This is a tribute to 160 years of tradition channeled through the cadre of upperclassmen.

"It has been a tough one and designedly so. There will be many others. West Point is tough. It calls for leaders who can stand straight and unyielding under the sternest of physical and moral pressures. The security of this nation cannot be entrusted to men of lesser mold.

"The history of the United States of America and the history of the United States Army and the history of the United States Military Academy are so closely intertwined as to be inextricable, one from the other. As goes the Army, so goes the nation. West Point is tough! It is tough in the same way war is tough. My constant theme, sirs, is that the history of the United States of America and the history of the United States Army and the history of the United States Military Academy are so closely intertwined as to be inextricable, one from the other. As goes the Army, so goes the nation."

"Lotta history," Ted whispers next to Kane, who shifts eyeballs right to see if their squad leader overhears. "If one gotta shit, do they all?"

The Commandant pauses, allowing his words to reverberate and sink in. He is back-dropped by Trophy Point with Battle Monument directly behind him. Forty-six feet tall and five feet in diameter it is reputed to be the largest column of polished granite in the Western Hemisphere.

On top of the column is a statue of a woman with wings, blowing a horn she holds in one hand and a wreath, much like Caesar's, in the other. She is supposed to represent 'Fame' and the New Cadets will soon learn the proper response to a piece of Plebe 'Poop', aka required knowledge, involving the statue. When asked 'How are they all?' by an upperclassman, the Plebe is required to reply: 'They are all fickle but one, sir.' To which the upperclassman asks: 'Who is the one?'. The reply: 'She who stands atop Battle Monument, for she has been on the same shaft since 1897.'

That piece of trivia, among much else, is in the New Cadets' future. At this moment, they face the commitment that will shape the rest of their lives. Even Ted falls silent as Commandant's tone becomes sterner.

"Men of '66," General Stilwell intones. "Your great adventure is under way. Now raise your right hand."

Kane, Ted, and the rest, automatically do so. They all repeat:

"I, William Kane, do solemnly swear that I will support the Constitution of the United States and bear true allegiance to the national government; that I will maintain and defend the sovereignty of the United States, paramount to any and all allegiance, sovereignty, or fealty I may owe to any state or country whatsoever."

*****

As night creeps over the Hudson and mist rises above the water, the exhausted, scared and bewildered New Cadets have one last task they are ordered to accomplish before Taps: write a letter home on their newly issued West Point stationery with their newly issued pen to reassure their parents all is well. The sealed envelope will be shown to the squad leader at 2155 hours.

There are only two desks for the three New Cadets but three chairs. Kane puts his stationery on a copy of Bugle Notes, the Plebe bible containing everything they are required to memorize and be able to recite verbatim. He leans it against the window sill and writes a brief missive:

Mom & Dad.

Alive. Much to do and must write this letter.

William.

Kane looks out, across the Plain and spots the flicker of lights from a train on the far side of the Hudson, trundling south for the city. He wishes he were on that train.

The football recruit has stopped crying but this requirement brings a sob, perhaps thinking of home, a girlfriend left behind, no longer being big man on campus?

Ted is writing away as Kane seals his envelope and puts it on the edge of the sink near the door. He returns to polishing his shoes, trying to emulate what the squad leader demonstrated earlier.

The door flies open at 2155.

"Attention!" Kane yells.

"Letters!" the squad leader barks. Kane hands his over as Ted and football recruit scurry to fold and seal theirs.

"In your racks at Taps, beanheads. No horsing around."

The door slams shut.

"'Horsing around'?" Ted repeats. "Either of you guys feel like horsing around?"

Football recruit doesn't respond, crawling into his bunk, sliding between the sheets. Kane keeps polishing. Taps echoes across the Plain from a Hellcat bugler standing at Trophy Point.

Kane turns off the lights and lies on top of his made bed, not daring to break sheets. They'd been shown earlier by the squad leader how to correctly make a West Point rack. It was Kane's luck that the example had been his and he figures he can't go wrong leaving it the way the squad leader made it. It is a habit he will keep for four years, never getting between the sheets except the night before the laundry goes out. Even on the most bitter winter night, when the radiators can't defeat the frigid wind coming off the Hudson, Kane will only huddle under his 'brown boy', a thick comforter. Making a bed each day takes too much time and time is the most precious commodity at the Academy.

Ted sits on the radiator near the window, reading something by the light of the moon. Kane is impressed his roommate dares the wrath of the roaming cadre who randomly open doors to assure compliance with lights out. Kane escapes his bed.

"What are you reading?" Kane asks. As he gets to the window, he realizes it's a letter. "Oh. Sorry."

"It's okay." Ted smiles. "My sister gave this to me this morning when she said bye. Seems like forever ago." He holds it out to Kane.

"It's personal," Kane says.

"It's all right."

Kane takes the letter, tilts it to catch the moonlight. There's a faint whiff of something enticing.

Dearest Theodore,

I use your full name because I know you don't like it. It's what older sisters do. They torment their younger brothers.

I tried to tell you what you're getting into it. You wouldn't listen to me. That's what little brothers do to their older sisters.

I know you don't have much time so I'll keep it short. Since you won't take my advice, I want to let you know two things.

1. *I'll always be here for you.*

2. *If you truly believe you've made a mistake, not just get depressed or tired or overwhelmed or homesick, but in your heart you know West Point and especially the Army, isn't for you? Quit. You're going to find that quitting is harder than staying. Everyone will think you failed. I won't. No matter what you do, you will be a success. You can call me, any time, and I will drive up immediately, no questions asked, and bring you home. I promise.*

Love,

Toni

Kane blinks a couple of times and pretends to read it a few seconds longer. He folds the letter and hands it back to Ted. They both turn their heads as the football team recruit sobs.

"We'd better get some sleep," Ted says.

They shake hands and go to their respective racks. As Kane stares at the ceiling he knows one thing.

His father won't come get him if he wants to quit.

The longest night of Kane's life to this point begins.

Monday Morning, 11 July 1977

MEATPACKING DISTRICT, MANHATTAN

Kane didn't put the five spot on the edge of the table, but folded it the way Dutch had taught him and kept it in the palm of his hand.

Morticia glided over, coffee mug, water with two cubes, raised a narrow eyebrow at the lack of the bill, but didn't say anything.

"Did you know Gansevoort aligns along the spring and fall equinoxes within one degree?" Kane asked her.

"Is this you initiating conversation?"

"Got to start somewhere," Kane said.

"No, I did not know that." She folded her arms over her chest. "But it is an interesting tidbit. Are you full of them?"

"I had a great history teacher in high school. Brother Benedict. He knew everything there is to know about New York City's history."

"A priest? Catholic school?"

"A Jesuit. Mount Saint Michaels in the Bronx."

"Wow, you're practically gushing with information this morning," Morticia noted. "I feel privileged."

"I probably know too much," Kane said.

"That's a burden the Gods bestow on certain people they desire to curse."

"Was that a sideways compliment?"

"No. An observation. People are full of all sorts of traits."

"Yeah," Kane said. "And sometimes people disappoint."

"No shit. Anyone we know?"

The Washington Street door jangled open and a partied-out foursome of lost discophiles staggered in. Morticia headed away to serve.

The Kid came in Gansevoort looking as rough as the foursome, paper tucked under his arm, wearing designer jeans, either the same or a similar lumberjack shirt with no sleeves and his brown boots. His hair was mussed and his eyes half-lidded, but he tried a smile nonetheless.

He tossed the paper close to the coffee and was reaching for the money when he realized it wasn't there.

"Have a seat," Kane said.

The Kid hesitated the offer, then slid in.

"You want some breakfast?" Kane asked.

The Kid shook his head. "I need sleep more than food."

"Coffee?"

"Messes with the sleep."

"I'm Will Kane." He extended his hand across the table.

The Kid automatically reached out and returned the shake, getting the five-dollar bill in the process. He looked at his palm. "Pretty slick, Will Kane."

Kane waited, but the Kid didn't offer reciprocation.

"I assume you have a name?" Kane finally said.

The Kid grinned. "Sure. But I like being the Kid. It's what my friends call me."

"I need a favor," Kane said.

The Kid waited.

"A fast car. I have to drive to a place near Boston. And back. Today."

"Faster than your Jeep, you mean? That won't be hard."

"Much faster."

The Kid nodded. "How much are you willing to pay to borrow a car for the day?"

"How much will it cost me?"

"Two hundred."

Kane peeled the money off his clip. Handed it over.

"You should learn to negotiate," the Kid said.

"How much would you have settled for?"

The Kid smiled. "Two hundred."

"Exactly."

"I'll have it here in thirty minutes," the Kid said, more energized. "See you in a bit, Will Kane. You're going to have a bright, sunny day for the drive. I'll make sure the car has air-conditioning."

Kane dropped the two ice cubes in the coffee and wrapped his hands around it. Resisted the impulse to stand as Toni came in via Washington. She was dressed for work, not looking like someone who'd partied the night away except for the big sunglasses. She made a beeline for the booth.

"I checked," Toni said as she sat. "No warrants yet, but its early. If Strong is pursuing this, he'll push forward today."

Morticia placed coffee in front of Toni without a word and retreated.

"What did I do to her?" Toni wondered.

"I don't know," Kane said. "Maybe she's intuitive."

"What's that supposed to mean?" Toni hadn't removed the sunglasses.

"You said your father doesn't know you're representing Mrs. Delgado, right?"

The coffee cup paused halfway to her mouth. She lowered it. Took off her sunglasses. "What's wrong?"

"You go dancing last night?"

"I did."

"Studio 54."

"What's with the interrogation?"

"That last one was a statement, not a question."

Toni pursed her lips. "You were following Delgado?"

"Yes."

"Once more, as I told you, no, my father doesn't know I'm representing Mrs. Delgado."

"Sofia," Kane said. "Seems you two should be on a first name basis at least."

Toni laughed. "Are you jealous?"

Kane blinked at the abrupt shift. "What?"

"Come on," Toni said. "I've felt it coming off you, Will. You aren't subtle. The other day in the office?"

"That was you."

"That was me responding," Toni said. She began lightly tapping the table with a long red fingernail, slowly, to a rhythm only she knew.

"Bullshit."

"Will." Toni shook her head. "All those years at West Point and afterward, I loved you like I loved Ted. My little brothers. All that changed after Dak To. Everything changed." She pushed on. "But there was Taryn. And Joseph. The accident. That affected everyone, not just you. Then there was Robert and my fucked-up marriage, although that was never really a factor for me."

"You screwed around on Robert?"

Toni laughed bitterly. "Will, you are really naïve. Even you said I shouldn't be working at the firm. In the man's world. I've had guys pull their dicks out in front of me in their offices. Somehow thinking that would turn me on."

"Bullshit. No one would do that."

"Oh, Will. *You* wouldn't. Stop judging the world by your standards. I get hit on every day, every place. I've had judges grope me in chambers, ask me to sit in their lap. Have to admit I did when it was important. I never went for the dick-waving though. That showed a lack of intelligence and, frankly, they're pretty gross. I deal with enough stupid in my job. So, yeah, I've screwed around. Selectively. So did Robert. Not so selectively. A point of contention between us as it showed he wasn't as smart as I'd thought he was." She shook her head again. "You haven't kept up with the world or your own life, Will. It's moved so far past you. It makes me sad."

"What's going on between your and Sofia Delgado?"

"She's a lot of fun," Toni said. "I don't think you know how to have fun, Will. What do you do for fun?"

"She's a client."

"A bonus. Getting paid *and* having fun. And she has connections."

"The Mob."

"Other connections. You'd be surprised who she knows. You'd be surprised who wants to know her. Who wants to experience the aura of the mafia by hanging around her. They're all thinking *Godfather*." She laughed. "Al Pacino was at Studio 54 a few weeks ago and wanted to meet Sofia. Al fucking Pacino came to our table."

"Why would you go back to that place after Delgado came after you there? And with his wife?"

"Told you. Fun. And business." Toni stopped tapping and leaned forward. "My father? He's into politicians. Builders. Contractors. Others. One sort of power. I don't want to spend the rest of my life doing dirty divorces for rich women. I want my own power.

"Studio 54? Do you know who goes there besides Pacino? Mick Jagger. Elizabeth Taylor. Cher. Bowie. Warhol. It's where the artists go. Actors. Singers. Writers. Every night there's famous people there. Movers and shakers. They're the ones I'm going to represent. I'm setting up my *own* firm in entertainment. That's my future. I want it to be honest. I want it to be successful. I want it to be exciting. That's why I go there. Contacts. Sofia helps."

"The bodyguard gigs you gave me," Kane said. "They didn't come through the firm. Those were from you. That's why Frank didn't do those jobs. They were entertainment people."

Toni nodded. "Sure. It's a way in to these people. When they come to the city from out of town they're worried about their safety, given all the bad press. Fear City. I send you. And every one of them thought you were great. You didn't try to talk to them, were unobtrusive and they all sensed you knew what you were doing."

"I thought I did," Kane said.

"Security will be an important department of my new firm and I need you in charge of it. Eventually we'll have a west coast office. Spend part of the year in the sun."

"You don't want to replace Ted?"

"I won't ever be able to. I accepted that from the start. It's reality. Something I'm good at and you aren't."

"You going to keep insulting me?"

Toni rolled her eyes. "Jesus Christ, Will. The truth is not an insult. I've tried to help you."

Kane didn't respond.

Toni sat back. "Did Ted ever tell you why he went to West Point? What put that thought in his head? Because father had already planned a path for his only son. The same path he'd followed. Prep school. Yale undergrad. Harvard Law. Then the prosecutor's office. West Point was a curveball father didn't expect."

Kane frowned, knotting the scar on his head. "Ted might have during Beast but that was a long time ago."

"Men and their memory," Toni said. She began tapping again. "Let me talk like a man then. Direct. So you understand where I'm coming from. I killed my little brother, Will. He went to West Point and ended up in Vietnam because of me.

"I started dating a cadet while I was in law school and Ted was in prep school. I took Ted up there one time. I thought he'd get a kick out of the place. I never imagined he'd fucking *go* there. By the way, that's another thing father blames me for. First, ruining his plan for Ted and then, of course, Ted dead.

"You know what's the worst part? That cadet liked me because he saw me one day in Manhattan while he was on weekend pass, and I quote the shithead after we got to know each other: 'First thing I noticed was that your legs go all the way to your ass, Toni'. We didn't last two months, but dating that guy changed Ted's life. It *ended* Ted's life." Throughout that her fingers kept tapping.

"What's going on, Toni?"

A tear rolled down her face. "I've kept up with *my* life, Will." She stopped tapping and reached across the table. Put her hand over his, wrapping it tight. "Walk away from this, Will. Ted's death carved out a piece of my heart that I'll never get back. Ted's, and then especially Lil' Joe's, did that to you too. I don't think I could bear something happening to you."

Kane turned his hand over, gripping her back. "Tell me, Toni."

"Jesus fucking Christ," Toni said urgently. "Don't you get it, Will? *I* don't know what's going on. I'm surrounded by secrets. And so are you. Don't pretend you don't have your own share. Your missing years? Whatever happened in Vietnam with that double agent? What happened to Ted in Ranger School? The scars on his face from that? Army training did that?"

Her voice took on an edge. "What really happened to Ted at Dak To? I never bought the official Army version on the Bronze

Star or your bullshit letter. Ted went down fighting? Weapon in hand? The closed casket? I tried to open it in the funeral home and it was sealed shut. Why do you seal a fucking casket? Father dragged me away. You're the one who talks about things getting deep. We're both in over our heads. Sometimes I wonder if Ted was the lucky one. Walk away, Will."

"Are you going to walk away, Toni?"

"Yes. Very soon. And I want you with me at the new place. I need you. Will you?"

Kane shook his head. "I gotta see this through. It's too deep now."

She pulled her hand out of his grip. Put her sunglasses on. "By the way, do you even know your waitress's real name? I'm sure you have no clue who her friend is you sent my way, do you?"

Kane didn't respond.

Toni left the booth, exited to Gansevoort and disappeared.

Kane slumped back, the cheap vinyl sticking to his shirt.

"Sending 'em away crying," Morticia said, appearing at the edge of the table. "You're a piece of work, Kane."

"I don't know what I am." Kane unpeeled from the vinyl and slung the map case over his shoulder. He entered the kitchen.

Thao worked the grill, but his attention was on a thick book propped against the service wall separating the kitchen from the behind the counter space. He was turning the pages faster than the omelets, eyes scanning. Just over five feet, he was lean with whipcord muscles. Dark brown skin, straight black hair, his face reflected the genealogy of the people who had been driven from their coastal lands in the ninth century by invaders and sought refuge in the mountains of Vietnam, making their home there for all the generations since.

He turned as the door swung open and grinned. "Dai-Yu."

Kane gave a slight bow. "Sergeant."

"Women are difficult," Thao said as he slid an omelet onto a plate and placed it on the service wall. He spoke precise English, slowly and carefully. Bacon sizzled and the exhaust fan rattled. It was ten degrees warmer than the diner, but Thao wasn't sweating.

"People are difficult," Kane said.

"Men are simple," Thao said. "They are either good, evil, or existing. Most just exist. It is women who are the great puzzle."

"Thank you for the peppers," Kane said.

"You are welcome." He expertly turned two omelets. "Those men Friday morning. They were evil. Especially the tall one in white. Very dangerous. He had a Browning Hi-Power under the table."

"My bullets are bigger."

Thao laughed. "That is so."

"Give me a break," Morticia said from the other side of the serving wall as she grabbed the plate and was gone.

Thao laughed again. "Women *are* indeed difficult." But he said it in a low voice, so she couldn't hear. He spoke in a normal voice. "Your sister, Mary, called yesterday. As she calls every Sunday morning. She kindly asked me to relay a message."

"She wants me to go to Mass?"

"Yes."

Kane didn't say anything.

"Family is important," Thao said. "Your sister seems like a good person."

"She's trapped there and can't escape," Kane said.

"Ah," Thao said. "As you escaped?"

Kane once more had nothing to say.

"The young woman, Farrah, also called," Thao said.

"What did she want?"

"She did not specify. She hung up when I told her you were not here."

"All right."

"The others send their thanks," Thao said. "They are all well. They ask about you."

"They don't need to ask about me."

"I tell them you are doing well. And Van Van left their usual tribute on Saturday."

"Did you tell them—" Kane stopped as Thao held up the spatula.

"One cannot tell them anything, Dai-Yu. They are in blood debt to you. The tribute assuages that debt. It is not about you. It is a selfish act on their part that appears otherwise. I deposited the money in the account." He served up another plate. "It has been suggested it would be advantageous for the business to replace the covers on the seats in the booths. They are in very sad condition. There are sufficient funds."

"By who? Morticia?"

"Yes. She is correct, of course. I have often thought the same."

"Then why haven't you said so?"

"I have just said so."

Kane shrugged. "Your decision."

"Your money, Dai-Yu."

"Our money. We agreed."

"It will be so." Thao nodded slightly. "She is more than she appears."

"Who? Morticia? She told me that's not her name. Do you know her real name?"

"Yes."

Kane waited but Thao wasn't forthcoming.

"Well, who is she?" Kane finally asked.

"She asked respect for her privacy," Thao said.

"Right," Kane said.

Thao changed the subject. "Van Van nowwork for the Ghost Shadow Triad."

"They told you that?"

"Of course not."

"How do you know?"

"The suits they wear." He reached out and Kane forced himself not to flinch as Thao lightly touched the visible part of the scar on his head. "You have a hard head. You were spared and you were marked. That means something." Thao nodded toward the front of the diner. "A car is outside. The young man is waiting on you."

Kane looked over the counter. A white Mustang with blue stripes was at the curb.

"That young man is also in debt to you," Thao said.

"What?"

"Not like Van Van," Thao said. "He needs your presence every morning as an anchor as he works through this difficult time in his life journey."

"I just give him money for the Times," Kane protested.

"He needs you," Thao said. "I will see you tomorrow?"

"Tomorrow," Kane said to Thao.

"Tomorrow," Thao repeated. "But Dai-Yu?"

Kane paused at the door.

"When I tell our friends you are well, I desire to be telling them the truth."

Kane left through the diner to the Washington Street door. The Kid cut the engine and got out, keys dangling from his fingers.

"You wanted fast," the Kid said. "'67 Ford Shelby, GT 500."

"What does all that mean?"

The Kid rolled his eyes. "It's fast, man. You didn't say anything about gas mileage."

Kane took the keys. "Where did you get it?"

"What's wrong?" the Kid asked.

"Nothing. Where'd you get it?"

"I didn't steal it," the Kid was aggrieved. "A guy I know is the concierge at the Washington Square Hotel. The owner checked in this morning and won't be using it for several days. Shacked up in a penthouse suite with a pile of coke and some company. His stays last several days if not a week."

"Won't he notice the odometer?"

"He'll be lucky if he notices the car by the time he's done with the binge," the Kid said. He pulled a cassette out of his pocket. "Some music for the road. It's got great speakers."

"I don't listen to—" Kane began, but the Kid slid the cassette tape in his shirt pocket.

"Don't worry. It's not disco. Some guys from Forest Hills. They have a new sound."

"Right."

"You going to be okay?" The Kid asked. "Want me to go with you? I can drive."

Kane tried to smile, but it didn't reach his face. "Thanks. But I got it."

"Bring it back to the concierge at the hotel when you're done."

Kane drove away. The Kid was still standing at the curb staring after him when Kane checked the rear-view mirror.

FORT DEVENS, MASSACHUSETTS

Kane speared the shovel into the ground with more force than needed. Threw the dirt to the side. The hole was three feet deep and he'd been digging for an hour. The two-hundred-mile trip to Fort Devens had blurred by in a little over twice that time.

Devens was a small Army post, split by Route 2 running from Fitchburg/Leominster to Boston. To the north of the road was a cantonment area housing an Army Intelligence School and the two battalions of the 10th Special Forces Group (Airborne) stationed in the States. The 1st Battalion was forward deployed at a former SS Barracks in Bad Tolz, West Germany. On the south side of Route 2, where Kane was digging, was a forested training area and in the midst of it, Turner Drop Zone, a large open field. He was beyond the southern edge of Turner, forty feet in the tree line.

"I can take a turn," Dave Merrick offered without much enthusiasm. He was sitting cross-legged, a six-pack of Bud next to him, one third consumed.

Kane wiped the sweat off his forehead, leaving a streak of dirt. "Almost there."

"Looks like," Merrick agreed, without checking.

Kane kept digging.

Merrick indicated the beers. "I'd offer you one, but I know you're not a fan."

Merrick wore OD green jungle fatigues, a crumpled and faded Green Beret stuffed in one of the pants cargo pockets. The insignia of a master sergeant, three chevrons and three rockers, was on the collar. Master parachutist wings and a Combat Infantry Badge with a star, indicating a second award via a second war, were sown above his nametag. A scuba badge was below. The left shoulders of the uniform had the Special Force patch, an arrowhead shape enclosing a dagger crossed by three lightning bolts, reflecting the three modes of infiltration: air, sea and land. A Ranger tab was above it. The right shoulder, combat unit, was the taro leaf of the 24th Infantry Division. He was a big man, six-four, well-muscled, with thinning red hair, almost fifty years old and projected an air of I-Don't-Give-A-Fuck that Uncle Conner would have envied. He'd enlisted in 1950 and experienced his first combat in the Korean War, one of the few survivors of the ill-fated Task Force Smith.

"How is Thao?" Merrick asked.

"Working hard, studying hard."

"Hell of a soldier," Merrick said. "Wish I had more of him on the team and less of these young douchebags coming out of the Q-Course."

"We had forty thousand in Vietnam," Kane reminded him. "We still lost."

"Fuck that," Merrick said. "*We* didn't lose. Fucking politicians lost. No will. The Army is gutted. Vietnam destroyed it. Most of your Infantry grunts are Cat Fours who don't know the difference between a doorknob and a grenade. A lot of the fresh meat we're getting in to Group are pushed through the Q-Course to fill the ranks. They wouldn't have lasted a week in the old days."

Kane didn't pick up the tired argument. Merrick was a warrior without a war.

"Does 10th still do joint training with the SAS?" Kane asked.

"We send a team over every so often on a JCET," Merrick acknowledged, referring to Joint Combined Exchange Training. "Usually with the SAS. Scuba teams with the SBS. Used to run an officer exchange program with them but haven't done it in a while."

"What about New Zealand SAS?"

"Nah. They had some guys in 'Nam, though."

"I remember."

"They also run that combat tracker school in Malaysia," Merrick said. "Hard to get slots, but it's a kickass school."

"You heard any rumors of a rogue SAS guy here in the States?" Kane asked.

Merrick frowned. "No. Unless you consider Charlie Beckwith. He did the exchange with the Brits in the early '60s."

"Fuck Charlie Beckwith," Kane said automatically as he continued to shovel.

Merrick laughed. "You've never forgiven him for Ranger School, have you?"

"He was crazy," Kane said.

"Still is," Merrick said.

"His RIs did shit that went way beyond the rules," Kane said.

"Yeah. You told me. That was fucked up what they did to your friend." Merrick shifted the topic slightly. "The word from Bragg is Beckwith's gotten authorization to form that unit he's always wanted."

Kane paused, pretending to be interested, but catching his breath, sweat dripping down his face. "What unit?"

"Counter-terrorism," Merrick said. "He's been bitching about it for years. Always thought the SAS walked on water and we needed a direct-action unit like them."

Kane went back to digging. "Why did the brass finally okay Beckwith?"

"That Entebbe raid the Israelis pulled off last year impressed everyone," Merrick said. "We have all these plane hijackings and bullshit terrorists setting bombs. Like those fucking Puerto Ricans in New York. Some generals finally got their head out of their collective ass and realized we need dedicated shooters to deal with it. Beckwith calls his unit Delta Force."

"Why?" Kane grunted as he tossed another shovel of dirt.

"He's a smart ass," Merrick said. "We've got our Operation Detachment Alphas, Bravos and Charlies in Special Forces. So he's going one better with Delta."

"That doesn't make sense. Ours are team, company and battalion."

"One of Beckwith's trademarks is not making sense. Our old unit, Fifth Group, formed a team called Blue Light at Bragg for those same missions. Some good people on it that we know. And several Det-A guys I worked with. I don't think Beckwith is going to do better than them from scratch. Not many guys are willing to leave the Groups to work with him. But it's all fucking politics these days. Who you know. Whose ass you kiss."

The familiar buzz of approaching turboprop engines crept through the woodlands silence. To the west a Hercules C-130 cargo plane was inbound to the drop zone at one thousand, two hundred and fifty feet above ground level. The C-130 was moving deceptively slow, 130 knots. As it crossed the trees at the far edge of the drop zone, bodies came off the ramp, one per second. Static lines reached their end, blossoming parachutes. The plane crossed and banked into a long racetrack over the Massachusetts countryside.

The shovel hit solid. Kane pushed dirt aside with his hands, uncovering wood. He shoveled and scraped, clearing the cache. "Rope," he said.

Merrick passed him a length. Kane looped it through a bolt in the wood. Together they lifted a heavy box out of the hole. Five feet long by two wide and two deep. Below it was another similar box. Kane hopped in and they repeated the process.

By the time he climbed out, Merrick was wielding a screwdriver, opening the first one. Kane joined him and they removed two-dozen screws. Took the lid off. Thick plastic sheeting protected the contents. They unpeeled, revealing smaller wood cases.

Merrick lifted one out. "Forty-fives." He unscrewed that lid. Pulled back the plastic and removed oilcloth from one of the guns. Handed it to Kane. "Feel better? I won't have time to work on the trigger or add a dual safety if you need it right away."

"I need it now. I can deal with the trigger." Kane checked the gun. "Safety will just have to stay off." The serial number was gone, acid burned. "Not as many as when we originally buried the cache," he noted as he pulled the slide back, inspecting.

"You're not the only one in need," Merrick said.

Kane glanced at him. "You selling them?"

"You buying that?" Merrick snapped, indicating the .45. "You know how long it's been since I've heard from you?"

"What do you mean?"

"I *mean* I'm only a couple of hours away and I haven't seen you in over a year. And that was when you wanted some range time. Now you need guns. I've got enemies I see more often. And Bahn wouldn't mind you stopping by and saying hi."

Merrick was married to a Montagnard, one of those who'd come with Thao, Van Van and the others.

"I'll make it back here," Kane promised. "For a visit. For real."

"Yeah." Merrick didn't sound convinced.

Kane pushed the release, the slide slamming forward. "Trent paid me a visit the other day."

"I don't want to know," Merrick said. "I'm not even here."

"I respect that. Giving you a heads up on a mutual enemy."

"I've been fucked over and I wasn't even on that chopper," Merrick said. "But we did plenty of other stuff that was off the official books. There're a lot of people who want all of that to stay deep and buried. Especially Countersign—" Merrick suddenly stopped. "I gotta ask you, Will. Are you wearing a wire?"

Kane wiped his face, leaving a muddy smear. He pulled off the sopping t-shirt, unbuckled his belt and dropped trou.

"Geez," Merrick said. "I didn't need to see that."

Kane pulled up his pants and buckled. "Yeah, you did. If you asked, you did. And you were right to ask."

"That shit is gonna follow us for the rest of lives. I got passed over for Sergeant Major. I checked with my branch. Told me, in so many words, forget about it ever happening."

Kane pulled his sweat-soaked t-shirt on. "Vietnam is our curse." He loaded a magazine with .45 rounds.

Merrick laughed bitterly. "Fuck 'em." Merrick was R.O.A.D. Retired on Active Duty. "I just want to get thirty, retire, and open up a gunsmithing place back in North Carolina near Bragg. Bahn needs to be around her people."

Kane inserted a magazine. Chambered a round, cocking the hammer. Ten dropped the magazine, added a bullet, and reinserted it. He pushed the safety into place. Holstered it.

"Feel better?" Merrick asked.

"A bit."

"Remember the pull will be tighter."

"Roger that."

Merrick extended another .45 still wrapped. "Might as well put this away for a rainy day."

Kane accepted it.

"Did Trent take your weapon?" Merrick asked.

"I'd like to see him try. I gave it up to a cop."

"Why?"

"He asked. Nicely. It's complicated."

Merrick was working on another case. "Cop take the High Standard? That's not good. Someone might wonder where it came from."

"That's a different story you don't want to know. The cops don't have it. Don't worry, no one is going to try to figure out where it came from."

"What did Trent want?"

"Me to be his asset."

"To do what?" Merrick asked.

"He didn't specify."

"Fuck him."

"Yep."

Merrick stopped unscrewing the lid. Reached into a rucksack and pulled out a bag of ammunition. "My latest batch." He handed it to Kane, then went back to the lid.

Kane looked inside. Several boxes of .22 caliber.

Merrick put the lid aside and handed another oilcloth package to Kane. He unwrapped a High Standard in mint condition. There was no serial number that needed to be etched away. These were made for direct consumption by the CIA. Diverted years ago from 1st Special Forces Group in Okinawa which had handled logistics for covert ops in Vietnam. How these ended up here was a long story.

"Check this out." Merrick unwrapped a larger item. "My weapons man would give his right nut to get his hands on this."

Twenty-two inches long with a folding metal frame stock, made of stamped metal, the Swedish K submachine gun was a classic among Special Forces. The box magazine held 36 staggered 9 by 19mm rounds, more than comparable submachine guns. It only had an automatic mode, but the cyclic rate was so slow, a capable gunman could fire single shot accurately via trigger control.

Kane held out his hand.

Merrick feigned surprise. "Seriously?"

"You wouldn't have shown it if you weren't offering."

Merrick laughed and handed it over. "Are you going to war?"

*****

Kane fired the .45, the recoil familiar and solid. Emptied and dropped the magazine as the slide locked to the rear. Reloaded, unlocked. Fired another magazine, shredding the silhouette they'd set up on the range. All head shots.

"For a city boy, you can shoot," Merrick acknowledged.

Kane picked up the magazines, wiping them clean. Then he policed the expended brass from thirty minutes of firing. He'd also fired the K, stitching 9mm into silhouettes, familiarizing himself once more with the feel of the trigger and single shot control.

"What's the scoop on the Colonel?" Kane asked.

"Last I heard he was retired in the deep woods in Maine," Merrick said. "His wife left him."

"That sucks. He got a raw deal." Kane separated 9mm and .45 brass into boxes for Merrick to take home and reload.

The C-130 circled overhead, race-tracking to drop another stick of parachutists.

"You have access to any smoke grenades?" Kane asked.

Merrick shrugged. "Sure. Back at the team room. Anything else? Tac nuke maybe?"

The latter wasn't exactly a complete joke. The most classified mission a handful of teams in 10th Group had was to parachute in, infiltrate a target, assemble a tactical nuclear weapon and arm it. The prevailing wisdom was that the delay they were told was built into the detonator didn't exist. A target that required a nuke was more important than a handful of Green Berets.

"If you're offering," Kane said.

*****

The team room was the top floor a worn World War II era two story barracks, built from a set of plans that had dictated the erection of tens of thousands of similar buildings on hastily expanded military posts all over the country decades earlier. The exterior was faded white planking. The interior had a concrete floor on the first level, where the latrine was, and creaking wood on the second. How many thousands of soldiers had passed through here was evident in the ruts worn in the wood stairs.

The team room contained a large wood table that could seat all twelve members. The team number, 225, was inlaid on top of it with tile along with a Special Forces crest etched into the surface, a labor of love and time by some past team member. A fridge was between windows, ostensibly issued to hold the team's radio batteries, but doing double-time with beer from which Merrick helped himself. There was, of course, no air-conditioning and the open windows did little to reduce the heat.

"Pretty much the same at it was in '68," Kane said.

Merrick pointed. "New log."

In one corner of the room was a six-foot high log. Assorted axes and throwing knives were impaled in it. Chips of wood from previous strikes littered the floor. The walls were covered with plaques from foreign units the team had trained and conducted missions with over the years. Norwegian Jaegers, Danish Fromandkorpset, British SAS, Italian Paras, German Fallschirmjager and GSG-9 and other countries elite units. Most of the plaques had some sort of edged weapon on them along with an inscription of martial brotherhood. Kane and Merrick had participated in some of those training missions before getting their orders reassigning them to Fifth Group in Vietnam in late 1968, a deployment that had embittered Taryn, who'd returned to New York City with Joseph while Kane went off to war for a second time. She'd hoped they could settle in Massachusetts for a few years, have a semblance of family life. Kane's return to the war had not gone over well. She hadn't believed his lie that it was the Army's decision, not his own.

Kane had dried off after a quick shower in the small stall in the open latrine. He'd shaken the dirt from his jungle fatigue pants and put on a fresh gray t-shirt. Slid on his denim shirt. The Swedish K, extra .45, and ammunition were in the trunk of the Shelby along with a half-dozen smoke and CS grenades. Merrick had given him several boxes of specially loaded 9mm rounds for the K. Along with hot loads for the .45 in the holster. The High Standard was in the map case.

"Have any det cord?" Kane asked. "Blasting caps? C-4?"

"How much shit are you in?" Merrick asked.

"I've got the CIA, the NYPD and a mafia enforcer all up my ass. Things have been better. I need to be able to defend as needed. My place has been broken into twice already"

Merrick looked uneasy. "We had some douchebag in Third Battalion try to sell C-4 to some assholes in Boston and get caught. The brass has done shakedown inspections since then."

Kane stared at him. "You don't have the goodies box?"

"This ain't 'Nam," Merrick muttered. But he led the way across the hall to a room that held a dozen wall lockers. Rucksacks rested on top, packed ready for deployment. There were several large, green wooden boxes with locks on them containing the team's radios, engineering and medical gear. Several barbells were scattered on rubber mats along with two benches. On the interior wall was a section of heavy pegboard with ten-inch wood pegs inserted in various holes.

"The old wall," Kane noted.

"A few of the guys still work out on this," Merrick said. Then he showed that he was one of those guys as he grabbed two pegs and stuck them in the highest holes he could reach. Pulled himself up with only his arms. Stuck out his right foot and rested it on a peg already in place. Advanced one hand up, then the other until his head just below the ceiling. Spread his feet to rest on pegs. Pushed upward on the ceiling and a section lifted out of place. The lines were so perfect it had been unnoticeable unless someone knew what they were looking for.

Merrick climbed into the attic dead space and out of sight. A minute later he lowered a box. Kane grabbed it and set it on the ground.

"I'll wait up here," Merrick said, tossing him the key ring.

Kane opened the box. An assortment of demolitions, grenades, mines, and ammunition, all of it illegal outside of the ammo depot or a war zone.

He took C-4, a box of blasting caps, a roll of det cord and put it in his rucksack.

"Engineer is going to be up my ass when he sees it gone," Merrick complained from the edge of the hole. "Took him quite a few range trips to scrounge this."

Kane checked the rest. Appropriated two frag grenades. Then a green bag containing a Claymore.

"Booby traps in a private dwelling are against the law." Merrick added: "I think."

"We both know about the law."

"No shit. Remember, front toward enemy."

"What if I'm surrounded?"

"Then you can attack in any direction," Merrick said.

Kane closed the box, locked it. He passed it to Merrick who pulled it into its hiding place, then replaced the ceiling and climbed down.

"You want to go to the Fort?" Merrick asked, referring to a bar right outside the gate in Ayer. "Some people you know from the old days will probably be there."

"Got a long day ahead," Kane said.

"Heading back to the city?" Merrick asked as Kane shouldered the ruck.

"Got a detour to make first," Kane said.

They walked outside into the bright sun.

"There's a bad heat wave coming this week," Merrick said.

"I've heard." Kane stuck out his free hand. "I appreciate your help."

Merrick reached past the hand, gripping his former teammate's forearm. Kane wrapped his hand around Merrick's forearm, the greeting they'd originated on the team in Vietnam after someone said that was how Roman Centurions greeted each other. Probably total bullshit, but the tradition had taken. As had the next:

"*Lions and tigers and bears, oh my,*" Merrick said.

Kane gave the reply. "*Yea, though I walk through the valley in the shadow of death I will fear no evil, for I am the meanest motherfucker in here.*"

"But watch out for the flying monkeys," Merrick warned. "They show up when you least expect them."

WEST POINT, NEW YORK

Despite four years of blood, sweat and tears while wearing Cadet gray, and the eventual bestowing of the Ring, a diploma, and a commission, Kane felt like an interloper as he drove the Mustang through the village of Highland Falls to the main gate and onto the hallowed grounds of the United States Military Academy. Of course, two of those three bestowments were no longer part of his life.

The battlements of the Thayer Hotel frowned down on him from the right, as disapproving in their own way as Mrs. Ruiz. To the left was Buffalo Soldier Field, where cadets played required intramurals during the Academic year. A sidewalk edged by a stonewall appeared on the right, overlooking the Hudson. Officer quarters were on the slope to the left as he approached the main 'campus' of the Academy.

Despite the air-conditioning as promised by the Kid, his hands were sweaty on the wheel. No matter how much time or distance a graduate chiseled out away from the Academy, most had a Pavlovian response upon returning. A twisted knot of dread that rose from the pit of the stomach and spread through the chest. Unbidden, the 'Sunday Night Poop', part of the plethora of irrelevant nonsense every plebe had to memorize, intruded unbidden into consciousness: *Six bells and all is well. Another weekend shot to hell. Another week in my little gray cell. Another week in which to excel. Oh, hell.*

The Academy even made its misery formal.

For Kane the feeling had initiated unbidden as he drove across the Bear Mountain Bridge from the east side of the Hudson via Route 202. He supposed there were graduates who grew excited as they approached their alma mater; MacArthur probably had a hard on as he'd been driven from the city to give his epic Duty, Honor, Country speech.

Kane slowly drove past the old hospital, then buildings named after significant figures in the Academy's history: Sherman Barracks which, interestingly, was across a courtyard from a mirror image: Lee Barracks. Grant Hall. Pershing Barracks. The buildings were sheathed in gray stone. He turned right after passing Bartlett Hall and parked on the roof of Thayer Hall, the former indoor riding hall overlooking the Hudson that had been converted to classrooms with few windows to enjoy the view.

Kane walked toward the Plain, stopping near Patton's statue. Old Blood and Guts, class of 1909, cast in bronze, had his famous pistols on his hips, a helmet on his head and his hands held a pair of binoculars as if he were searching for a new enemy; another warrior who'd wilted without a war to fight.

Kane gazed across a tennis court. There were new barracks flanking the Mess Hall and the statue of George Washington; they'd been under construction when he'd graduated. In front of them was the flat green parade ground. He could smell the freshly cut grass. Kane was trying to recall and drawing fuzzy images.

Even in summer, the Military Academy was bustling with activity. Beast Barracks for the future class of 1981 was a week old. Squads of New Cadets were drilling on the Plain under the harsh supervision of upperclassmen. The latest additions to the Long Gray Line stumble-marched, hair shorn, brains overloaded, emotions savaged, most of them in a condition approaching shock, the infamous tearing down to build something new, not just a warrior, but a leader of warriors.

That was the theory since the Academy's founding in 1802 by Thomas Jefferson, a surprise move by a mostly anti-military President. His goal had been three-fold: to establish a cadre of officers for the fledgling Army that wasn't aristocratic; one drawn from all parts of the nation to avoid being politicized; and finally to train engineers for a country that was rapidly expanding.

The members of '81 weren't Plebes yet, having to get through the hell of eight weeks of Beast in order to gain that lowly title. They were New Cadets. Beanheads. Smacks. Crots. Among the nicer things they were called by the cadre, many bent on regurgitating the abuse they'd suffered a few years earlier.

An anomaly caught his eye. Some of the New Cadets were different. It took Kane a moment to understand. A new wrinkle that had started with the class of 1980, which had entered the previous year in 1976, was a sprinkling of women among the New Cadets. Their forms singled them out from their peers. He experienced a moment's compassion because if they could be spotted so easily, it meant they couldn't 'ghost', a key survival tactic for Beast and plebe year. That was one area in which Kane had actually had an advantage due to his childhood in the Bronx. He'd mastered ghosting when taking the subway to high school, where one never made eye contact or drew attention. It didn't occur to him he'd learned it at an even younger age when everyone in the home whispered and walked on tiptoes when the head of the household worked night shifts and slept during the day.

The Yearlings, sophomores, were further west on the military reservation at Camp Buckner, receiving training on the various combat arms by a contingent from the 101st Airborne.

Third year cadets, the Cows, were scattered around the world, training in regular Army units as a form of sub-lieutenant. The 'cow' designation dated back to the old days, as did most things at West Point, when the only leave the cadets received in their four years was a long break between the second and third years. The cadets would travel home by train, horse, boat and foot, to mother's cooking and come back to the Academy overweight and out of shape; thus Cows.

The newly minted Firsties were the leadership cadre at both Beast and Buckner. Top of the heap, keeping the cycle churning as it had for 175 years. They swaggered as if they owned the world, with little inkling of the dark possibilities ahead.

Kane turned away from the spectacle. He pushed open the door to the library next to Bartlett Hall and entered this bastion of knowledge. It was practically empty since the Academic Year was weeks away, not that it was packed then either. A single, matronly woman manned the front desk. She glanced at him, then went back to cataloguing.

Kane took the wide steps to the fourth floor. Some of the dread had dissipated upon entering the library, a sanctuary for all cadets, where hazing was forbidden and most cadets spent as little time as possible. Kane had been an exception to that.

The large wooden door to the Archives on the top floor was locked. Kane pressed the button and waited. A few seconds later the lock clicked. Kane pushed the door and entered the climate-controlled section that held the Academy's original documents, along with all that various distinguished graduates had bequeathed over the years. Large flat tables with drawers below them crowded the room. A number of the tables held maps, most hand-drawn. Many were the work of early graduates from when they spread out into the American west, surveying and exploring. All cadets still took drawing as a required course despite the invention of cameras and satellites. The walls were lined with shelves filled with carefully catalogued titles protected behind glass.

An older man sat at a desk in the far corner with a view of both the Plain and the Hudson River. His desk was huge, twelve feet wide by six deep. There were weights in the shape of small cannons that could be used to hold documents in place. Attached to the desk was a large magnifying glass on a long, moveable arm with a circular light built around the glass that could cover any part. At the moment, though, the surface held only a thick hardcover book.

"Good afternoon, Mister Kane."

"Good afternoon, Mister Plaikos."

Plaikos stood up, slightly canted left, and walked around the table, hand extended. The reason for the cant became obvious: his left leg was gone below the knee and a peg leg made of worn and pitted dark mahogany thumped on the floor. He was short and compact, well-tanned, silver-haired and looked younger than his 58 years. He wore khaki pants and shirt, and no insignia. A government employee, he held the equivalent GS pay grade of a one-star general yet received none of the homage that star garnered.

The two men shook hands and two Montagnard bracelets jangled on Plaikos's wrist. He was from a generation before Kane, a graduate of the class of 1941. He'd joined the Infantry and chosen what was considered the plum assignment in June of that fateful year: the Philippines where the already legendary Douglas MacArthur was the Field Marshall of the Philippine Army. The plum turned rotten when the Japanese invaded.

Plaikos fought in the retreat to Corregidor and watched MacArthur ride away in the middle of a night on a PT boat, earning a Medal of Honor for the trip in the wrong direction. When MacArthur's unlucky successor in command, Wainwright, capitulated, Plaikos initiated his long career of disobeying orders and took to the jungle along with fellow American and Filipino soldiers. For four long years they'd fought a guerilla war, learning blood lessons as they went, often at the cost of lives.

Instead of returning to the Regular Army once the Philippines were liberated, he was recruited by Wild Bill Donovan into the OSS—Office of Strategic Services. From there, he'd matriculated into the fledgling CIA and established a career traveling around the world, wherever his hard-earned insurgency skills were required. That career ended in 1961 when an Air America plane was shot down in Vietnam and his left leg crushed in the crash. That was as much of his story that Kane had been able to glean from him over the course of four years and numerous hours in the quiet of the Archives. Plaikos was a man who'd done much, but said little about those endeavors.

Plaikos returned behind his desk and sat down. Kane took a seat on the side of the desk.

"What can I do for you, Mister Kane? I was pleasantly surprised by your phone call. It's been a long time, but I find your rare visits interesting. Do you need me to retrieve something you've dispatched for safekeeping? You understand, of course, that the material is not at hand and would require some time to retrieve."

"No, sir. I need your expertise on a certain matter."

Plaikos tapped the book. "I was perusing this. A rather intriguing tale about covert operations in the Second World War, mainly focusing on British and American work in Europe. I had no experience in that theater during the war, but met quite a few of the players, those that survived, afterward." He lifted the book so Kane could see the cover. *Bodyguard of Lies.*

"Good title, sir," Kane said.

"From a quote by Churchill," Plaikos said. "*'In wartime truth must always be attended by a bodyguard of lies'.* Very appropriate." He marked the page with an index card and closed it. "The author draws some intriguing conclusions and some not quite accurate ones. The irony is that some of what is written is part of that very bodyguard, misinformation and cover stories designed to hide what actually happened. Nevertheless, a worthwhile read and insight into some nasty business. That is the way history is recorded." Plaikos returned to the reason for Kane's appearance. "So. What might I help you with?"

"I had a visit on Saturday from your former organization, sir," Kane said. "Trent wanted me to be his asset."

"Phil King's errand boy," Plaikos said. "King and I crossed paths over the years."

"He mentioned King, sir," Kane said. "Called him the Gray Ghost."

"That can be taken several different ways," Plaikos said. "I met King in Berlin before the blockade and we were there during the Airlift. We were trying to establish our networks in the east." Plaikos shook his head. "I sometimes believe the Airlift was our greatest post-war moment. You should have seen it, Mister Kane. I give those flyboys all the credit they deserve. True heroes. They had that running like a machine. I wish I could say as much for the Agency's efforts. What kind of asset?"

"He talked about the United Nations but his focus was Wall Street and money, sir. He said that was the key to everything."

"That's true. I never met Trent although I checked into him because of your dust up in 'Nam. He did field work in Central and South America, then shifted to Vietnam when that heated up, as many of us did. But he was in-country after my time."

"I appreciate everything you did, sir," Kane said. "And still do for me."

"I didn't do much," Plaikos lied. "An operator like King needs a person willing to take the slings and arrows as his front man. He's DCO now." Plaikos paused. "You know, it just occurred to me that the saying should be slings and bows or stones and arrows, otherwise it's inconsistent. Either the weapon or the projectile. Ah well. Trent does the dirty work that King can't sully his hands with, such as testify at your trial. I assume you turned him down?"

"Yes, sir. But I don't think it's the last I'm going to be hearing from the Agency. Trent said they have me flagged."

"What popped the flag?" Plaikos asked.

"A little trouble with the NYPD, sir," Kane said. "The cops ran my name through the FBI criminal database. Trent said they picked it off that. He mentioned readers and computers and that the movie *Three Days of the Condor* was relatively accurate."

Plaikos folded his hands together on the desk. "Interesting. What specifically do you want to know?"

"How much trouble can Trent, and the Agency, cause me? They already destroyed my career in the Army, although Trent mentioned being able to erase the dishonorable."

"I don't see why the Agency would go out of its way to cause you further problems," Plaikos said. "The flag popped and Trent saw an opportunity to recruit an experienced asset. It's standard procedure to exploit a potential's problems. Unless you cause the Agency trouble, they'd have no reason to continue. In fact, there are aspects of your Vietnam experience with them that they'd like to keep quiet, so you do have leverage." Plaikos smiled. "Which, of course, you already know since you sent your files and recollections about Phoenix, Gamma, Countersign, and other applicable data to me for safe-keeping."

"Trent doesn't know all that, sir," Kane pointed out. "Especially Countersign. At least, I hope he doesn't. That op was kept tight."

"Forget about Trent. Phil King would assume you've protected yourself on the back end. In fact, he might not be happy that Trent kicked a quiet hornet's nest."

"He said King sent him and sent his regards."

"That doesn't mean he spoke the truth," Plaikos pointed out. "If I was in King's position, I would know you've covered yourself," Plaikos said. "I think you'll be fine with your answer to Trent. Unless, of course, you wish to have your discharge changed? It was a miscarriage of justice."

"I'd be trading one problem for another, sir," Kane said.

"Likely." Plaikos nodded. "You've gotten a bit wiser with the years, Mister Kane. You're not the same young man I found wandering lost in the stacks as a plebe, but life has a way of forcing us into maturity. A handful actually learn from their experiences and I'm glad to see you have."

"Thank you, sir. I just wanted to double-check."

"Anything else?"

"That was it, sir." Kane put his hands on the arms of the chair to get up, but paused. "Can I ask you something?"

Plaikos nodded.

"Why did you talk to me the first time?" Kane asked. "Most plebes come to the library to ghost. Catch a nap in some corner."

"True," Plaikos said. "But you were doing more than ghosting. You were actually searching the stacks. And reading. I observed you for a while. On top of that, you were checking out books that weren't mandatory for a course assignment, which is most unusual. A considerable amount of nonfiction. Your array of interests was intriguing. It seemed as if your mind sought enlightenment beyond the rigid mental walls the Academy drops around cadets. Very few of your fellows avail themselves of the treasures in this building."

Kane smiled. "I have a friend you should meet, sir. He was a reporter for the Post. He speaks of the main branch of the New York Public Library with the same reverance."

"Reporters and spies, ex-spies, are not that different," Plaikos said. He changed the subject. "Did you see the split-tails?"

"Excuse me, sir?"

"The female New Cadets," Plaikos said.

"I saw some out there."

"What do you think about it?"

Kane shrugged. "It was inevitable, sir."

"Lots of old grads are up in arms," Plaikos said. "Class of '79's motto is LCWB—which ostensibly stands for loyalty, courage, wisdom and bravery but is actually last class with balls."

"Yes, sir."

Plaikos laughed. "You don't know how I feel about it, so you're withholding your opinion, aren't you? Afraid you might piss me off?"

"I imagine it's a sensitive subject around here, sir," Kane said.

"Some things you have to take a stand on," Plaikos said. "But your answer is correct. It was inevitable, it's the law, and that is that. Some professors stood against the inevitable and they are no longer with us."

"How do you really feel about it, sir?"

"When I was in the jungle in the Philippines," Plaikos said, "the women who were with us fought as well the men. And they died the same as the men. I imagine female graduates will do the same. The Army isn't very popular right now, Kane. With the cheating scandal last year, the Academy suffered a black eye. We need the best, whatever the gender."

"Yes, sir."

Plaikos teetered to his feet. "Are you going to pay your respects?"

Kane stood. "Yes, sir."

"They should make the cemetery part of the recruiting tour," Plaikos said as he limped Kane out. "That would be a dose of reality. My class earned the moniker Black '41 for our miscarriages of etiquette while cadets, but it fits what happened to a number of my comrades after graduation. Many suffered and died on the Death March and then the poor souls who survived that ordeal drowned in POW ships sunk by our own planes. They rot in unmarked graves in the jungle or on the bottom of the ocean, not in the cemetery." He hit a button and the door swung open. "Tell me one thing. Do you miss it?"

"The Army?" Kane shook his head. "No, sir. They used me and threw me away."

"Interesting," Plaikos said. "Good luck, Mister Kane."

*****

Kane was in a quiet zone on the main post, shielded from activity by the solemn presence of death. The West Point national cemetery is on a river bluff, surrounded by a stone wall and thick hedges. The Hudson, hundreds of feet below, flows southward toward Manhattan, fifty miles away.

Soldiers from every war in U.S. history are buried here, beginning with the Revolution. The small Cadet Chapel from 1836 was moved here stone by stone when the larger, newer one was built on a hill overlooking the Academy. It's composed of dark stone and fronted by white Ionic columns. The interior walls are covered with marble shields, each memorializing a general from the Revolution. One, emplaced choir left, nearly hidden from sight, has the name scratched out, leaving *Major General ------ Born 1740*. The only vestige of the man who commanded the key Army post here during the Revolution and attempted to sell the plans for its defenses to the British: Benedict Arnold.

As was his habit, Kane diverted from a direct path to his destination to walk on the grave purportedly containing Custer's remains, although who knew what had been scavenged off the Little Big Horn battlefield after the bodies had been scattered and reduced to bone by carrion? A white obelisk marked the spot, where his widow, Libbie, keeper and spreader of his flame of infamy, had been laid to rest in 1933.

Killed With His Entire Command in the Battle of the Little Big Horn, June 25, 1876.

That wasn't true. Half the Seventh Cavalry, under the command of Reno and Benteen, had fought off repeated assaults for a night and day after Custer went down, and most of their troopers survived. 'When the legend becomes fact, print the legend.' The line from the *Searchers* applied to everything at West Point. The cemetery is beautiful, meticulously maintained, a celebration to the concept of duty, honor and country.

There was a slight breeze from the north, along the Hudson, between Storm King Mountain and Cold Springs on the other side of the river. It was hot and humid, the thick air weighing on Kane as he walked toward the northern quadrant, a four pack of Harp beer in hand. Birds chattered and cars passed a hundred yards away on Washington Road.

Kane approached a large stone pyramid mausoleum twenty feet high, guarded by a pair of stone sphinxes. The resting place of General Viele, class of 1847, and his wife. Viele had shown some concern in his death plans as he'd had a buzzer wired from the interior of the mausoleum to the Superintendent's quarters so he could be rescued if accidently entombed while still alive. On the more practical side, Kane owned a print of the *Viele Sanitary & Topographical Map of the City and Island of New York*, something he'd been directed to study by Brother Benedict. Besides his military service in Mexico and the Civil War, Viele had been Commissioner of Parks for the City and his map was a basis for designing Central Park.

Kane admired Viele's unfounded optimism about the buzzer. Kane was, of course, putting off the task. To the left of Viele's pyramid was Section XXXIV, where Ted and others from the Vietnam era lay.

A row of markers, a number of them the standard Government Issue white stone, 24 inches tall, formed the rows. These were the majority of the thirty members of the Class of 1966 killed in Vietnam who had chosen the Academy as their final resting place. Eight classmates had reported to the 173rd Airborne and been involved in the battles at Dak To over the course of 1967. Four were killed. Kane and one other were wounded.

Kane sat cross-legged in front of a marker. He opened a bottle of beer and poured it onto the grave, the parched ground and struggling grass absorbing it. He took a deep draught from the other one, then emptied it too.

"Irish beer, Ted. You gave me shit about it. A four pack. Said it summed up the Irish. Couldn't even get a six pack right."

THEODORE
JOSEPH
MARCELLE

NEW YORK
CLASS OF 1966 USMA
A CO. 2/503RD INF
VIETNAM
SEPTEMBER 29, 1944
22 JUNE 1967

The breeze picked up. Kane's nose wrinkled at the foul odor. "They put our class close to the sewage treatment plant, Ted. You'd like that. Remember the two-mile run test? The turnaround at the plant?"

Two cadets in gray pants and starched white shirts were walking through the cemetery, taking a short cut from the PX. They saw him, paused, and angled away, avoiding a possible future truth, living or dead.

Even though Kane and Ted had been assigned different companies in the Corp at the end of Beast Barracks, they'd maintained their friendship, even visiting as plebes, venturing into each other's companies. This was an ultimate sign of plebe comradeship, daring to foray into the hostile environ of a different company as an unknown beanhead. Each had spent many hours over that plebe year braced against a wall being hazed by upperclassmen, just yards away from the safety of their friend's room. Once that first year ended, it was easier to spend time together.

Kane reached out and traced his fingers over the letters and numbers carved in the stone. "We thought we were on the side of the angels, Ted. Turns out we weren't. But I hope you're with them now. I don't believe they exist, but if they do, know you're with them. The Academy prepared us for what it thought was everything. But there's some things it left out, Ted. Two in particular. They didn't teach us about losing. We were convinced we were always right, all the time, and always going to win. And they didn't teach us about evil."

There was no buzzer wired from Ted's grave.

Kane poured the last two beers for Ted.

They are here in ghostly assemblage.
The men of the Corps long dead.
And our hearts are standing attention, while we wait for their passing
tread.
We Sons of today, we salute you.
You Sons of an earlier day;
We follow, close order, behind you, where you have pointed the way;
The long gray line of us stretches, thro' the years of a century told
And the last man feels to his marrow, the grip of your far off hold.
The Corps
Written by West Point Chaplain, Bishop H.S.
Shipman, 1902

Friday, 22 June 1967

HILL 1338, DAK TO, SOUTH VIETNAM

The first American casualty this day in the Central Highlands belongs to Charlie Company, 2/503rd Battalion of the 173rd Airborne Regiment.

Just after first light a fucking new guy, FNG, leaves the perimeter to take a piss and is shot by a nervous sentry as he blunders back. It's going to be that kind of day. Everyone is jangled, the combat vets most of all. The previous night one of the CIDG, civilian irregular defense group, a Montagnard tribesman trained by Green Berets, had been killed at a listening post after a brief, uncertain contact with the NVA. His body lay in the center of the company's position all night, a harbinger of nothing good to come.

It's a hot and humid morning. Low clouds loom over Hill 1338 of the Dak To Mountains in the Central Highlands of the Republic of Vietnam. Thick fog saturates the triple canopy jungle which presses like a thick green, multi-layered almost impenetrable blanket on the steep terrain. Visibility averages less than ten feet.

The FNG's body is brought into the perimeter, wrapped in a poncho and trussed so it can be carried by two men on a pole when they move out later in the morning. It is placed next to the dead CIDG.

The CIDG and the FNG are the first dead men William Kane has ever seen outside of a funeral home.

It is an initial chipping away of his mirage of war and John Wayne heroics. It is a reckoning of his mortality. Because he realizes a profound truth that seems obvious but not to the core until experienced firsthand: dead is dead.

The Captain reminds Kane and the other platoon leaders, who remind their NCO's, who remind the soldiers, DO NOT BE FUCKING STUPID which summons echoes of Chargin' Charlie Beckwith and Ranger School which Will Kane had graduated from just eight months earlier.

Kane is 22 years old and responsible for a platoon of men, 33 plus him, most of them younger, with an average age of 19. They range from FNG's to a handful of experienced NCOs, a couple of whom were with the original Sky Soldiers on the first 173rd deployment to Vietnam in 1965, rotating back on a second tour.

There aren't many of those.

Fifteen hundred meters, in military jargon a klick and a half, in civilian distance roughly a mile, from Charlie Company is Alpha Company to which Kane's best friend, West Point roommate and Ranger School buddy, Ted Marcelle, is assigned. Given the difficulty of the near vertical terrain of Hill 1338 and the denseness of the jungle, they might as well be in separate countries. However, on a map in the safety of Battalion Headquarters someone might theorize that the two companies hold mutually supporting positions. Especially given that headquarters looking at maps have often held such theories regarding deployed units not directly in sight throughout millennia of warfare.

Nothing is impossible to the man who doesn't have to do it.

The hill takes its designation from the elevation of its peak on the map. Surely the local mountain people, the Montagnards, have a name for it, but for this Army's purposes 1338 works. The name possesses none of the punch of earlier American battlefields such as Saratoga, Shiloh, Gettysburg, Belleau Woods, D-Day or even Chosin, but Vietnam is that kind of war.

Charlie Company spent a nervous night near the top of 1338. Alpha is lower, near a landing zone they'd carved out of the jungle the previous day. The two companies are part of a larger stumbling movement by the 173rd code named Operation Greeley. Kane's West Point training never taught the tactics of advancing through jungle with no specific goal other than making *contact with the enemy and killing more of them than they kill of you. But Vietnam has devolved into that kind of war.*

"Saddle up!" the Captain calls out.

The command is passed down. Rucksacks are shouldered, the foot soldier's familiar burden. Each man carries more than the basic load of ammunition as proscribed by Infantry doctrine; hundreds of 5.56-millimeter (mm) rounds for their M-16s. While the magazines are designed to hold 20 rounds, no one loads them with more than eighteen or else there's a likelihood over pressure on the spring will cause a misfeed. A Claymore antipersonnel mine adds to each soldier's load. To feed the pig, the M-60 machinegun, each man carries a belt of one hundred rounds. Every man also has a round to feed the two mortars in the weapons platoon. An entrenching tool. C-Rations broken down from their cardboard boxes and loaded tightly in socks to keep the cans from making noise. When a soldier chooses between food and ammunition, the more experienced go with ammunition. Extra plastic spoons are tossed to save weight, since a man only needs one.

On their LBE, load bearing equipment, besides ammo pouches and a first aid kit, each man has fragmentation and smoke grenades and as many canteens as they can clip on the web belt and still carry the ruck. Water is life in the heat and humidity. Resupply uncertain.

A few unlucky souls, the RTOs, carry the PRC-25 radio adding 23 pounds, along with the weight of spare batteries. The antenna rising up over their shoulder is akin to a bullseye. The flex portion is pulled down, stuck through the front of the LBE pulling in one horn of the bull, but not by much.

The individual load averages between 75 and 100 pounds. Not including weapon, helmet and uniform. The rucksack settles on top of the LBE, an arrangement soldiers spend hours adjusting, tying, and taping, until it clings to their body. It will never be smooth or comfortable. The goal is functional.

"Move out," the Captain orders.

The jungle is primordial. Some trees are so old their trunks are wider than a man is tall. Clumps of bamboo cluster impassably. Horribly lush undergrowth crowds the ground so thick, its questionable how far a bullet can go, never mind a man. Despite their training and knowing better, soldiers are forced to eventually use the trails, where death awaits.

Distant pops, muted by the jungle between, reach the men of Charlie. Downhill, Alpha Company is in contact.

It begins raining.

The lead elements of Charlie head toward Alpha but its fifteen hundred jungle meters. Alpha is enemy territory away, requiring the lead squad of Charlie to move with fear and trepidation of the inevitable ambush. The point man is a sacrifice to the God of body count. Rather than add alacrity, the increasing volume of fire from Alpha's location slows Charlie Company.

There is enemy ahead. Many enemy. The pops are merging into a fearsome crescendo. Veterans initially recognize the distinction between M-16 and AK-47, but now they are as one. Machineguns, American and Communist made, add their own fast paced chatter. The crump of artillery.

A fearsome keening of lead and steel.

Kane holds his newly issued and zeroed M-16 in one hand, radio handset wrapped in plastic in the other. Initially he'd wanted to carry the 'prick' himself, but his platoon sergeant, months more experienced in war, talked his fresh-faced platoon leader out of committing suicide. The RTO is close behind Kane, the handset cord stretches between them.

Kane's on the company net, so he can receive the Captain's orders. But he has the RTO briefly switch to the second preset frequency every so often to catch glimpses of the Battalion net. On the airwaves, Alpha's company's commander is initially calm, transmitting with the rattle of battle lurking in the background. But as the cacophony of the firing increases and approaches, so does his urgency, calling for artillery and air support.

Nevertheless, Charlie advances slowly. The Captain is correctly afraid of ambush and keeps a tight rein on the movement.

Then, oddly, the Captain receives orders from Battalion to halt. No one is quite sure what's going on. Battalion needs time, and less rain and fog, to sort it out, only able to make decisions second-hand via the radio and the map.

Kane kneels, rucksack on his back. More experienced men do the rucksack flop on their backs, knowing a halt can last seconds or hours. Hurry up and wait is the Infantryman's mantra.

Charlie Company waits.

Kane worries about Ted, assigned to Alpha, yet a small part of him envies his best friend getting his combat cherry busted first. Both of them are only weeks in-country and days in the field.

The sound of battle in the distance is lessening. Contact broken? Enemy withdrawing?

As the morning wears on, silence settles.

Battalion orders Charlie to move to Alpha's location. Link up is the order.

Kane takes that as a positive. They'll join forces.

The Captain once more warns they can expect to make contact. The point squad leads. The rest of the platoon follows. Kane's platoon has the left corner of the diamond formation, stumbling on the side of the steep ridge. The other line platoon is to the right. Weapons brings up the rear with its two 60mm mortars and company headquarters. The FNG's body and the Montagnard's are carried in the middle by the dumb fucks the first sergeant has chosen, one of them the shooter of the man he carries. Theoretically the formation is a diamond. The jungle and ridgeline say otherwise, forcing the company tighter than the Captain likes and the center is inevitably pushed onto the trail running along the crest of the ridge. The same one Alpha is astride in the lower ground. They move slowly.

Kane isn't certain how much of his soaked jungle fatigues comes from sweat, humidity or the lessening rain. Men slash at bamboo with machetes. Soldiers grasp at undergrowth and trees to keep from sliding down the side of the muddy ridgeline. Like warriors throughout history, they are dirty, wet, tired and scared.

It takes the afternoon to make the distance. They reach an open area, the helicopter pick up zone Alpha had hacked out of the jungle the previous evening. Unfortunately, to keep the enemy from using the clearing as a base for mortars, Alpha, once it finished getting resupplied via the PZ, had salted it with CS crystals.

Kane dons his gas mask, realizes the filters have been soaked and the mask is worthless. The soldiers push through, the lightest step producing a cloud of CS gas. By the time the company crosses the clearing, every man is coughing, eyes pouring tears and many are vomiting.

It is growing late. Darkness is only a few hours off.

They find the first element of Alpha—the weapons platoon which had salted the PZ, along with the company commander who'd been supervising. The line platoons, over 100 men, are further on. Somewhere. The company commander isn't sure.

Taking advantage of a break in the clouds, the battalion commander hops off his helicopter. His orders to the Captain aren't something Kane was taught at West Point: "I want you to try to probe down the hill, but break off if you have any contact. Don't throw good money after bad."

Try? Break off if you make contact? Good money after bad? Kane doesn't drink in the aura of Grant, Pershing or Patton in those edicts.

The Captain orders his men to press on, to find the rest of Alpha. But the enemy is waiting. The lead elements are engaged.

Kane fires his first shots in combat as he gets his squads on line.

But he fires blindly, toward the uncertain location where the enemy fire is originating. A considerable amount of enemy fire.

They can't push through. There are too many. The Captain decides to err on the side of 'good money'.

The order is passed to form a perimeter. Expect an assault from a large NVA force some time during the night.

The longest night of Kane's life to this point begins.

He crawls from man to man in his platoon, making sure they've done the best they can digging in, scratching out whatever cover possible. Reassuring what he doesn't feel. Thoughts of Ted ahead, somewhere.

Some men sleep. Many wait for death to come sweeping over them.

As darkness falls, frayed nerves are scraped as men outside the perimeter scream for help. For a medic. For their mother. Some just scream, inarticulate pain, the jagged melody of the wounded that echoes with a man the remainder of his life.

It is what is left of Alpha Company.

Gunships blade by, spurting rockets and machine gun fire. Artillery sprinkles throughout the night, a protective curtain for Charlie Company.

Kane sits with his back against a tree, peering into the darkness, weapon across his knees. The handset clipped to his web gear. His RTO curls in the hole a few feet away, pretending to sleep, the radio between them within mutual arms reach. There is no contact on the battalion net with anyone in Alpha. Only Bn HQ talking to the artillery and gunships.

Not long after nightfall the melody of the unseen wounded intermingles with something worse. The cries of those about to die, begging for mercy. The pleas are always followed by the single crack of a shot. Another shot. And another.

A few stragglers from Alpha crawl into the perimeter over the course of the night. Most wounded. All in shock.

None are Ted.

Kane envisions Ted lying low, waiting for reinforcements.

As BMNT lightens the sky, the shooting dwindles. By dawn silence. No firing. No lament of the wounded. Even the jungle is quiet. No sign of the NVA. The men of Charlie company are hushed, relieved to be alive, fearing the day ahead.

The Captain's order is subdued. "Move out."

They find the remnants of Alpha Company. Clustered along the trail. Seventy-eight men.

Kane stumbles among the bodies. Many are naked. Mutilated. Eviscerated from navel to sternum. Eyes dug out. Intestines strewn about. Fingers cut off for the rings. Some had their hands tied, indicating they'd surrendered before being executed.

A soldier is found alive among the carnage. He'd been shot in the back several times, but played dead. Even when his finger was amputated and his wedding band stolen. Medics tend to him.

Kane is searching. Forcing himself to stare at death in an array of ugly, horrific guises.

This is Little Big Horn, he thinks. This is what it was really like. Nothing gallant or noble in a massacre. No one had told him about the smell. Of urine, shit, viscera, blood, fear and desperation.

He finds Ted. His gear, his weapon, his boots, his clothes, gone. His pale chest is still. His dog tags remain, stained with blood. His eyes are cloudy, lips curled back in a frozen grimace. His hands are lashed behind his back with a strand of barbed wire. Surprisingly, missed in the darkness, his watch is still on his wrist, hidden by the green Velcro band.

Kane stares at the barbed wire for several long moments, then unwraps it, not noticing he's ripping his own flesh. He frees Ted's hands and places them on his chest. Takes the watch off and puts it in the cargo pocket of his jungle fatigues. Like the others, Ted's finger is cut off. His West Point ring gone. A trophy of war.

A small dark hole in his forehead; the back of the head a crater. Most of the brain with it. An empty enclosure where Ted had once existed: his laughter, his loves, his memories and his future are all gone.

Kane removes one of the dog tags. He puts it on the chain around his own neck. The other he leaves for the casualty officer. He cradles Ted in his arms, surprised how heavy a dead man weighs, and carries his friend to the body bags.

Monday Evening, 11 July 1977

GREENWICH VILLAGE, MANHATTAN

Kane dropped off the ammunition, grenades, demo, backup .45 and Swedish K at his apartment before returning the car to the Washington Square Hotel. He tipped the concierge forty. In exchange he got a name and another point of contact added to his notebook.

Night settled uneasily over the city, the specter of Son of Sam purging the streets. The bright lights fought against the darkness, putting a glow into the sky, a false halo over a city teeming with sin and fear.

Kane packed the map case. High Standard. Night vision goggles. Camera. The .45 was on his belt, two extra magazines in a holder behind the holster.

He opened the front door, stepped out, locked the door and put the matchstick in place, the piece of tape at the top. When he turned around, Detective Strong's wide bulk was silhouetted at the top of the stairs against the dull light from the closest street lamp.

"Paranoid?" Strong asked.

"You're on my case," Kane said. "Shouldn't I be paranoid?"

"Not if you're innocent."

"Do you have a warrant?" Kane asked, taking a step toward his door.

"I'm not here about that," Strong said. "Someone is asking for you. At *another* crime scene. Seems you're very popular where bodies are involved."

"Whose body?"

Unlike Uncle Nathan, Strong didn't need to keep the victim a secret. "Malcolm Dixon. Elevator operator at 7 Gramercy.

Disabled vet with no legs in a wheelchair." The disgust in Strong's voice over the crime was obvious.

Kane stepped up to the gate. "What happened?"

Strong crooked a finger. "Come."

"Is his father all right? James?"

"His father is grieving which is what family members tend to do. He's not the one asking for you. Some high-class hooker named Farrah. She's refusing to leave the crime scene until she talks to you and I'd prefer not to drag her out. Are you coming?"

Kane followed Strong to the unmarked. He got in the passenger side while Strong took the wheel. Unlike Conner's, and like Nathan's, the interior was spotless. Strong put a red bubble on top, the light rotating. Pulled out and drove east across the island toward Gramercy.

"You're wearing a gun," Strong noted. "Which is odd because I took your gun."

Kane stared straight ahead.

"I also took your permit. I could arrest you now. Save myself some trouble."

Kane didn't respond.

"I checked on you," Strong said. "Ran you through the Feds. You've got no criminal record. Talked to your Uncle Nathan for more background. I remember that Green Beret fiasco in Vietnam. The trial. Made all the papers."

Strong turned left off 14th onto Park Avenue.

"You got anything to say?" Strong asked.

"I'm exercising my right to remain silent."

"I haven't Mirandized you," Strong said.

"That's been noted."

Strong slammed on the brakes and Kane had to use both hands to keep from eating the dash as horns blared behind them.

The detective turned to him. "You're a shit magnet, Kane. Some people are born one, some people become one. I don't know which you are. But your history is full of it and your present is full of it and unless you want your future to be full of shit, you better understand one thing. You can be with me or against me. There is no middle ground. Decide now."

Horns blared, middle fingers were extended from taxis and cars edging around. Curses screamed. Strong was one hundred percent focused on Kane.

Kane returned the stare. "What does that mean? With you or against you? What are *you* for, Strong?"

"The law. The truth."

"Give me a break," Kane said. "What world are you living in?"

"The world where I could have slapped cuffs on you the moment I saw that gun on your hip," Strong said.

"Are you threatening me?"

Strong shook his head in amazement. "What is wrong with your brain?" He pointed. "I see the scar. You uncle said you took a round in the torso and one that glanced off your skull at Dak To."

A taxi driver stuck behind them leaned on his horn for five long seconds, a New York Hour, not deterred by the flashing light.

Strong poked Kane in the chest. "What are *you* for, Kane?" Waited a few seconds. Poked him again. "Getting angry, Kane? Going to hit me?"

"No."

"But you're pissed."

"You are irritating."

"I can be a lot more than irritating." Strong poked.

Kane looked ahead. "Can we get to where we're going?"

"You can't ask me to do a damn thing," Strong said. "I came to get you as a courtesy. Did you know Malcolm? His father, James, said you were a friend."

"I knew him," Kane said.

"Were you a friend?"

When Kane didn't respond, Strong went on. "I don't think you were. Because if your friend is dead, you don't act like an asshole. You would want to know who killed him."

"Who killed him?"

"The suspect is claiming self-defense. Against a guy in a wheelchair."

"What?"

"Got your interest now?" Strong turned away and sat back the seat, large shoulders dropping. "With me or not?"

"The law? Truth?" Kane said. "How about one of two? Truth."

Strong put the car into gear. "Good enough for now."

Kane spoke. "I didn't take a round in the torso at Dak To. It was shrapnel. From a bomb dropped by a plane. A Marine plane. Killed a lot of good men."

"I wasn't flying it," Strong said.

Park Avenue, right onto 20th.

"Two of Delgado's crew jumped me last night," Kane said.

Strong glanced over. "You seem none the worse for it."

"They are. They thought I killed Cibosky."

"It's still a possibility. But you didn't kill them, right?"

"Nope."

"So you probably didn't kill Cibosky."

Several patrol cars were scattered on Gramercy Park West, in front of the condominium. Lights were flashing. A killing here drew more attention than other places in the city. A patrolman waved Strong through.

They pulled in front.

"Where's James?" Kane asked.

"We had to send him to the hospital," Strong said. "He's taking it hard." He opened his door and got out. Kane joined him.

"Was he hurt?"

Strong glanced at Kane as they walked to the door. "His son is dead. That's hurt."

"I know *that* hurt."

For the first time, Strong was shaken. "Truce?"

Kane nodded.

They went in. Two patrolmen stood next to the open elevator. Strong and Kane got on. Strong did Malcolm's job, pushing the lever to Farrah's floor.

Silence as the elevator shuddered upward. The doors opened to the corridor. A tipped over wheelchair was pushed against one wall a few feet into the corridor. A pool of blood under it.

Kane waited as Strong didn't exit.

The detective recited to himself: "*'Life is for the living. Death for the dead. Let life be like music. And death a note unsaid'.*"

"Langston Hughes?" Kane said.

Strong was surprised. "One for the white guy. Maybe you're not that dumb."

"Is that what you said to yourself in the Village, before coming under the crime scene tape?"

"Words keep me sane in an insane world." Strong pointed at the bloodstain. "Three rounds to the chest."

"Where's the body?"

"On the way to the morgue."

A blood spatter led from a spot five feet farther on to Farrah's open door. Someone else's blood.

"The shooter is at the hospital," Strong said. "Several superficial cuts. Nothing life threatening."

"Fuck," Kane muttered.

"Come on." Strong led him into Farrah's apartment.

Blood was speckled, but not in significant quantities. Farrah sat on the couch, dressed only in panties, a towel held to her chest as a paramedic tended to her back. Flesh was split, blood oozing through gauze.

"Coat hanger," Strong said.

"Will!" Farrah tried to stand, but the paramedic put a hand on her shoulder.

Kane knelt in front of her, Strong hovering behind. "What happened?"

She reached out and grabbed his hand. Her eyes were unfocused. "He crossed the line, Will. He did. I didn't want to scream, but I couldn't stop."

"I know."

Farrah was shaking her head. "He didn't have to hurt me so bad. He didn't. I told him the belt was okay. But not the hangar. He never did that before."

"It's all right," Kane said. "You'll be all right."

"They said someone got shot in the hallway," Farrah said. "I told them I wouldn't talk to anyone but you. Did you shoot him?"

Kane glanced up at Strong, who shook his head. "No. I didn't shoot anyone."

"Good. I'm glad you didn't shoot him, Will. I'm sorry I called the diner earlier today. I shouldn't. I don't want you in trouble. This is my problem."

Strong was nodding toward the door.

"Let them take care of you, Farrah," Kane said. "Go to the hospital. You're going to need stitches."

She numbly nodded. Got up with the paramedic.

They walked out.

Kane remembered a few seconds too late.

Farrah screamed in the hallway. "No! Not Malcolm!"

Strong held out a hand, stopping Kane from going out there. "They'll take care of her."

"You didn't tell her who was shot," Kane said.

"She wasn't a witness to that," Strong said. "She's high and not thinking straight so it doesn't matter what anyone tells her. And she's in pain."

"High? Fuck."

"We're not sure what went down out there," Strong said. "The only witness for the hallway is the suspect with the gun. He has his version."

"He gunned down a guy with no legs in a wheelchair," Kane said.

"Who he says was armed," Strong said. "We found a gun in the vic's hand. It didn't look like it was planted. I've seen that. Do you know if Malcolm carried a gun?"

Kane shook his head. "No idea."

"Truth," Strong said.

"I got no idea," Kane said. "Doesn't everyone have a fucking gun in this city? Knowing Malcolm, yeah, he probably had something under that blanket where his legs used to be. Did he get a round off?"

"No. He was alive when the ambulance got here," Strong said. "But couldn't say anything. Died as they were loading him. I arrived at the same time. They'd ripped his clothes off working on him. He had tracks in his stumps. I've seen a lot, but that's a new wrinkle. Did you know he was a junkie?"

Kane walked to the chair he'd piled his clothes on the other day and sat down. "His dad thought it was his meds from the VA. I did too."

"The VA doesn't dispense heroin," Strong said. "Not yet," he added, almost to himself.

Kane looked up at Strong. "Who shot Malcolm? Who beat her?"

Strong grimaced. "Sean Damon."

Kane was perfectly still.

"You know who that is?" Strong asked.

"Yes."

"You're acting like it's more than just know who it is. Have you seen him here before?"

"No."

Strong indicated the apartment. "How are you involved in all this? Why'd she ask for you? Why'd she leave a message for you earlier? She seems a little out of your price range."

"I had to handle something here for the job."

"For the firm? Antonia Marcelle?"

Kane nodded.

"What was the job?"

"That's supposed to be confidential," Kane said without much energy.

"Truth."

"Toni told me someone was trying to shake down a friend. The doorman, James. Seems it was against his job description to cover for an escort working out of an apartment in the building."

"She doesn't own the apartment." Strong moved a stuffed pony aside and sat on the edge of the bed, checking his notebook. He wrote in it, then flipped a few pages. "That's the other problem. The name on the lease is a company, Advantage LLC. When I asked her, I didn't get anything coherent." Strong looked up from the notebook. "I would assume there is some connection with the Marcelle's given you were sent here by them. Which makes me wonder if the hooker is working for Marcelle?"

"More likely a client of the Marcelle's," Kane said.

"Still doesn't make sense," Strong said. "Why would your boss, Antonia Marcelle, give a damn about some doorman? Did you ask her?"

"No."

"Were you curious?"

"It's a job," Kane said. "I helped someone out."

"That's when you met the hooker?"

"Farrah. James introduced me," Kane said.

"Are you involved with her?" Strong waited. "I'll take your silence as assent. How long ago did you first come here?"

"I think it was in February."

"When was the last time you met the hooker?"

"Friday."

"You're in the wrong line of work, Kane." Strong wrote in his pad. "Did it ever occur to you that the real client was whoever owned the apartment and the hooker?"

"What's Damon's story?" Kane asked.

"She pulled a knife and he defended himself," Strong said. "She cut him. Not bad, but a couple of times. We've got the knife. He's got the cuts. Not like he did that to himself. She didn't deny cutting him. Said she did it after he hit her with the hanger. He says he hit her with the hanger after she cut him. He said, she said."

"Who do you believe?"

"It doesn't matter," Strong said. He snapped the notepad shut. "Guess who Damon's attorney is?"

"Thomas Marcelle," Kane muttered.

"You want truth?" Strong said. "Damon won't get charged. Self-defense. Even if it wasn't, it is."

Kane stared at the detective. "That's the law?"

"That's the truth." Strong nodded. "That's a point for you, Kane. But you're holding something back."

"My Uncle Conner says there's two levels to the law. Says he's a collar man. Are you?"

"I'd take what your Uncle Conner says with some skepticism."

"What happened between you two?"

"Ask him."

"Did you arrest Damon?"

"No. He's at the hospital getting stitched up."

"So you didn't collar him."

"Already said that was a point for you."

"Who is Advantage LLC?" Kane asked.

"Could be the Marcelle Firm," Strong said. "Could be Damon. Could be both. Which means the hooker is owned like the furniture in here. Given he felt he could beat her like that, I'd go with Damon. He's a wicked piece of work. Him and his Irish thugs, the Unholy Trinity." He stood. "There's something you should see."

Strong walked into the hallway, Kane following. Opened the door across the way. The bedroom had a large, king-sized four-post bed in the center. There were straps secured to bolts on each post of the bed leading to padded cuffs. The ceiling above the bed was covered in mirrors. There was an assortment of oils, gels, dildoes, and other objects of the carnal art on a large dresser. It had a tall mirror on top of it.

"This is where she worked," Strong said. "The way you're looking around, she didn't bring you in here?"

"No."

"That's interesting." He went to the dark wood paneling to the left of the dresser. Shoved the palm of his hand into the edge of the wood, next to the mirror and a tall panel popped forward on hinges. He opened it and indicated for Kane to look. A 16mm camera was set on a short tripod facing the room, angled through the mirror's one-way glass.

"There are mikes," Strong said. "The on switch for the camera and mikes is here." He indicated underneath the top edge of the dresser which extended a couple of inches to either side.

"How did you find it?"

"I worked vice for fourteen months," Strong said. "This could be one of a couple of things. Could be making movies and selling them to the peep shows around the Deuce. But I very much doubt that. It's for whoever owns this place and her."

"Why?"

Strong gave Kane the look. "To film whoever was in here. Blackmail, Kane. That's what people like Damon are all about. Be glad she didn't bring you in here or you'd be on film."

"It wouldn't be much of a film," Kane said. "Why did Damon really beat her?"

"Who knows?" Strong said. "Some guys get off on it. Or he found out she was entertaining unsanctioned people. Like you. Since you were here last Friday."

"She'd been choked recently. Hard. Left marks on her throat."

"I saw them. Did she tell you who did it?"

"Just some client."

Strong sighed. "We've both seen some shit, haven't we, Kane?"

"Yeah."

Strong indicated the camera space. "Notice something else?"

"No films."

"No films," Strong agreed. "We searched the place. Not a single one. That seems odd. The camera is loaded, though. Ready to roll."

"The films are taken away."

"You're catching up," Strong said.

"You said you've got no case against Damon in regard to Malcolm. What about for what Damon did to Farrah?"

"She cut him with a knife."

"Is he pressing charges against Farrah?"

"I very much doubt he wants any part of this in a courtroom," Strong said. "Where did she get the knife?"

"I gave it to her."

"Thought so after seeing it. Professional, with perfect edges. Man, you're a shitstorm, Kane."

"Why are you showing me this?" Kane asked.

Strong led the way to the door. "To give you an idea what you're involved in working for Thomas Marcelle. The kind of people he represents."

"I don't see the connection," Kane said, "other than Toni asking me to help here one time and Damon being Marcelle's client."

"Are you deliberately playing dumb?" Strong asked.

"I've got a lot going on," Kane said. "Sorry I'm not at your speed, Detective."

"Actually," Strong said, "I think you might be ahead of me on some things. You know more than you're telling me."

"Why tell you anything?" Kane asked. "You've already said the law isn't going to apply."

CIVIC CENTER, MANHATTAN

Strong didn't offer a ride back to Kane's apartment, which was fine because that wasn't where he wanted to go. His original plan, to follow Delgado once more, was gone. Strong hadn't taken the .45 or checked the map case, which had implications.

Kane paused for a moment outside the building where a pool of blood indicated the spot where Malcolm had been loaded into the ambulance. And where he'd died. A man in the same uniform James and Malcolm wore, had a bucket of water and he tossed it on the blood, dispersing it toward the sewer. Another bucket and there'd be no sign of what happened.

Kane walked south from Gramercy on Park Avenue, among the scattering of pedestrians, inadequately juggling the pieces of his life and recent events. He reached Union Square Park and angled through when an image of Lil' Joe flashed in his consciousness. It hit like a punch in the heart and Kane had to stop, just in front of the large statue of George Washington on his horse.

Consciously he knew this sudden reaction was because some synapse had connected this location to death: Union Square had been built upon a former potter's field. Brother Benedict had articulated a particular interest in places that were built on top of sites used for very different purposes, from graveyards to swamps to slaughter-pens to former garbage pits. Kane put a hand on the iron fence around the statue to steady himself. Closed his eyes and took several deep breaths. He spotted a payphone.

Kane inserted a dime and punched the numbers.

It was answered on the third ring, the voice tinged with drunk. "Riley."

"Uncle Conner, it's Will. Why did you call Toni Marcelle a dyke?"

"What?"

"The other day, at the yacht club, you called her a dyke. Why?"

"Geez, kid. I don't know. I heard something, somewhere. I don't know."

"Think. Who told you?"

"Scuttlebutt, Will. Not many female lawyers. She's divorced. You know how guys talk."

"What do you know about Sean Damon?"

"Ah, fuck, Will. What you into? Leave it alone if it involves that old fucker. He'll have his mick friends cut your nuts off. Don't you have enough trouble already?" A shrill voice was slicing Conner in the background.

"I'm trying to figure out what exactly the trouble is," Kane said. "I'm involved whether I want to be or not. You know that."

"Damon is bad enough by himself. But he's got three buddies from his old neighborhood in Hell's Kitchen that have been with him since Christ was a corporal. The Unholy Trinity. Nathan can give you their names, but they're stone cold killers."

"They got to be in their seventies," Kane said.

"Which means they been killing folks since before you were born," Conner shot back. "They can still gut you and dump the body with the best. Stay away from them. Hell, they're holding their own on the West Side against the Genovese Family. Fucking whackjobs." Several seconds of silence. "Listen. There's not much I can do to help. But if there is, let me know."

Kane was taken aback. "I'm all right, Uncle Conner. Don't worry. I'm sorting it out."

"Okay," Conner said.

Several more seconds of silence except for Aileen's screeching in the background.

"I've got to be going," Kane said.

"Be careful, kiddo."

WEST SIDE HIGHWAY, MANHATTAN

Kane needed darkness for his next act. Since it wasn't dusk, he jogged over to the West Side Highway, skirted the barrier, went up the ramp and onto the roadway. By the time he was on the highway, his gray t-shirt was soaked with sweat. He removed the denim shirt and tied it around his waist.

He walked around the plywood barrier. There were several homeless about, all giving Kane varying looks ranging from wariness to sizing him up to the equivalent of the hatred of South Vietnamese whose village had been 'pacified'.

Wile-E looked considerably more human, sitting on the edge of the railing, feet dangling, facing the Hudson. His hair was still long but it was clearly blond. He was clean shaven. His field jacket was a shade less dirty. He was drinking from a bottle in a paper bag and had a cigarette in the other hand, smoke curling into the air.

"How'd you like Soldiers and Sailors?" Kane asked as he came up next to him.

Wile-E glanced at Kane then took another slug. "It was a bed and a hot shower. I appreciate it." He held out the bag, hand shaking. "Want some?"

"Got to work tonight," Kane said.

"You're not a cop," Wile-E said. "But you carry a gun. What's the story?"

"I work for a lawyer."

"Must be a tough lawyer."

"She is. Are you off the needle?"

"Why do you care?" Wile-E asked.

Kane didn't say anything.

Wile-E sighed. "Trying. It's hard. What's the point?"

"That's something you gotta figure out," Kane said, "but you can't do it while you're using."

"That's, what-do-you-call-it? A Catch-Two?"

"Yeah," Kane agreed. "It's fucked."

"Maybe," Wile-E muttered, more to himself than Kane.

"You want a job?" Kane asked.

"I get disability."

"That's not an answer," Kane said.

"I get a job, I lose the VA disability," Wile-E explained.

"Who told you that?" Kane asked. "That's not how it works. You get a job, you get structure. You get structure, it gives you a better shot at staying off the needle."

"How do you know? What are you some do-gooder?"

"That's the last thing anyone would call me," Kane said.

"You hang out in the mornings at that diner at the end of the High Line," Wile-E said, not a question.

"How do you know that?"

"I asked around about you, Cap'n," Wile-E said. "Trying to figure out your angle. Nobody does something for nothing. Now you want to get me a job. Get me straight. What's your angle?"

"I'm not a captain anymore." Kane sighed. "Someone I knew, a veteran who lost his legs in 'Nam, was killed earlier today."

"A friend?" Wile-E asked, giving him his complete attention.

"I guess."

"You guess he was your friend?" Wile-E shook his head. "Someone is either you're a friend or they ain't."

"How many friends do you have?" Kane asked him.

"None anymore and I ain't pretending to, neither. Was this guy a Sky Soldier?"

"First Cav."

"What was his name?"

"Malcolm."

Wile-E held up his paper bag. "Here's to Malcolm. He's probably in a better place." He took a long slug, draining it. Tossed it off the Highway. It hit the ground with a muted smash. "A friend would loan me some money for a refill. Booze, not smack."

Kane peeled a twenty off. "Think about the job, all right? At the diner. Talk to a Montagnard named Thao. He's a good man."

"Sure, I'll think about it."

*****

Kane took a detour south to Dino's Pizza. The same kid was behind the counter, listening to the Yankees losing to the Baltimore Orioles on a transistor radio. Kane bellied up to the counter.

"Slice?" the pizza maker asked.

"How much do you have in the register?" Kane asked.

"Oh, come on. Give me a break."

"Get a new line," Kane said to him. "You remember me?"

The pizza maker squinted. "Yeah."

"I'm not robbing you. How much in the register?"

The pizza maker checked. "Fourteen bucks and some change."

"You slip anything over twenty in the safe, right?"

A frown. "Yeah. So?"

"You told me you lost eighty-two dollars the other night."

The youngster took a step back. "Did I?"

"How much did I leave you?"

"One-twenty."

"You abused my kindness, didn't you?"

"Hey. Come on. I been docked twice this month."

"Did you abuse my kindness?" Kane repeated.

The pizza maker hung his head. "Yeah. Sorry."

"Okay. Don't do it again. Stuff like that makes me lose faith in people." Kane turned for the door, but spoke over his shoulder. "Put more cheese on your pie. It'll help."

CIVIC CENTER, MANHATTAN

Dutch had taught Kane how to pick a variety of locks. One of the places where he'd demonstrated techniques was the rear maintenance door to the Chambers-Broadway building. That made entry simple.

Kane took the staircase to the top floor. Entered through the fire door. It was quiet, but most lights were on. Kane did a circuit of the floor, checking to see if anyone at *Marcelle, van Dyck, Feinstein and Marcelle* was working late.

He entered the boardroom. The ornate oak table was big enough to mimic an aircraft carrier. The walls had more old

white men frowning. He poked his head into the library. Lots of
law books, but nothing unusual.

He moved through the library to another room. The
executive lounge. There wasn't just a shower; there were four
private showers. Lockers. Enough marble to make a dent on a
quarry. Not exactly a World War II wooden barracks with open
stalls.

Kane returned to the main corridor, which circled the floor.
Looked at the door to Toni's office. Passed. He chose to start
with the top.

The door to the inner sanctum was locked, but interior locks
were simpler. Thomas Marcelle's office was twice the size of
Toni's, in the southeast corner. A large desk commanded the
room. A table that sat four was to one side. A couch and several
comfortable chairs along the wall. A wet bar. A small private
bathroom in case Marcelle couldn't make the walk to the
executive lounge or deign to shit with lesser-than's.

The lights of the Brooklyn Bridge glittered a quarter mile
away. Closer, City Hall was dark, a few feeble lampposts battling
darkness and losing. The building lights were off to save the city
money. From his desk, Thomas Marcelle could look down on
the mayor's office. To the southwest, the Twin Towers
shimmered. Aircraft warning lights on top blinked.

The walls were covered with pictures. Thomas Marcelle
meeting dignitaries. Many were from his time in the US
Attorney's office, but others were recent. The various mayors
he'd outlasted. Governors, senators, congressmen, developers,
sports figures.

None with any mafia boss's or capo's.

There were several awards honoring Thomas Marcelle for
this or that.

No plaques with edged weapons.

There was one weapon, though: Ted's saber, mounted on
hooks.

Kane sat at the desk. The surface was clear, the in-box
empty, as was the out. The drawers were locked. Kane opened
them and searched. Nothing perked.

Relocked the desk. Contemplated the single three-drawer filing cabinet behind the desk. It had a tumbler lock, much like the ones they'd had back in Vietnam at HQ for classified material. Dutch had introduced him to such locks, but told him that if he had to do a tumbler, he'd be better off finding the combination or bringing some C-4. Safe cracking was a skill even Dutch hadn't taken on.

Kane checked the desk blotter, lifting it, hoping the combination might be there. Then he saw the footlocker. It was almost hidden on the far side of the couch. Kane walked over and knelt in front of it. The stenciled name was faded and scratched but legible:

MARCELLE, T.J. LIEUTENANT

The clasp was secured with the same Army combination lock they'd been issued during the first week of Beast. Kane dialed the combination for Toni's birthday and it clicked open. All these years and neither Ted nor his father had changed it.

He swung open the top. In the upper tray, on the left of the single partition, were several blue boxes. Kane opened them, one by one. Purple Heart. Bronze Star. Vietnam Service ribbon. Less than two weeks in country and this was the result. The first week had been the 173rd's orientation for newbies and jungle training, along with zeroing their weapons. Then he and Ted had been choppered to the 2/503rd as it was deploying to assault the mountains around Dak To.

Two days later Ted was dead.

The right side of the tray held some letters, and a Combat Infantry Badge, the 'holy grail' of the Infantryman. It's a rectangle of Infantry-blue enamel, with a silver musket, Springfield Arsenal, Model 1795. The rectangle is super-imposed on an elliptical oak-leaf.

After branch night at West Point, when cadets picked their future niche in the army according to class rank, Kane and Ted and others who'd chosen the crossed rifles of the Infantry had discussed the CIB as a necessary accouterment to an Infantry Officer's resume, even more so than Ranger School, given that the country was at war.

Posthumous had not been in anyone's plan.

Both had also noticed that with Vietnam heating up, a classmate who'd talked incessantly about Infantry for four years had chosen another branch of service, less likely to put him in harm's way. Nevertheless, there had been more than enough eager for combat that ninety-eight added the option to volunteer for assignment to Vietnam after a short state-side shakedown tour as a platoon leader.

A few letters were from Ted to his father over the four years at West Point. Not many but more than Kane's single one from R-Day taps. Kane spotted a familiar envelope. The letter he'd written to Thomas Marcelle after Ted was killed. The twisted story he'd inscribed about how Ted had died, fighting to the last bullet. How he'd found Ted's body with weapon in hand, a single unlucky round in the head, in line with the lies the Regimental Surgeon had written on the numerous hasty autopsy reports after the battle on Hill 1338.

Underneath, in the lower portion, was Ted's full-dress gray coat with its rows of brass buttons. His tarbucket. Red sash. Kane put everything back and closed the locker.

As he walked toward Toni's office, something occurred to him. He went back into the boardroom. There was a pair of large blackboards set on rollers. They'd not only been erased, but wiped clean, much like a student had been assigned to do in the classrooms at Holy Rosary, using a bucket and a sponge. He pushed the boards apart, revealing a screen. Reversing direction and crossing the room, he found a narrow door built to look like part of the wood paneling. Inside was just enough space for a chair and a table. An overhead projector, slide machine and projector were on the table. A panel in front of them was designed to be pulled back and slid down. No film was loaded in the projector and there were no film canisters.

Kane walked back into the room, thinking about the barebone spaces A-teams isolated in prior to a mission. Often lined with plywood on which maps and recon photos were tacked for mission planning. Thomas Marcelle had brought Sean Damon in here. Why? Marcelle, Toni and Damon could as easily have convened at the table in Marcelle's office.

Kane went to the blackboards, checking the tracks they were set in. He pulled a small flashlight out of the map case and shone it in the two-inch space behind them and the wall.

There was something on the back of the blackboard. Kane went to the front and lifted it. The bottom rollers came free of the slot. He turned it around. The reverse side was corkboard. Flat thumbtacks held a construction plan. The plan was six feet long by two wide, taking up the center. Much like the Son of Sam maps, other thumbtacks held strings going to colored index cards pinned on either side. The map projected the future of the lower west side of Manhattan, from 42nd Street to the Battery.

Westway.

The ambitious plan to replace the West Side Highway. 4.2 miles. For most of it a six-lane roadway would be buried underneath landfill along the Hudson after all the dilapidated piers were removed. Parks, shops, and apartment buildings would be constructed on top.

The index cards had numbers written on them and letters in some sort of shorthand that Kane couldn't make sense of. Except for the dollar signs. Even those were a form of shorthand and it took him a moment to realize the amounts were in millions, ie $1.2 was $1,200,000.

There was considerable money totaled on the cards, over a billion dollars. Construction contracts. The colors and codes? Different companies? Different plans? Different payoffs? Different mafia families?

Kane checked the back of the other board. It had a map of the same area as it currently existed. There were also thumbtacks threaded to index cards on the edges. But the strings went to various, existing locations all about the lower west side of Manhattan.

Kane retrieved his camera and took pictures of the maps, both in total and then sections in detail so the writing would be legible. Finished, he reversed the boards and put them back on the track.

He left the boardroom. Kane could sense Mrs. Ruiz's absent disapproval as he picked the lock on Toni's door. Her office was as neat and tidy as her father's. Empty desk, in and out boxes, no files scattered about. Her desk was easily picked.

A vial was buried in the middle right drawer. Kane opened it. White powder. He put it back. Her engagement ring and wedding band were pushed to the rear of the drawer, neglected. In the bottom right drawer was a stack of faded envelopes, tied together with a red piece of yarn. Kane pulled them out and fanned through, checking the return address. Over five years of Ted's life. From the one he'd written that first night in Beast through four years at the Academy to Infantry Basic, and a scribbled note during Ranger school. Two from Vietnam during in processing. Kane was surprised to see several in there from him.

There was another letter from in-country. The return address was the unit and its APO:

C CO: 2/503rd Airborne

The stamp was 17 June 1967. The day the battalion had moved out of Dak To on the sweep that would end with the battle on Hill 1338. Two days before Kane and Ted had choppered in and joined the battalion in the field on the 19th.

Kane slid the letter out. The handwriting on the brief note looked familiar. He checked for a name at the bottom, but there wasn't any. Kane reached out and grabbed Toni's chair to steady himself as he read:

Toni,

Got word from Bn S-1 that your brother is inbound to us. Bn slotted him for a rifle platoon in my company. No way. Did you have anything to do with this? Your father? Some sort of sick revenge?

You'll be happy to know I swapped him out with Alpha. Getting their West Point butterbar instead. So don't expect reports on me from little Teddie.

Fuck You and Your Father.

Again.

Kane knew who wrote it: his commander in Charlie Company.

He shouldn't have been in Charlie. Ted should have. Kane shouldn't be alive. Ted should be.

Kane leaned back in the seat, closing his eyes, forcing himself to continue breathing despite the hole that was ripped through his chest.

The dots lined up. This was the man Toni said she'd briefly dated when he was a cadet. The reason Toni believed Ted went to West Point. The reason Ted ended up in Alpha Company and Kane in Charlie.

Kane dropped the letter, strode out of the office. Down the hallway, to the right. He circled the top floor several times, trying to gain equilibrium.

He re-entered Toni's office. Put the letter in the envelope, then pocketed it.

Returned the other letters to the drawer.

Searched the rest of the desk. Relocked it.

He turned to the filing cabinets. They had a different, simpler lock than her father's. Six numbers.

Kane dialed Ted's birthday.

The lock clicked open. The Marcelle siblings were nothing if not predictable in certain areas.

The files were in some sort of order, but Kane couldn't figure it out. Not alphabetical. He searched the labels. Lots of names he didn't recognize. Some cases he'd worked on. He found Delgado, pulled it out. Standard divorce crap, along with his brief reports; lacking, of course, his recent photos. Put the file back.

Opened another drawer. Scanned the labels.

Another drawer. Nothing on Damon. Nothing on Farrah or 7 Gramercy.

He knelt and opened the lowest drawer. Thumbed file after file, checking the tabs. Stopped when he saw KANE.

He withdrew the manila folder. It was thin. Sat at Toni's desk and opened the file.

It wasn't about him. It was a divorce settlement initiated by Taryn. On top was a copy of a notarized version, signed by Taryn with Antonia Marcelle as attorney and Mrs. Ruiz as witness and notary.

Kane tried to process it. Toni hadn't handled their divorce. He'd signed the form Taryn had mailed him, agreeing to everything she wanted, which wasn't much of anything except to be divorced and left alone. This was different.

He read through. It requested sole custody of Joseph, citing William Kane as an unfit father. The list of supporting facts was a chronology of Kane's military service and absences; a claim from a doctor that a head wound like the one he'd received could cause mental instability; and finally the murder charge in Vietnam and the fact he was in military prison.

Kane turned back to the first page.

Dated 14 November 1969. The day before he landed at LaGuardia.

Tuesday Night, 12 July 1977

GREENWICH VILLAGE, MANHATTAN

The .45 rested on Kane's small kitchen table, sandwiched between a copy of the divorce decree and the letter Kane had stolen from Toni's desk. His copy of the same photo she kept on top of her desk: Kane, Ted and Toni at Trophy Point right after graduation parade, sabers crossed, was under the pistol grip. A single bulb in a table lamp projected a cone of light around the objects on the table. The remainder of the basement was dark.

Beyond the .45 was a tattered shoebox, the corners crumpled, the writing faded. The top was off. Inside was a stack of photos of various sizes and a handful of letters.

It was three in the morning, the time when sentries are the drowsiest. When only the night shift or the restless are awake.

Kane reached over the .45 and retrieved a picture from the shoebox.

Wan, bleary-eyed, but smiling brightly, dark-skinned Taryn held a newborn Joseph in her arms. In a clinic in bumfuck Alabama, while Kane was doing pushups in the sawdust pit at Camp Darby, Fort Benning.

Kane put that picture on top of the .45.

He ran his fingers over the smooth surface of the polaroid, to the rough grip of the pistol, then back, lingering on Joseph's face. Ted's middle name. Taryn had outright refused Theodore and grudgingly given in on Joseph. Kane had nicknamed him Lil' Joe, but Taryn had never liked that. He hadn't been around enough for it to really get under her skin.

'It ended Ted's life.'

Toni had been honest, yet withholding, when she said that at Vic's. Not just introducing Ted to West Point, but that cadet, that man, who had been Kane's company commander at Hill

1338. He *should* have been Ted's commander. Kane reached inside his shirt and pulled the dog tags off. One was his. One was Ted's. Kane *should* have been the one lying dead in the blood, urine, feces, and viscera with the back of his head blown out. Stripped of his equipment and uniform. Hands bound by barbed wire.

Why hadn't Ted told him who the Charlie company commander was? Why hadn't Toni? Something had been off from the moment Kane and Ted choppered in to the 2/503rd during that movement to contact. Kane had sensed it and reflected on it often, never being able to pinpoint, always ascribing it to the randomness of which company had been ordered to be in what place in the attack. But it went deeper than that. It came all the way back here to New York.

'We're both in over our heads. Sometimes I wonder if Ted was the lucky one. Walk away, Will.'

Kane knew there was no walking away. He'd tried running to the other side of the world, drinking away, drugging away, fighting away, sexing away, working it away and nothing had served. It was just getting worse, faster and faster.

'Man, you're a shitstorm, Kane.'

Strong was right about that.

'Here's to Malcolm. He's probably in a better place.'

Kane slid the picture of Taryn and Joseph aside.

He scrawled *I'm sorry, Toni* on the bottom of the letter from his company commander.

He picked up the .45 and put it to his temple. Put his finger over the trigger. Closed his eyes. Saw Ted lying there, brains blown out.

Remembered the mess and he couldn't make Pope clean up that up.

Kane walked to the small bathroom, flipping on the fluorescent. The lip of the stained sink was crowded with the chemicals he used to develop pictures. He stepped into the tiny shower stall. The light was unsteady, as it always was, flickering.

Another mistake. The round would go through his head, through the wall. And the bullet was the one Morticia had caught.

Kane went back to the kitchen, laid the .45 on top of the letter and retrieved the High Standard. Returned to the shower stall. He'd bleed, but like Cibosky, there wouldn't be any brain matter for Pope to deal with or bullet through the skull and wall. Pope could simply turn on the shower and wash away the traces of Kane once the body was carted away.

As Malcom's blood had been hosed away on a grimy New York street.

Kane made sure there was a round in the chamber. Turned the bulky suppressor toward his right eye and reversed his grip, thumb on the trigger.

Amazed that the tiny .22 bore could appear so big. A black hole waiting to engulf his life.

Kane focused his left eye in the distance, through the door, into the bedroom, which blurred out the other eye's image of final darkness.

As his thumb put pressure on the trigger, the stack of NY Times next to the bed came into focus.

Tuesday Morning, 12 July 1977

GREENWICH VILLAGE, MANHATTAN

Kane lay on his back, the .45 on his chest. He stared up through the plant leaves at the hazy smog, imagining there were stars above. The smell of the tilled earth almost held back the incessant odor of the city, but not quite. Rotting garbage, vehicle exhaust, industrial smoke, and a whiff of salt water as the breeze wound through the buildings from the west. At two in the morning, the noise level was at low cycle; a distant siren, a ship's horn in the harbor, the rumble of a descending plane arriving late to Newark across the river. A car passing, tires chattering on cobblestone.

The sound of glass breaking.

Kane rolled and knelt, safety off. A beam of light flickered through his kitchen window. He scurried to the back door, keeping low. The wood door was open, the screen door closed. Hushed voices crept through the screen.

"Where is he?"

"Fuck if I know. Maybe upstairs?"

The sophisticated level of vocabulary indicated two fools blundering about in darkness and ignorance. It wouldn't take them long to search the tiny apartment. Their dark forms and lights entered in the kitchen.

"Outside?" one whispered.

"Why would he be outside?"

Kane could see them on an angle as he pressed against the brick, peering through the screen door. They had flashlights in one hand, guns in the other.

"Door's open," the other keenly observed.

Kane felt the weight of the .45 in his hand. He slid it into the holster. The screen door creaked open, a revolver leading, then an arm.

Kane grabbed the wrist, applying pressure on the joint while simultaneously twisting and dragging it down and around the man's side. The gun fell from the man's hand as he let out a yelp. Kane kept the momentum on the wrist, into the small of the man's back, then up, tearing ligaments in the shoulder as it bypassed the normal range of motion. That elicited a scream.

Kane pushed forward, shoving the man into his partner.

"What the fuck!" the second intruder yelled, stumbling back into the kitchen, flashlight beam wildly arcing.

Kane threw aside the disabled gunman and kicked at the second guy's gun hand. The toe of the jungle boot hit and the revolver went flying.

"Who the—" the guy began, but Kane knocked the rest of the sentence out of him with a sidekick to the solar plexus that sent him flying out of the kitchen into the bedroom.

Kane spun about, his internal clock warning him. The first intruder was on his knees, trying to locate the gun with his good hand.

Kane stomped on that hand, bones crunching. Another scream. Snap-kicked the gunman in the side of the head and he was out.

Kane walked to the bedroom. The second idiot was curled in the fetal position, moaning.

"It was only one kick," Kane said, shaking his head. They didn't make henchmen like they used to.

The guy raised a hand. "All right! All right!"

"What's all right?" Kane asked. He flipped the light on, did a quick check behind but the first gunman was still unconscious. "Just two of you?"

"Yeah."

"Anyone waiting outside? In a car?"

"Nah."

"What are you doing here?"

"We're looking for Alfonso."

"Delgado? You think I keep him in the kitchen?"

The guy sat up with his back against the bed Kane had never slept in. "He's gone. Nobody can find him."

"I don't think he's gonna be found," Kane predicted. "Who sent you? Cappucci? Quinn?"

The guy shook his head. "He's our capo. We been looking all over town for him."

Kane's hand went to the .45 as the screen door creaked, but relaxed when he recognized Pope in a robe, skinny, pale legs above fuzzy slippers.

"I heard a scream," Pope said. He looked about. "I see the reason. I assume these are not friends of yours?"

"From Alfonso Delgado," Kane said. He returned his attention to the guy against the bed. Drew the .45 and aimed it. "Any last words?"

"Hey! Hey! Hey! No, man, no. We was just looking for the boss."

"You came with guns," Kane said. "A gun for a gun."

Pope stood behind Kane's shoulder, but silent.

"We wasn't going to do nothing," the guy pleaded. "You got a bad rep."

"Is that a good thing?" Pope asked.

The guy shifted his attention to the ex-newspaperman. "Come on, old fellow. Help me out."

"I should ask him to shoot you for the 'old fellow' comment," Pope said.

"You drive here?" Kane asked.

The mobster nodded.

"Keys?"

He dug the keys out of a pocket and tossed them to Kane, wincing as he did so.

"What kind of car?"

"Caddy."

"Where is it parked?"

"Across the street. Down the block."

"Which way down the block?" Kane asked patiently.

"What?"

"Toward the river or city?" Kane asked.

"City."

Kane snap kicked the guy on the jaw. His teeth smashed together with a loud clack and his head bounced back against the bed. As it came forward, Kane executed a turn kick into the side of the head, knocking him out.

"That didn't hurt your foot, did it?" Pope asked.

"Nope."

"What now?" Pope asked.

"They should be out for a while," Kane said. He held up the keys. "I'm going to bring their car out front. Then I'll load them and take 'em away."

"Will they remain in their current condition?" Pope asked.

"I would hope they eventually feel better," Kane replied.

"I was concerned about the breathing part," Pope said.

"They'll remain breathing," Kane assured him.

Tuesday Morning, 12 July 1977

GREENWICH VILLAGE, MANHATTAN

"Morning, lad." Pope was sitting on the stoop as Kane exited his apartment.

"Good morning," Kane said as he closed the lower level gate. "You're up early."

"It was a somewhat abnormal night," Pope said. "I wanted to catch you before you're off to breakfast."

"They're fine," Kane reassured Pope. "Well, not fine, but alive. I dropped them near the emergency room." He had the map case looped over his left shoulder and wore his daily attire of black jungle fatigue pants and gray t-shirt under denim.

"Did you get any sleep?" Pope nodded toward the brownstone. "I noticed you spent the other night in the garden. That's taking the not being in the bed thing a bit far or do you prefer nature?"

"I got a couple of hours. And it was a good thing I wasn't in my bed last night."

"True," Pope said. "You seem troubled."

"Is that your reporter sense?" Kane asked, trying out a smile.

"My old man sense," Pope said.

"Shouldn't I be, given recent events?"

"You handled those two hoodlums with relative ease. I sense you're troubled by something deeper. I noted earlier this morning during the kerfuffle that you had photographs spread on the table."

"I learned some disturbing things about the past last night prior to the encounter," Kane said.

"Interesting," Pope said. "So the history is the same, it's your perception of the history that has changed in light of new knowledge."

Kane checked the street in both directions. "Say again?" He sat next to Pope.

"Whether we know something or we don't," Pope said, "the reality of the past is the same. What happened, happened. That's the goal of a reporter. To uncover and report on the facts, not the perception of the facts. You're viewing the past differently based on new information, but that doesn't change what happened. You just didn't know all the facts."

"I still don't," Kane said. "Do we ever?"

"Not really. But we muddle through the best we can."

"Muddle is an appropriate word for it," Kane said. He noticed that Pope had his notebook on the stoop. "What's going on?"

"Sean Damon," Pope said. "Associate of mine at the Post sent a messenger by yesterday." He waved a hand. "It slipped my mind in the hub-bub of the moment while you were dealing with those buffoons and then I thought it could wait and we both needed some sleep." He picked up the notebook. "Quite interesting. Seems Mister Damon got closer to his roots."

"How so?"

"Quick version. Damon's parents came from what many like to call the 'old country'. He grew up in Hell's Kitchen, and ran with an Irish gang of hooligans called the Westies. He had higher aspirations and used his street smarts to connect the political machine with the street gangs for the benefit of both. He rose steadily until he ran the machine."

"I was told by my uncle that a few of his friends from the Westies are still with him."

Pope nodded. "The Unholy Trinity. A bad lot." He rummaged through his notebook and retrieved an old newspaper clipping. "One of the few photos of the triumvirate."

Kane leaned over. He recognized them from his visit to Toni's office last Friday. The muscle waiting next to the gold limo.

Pope pointed, one by one. "Winters. Dunne. Haggerty."

"They look a bit long in the tooth."

Pope passed the clipping to Kane who studied the three. "There's many a departed soul whose last vision on this planet was these fellows' ugly countenances. Don't underestimate them."

"I'll keep that in mind." Kane pulled out his notebook and wrote the three names along with a brief pertinent so he'd be able to connect name to person.

Pope continued. "Damon always paid lip service to various Irish-American organizations in the city as needed, but his real focus was politicians, city hall, the street vote, the Irish gangs and the Italian mafia. In the years since he's come back from prison, though, he's become closely involved with Noraid, the Northern Aid Committee, under the guise of his newly resurgent faith."

"You say 'guise'," Kane noted as the first streaks of sunlight slanted over Manhattan. It was already hot and the day promised to be sweltering. The forecast was grim for Wednesday: a massive heat wave threatened to boil an already over-heated city.

"There's money in it now," Pope said. "The grail Mister Damon worships above all else."

"Tip jars on bars," Kane said. "I saw one the other day."

"It's the Irish," Pope said. "There're lots of bars."

A woman walked her dog by. It paused to piss on the tree in front of the brownstone. The walker didn't look at either of them, following the time-honored city tradition of never make eye contact. The dog however, gave them a disdainful once over before finishing its business.

"For widows and orphans," Kane said.

"That, my young friend, is bollocks. The majority of the money never leaves the United States. It's used to buy weapons. My source says ninety percent of IRA guns are smuggled from the States. They have a particular fancy for your AR-15. Purchased with Noraid money. Damon is rumored to be brokering quite a few of those deals, since he has the connections."

"And he takes a cut."

"Exactly. Those guns kill British soldiers and Irish civilians. Hundreds have died in the Troubles."

Kane nodded. "Someone told me recently that money is at the root of all wars and rebellions."

"True, but it's the guns and bombs that kill."

"How much are we talking about?" Kane asked.

"Best estimate around ten million a year."

"What percentage would be Damon's?"

"Perhaps a third."

"That much?"

"It's illegal," Pope said. "Cost of doing business. The Provos maintain the widows and orphans façade, but it's the guns they want."

Kane stretched his legs out. "Seems Damon has his fingers in a number of pies, not just Noraid."

"What have you learned?" Pope asked.

"Based on the numbers, Damon's big prize is Westway. I have photos of maps in Thomas Marcelle's conference room of the proposed project. Looks to me as if he and Damon plan to carve up the work to various contractors."

"Intriguing," Pope said. "The potential for graft is sizeable."

Kane retrieved a manila folder from the map case and slid out the stack of photos he'd developed. Passed them to Pope. As the old man perused them, Kane watched the sun creep long westerly shadows along the street.

"Intriguing," Pope said after shuffling through. "Appears to be a two-tier strategy." He pulled a magnifying glass out of his satchel and peered closely.

"What do you mean?"

"One map is obviously the contracts for construction of Westway and affiliated programs based on the current plan. Which means Marcelle and Damon assume they'll get the authority from the Mayor's office to do so. I'd say they're very much against Bella Abzug for the nomination given she's anti-Westway."

"Yeah, I learned that."

"The other map, though, indicates foresight. It's for properties that will be purchased for Westway's right of way, or remain, but be adjacent. One can assume the value of both will appreciate considerably once the project gets the green light. As best I can tell from my brief study, Marcelle and Damon are in the process of buying up as much as they can.

"If I put on my reporter hat, I'd be most interested discovering where they're getting the money to do this. They've already sunk quite a bit of capital into buildings and land of dubious current value. It would take time to decipher their shorthand. But from the glance, I'd say Marcelle and Damon aren't cutting others in on that part of the operation. They must be leveraged to the hilt."

"Greedy."

"I wonder who is fronting the money," Pope murmured. "It has to be a significant amount." He finally looked up. "Is this information proprietary or may I give a sniff to a friend? She'd love to, as the mobsters say, dip her beak into it."

Kane shrugged. "I don't care. Just don't quote me as the source."

"Eminently understandable," Pope said, "as it affects your place of employ. I don't suppose I could get a copy of these photos from an unnamed source?"

Kane considered it. "Let me think on that. Depends how things go the next couple of days. I'll probably be looking for a new job anyway."

"I can't say I'm sorry to hear that," Pope said. He handed back the Westway plan photos. Tapped the property ones. "These would facilitate gathering the information on Damon and Marcelle's current situation. I have a friend who could help me dig and peel through what are obviously front companies they're using the buy the properties, but it would be easier having the specific addresses that you've captured. Perhaps time might be a critical factor, given your early morning visit?"

"Those two bozos weren't connected to Damon," Kane pointed out. "But yeah, I'd like to learn more about what Damon is up to. And how deep Thomas Marcelle is involved. And anyone else. There's an apartment at Seven Gramercy owned by a company called Advantage LLC. I'd like to know who that is."

"I appreciate your confidence in me, lad," Pope said. "One tidbit my source did pass on is something to factor in. He said that Damon is considered bullet-proof in this city."

"What does that mean?"

"My source does not use that term lightly," Pope said. "In essence, he says Damon is considered hands-off by all levels of law enforcement."

"Why?"

"He has very powerful friends in high places."

Kane stared down Jane Street, early morning sunlight illuminating the leaves a shimmering mélange of green. "I'll keep it in my mind." He stood. "But there is another reality."

"And that is?"

Kane tapped the .45. "No one is truly bullet-proof."

MEATPACKING DISTRICT, MANHATTAN

Kane leaned against the wall, the handset for the payphone next to the entrance to the kitchen cradled between ear and right shoulder. He'd dropped copies of the photos in a mailbox on the way to the diner to be delivered to Plaikos at West Point.

It was answered on the third ring. "Riley."

"Uncle Conner, it's Will."

"Hey, kiddo. What's going on?"

"You went to the accident, didn't you?"

A few seconds of silence ticked by. "Yeah."

"Did Taryn have any documents with her?"

"What? What are you talking about?"

"Paperwork. A file folder. An envelope. Anything?"

"Geez, Will. I wasn't looking for stuff like that. When I got there, they'd already taken Taryn to the hospital. And Joseph, well, Nathan had covered him with his jacket."

"Nathan was there first?"

"Yeah. He was at your parent's place, helping set up the party for your homecoming. I was on duty. But the precinct sergeant called both of us right away. Nathan was only a few blocks away. Will, we weren't looking for stuff. All we cared about was Taryn and Joseph."

"All right."

"What's going on?"

The Kid came in, smiling and bopping. He paused when he didn't see Kane in his usual spot, then spotted him by the phone and waved. Kane gestured for him to go to the booth.

"I'm checking on something. I gotta go. I'll talk to you later."

"Will?"

Kane hung up and sat in the booth. Pulled a five off his money clip and passed it to the Kid. He put the paper next to his map case on the table. "Thanks."

"How'd you like the GT?" the Kid asked.

"The what?"

"The car."

"Oh. It was nice."

"The music?"

Kane extracted the tape from his shirt pocket. "Sorry. Didn't get a chance to listen to it."

The Kid was crestfallen.

Morticia slid over, depositing coffee, water/two cubes. "Would you like anything, sweetie?" she asked the Kid.

"No thanks," the Kid said. "Long night. Gotta get some sleep."

"Where do you live?" Kane asked.

The Kid's eyes grew guarded. "Not far. Usually Tribeca in the abandoned buildings."

"Nothing certain?"

The Kid laughed. "Nah. Can't afford rent. I crash where I can."

"Why are you asking?" Morticia challenged Kane.

"I was making conversation," Kane said. "But, Kid, if you ever need a place, 233 Jane Street. The bed is always free in the basement bedroom. The old man upstairs is there most of the time. Name's Pope. He's a good guy. He can let you in. But it's probably not the safest right now. I've had some not so good people show up there recently."

"You've had some not so good people show up here," Morticia threw in. "You're becoming popular with the not so good crowd."

"Okay," the Kid said tentatively.

Kane waited until Morticia moved off to serve a table on the far side. "Listen, you know someone who can take care of a car?"

"'Take care of?'" The Kid repeated.

"Make it disappear."

"You mean a stolen car?"

"Not stolen," Kane said. "Dispossessed and the owners won't need it anymore."

"Yeah, I know a chop shop," the Kid said.

Kane pulled out the keys. "Cadillac. It's parked on Jane Street, near Greenwich."

"They'll pay for it," the Kid said, taking the keys.

"Keep whatever you get," Kane said.

"Thanks," the Kid said, edging out of the seat. He scurried out of the diner, leaving the cassette on the table.

"You should at least have listened to the music," Morticia said. She picked up the cassette. "Oh, the Ramones. You'll like this. A new sound."

Kane fought a flinch as she slipped it back in his shirt pocket. "I got a lot going on, as you've noted."

"It's not going to get better," Morticia said as Toni entered via the Washington Street door.

"Coffee black?" Morticia asked Toni as she walked by.

Toni nodded. "Thanks." She sat across from Kane and removed her sunglasses. "How do things stand with Strong?"

"We have an understanding," Kane said.

Toni raised an eyebrow. "Care to share?"

"Strong and I made a pact to exchange the truth," Kane said. "It's more than I can say for most people in my life."

Toni's eyes narrowed. "My personal life is my business."

"It is," Kane agreed. "What's going on with Westway and your father and Sean Damon?"

Morticia placed a cup of coffee in front of Toni and moved away. Not very far.

"That's not your business," Toni said.

"Are you involved in it? Damon was at the firm the other morning. When you had to go to the conference room."

"Again. Not your business."

"I can't help you if I don't know what's going on," Kane said.

"Will, the list of things you haven't been able to help with is quite long."

"As long as the list of things I don't know about."

"Longer."

Kane didn't say anything.

"You haven't asked why I'm here," Toni said.

"No. I haven't."

"Mrs. Delgado is in the hospital."

Kane waited for the rest.

"She was beaten," Toni said.

"How do you feel about that?"

Toni blinked. "What?"

"Mrs. Delgado getting beaten," Kane said. "How do you feel about that?"

"It's terrible," Toni said.

"Do you feel responsible?"

"No. And you haven't asked me who did it."

"I assume Alfonso Delgado," Kane said. "Did she tell you?"

"I saw her briefly in the ER. She told me, but she won't tell the cops."

"Why not?"

"Because the mob doesn't invite the police into their business," Toni said.

"Has she informed her father, Don Cappucci?" Kane asked.

"I don't know."

"But she will or already did since you talked to her."

"Most likely."

The pay phone rang. On the third ring, Thao exited the kitchen and answered. He began writing five letter blocks on a meal ticket as he listened.

"So she won't need a divorce," Kane said. "Case closed."

"What is wrong with you?" Toni demanded.

Thao handed two meal tickets to Morticia.

"You haven't been to your office yet, have you?" Kane asked Toni.

"No. I stopped by here on my way. To let you know."

"What hospital is she in?"

"Mount Sinai."

"Same as Farrah."

Toni blinked. "What happened to Farrah?"

Kane removed his two ice pellets and dropped them in his coffee. "She was beaten. Seems to be catching."

"What's wrong, Will?"

"That's a long list too, Toni. The short list is what is right?" He took a sip of coffee, put the mug down and leaned back in the booth. His shoulders drooped and he rolled his head back, eyes half-closed. "The doorman's son at Gramercy? Malcolm. Did you ever meet him?"

"I don't know."

"You'd know. He had no legs. Ran the elevator from his wheelchair."

"You used the past tense again."

"He's dead."

"Fuck," Toni said.

"Sean Damon shot him, after he beat Farrah. Surprised you haven't heard. Given your father is his lawyer."

Toni also sat back against the worn vinyl.

"Those years I went missing?" Kane said. "I went quite a few places. Did a lot of different things. Spent a lot of time trying to forget. There's only one way that really works and since I'm here, you can assume I didn't succeed on that path. I tried, but in ineffectual ways. Drugs, alcohol, stupid fights in bad places. Which means I was either a coward or it wasn't to be my path, at least according to Thao. So I cleaned up and I spent time learning from the masters."

"To meditate?"

"No. I learned what you saw the other day with Cibosky. I thought it might help with my anger issues."

"Doesn't seem to have."

"Oh, you'd be surprised."

"You feel better?"

"No," Kane said. "And nobody is going to feel better now either."

"What does that mean?"

"Whatever you want it to," Kane said. "To be honest, I'm not sure. Yet. But too many people are pushing me, too hard. I shouldn't have come back to the States. Especially not to the city. Too many ghosts. I thought I might be able to fit back into society in some way. I'm leaning toward that being an error."

"Get off your weepy wagon, Will," Toni said. "We've all had tough times. We've all suffered losses. We've all known pain. You. Me. The waitress who is trying to listen in." Toni slid out of the booth. She leaned over so only Kane could hear. "You don't know me. You don't know the things I've gone through. Just as I don't know a lot about you. But grant me one thing. It's something I've given to you from the start."

"What's that?" Kane asked.

"Respect without having to know." Toni walked out without looking at Morticia or back at Kane.

"I'm sorry," Morticia said.

"For listening in?"

"Nah," Morticia said. "It's a public place. She could have called you into chambers or whatever it is lawyers do if she wanted privacy. I'm apologizing for being hard on you. That was nice of you to tell the Kid where you live and offer it."

"You don't know his real name either, do you?" Kane said.

"Oh, I know it," Morticia said. "It's his prerogative whether he wants to tell you or not. You know why you don't remember people's names, Kane?"

"Why?"

"You don't care that much about them."

"I thought you weren't going to be hard on me?"

"I apologized past tense," Morticia said. "Besides, that's not being hard on you. It's advice. You can change that."

"What's your real name?"

"Nice try."

"Did Toni help your friend?"

Morticia grew guarded. "Sort of. Why? What did she say to you?"

"Nothing," Kane said. "Actually, the same as you. That I don't know anybody's name."

"As I said. You can fix that."

"Not if they won't tell me their names."

Morticia held up the meal tickets. "More cryptic messages from Thao. These things don't make sense. One is from yesterday."

Kane took the tickets. "You get into everyone's stuff, don't you?"

"Only when I'm put in the middle of it. What's with the blocks of letters?"

Kane put the tickets on the table and pulled out his notebook, opening to the trigraph. "It's a secure commo system we use in Special Forces." He tapped the notepad. "Thao has this trigraph memorized. I've got to use one. Sort of like I need this to keep track of names."

"Names are easier," Morticia said.

"True."

"Thao's a genius isn't he?"

Kane nodded. "Yeah. He's got special talents."

"Why's he a cook?"

"Why are you a waitress?" Kane shot back. "He's studying to be more."

"Good for him," Morticia said. "And your friend, Toni? She's too thin. Probably cocaine."

"It is cocaine," Kane agreed. "And stress. Any other words of wisdom?"

"Take care of yourself, Kane. This place would be boring without you." Morticia glided away to serve some new customers.

MOUNT SINIA HOSPITAL, MANHATTAN

A hospital can be approached as a beacon of healing and hope or a pit of pain and death. Kane leaned toward the latter. He avoided them as much as possible. As a child the few times his mother had been in the hospital, he'd gotten nauseous, even running out once. He'd been chased down by his father, who'd publicly castigated him in the lobby.

That hadn't helped his attitude toward hospitals.

Neither had his own hospital stay after his first tour.

Farrah and Sofia Delgado were on different floors. Kane checked on Farrah first. She shared a room with three other women, all in various stages of battering. Her eyes were closed. Her face had been scrubbed of makeup and she was lost in the hospital gown and blanket. Kane paused, staring at her for several seconds.

She opened her eyelids. "I saw you coming. I was hoping you'd keep going." Her brow was covered in sweat.

He sat down on a chair next to the bed. "Why is that?"

"I don't want to cause anyone else trouble." She wasn't focused, the pain meds on top of withdrawal.

"You'd have to get in line. And you'd be pretty far back."

Farrah sighed, then winced. "They kept me here. My back is worse than I thought. He really laid into me."

"Sean Damon."

Farrah nodded. "But you can't tell the cops!"

"They know," Kane said, realizing she couldn't recall some of what happened. "He killed Malcolm. But he's claiming self-defense. Nothing will come of it."

"Oh," Farrah sighed defeat. She gathered some strength. "Don't you do nothing!"

"I'm here to see how you're feeling," Kane said.

"How is James?" Farrah asked. "Malcolm was everything to him."

Kane wiped her forehead with a hand towel. "Are you detoxing?"

She closed her eyes tight. A single tear appeared at edge of each eye. A terse nod. "It's not too bad. I wasn't using much. The hospital meds are hitting me more than anything else. Hard to stay awake."

"Malcolm was supplying you?"

Another terse nod.

"Is that why Damon beat you? Because you were using?"

Her eyes opened. "I was sloppy. He saw a needle mark. I crossed the line."

"His line. Did you tell him Malcolm was your supplier?"

She looked away. "Not at first. But then it hurt so bad. I tried to defend myself like you said. I cut him a few times, but he got the knife. And really laid into me. I finally told him. Then he went out and I heard the shots a little bit later. I was hoping it was you shooting. And you'd killed him."

"He ambushed Malcolm," Kane said. "The way it must have played out is he called for the elevator, backed up holding the gun ready and when Malcolm drew his, killed him."

"I'm so sorry," Farrah whispered.

"You didn't kill him," Kane said. "Malcolm died years ago. He was just hanging on." He reached out and awkwardly took her hand in his. "I got in trouble asking this the other day, but how old are you?"

She looked down. "Nineteen."

"For real?"

"For real."

"How long have you been working for Damon?"

"Two and a half years."

"Okay. Were you saving money, like you said?"

"I tried," Farrah said. "I had a stash. Six thousand, four hundred, and thirty-two dollars."

"Damon found it." Kane made it a statement.

"How did you know?"

"Were you using before he found it?"

"No. I swear. But once the money was gone . . ."

"'Hold fast to dreams'," Kane whispered.

"What?"

"Something a wise man once wrote," Kane said. "Damon didn't want you getting away. You knew about the camera?"

"Yeah. Film whoever Damon sent."

Kane pulled a picture of Thomas Marcelle out his map case. "This guy?"

"No."

Another picture. "His daughter, Toni?"

"No. Always men. But some of the men, Damon would tell me to bring in a friend. Sometimes another girl. Sometimes a guy. You'd be surprised how many of them wanted a guy."

"Not really," Kane said. "Was one of them a tall, thin, red-head guy? New Zealander?"

She shook her head. "I think I'd remember someone like that."

But Kane caught the shift in her eyes. "Is he the one who choked you?"

"Told you. Nobody like that was a client."

"What happened to the films?" Kane asked.

"Damon or one of those creepy old guys who work for him would get them. At least once a week. Sometimes right after if it was someone special, I guess."

"Do you know the names of the people he had you entertain?"

"A few told me, but not many. I can't give you names, Will. He'll kill me."

"He'll kill you one way or the other. Eventually."

"No. He's promised to give back the money. Six more months. Then I get the money and I can leave."

"Why would you believe him?" Kane asked.

"There was a girl in the apartment before me. Tammy. She taught me how to use the camera. Other stuff I needed to know. She said her time was up once I was ready. And she did leave. So I'll train my replacement and leave. Just six months. I can do six months."

"Ever hear from Tammy again?" Kane asked.

Farrah closed her eyes and swallowed back a sob. Her hand tightened inside his. "Oh, Will. What am I going to do?"

"How long is the hospital keeping you?"

"They said they'd let me out tomorrow."

"Where's home?" Kane asked.

"I can't go back there," Farrah said. "I'll die there. Just differently."

"Ever been to North Carolina?" Kane asked.

She shook her head. "What's in North Carolina?"

"I know some people there. Good people. Families. They'll take you in for a while. Help you get a job. A place to stay. Of your own."

"I've got nothing to—" Farrah stopped as Kane let go of her and reached into a pocket. He pulled out a thick envelope and held it in front of her.

"Five thousand. I'll add one thousand, four hundred and thirty-two dollars to it. But we need to leave now."

Farrah indicated the IV drip. "I'm hooked up. And they said they had to put on different bandages before I can leave. I don't think I can walk."

Kane frowned. "All right. It will take me a little time to set this up anyway. I'll be here tomorrow morning, early, before dawn, and get you checked out. I'll have the money and a bus ticket to Fayetteville, North Carolina. I'll take you to the Port Authority even if I have to carry you. Someone will meet you when you get to Fayetteville." He put the money back in his pocket. "Yes or no?"

Farrah whispered: "Yes." Her eyelids were drooping.

Kane stood, gently removing his hand from hers. "Good. Everything's going to be all right. I promise. Get some sleep." He walked out without looking back.

Took the elevator up two floors. Mrs. Sofia Delgado, the former and once more Sofia Cappucci, mafia debutante, was in a private room. A no-neck very big guy in a tailored black suit was outside the door. He was several degrees up from Delgado's crew in terms of obstacle and could get in Studio 54 guarding the right person.

As Kane considered ploys for talking his way past, the door opened and Detective Strong exited. He spotted Kane and changed course toward him.

"What are you doing here?" Strong took Kane by the elbow and moved him out of earshot of the muscle.

"I checked on Farrah."

"The hooker. She didn't tell me anything more." Strong reached into a pocket and pulled out the boot knife. "You want this back?"

Kane took it. "The case is closed?"

"It never opened." Strong nodded toward the bodyguard. "What do you want with Mrs. Delgado?"

"I was going to ask her where I might find her husband," Kane said.

Strong snorted. "You really are a funny guy, Kane. You're like a combination of your uncle's. All the worst parts. Didn't you get anything from your father's side of the family?"

"A lot of anger. Toni Marcelle says Mrs. Delgado told her that her husband beat her."

"I'm sure he did," Strong said. "But those people don't talk to my people. They handle their own problems. I'd say the Delgado divorce case is no longer a case."

"Where's Delgado?"

"Who knows?" Strong said. "If he's smart, he's on a plane out of the country. More likely, though, in the East River. Old Man Cappucci was here earlier. He was in a rage. Made enough commotion the cop assigned to the hospital had to come up. Recognized him. Called it in. I came over, since all of this bullshit seems connected." He pointed at Kane. "With you in the center."

"I'm not in the center," Kane said. "I'm sort of underneath it all and catching the shit that drops."

Strong smiled. "A more apt description."

"Mrs. Delgado didn't tell you anything?"

"Said she tripped and fell down the stairs. That's it."

"Not much law going on with any of this," Kane observed.

Strong stared at him for several seconds. "You got a point, Kane. I told you that the other day. Don't push it. Eventually the law catches up to everyone."

"I don't think so. You're an idealist, Strong. Which isn't good for your profession."

"I'm not an idealist," Strong disagreed. "I'm a pragmatist. Let me tell you a little something, Kane, so you understand that you and I, while we share some things, we're not the same. When I got back from 'Nam in 68, I wore my uniform. I was pretty clueless what was going on here in the States. I was proud of that uniform and being a Marine. Still am."

Kane nodded. "Gotta admit Marine dress blues are much sharper than Army greens."

Strong continued. "I flew into LaGuardia. No one spit on me like you hear about. But no one would look at me either. When I went outside to get a cab, none would stop. Not a one.

They'd go right by and pick up some white person. The cop on duty, moving the loading and unloading, finally stepped in front of one. Told the driver he had to take me. When I told the driver the address in Harlem, he tried to pull away but the cop stopped him again. Held him until I got in. Here's the really funny part of the story, Kane. The driver was black."

"Is that why you became a cop?" Kane asked.

"Not in the way you think," Strong said. "The driver's livelihood was in his medallion. He had a family to take care of. After a few weeks being back in the old neighborhood, I couldn't blame the guy for not wanting to drop me off there. But the cop getting me that ride? He made a difference. I figured I wanted to make a difference. If I could help just one other person, I figured I could break even in life. More than one, I start paying back what I lost in 'Nam."

Kane absorbed that. "You wanted to be a force multiplier."

"A what?"

"That's what we were in Special Forces," Kane explained. "We were twelve guys on a team, but our true job was to teach others, to build a larger force. We could train a battalion of irregulars."

Strong shrugged. "If you want to use that term, then a force multiplier for good."

Kane nodded. "Okay. That makes sense. Truth. I did have to ask to find out that the line you say before going to a body was from Langston Hughes. But in elementary school, an English teacher made us memorize some poems. I actually remember part of his. Something about '*hold fast to dreams*'?"

"'*For if dreams die, life is a broken-winged bird that cannot fly*'," Strong finished.

"Yeah." Kane pointed at the floor. "There's a broken-winged bird down there."

"Lots of them in here," Strong acknowledged. "I ran the hooker's prints. Nothing. Never busted for soliciting which is unusual. One of Damon's people must have gotten her right off the bus or the plane or the train. However she arrived in the city. But she got a ride right away to the wrong place."

"When she was seventeen."

"I've picked 'em as young as eleven on the streets," Strong said. "I've seen them in the morgue that young."

"Close all those cases?"

"Don't push it."

"Can you put a guard on her?" Kane asked.

"Who? The hooker?"

"Farrah. Yeah. Until around five tomorrow morning. Then I'll get her out of town. She can't leave yet, too medicated."

"You think someone will come after her?"

"Possible."

Strong grimaced. "I see the need, but the reality is it would require overtime and we don't have the authorization for the funds. Son of Sam, your Uncle and his folks, are eating all that."

Kane pulled out his money clip. "How much would it cost to put a cop, a good cop you trust, on her until tomorrow morning off the clock?"

Strong thought for a moment. "One-fifty."

Kane peeled off two hundred. "Thanks. Am I still under investigation for Cibosky?"

"Not unless something comes up," Strong said. "As far as I'm concerned, these pieces of shit can kill each other until there are none left."

"That would be nice. What about my Jeep?"

"I'll authorize its release."

"Thank you."

Strong pulled out an acetated card. "Your carry license. Since you're strapped at the moment, you might want to be legal."

"Thank you again."

"Get a driver's license."

"Right."

"Be careful," Strong said.

"Semper Fi," Kane said.

Strong walked away and got on the elevator.

Kane held the license in his hand as if weighing it, then put it in his money clip. He went to the far side of the nurse's station and edged into an alcove with some empty seats. He sat down, un-bloused the pants leg and threaded the knife sheath back inside his boot.

The other elevator dinged open. Kane froze, bent over, as Quinn exited and made a beeline for Mrs. Delgado's room. The bodyguard opened the door for him and followed.

"*Curioser and curioser*," Kane muttered. Done with the knife, he walked around the nurse's station to the door. Peered through the narrow glass.

Quinn leaned over Sofia Delgado, one hand on the side of her head. Quinn kissed her, not in a friendly, concerned, how-ya-doing Mrs. Delgado manner, but a mirror of Toni's kiss the other night at Studio 54.

The door was shoved open, knocking Kane back and the bodyguard grabbed him by the throat, squeezing, lifting him off his feet. Kane reacted, grabbing the wrist in exactly the right place, exerting pressure, twisting hard. The guard released as pain from pinched nerves jolted him. Kane kept hold of the wrist, pushing the guard into the room, the door swinging shut behind them.

Quinn straightened, observing.

Kane continued to torque the wrist and bring it up, extending the bodyguard's arm, while staring into Quinn's eyes. A small bone cracked and the guard cursed, but held his position, officially certifying as a tough guy.

Kane raised an eyebrow at Quinn, who didn't respond.

"Who the fuck is this?" Sofia Cappucci demanded.

"Kane," Quinn told her.

Kane struck with his other hand, an upward blow into the bottom of the over-extended elbow. It snapped upward and the bodyguard finally let out a gasp of pain, the equivalent of a normal person's scream.

"Enough," Quinn said.

Kane let go. The guard scooted back, functional hand going inside his jacket.

"No," Quinn ordered.

The guard's hand froze. He looked at Quinn, waiting.

"You gonna let him do that to Matteo?" Sofia Cappucci demanded.

"It was a fair fight," Quinn said. He indicated the door. "Get someone to fix that."

Matteo left, unnaturally canted arm hanging at his side.

Quinn sat in the chair next to Sofia, taking her hand in his. "What can I do for you, Mister Kane?"

Sofia had a black eye, an arm in a cast, but otherwise seemed in decent condition. Her lips certainly weren't bruised or split from a beating or the passionate kiss.

"Where's your husband?" Kane asked her.

She met his eyes. Hers were cold anger, unflinching, not quite a mirror of Quinn's but the two of them were from the same twisted branch of the human race. "Not here."

"I was going to ask you that," Quinn said to Kane, "given as you've been following him. If you'd been on the job, you could've prevented this."

"You told me to stop."

"Has anything I've said changed your actions?" Quinn asked.

"You have something of mine," Kane said. "I need it back."

"Why would I do that?" Quinn asked.

"I'm on a roll getting things back," Kane said. "Thought I'd keep playing."

"I told you not to play anymore," Quinn said.

Kane held his hands up. "I'm good with that, but you're the one who still has the hook in me. Cut me loose."

Quinn smiled. "I've got everything I want. No need to continue this." He waved toward the door as dismissively as he had for the guard. "All right, mate. Consider the hook gone."

Kane walked out.

GREENWICH VILLAGE, MANHATTAN

A note was taped to Kane's door: UPSTAIRS.

Toni's precise handwriting.

Kane went up. Opened the front door. Toni and Pope's voices echoed in the hallway. Kane took a deep breath and entered the kitchen.

"There you are, lad. A lovely friend of yours is visiting." Pope smiled, but his eyes were shifting back and forth.

"William," Toni said, a teacup in front of her.

Pope cleared his throat. "If you'll excuse me, I hate to be an inconsiderate host, but there are some weeds that desperately need pulling out back."

Toni graced him with a forced smile. "Thank you for your hospitality, Mister Pope."

"Just Pope." He exited the back door without his usual name spiel.

Kane reluctantly took the chair facing Toni, uncomfortable with the door behind him.

"You going to say anything?" Toni asked.

"About?"

"You broke into my files?"

"Why do you think it was me?" Kane asked. "Someone has broken into my apartment twice this past week because of the Delgado case. Maybe that someone broke into the firm?"

"You asked me if I'd been to the office this morning," Toni said. "It was a weird thing for you to ask."

"I'm a weird guy."

"Fuck you, Will."

"We already discussed that," Kane said. "We have different versions."

"What do you want to know?"

"About?"

"You want to play games?" Toni asked.

"You're the one doing the lawyer thing," Kane said. "Asking questions. Giving nothing up. Tell me about Taryn. I heard a rumor she filed for divorce before I came back from Vietnam."

"You left your file on my desk."

"Technically, my wife's file."

"You know how she heard you were up on murder charges in Vietnam?" Toni didn't wait for an answer. "A reporter called her. Asked what she thought. She was clueless."

"I was in jail. They didn't give me a dime for my one call. In fact, I didn't get any calls. Military justice is like military intelligence. An oxymoron."

"How much time did you spend thinking about how it affected her? And Joseph?"

"Don't tell me what I thought," Kane's voice went up a notch. "You weren't there."

"You weren't *here*. I was. With her. When no one else was. Not your family. They never cared for your dark-skinned Persian wife, did they? Or as your Uncle Conner called her on more than one occasion—the sand nigger-- which is kind of pathetic coming from drunken Irish trash. Your father barely acknowledged Joseph as his grandson. I'm sure your mother would have done better if he'd let her although the fact Taryn was Muslim didn't go over well with her at all. Did you marry Taryn just to piss *everyone* off?"

Kane's nostrils flared as he took a deep breath. "I married her because I loved her."

"Here's what should really worry you," Toni said. "Taryn thought you could have done it. Just the fact she considered it a possibility meant you weren't the person *she* loved. Whom she married. You weren't then and you aren't now. I don't know who you are." Her fingers began their drum roll on the wood table.

"Stop that."

"Fuck you."

"What about the custody thing?" Kane demanded. "Did she come up with that or did you help her?"

"That was her," Toni said. "And she had valid points. I agreed with her."

"Fuck *you*," Kane said.

They sat with the drum roll for several seconds.

Kane gripped the edge of the table, knuckles white. "The guy who was harassing James at Gramercy. Was that a set up to get me there? Hook me up with Farrah?"

Toni rolled her eyes. "You know what the word obtuse means? Did they teach you that at Hudson High as it relates to more than just a triangle in engineering?"

"Answer the question."

"Yes and no." She glanced down at his hands. "Mad? Going to hit me, Will?" She rattled the table with her nails harder, much like Ruiz typing in response to Monty Python.

Kane closed his eyes briefly, removed his hands from the edge of the table, put them on his thighs and squeezed hard into his own flesh. Took a deep breath. "Never."

Toni stopped tapping. "I know. Taryn thought you might have killed someone in cold blood in Vietnam but one thing she was certain of: you loved her and Joseph. At least in the fucked-up way you thought love was. Is. Whatever. You'd never hurt them deliberately. It was the *not deliberate* stuff that destroyed her. I know you're my friend. You've got a lot of faults, but dependability isn't one of them. That's never changed. But there's only so much you can do, isn't there? Your dependability didn't help Ted."

Kane's voice was harsh. "Don't go there."

"You're right. That was mean."

Kane veered from analysis. "What did you mean 'yes and no' about Farrah?"

"Yes, it was a set up. But not by me."

"You called me to go there." Kane leaned back in the chair, freeing his thighs from his fingers.

"You know what goes on in that apartment?" Toni asked. "What really goes on?"

"Strong showed me the camera."

"You know who owns the place?"

"A company called Advantage LLC, which I'm guessing is Sean Damon."

"Very good." Toni nodded. "Okay, you're up to speed a bit. The next part should have been simple deduction. Damon set you up."

Kane shook his head. "Why? I first went there back in February."

"It's what Damon does," Toni said.

"I still don't get why he'd want to set me up?"

Toni repeated herself slowly. "It's what Damon does."

"Why did Damon give a shit about me in February? He never met me. How did he even know I existed?" Kane twisted in the chair and his hand went for the .45 as the back door swung open.

"Relax, lad," Pope said, holding up his cup. "Forgot my tea."

They both waited as Pope poured himself a generous jolt, then leaned the bottle toward Toni. She nodded and he topped her off. "William?"

Kane shook his head. "No, thanks."

"Apologies for intruding," Pope said. He exited.

As soon as the door shut, Toni explained. "Don't take it personally. Damon learned we had a new investigator working for the firm. He wanted leverage on you, like he wants leverage on everyone in his orbit. Just in case."

"I thought I was paranoid," Kane said.

"You are. So is he. Except he likes staying *ahead* of the power curve. When I was ordered to send you there, I called Farrah. Asked her not to film you. Because unlike many people, I happen to like you."

"She didn't film me."

"And she probably got the shit beat out of her for that. When Damon checked his archives, because *now* he wanted it, he discovered the film with your name on it was blank."

"Fuck. Where are his archives?"

"Lots of people in the city would love to know that."

Kane tried to understand. "Who actually told you to send me there in February? Damon directly?"

"Father. On Damon's orders."

"Fuck."

"That's a lot of fucks," Toni said, an attempt at a smile.

"Why is your father doing what Damon wants?" Kane asked.

Toni looked past him, out the window at Pope, whose weeding consisted of sitting on a wood bench and sipping from the cup while sweating.

Kane rubbed his forehead. "Okay, I'm slow but I'm catching up. Damon has dirt on your father? He was ahead of him when he was the prosecutor. That's why you father cut the deal."

Toni nodded, but still didn't look at him.

"Your father threw everything away just 'cause he was caught on film screwing a hooker?"

Toni finally faced him. "It's worse than that. First, my mother has the money. She brought it into the marriage. So a divorce would have gutted father financially. But I think he could have survived that. Downgraded his life-style. He would have been fired by the Feds. Even that he could have survived."

"What was it, then? What was worse?"

Toni shook her head. "What else did you go through at the firm?"

"You guys don't leave much lying around," Kane admitted. "Your combination was easy to figure out. And Ted's footlocker in your father's office had the same combo from West Point."

"And?"

"The Westway plan in the boardroom on the back side of the sliding doors."

"Shit." Toni let out a deep sigh. "You took pictures?"

"Of course."

"That's a bomb you're sitting on," Toni said. "People get vicious when that much money is involved."

"And your father and Damon are slicing it up and will be passing it out. And they're buying up property."

"Wait?" Toni was surprised. "What do you mean buying up property?"

"Where Westway will go," Kane said. "And next to where it will be. There's two maps in the boardroom."

"I've only seen the one with the plans," Toni said. "And that was just briefly."

Kane stared at her.

"Fuck you," Toni said again.

"Your father isn't letting you in on that?"

"Apparently not," Toni said.

"And you talk about my family?"

"Have you told anyone? Shown anyone the pictures?"

"Not yet."

"Not ever," Toni said. "You're way out of your league, Will. I've been trying to tell you. The Delgado case is closed. If you have a deal worked out with Strong, then the Cibosky killing will go away. Do *not* get involved with my father or Damon or Westway."

"Or you?" Kane asked, "You're in on the Westway contracts, right?"

"I'm not *in* on anything," Toni said. "Told you. I've set up my own place."

"You're the second woman who's said that to me today," Kane said. "That she has a plan to get out. Her plan didn't work well."

"Burn the photos," Toni said. "Destroy the negatives. Do not send to your fucking cut out."

"Who else knew?" Kane asked.

"Knew what?"

"About Taryn filing for custody and the divorce? Who else knew?"

"Whoever she told. I certainly didn't tell anyone."

"Except Mrs. Ruiz," Kane said.

"I trust her."

"Yeah, but now I know why she doesn't like me. You know who I saw this morning at the hospital?"

"Farrah."

"And Mrs. Delgado," Kane said. "Know who was with her?"

Toni folded her arms across her chest.

Kane gave it a few more seconds, but she didn't bite. "Quinn. The Cappucci family enforcer. And he was kissing her. Much like you were at Studio 54. Seems Mrs. Delgado, or we should say Ms. Cappucci now, gets around."

"So?"

"You don't care?"

"Why should I?"

"I assume the Cappucci family is in on Westway?"

"They get some contracts. Everyone gets a taste. Which is why you need to stay away and burn those pictures. This is so much bigger than father and I."

"Yeah. I'm picking up on that. Did you tell Sofia Cappucci about me? That I was on the case?"

"We already discussed that."

"We discussed it before I knew that both you and Quinn were fucking her."

"Technically, I'm not fucking her."

"I'm not in the mood for bullshit," Kane said. "Here's the thing. I wondered how Quinn knew about me. About the Army.

More importantly about Taryn and Joseph. And now I know, don't I?"

For the first time Toni didn't meet his eyes. "I might have said something. I honestly can't recall."

"Because you were high on cocaine? Drunk on champagne?"

"I think we're done here."

"Hold on." Kane backtracked. "Was Taryn going to serve me at the airport?"

"I don't know," Toni said. "Really. I don't." Her shoulders slumped, but she met his eyes. "She might not have served you at all. She might have torn it up. She was going to make her decision when she met you. What she felt when she finally saw you. It was hard for everyone."

"Really?"

"Really," Toni said, fire sparking in her eyes. "Don't fuck with Damon. I'm not 'going along' with Westway, Will. That would be like saying you went along by going up Hill 1338 or the next worthless hill where you got shot six months later."

"I'm going to be sick," Kane said. "Excuse me."

Toni was shocked. "What?"

Kane put a finger to his lips and indicated for her to remain where she was. He went to the bathroom and shut the door loudly, remaining outside, then moved silently to the back door, gently opened it and slipped outside.

When Pope looked up at him, Kane indicated for him to be quiet. He hopped the wood fence into the yard behind the next brownstone. Then the next fence into the narrow alley between it and the building next door. He ran to the front and stopped. Peered out at the tree-lined street. A Con-Ed van was parked on the far side of the street, forty yards away. But there were no open manhole covers or, per Con Ed SOP, a cluster of guys standing around chatting while one worked.

Kane drew the .45 and sprinted for the van. He jerked the back door open, leveling the gun at the man sitting at the electronics console that lined one side.

"Whoa! Whoa!" the guy yelled, ripping the headphones off and holding up his hands. "Take it easy, cowboy."

Kane climbed in, shutting the door behind him. "You alone?"

The guy nodded. He wasn't Robert Redford. A lanky man in his thirties, he sat on a rolling chair, shirt soaked in perspiration. It was sweltering inside the van and stunk of sweat, bad fast food, and boredom.

Kane looked over the gear, keeping gun on target. Receiver, two tape recorders, both reels turning. Radio. "What's your name?"

"Fuck you. You got no right to be in here."

"Okay, mister 'fuck you', you had a choice which way to take this and that was the wrong answer." Kane returned the .45 to the holster.

The guy dropped his hands, his right one angling toward a backpack. Kane snatched the guy's left hand, snapping him forward away from the backpack, while simultaneously executing a short, side-kick into the armpit. With the force vectors in opposite directions, the arm popped from the shoulder socket.

The guy screamed and Kane hit the solar plexus with his other hand. That increased the pain and cut off any more screams as the guy doubled over, left arm dangling.

Kane shoved the chair to crash into the other side of the van. It wavered, then tipped over. Kane ignored the gasping and inarticulate sounds. He opened the backpack. A lunch pail and a High Standard .22. Kane removed the lunch pail. He pulled the spools of tape off the spindles. Checked a cabinet below the console and found six more reels. He tossed them in the backpack.

The guy regained his breath. "You know who I work for?"

"That's why I'm in here," Kane said. "Tell Trent I say hi."

The acknowledgement was in the guy's eyes and his words: "You're fucking with the wrong people."

"You know who I work for?" Kane said.

The guy didn't respond.

"I work for me," Kane said. "I don't have to answer to anyone. That makes me unpredictable." He removed the High Standard from the backpack, made sure there was a round in the chamber. Pointed it at the guy. "Still the best available, isn't it? A classic, I tell people."

"I go missing they'll send someone."

Kane pointed at the FM radio. "How often do you check in?"

"I don't. That's for emergencies and for updates from higher."

"You don't check in?"

"What for? I'm on surveillance for data, not action. This fucking shoulder is killing me, man."

Kane asked: "Where are the transmitters?"

The guy cradled his dislocated arm. "You won't shoot me."

Kane cocked his head as if considering the decision. "Yeah. You're right. You're not worth the bullet." He put the gun in the backpack. "But you have two shoulders." He took a step toward the technician.

"Hold on!"

"Tick tock."

"Four."

"Where?"

The tech rattled off their locations.

"Anything else I need to know about this surveillance op?" Kane asked. "When is shift change?"

"Two hours. I gotta get to a hospital, man."

"It's dislocated," Kane said. "Pops back in. I'd do it, but I don't like you." Kane grabbed the bad arm.

The guy squealed. "I told you everything!"

Kane slapped one cuff on the wrist, then locked the other end to a stanchion, out of double arm's reach of the radio. "You got any balls, you can pop it back in. Don't come back here."

He exited the van, the pack on his shoulder. Went in the front door. Pope and Toni waited in the kitchen.

"Here." Kane dropped the pack on the table. Removed the transmitter from the floor lamp behind Toni, and where he usually sat, and handed it to Pope. "There are three more in my apartment. I'll get 'em later."

"What's going on?" Toni demanded.

"Very Watergate." Pope was looking at the device. "Nice engineering. They get smaller every year."

"*Who* is bugging you?" Toni asked.

"CIA." Kane opened the backpack and retrieved the High Standard. Held it out to Pope. "You know how to use it?"

"Well enough. Is it silenced?"

"No gun is silent," Kane said, "but if you shoot it in here, it won't be heard in the parlor."

Pope accepted the gun.

"'CIA'?" Toni said. "Why is the CIA bugging this place?"

"To see what I'm up to," Kane said. "They came with a job offer a few days ago. I turned them down."

"They seem to take rejection poorly," Pope said, holding up the bug and gun.

"They take everything poorly," Kane said. He looked at Toni. "Where were we? Oh yeah. Whether my wife was going to divorce me and take my kid away as I got off the plane from Vietnam after I got out of prison after being accused of murder."

"You forgot to say 'falsely' accused," Toni said.

"I hear my garden crying out for me." Pope grabbed the bottle.

Kane sat down and Toni took that as her cue to stand up. "We're done here, Will. Stay away from Westway. Stay away from Damon." She indicated the bugs. "You've got enough problems of your own. I don't know what you're into."

"Ditto."

She walked to the back door. Pushed the door partly open. "Thank you for your hospitality, Pope."

"You're welcome, lass."

Toni left via the front door as Pope came in the back, rivulets of sweat on his face, bottle in hand.

"It's damn hot out there," the old man said, taking off his hat. He turned on the fan in the window. "Not much better."

"My sister and I tried sitting in front of the open refrigerator with a fan to cool off one time," Kane said. The front door slammed shut. He switched seats.

"How did that work?" Pope sat with a weary sigh.

"Fine, until my dad came home from work. The beating negated the upside." Kane was staring out the window, but his eyes were unfocused.

"What are you going to do?" Pope asked.

Kane gave an abrupt laugh. "About what? I've got several problems."

Pope picked up the bug. "This seems the most immediate."

"Not really. Trent was just gathering information to try to get me to say yes."

"Are you going to?"

"Hell, no."

"And if he doesn't accept that?" Pope asked. "How is he going to feel about what you did to his person in the van? I assume whoever is out there didn't give up the reels and gun willingly. You didn't kill him did you?"

"No," Kane said. "Trent doesn't give a shit about anyone."

"But he is going to show up here." Pope made it a statement.

"I imagine."

"And? What then?"

"I've got his number," Kane said. "I'll call him and set up a meeting. Away from your place."

"I'd appreciate that."

"You called the diner this morning. Left a message that you had something?"

Pope reached over and retrieved his leather satchel. "I researched the properties in the photos." He removed the rubber bands from the Scholastic notebook, putting them on his wrist. "A number of shell companies."

"Advantage LLC?" Kane asked.

"Damon's." Pope ran his finger down the notes. "Some of the oldest properties are under that umbrella. Damon's had one place since the forties. Surprised the Feds didn't find it when he was convicted but it was hidden pretty well."

"Seven Gramercy Park," Kane said.

Pope raised an eyebrow. "Indeed. You are familiar with it?"

"Somewhat. He keeps an escort there and she films her clientele."

"Ah, that makes sense," Pope said. "Explains his leverage." He thumbed through pieces of paper. "And this one is curious and his second purchase. By a company called Trinity Holdings. He purchased part of the old Nabisco plant in 1960, after the company moved out of the city."

That was several blocks north of Vic's. A sprawling factory complex that had been the birthplace of the world's most famous cookie, the Oreo. It covered a couple of city blocks. Skyways over streets connected the parts of the complex. The High Line ran through one of the buildings.

"It's abandoned," Kane said. "Hookers and dealers own that area." He thought about it. "Trinity. That's what his three enforcers are nicknamed. Is that the only property he has under Trinity?"

"I haven't completely cross-referenced all the properties and holding companies," Pope said as he scanned the pages he'd accumulated. "But I don't recall seeing it elsewhere." He looked up. "That area has a bad reputation. I don't understand why Damon would have bought in there."

"1960? It's not connected to the Westway project," Kane mused. "He bought it for another reason."

"What's that?"

"If it was his second buy and he still has it, it must be important. Did you find out where Damon lives?"

"He bought a penthouse suite on Fifth Avenue after getting out of the pen. Built in 1968."

"He wouldn't shit in his own yard," Kane said.

"Pardon?"

"Damon stores those films somewhere. He wouldn't keep them in his home." Kane looked north, as if he could see through the buildings in between. "The Nabisco Factory is his ERP."

"His what?"

"Emergency Rally Point. It's a military term. More accurately, I think it's where he keeps his secrets." He returned his attention to Pope. "What about Thomas Marcelle?"

Pope extended a sheet of paper. "There are his properties. Mostly abandoned warehouses and pier property on the west side."

"Toni Marcelle?"

Pope shook his head. "Nothing in her name."

"What about under her ex, Robert Jenkins?"

"Nothing. Just property for shells owned by Damon and Thomas Marcelle. Even though a number of them are abandoned or in bad shape, there's a lot of money invested."

"How much?"

"Conservative estimate? Fifteen to twenty million. I doubt either have that amount lying around. They've got a backer."

"Who?"

"No clue," Pope said. He thought for a second. "But someone putting that amount of money into this, there would be a back door."

"What does that mean?"

"A way of getting control if either Damon or Marcelle renege or try to cut whoever backed them out of the deal. There is no honor or trust involved in such deals. I'll check into it."

"I appreciate all this," Damon said.

"Ah, you should really thank Maggie. A most pleasant woman in city records. She is a font of information."

Kane reached for his clip, but Pope stayed him. "Maggie would never accept money. She has ethics, although she does associate with me. She loves the theater though. Tickets to a show or two on Broadway would make her quite happy."

"I wouldn't know what shows to—"

"I'll take care of it," Pope said. "I'll let you know the tab once I procure tickets."

Kane stuck out his hand. "Thank you, Pope."

"You're welcome, my young friend."

PIER 52, LOWER WEST SIDE MANHATTAN

The late afternoon city was somnambulant, oppressed by the surging heat and the specter of Son of Sam. The sun was sliding toward the Hudson, above murky, smog-smeared clouds. Air conditioners and fans were working overtime, taxing the power grid. On streets in the outer boroughs, fire hydrants were open and children were running through the spouting water, desperate to cool off and lowering the water pressure in the system. In the Bronx abandoned buildings burned as owners grasped for insurance money and the fire department stood by, not risking life and limb. The New York Yankees were in Milwaukee defeating the Brewers as they continued to chase the Red Sox for the pennant. The Mets were the Mets.

The Jeep was parked on Pier 52. Vic's was a couple of blocks due east on Gansevoort, on the other side of the broken West Side Highway. Farther out on the pier were two tall smokestacks and an abandoned warehouse with a faded *Baltimore and Ohio* painted on the side. Five large pieces of the metal side of the warehouse had been cut out, including a half-moon facing the river, the result of an unsponsored work of 'art' by a local sculptor in 1975. Few people appreciated it, because not many wandered here. Kane didn't quite grasp how putting holes in an abandoned building was art: with some C-4 he could do the same although the lines wouldn't be as neat and it would be called destruction.

To the north, several blocks away, was the Nabisco Factory. The building closest to the highway and the water was eleven stories high with faded large white letters on top lamenting *NATIONAL BISCUIT COMPANY*. A lower, but larger building across from it on the other side of Tenth, with the High Line running through its second floor, remembered *RITZ CRACKERS*. From the pier, most of the windows in the buildings appeared boarded or broken. Similar to trying to get through the jungle in the Central Highlands, Kane couldn't see much, but he knew there was danger inside those brick fortresses. Like the waterfront, the meatpacking district and the West Side Highway, it was another indicator of a decaying city shuddering forward to an uncertain but obviously bleak future.

Kane stood among the weeds, scrub brush and dirt on top of the pitted concrete as the large car approached. The black Lincoln Continental Town Car was a boat compared to the Jeep. The windows were tinted and the engine rumbled with power. It stopped thirty feet away and the front passenger door opened. A man exited, overdressed for the day in a long tan raincoat that partially hid the Uzi on a sling on his right side from the casual observer. He moved several feet to his right, getting the angle on Kane and out of the direct line of the muted glare of the drooping sun.

The engine continued throbbing as the rear left door swung wide. Trent exited accompanied by a cloud of smoke. He wore his usual rumpled suit, the tie partly undone. The inevitable cigarette was in his left hand. His shades were darker than the previous ones.

"Captain Kane," Trent said, halting eight feet away.

Kane indicated the security. "Do I make you nervous?"

"Your propensity for violence has reared its ugly head once more," Trent said. He indicated the car. "Like it?"

"No."

Trent laughed. "V-8, 460 cubic inch engine with four-barrel carb. It's very comfortable on the inside. Nice and roomy."

"I know someone who would understand what those numbers mean. Perhaps even be impressed by them. But that someone isn't me."

"What does impress you, Kane?"

"Did you pull the surveillance?"

"Sure. Given that you asked so nicely."

"Why did you have it in the first place?" Kane asked. "I've got no secrets."

"Oh, I disagree on that," Trent said. He squinted at the sun over Kane's shoulder. Trent took a few steps to his left to get out of the direct light and maintain the open field of fire for his security. "You know what's strange? Never picked up a word in your apartment except for the other night when you had some visitors. You don't even talk to yourself. I thought I detected some sobbing the other night, though, before those guys showed up. Crying yourself to sleep?"

"I'm never going to work for you," Kane said.

"Never is a long time in the big sense, but relative when it comes to individuals. Never ends when you die."

"Are you threatening me?"

"I know you don't threaten well," Trent said. "You proved that in LBJ. I misjudged you initially. Thought you'd be easy to break."

"You're still misjudging me."

"I learn from my mistakes. You should too." Trent chained another cigarette. When the new one was fired up, he held up the pack in offer.

Out of the corner of his eye, Kane saw the security man reach inside the coat, hand on the pistol grip of the Uzi. "Is he twitchy?"

"He's got a job to do. He's heard you're dangerous with your hands." Trent lowered the pack.

Several seconds ticked by. There was no timer on this chess game for the next move.

Trent finally broke the silence. "I'd love to stand here and sweat, but you did call me. What's on your mind, Kane?"

"You brought me here," Kane said. "By putting surveillance on my place. You knew I'd spot it."

"I hoped you would," Trent said.

"It was a test?"

"It was surveillance. Took you several days. That was disappointing."

"You lie so easily," Kane said. "It would be impressive if it was an admirable trait."

Trent looked around. "Where are your people? Do you even have people?"

"Thao is in the warehouse with his crossbow."

"And?"

"That's enough for you and your man."

Trent smiled, exposing his yellow teeth to the slanted rays of the sun. "The Yards and their crossbows." He made a show of looking at the dark windows and doors, then at his security. "Forty yards from there to my man. Does that archaic weapon have the range?"

"It has better accuracy at the distance than that Uzi. It's basically an over-hyped bad pistol."

"I'll take your word on it. And you and I? What? Doing the Wyatt Earp thing?" Trent flapped his jacket. "See? I'm not armed. Now the driver, that's a different story. And who knows how many other people are in the car?"

"Money."

"Is that an interrogative or a statement?" Trent asked.

"Both. You said money is the key to everything. You came to me because of money."

"I'm listening."

"Westway."

"Took you long enough."

"I've had other things going on."

Trent fired up another cigarette even though the current one wasn't yet a nub. He flicked the still burning one away. "By the way, don't overly flatter yourself about the gun man. This city is a fucking cesspool. I don't go anywhere without security. Hell, cops don't even answer emergency calls unless its officer down."

"The Robert Redford line was a nice touch," Kane said. "Had me going there."

"Oh, we have people doing that. Once you get on our radar, as you did in Vietnam, you only get off it by dying. Which we actually thought might have happened when you departed the reservation in late '69, early '70. You didn't come back for five years. There's a significant gap in your history. Where did you go?"

"Wherever I went, there I was."

"Cute. Regardless, your name came up on the FBI database check by the NYPD. Carpe the opportunity, I always say."

"How do I fit in?" Kane asked.

"We want to know where the Westway money is going," Trent said. "One point five billion, you don't think that gets some attention? Plus, by the time all the graft kicks in, the strikes, slowdowns and other union bullshit, it'll easily top two billion. Has the government ever done anything that came in under budget?"

"Why do you think I know anything about it?"

"We've been having an adult conversation so far," Trent said. "Let's not derail."

"Thomas Marcelle and Sean Damon are slicing it up," Kane said.

"We know that. That's why we're talking. We want the details."

"What do I get?"

"Now you're acting as mature as the conversation," Trent said. He lit another cigarette, tossing the old aside. It landed in a dry bush. A small flame flickered. Both men ignored it.

Trent continued. "The murder charge disappears."

"I already took care of that."

"Bully for you. That's one of the reasons I want you to work for me. You get things done, Kane. It's a rare trait in this modern world riddled with incompetence. How about honorable discharge?"

The bush flared, then the flame quickly died.

"Too hot for fire," Trent observed.

"What else?"

"Greedy, eh? Let's see what you get us first. We'll start with the discharge."

"All right."

Trent laughed. "You should learn to negotiate."

"Someone else told me that, but you were only going to give me the discharge and you already knew the murder charge was dead. You don't negotiate with people you want working for you, do you?"

"No, I don't. Sets a bad precedent." Trent turned and headed back toward the Town Car. "Talk to you soon," he said over his shoulder. He got in, slamming the door. The security entered and the car backed up, turned and drove away.

Kane waited until the car was out of sight, then headed for the Jeep. He started it and put it in gear. Before he let up the clutch he glanced at the empty warehouse, then drove away.

Tuesday Night, 12 July 1977

MEATPACKING DISTRICT, MANHATTAN

Muggy, smog-laced air cloyed around buildings and people. The glow from the few working streetlights was dissipated, murky, not penetrating into the darkness as far as it should. Kane's hand brushed over the butt of the .45 as he stared at the dark bulk of the Nabisco Complex. He had his external frame army rucksack on his back, bulging with an array of contingencies for a multitude of possibilities. He could have worn a clown suit and no one in the city, particularly this section, would have given him a second glance.

The steel centipede of the High Line stalked across 15th, adjacent to Tenth Avenue and passed into the western edge of the Nabisco complex which encompassed the entire block bordered by 15th and 16th, and east-west between Ninth and Tenth. Pope's friend, Maggie, had pinpointed where Damon had bought into: the top two floors of the separate building at 85 Tenth Avenue, across the street and facing the waterfront. It had been the headquarters of Nabisco and also a state-of-the-art cookie factory in its prime. An abandoned skybridge crossed over Tenth between the building and the complex to the east.

"Hey, sweetie, wanna go camping with me?" A hooker teetering on six-inch platform shoes looped around Kane, lacing the air with perfume during her pass. Given she was six feet tall, the shoes gave her a significant height advantage. She wore stockings held up by garters that covered muscular thighs below satin short shorts. Well above average breasts pushed against a thin, midriff cut t-shirt.

"No, thanks," Kane said.

"I can give a you good time like you've never had." The hooker pulled aside the bottom of her shorts and exposed a penis that was equivalent to the breasts in size if not congruent in sex.

"Sorry," Kane said, "I've already got a date."

"Oh, you're missing out," she lamented as she prowled in search of fresh meat.

A station wagon with Jersey plates crawled by on Tenth, headed north. A group of teenagers from across the river passed quart beers and ogled the prostitutes. They'd be lucky to get back over the GW Bridge with the wheels and their wallets.

Kane did a walk around of 85 Tenth. The eleven-story building was dark. There were several entrances for trucks to deliver and pick up goods, but they were sealed with long-locked rusting gates. One was open, on 16th, a black hole descending into the brick. Kane edged in, out of sight of anyone on the sidewalk, then put on the night vision goggles. He walked into a dark loading bay, forty-five at the ready. There was one vehicle: a panel truck. Trinity Meats was stenciled on the side.

A cargo elevator was to one side abutting a loading platform. Kane pressed the button. Rusting machinery creaked and rattled. Kane had the .45 in hand as the elevator arrived with a solid thud. He pulled on the strap, opening the horizontal doors. He took off the goggles as a light bulb flared them out. The interior was empty. The elevator was old, but the steel panel wasn't. There was a keyhole next to the top two floors. Kane tried both buttons and the machine didn't respond.

Kane exited the elevator and searched for fire stairs. They were in a dark, smelly corner. The door was unlocked. Based on the smell of urine and vomit, the stairs were used as a public toilet. He took the steps two at a time.

The fire doors to the top two floors were locked, which was against code, as if anything in this building was up to it. Drew the .45 and pushed open the door to the roof. He reconned it. There were several spots with deposits of needles and/or used condoms, but nobody recreating at the moment.

He paused, looking past the rooftop. The Twin Towers glittered to the south. Beyond and to the right, the Statue of Liberty appeared forlorn and lost in the dark, the torch barely visible. To the north lights on top of the two suspension towers of the George Washington Bridge were barely visible. The Hudson flowed dark and murky directly to the west around Pier 57, just past the empty West Side Highway. The pier had a few lights on but was unmanned this time of the night, as it was a depot for New York Transit buses.

Kane went to the north side where a number of exhaust pipes came through the roof. He looked over the edge. It was ten feet to the window on the floor below, which was covered with quarter-inch diameter iron bars eight inches apart bolted into the brick. Kane walked the entire perimeter. Every window on the top two floors was secured the same way, a good news-bad news scenario. The bad was getting through it. The good was that if Damon felt the need to fortify the floors there was something inside he didn't want intruded upon, which Kane viewed as an invitation.

Back at the north side, Kane leaned over the railing and studied the bars. Sat down and opened the backpack. He geared up. Put his LBE on over his shoulders, hooking the web belt. Slid the .45 in the supple leather holster on the left side. The shoulder straps were already set and tight, loose ends secured with black electrical tape. The ammo pouches held spare magazines for the Swedish K. He looped two fragmentation grenades on the right shoulder strap, below the first aid pouch on bands he'd had sewn on in Vietnam. The pins were secured with paper tape, a blood lesson learned in the jungle, where a branch could poke through and pull out a loose pin, guaranteed to ruin the wearer's day. He placed smoke grenades in the empty canteen pouches. He pulled the Swedish K out and unfolded the wire stock, securing it in place. Locked the bolt to the rear and inserted a magazine, making sure it was seated properly. The bullets were Merrick's 9mm specials.

He took out detonating cord, fuse and four blasting caps. He knit together what was needed for the bars. Partly buttoned up his denim shirt and carefully put the explosive rig inside.

Kane pulled a thirty-foot length of rope out of the backpack. Checked the exhaust pipes, found one that was solid and directly above a window. He secured the rope to it. Took another twelve-foot length of rope and quickly fashioned a Swiss seat between his legs and around his waist, squatted to tighten it, and locked a snap link to the front. All those days in the rope corrals in Ranger and Special Forces school had ingrained a number of various knots into his muscle memory. He wound the longer rope through the snap link. Slung the K over his back.

He climbed over the railing. Feet against the building, using his right hand as a brake, he walked down the outside of the building to the window. When he reached it, he saw what he hadn't been able to observe before: plywood inside the bars closing off the window.

Kane re-evaluated. He had no idea who or what was on the other side of the plywood. He pressed against the building, trying to hear, but the ambient New York noise was too loud and he couldn't get his ear next to the wood because of the bars. A positive was that the plywood was on the inside of the frame. Unless of course it was reinforced on the interior with something bulkier.

The plan always lasts until one crosses the line of departure. A mantra of the Infantry and combat.

Kane could hear Beckwith screaming '*Do it, Ranger!*'

Kane took Ted's advice. "Fuck you, Beckwith." He reached up. Climbed, pulling with his arms and locking the rope between his feet. He made it to the roof. Retrieved the rope and untied it, coiled, and put it back in the pack. Took apart the explosive rig for cutting the iron bars, storing the blasting caps in their padded case.

He shouldered the ruck and went to the twelve-foot high square housing the overhead machinery for the elevator. A service hatch opened with some effort. Kane peered inside but couldn't see much. He activated the night vision goggles and pulled them on. Cables looped over a large wheel above and descended to the roof of the freight elevator, which was still at the ground floor.

Kane attached the rope to the exterior, re-rigged, and rappelled the elevator shaft to the top floor doors. He stood on the narrow lip. Found the manual release and tripped it. As the doors opened, he brought the K up with his left hand, while he had his right on the goggles.

The space beyond was dimly lit, but it was enough to blind out the goggles so he shoved them up, blinking, aiming.

Kane held position as he got oriented. Naked low wattage lights bulbs dangled from wires looped through trusses bracing up the ten-foot high ceiling. They revealed a large open space with supporting columns evenly spaced. Internal and external brick walls. Wood floor composed of wide, worn planks. The window route would have been a problem as the plywood sheets were solidly crisscrossed with two by fours on the interior. There were also small white blocks on each window, attached to the center two by four. Explosive, wired to go off if the plywood was breached. Enough to take out anyone coming through. Someone was being appropriately paranoid.

The aura was worse than a hospital. No one came here for succor. The heat was overwhelming given this was the top floor and there wasn't any circulation. It was over one hundred and ten degrees and stifling. Whatever baking smell had once permeated the place had been overtaken by something else so strong it wiped out forty-five years of cookies.

Lions and tigers and bears oh my.

The open area held a scattering of wood crates, some old machinery. Along the wall to the left were rows of large, industrial ovens. They had wide doors on blackened iron bellies, exhaust pipes extending to the ceiling. This baking space took up two-thirds of the top floor. To the right were stacks of long wood boxes with rope handles on either end that Kane recognized: weapons containers. There were two doors in a brick wall thirty feet ahead.

Kane looked up, checking the ceiling. Metal trusses crisscrossed, wiring and exhaust pipes exposed. Nothing untoward.

Kane looked down. A fishing line stretched across the exit from the elevator. Six inches off the ground. He checked left and right and visually tracked it to a piece of rebar stuck in the wood floor, where the almost invisible line turned ninety degrees to the right, going out of sight around the exterior of the elevator shaft.

Kane stepped over the wire. It was attached to a homemade pipe bomb screwed into the wall. Filled with nails and screws it was a field expedient Claymore and would kill people getting off the elevator just as efficiently.

Kane moved forward slowly, feet sliding lightly, submachinegun stock tight to his shoulder, nerves on fire. Where his eyes went, the muzzle of the K tracked. Fifteen feet from the wall, Kane halted. Something was off. He scanned up, left, right, down, but couldn't pinpoint the cause of his disturbance, but he trusted it as he always had on patrol.

Sweat was trickling down his face and his t-shirt and shirt were soaked. He was breathing harder than normal, not just from stress, but the hot air seemed inadequate.

Kane reversed his thinking, putting himself in the position of Damon. If someone infiltrated this far, they'd gotten past the tripwire, which meant they were aware of the possibility of more wires and doing exactly what Kane was doing: sliding their feet.

The floor consisted of well-worn eight-inch wide wood planks, perpendicular to Kane's approach. He knelt down and while keeping the K in one hand, ran his fingers over the floor. The next board was slightly off, something one wouldn't notice unless they were searching carefully and close to the floor. Barely an eighth of an inch higher. That could be warping from age.

Or.

Kane drew his knife. Put the tip in between boards and leveraged. The plank moved easily. He put his fingers under it and gently lifted. A pressure activated anti-tank mine, large enough to obliterate everything in this space, was in a cavity below the wood. Kane put the board to the side. Stepped over the mine and continued toward the doors.

The booby traps were good news on two fronts. First, it meant there was something of value. But more importantly, something of so much value that only Damon and the Trinity knew of the location because there were no guards. Damon was counting on the static defenses for protection because he couldn't trust anyone else with the secrets inside.

If that were so . . .

Kane looked about once more. Spaced along the base of the exterior wall were pipes painted black. They were connected with fuse. He checked one. Thermal, designed to burn, not explode. This floor was primed to incinerate everything inside to ashes.

Kane went to the weapons cases. Twenty-four. The stenciling on the side was US Army. M-16s. Ten per. A lot of firepower destined for Ireland. Kane took pictures of the stenciling and lot numbers.

Kane went to the door on the left side of the interior brick wall. Several sheets of three-quarter inch four-by-eight-foot plywood were stacked to the side of the door. Eyebolts were screwed into the four corners of each.

Kane picked the lock. Checked for tells. Eased it open an inch. Used a finger to probe for trip wires. Nothing. Opened the door a foot. Checked. Opened it enough to get inside. Darkness beckoned. He pulled the NVG's down. A square room, fifteen feet to a side. Kane slid his foot forward. His heart surged for a moment as his foot hit something. He knelt, reaching out. Some soft material covered the wood floor. He felt as far as his arm could reach.

Kane edged inside. A set of work lights were to his right, unplugged. Kane took a chance and plugged them in as he pulled up the NVG's.

The brick walls, ceiling and floor were layered with old, stained soundproofing, much like a recording studio. It looked like it had been emplaced when Damon had purchased the place seventeen years ago. Kane doubted any noise in this room could be heard outside the building, but there had been other businesses initially established on lower floors after Nabisco left before the building eventually emptied.

A wide roll of thick plastic sheeting lay along one wall. Several rubber bags were stacked in a corner—body bags. Two trestles four feet apart were bolted to the floor in the center of the room. Kane walked up to them. A large plastic bucket to the side held assorted chains and manacles. Another contained various tools: saws, pliers, rasps, and more. A power drill and jigsaw were on the floor next to it. Along with a chainsaw. Several jugs of bleach and a large plastic tub.

Kane stood there for a moment and processed the implications. Added in the sheets of plywood.

How many people had this room taken?

He removed the ruck, took pictures, put the ruck back on, unplugged the light and backed out of the room.

He paused and looked over at the ovens. "Fuck," he muttered. Murder incorporated.

Went to the next door. He repeated the tedious opening process.

This room was the same size, also with work lights. He plugged them in.

A 16mm movie projector rested on a metal cart, pointed at a screen on the wall. Next to it were sixteen long wooden boxes, each three feet in length and the correct width and height to hold film canisters. Five folding chairs faced the screen. Against the far wall was a film-processing machine. The required chemicals were stored on shelves above it.

A reel was loaded on the projector's arm. Kane checked the name on the empty canister. His.

Kane shrugged off the ruck. He flipped open the top of the nearest box. The canisters were packed vertically, a label facing up. Name, date.

He photographed the content of all the boxes. The dates stretched back three decades. Kane recognized some names but didn't loiter. He could read more carefully once he developed the pictures. However, it was obvious that Damon owned a good portion of the upper layer of New York City. There was no going to the authorities with this evidence because enough of the authorities were in these boxes to stop any investigation cold.

Bulletproof.

Kane appreciated Damon's organizational skills. The films were in strict date order, but also cross-referenced in smaller writing on the labels to the other films by date, depending on the subject.

There was one film for Thomas Marcelle. Dated 1966.

Kane shook his head as he saw three with Robert Jenkins, dated from 1970 through 1972. Toni's ex. That meant the operation was working even while Damon was in prison. The Unholy Trinity keeping the home fires lit.

The one he focused on, though, was for Antonia Marcelle. Dated 1973.

He turned the projector on. The motor whirled and his loaded film began to play. Blank. That confirmed the cause of Farrah's beating. It had nothing to do with the drugs, which Kane had suspected; after all, Damon would have preferred her on them as it made her more pliable. Farrah was lucky Damon hadn't killed her immediately. Malcolm had heard her screams and been coming to her rescue when he was gunned down.

Kane rewound his film. Removed it. Put Toni's reel on the camera. Threaded the film. Turned the camera on and the lights off.

Farrah's—rather Damon's—working bedroom. A few things were different but the bed was the same. The mirrors. Bad taste never went out of style. There were no sex toys in view or tie-downs on the posts.

The film continued with no one in the frame for over a minute, indicating the camera and mikes had been turned on early. Then there were voices. Toni and a man.

They were indistinct until Toni entered the room. She stopped and turned. "This is a business meeting." She indicated the bed. "This is ridiculous."

"Oh, it's not what you think, lass," Damon said, off-camera. "This is indeed business. Of a most serious nature."

Toni folded her arms. "Leave my father and husband alone. They've done enough for you."

"It's never enough." Damon's voice was gravelly. The old man was keeping out of the field of the camera. "I had to do time, so he has to pay for that."

"He's already paid." Toni was wearing a conservative gray business suit. "We've done all you wanted. Father took care of your legal business while you were away so—"

"Away?" Damon laughed. "Is that what you call it?"

"Father got you the best possible deal he could manage," Toni said. "The evidence was overwhelming. You should have gone away for life."

"You'd have liked that, wouldn't you?"

Toni's eyes shifted, looking past Damon as the sound of voices echoed into the room. "Who's that?"

"Some business associates of mine," Damon said. "As you said. This is a business meeting. Did you watch the films I sent you? Your father? Your husband?"

Toni nodded.

"Do you want me to release them? Destroy your firm? Think how your mother will react? Or do you want business as usual? Money pouring in. Everyone happy."

"I'm not happy," Toni said. "Father isn't either."

"I don't give a damn, you fucking cunt," Damon replied in a harsh, even voice. A single, out of focus finger appeared at the edge of the frame, pointing at Toni. "You called me. Threatened me. You should have let well enough alone. Now I don't trust you. That forces my hand. But I'm in a benevolent mood, lass. You've got a choice. You can depart this place one of two ways. Alive or dead. The latter, you'll just disappear and not in an easy way. Your father and husband and mother will never know what happened to you. No one will. Or you can walk out alive, but only if I trust you."

Kane had his hand on the switch for the projector. He wanted to turn it off, but he had to confirm. As Pope had pointed out: know as much of the reality of the past.

"Fuck you," Toni said. "You wouldn't dare hurt me."

Damon laughed. "Why not? Your father or husband can't protect you. Who can? You think your father and husband's films were it? I've got something else for you to see so you have a precise understanding of the nature of the decision you're facing."

A man walked into the frame wearing a ski mask and carrying a projector. He was dressed in black slacks and long-sleeved turtleneck. Based on his size, Kane estimated it was Haggerty, the ex-boxer, one of the Trinity. He put it on the night table next to the bed, and pointed it at the wall to the left. Plugged it in. A film was already loaded.

Haggerty flipped the on switch and left. Whatever was being projected was off frame. Toni was staring. The sound was faint, but it was a woman begging, screaming. Toni took a step back, her legs hitting the edge of the bed. She sat down in slow motion, mesmerized by the images playing on the wall.

The volume was turned down, but the screams rose, something Kane hadn't heard in a long time. The begging for mercy, then for death.

This went on for long, echoing minutes. The sound of power tools. More screaming, begging, animal-like whimpering.

Then the sound abruptly ceased.

Toni, face pale, slid off the bed to her knees and vomited.

"Strip," Damon ordered. "Or you end up like her. The only way I can trust you is to have the same on you as your father and husband. Or to have you dead. And if I have to finish you, you'll go in the same manner as the girl on the film. Then I'll release the films of your husband and father and destroy your family."

Male voices intruded on the sound track, low, rumbling, anticipating. Toni was on her knees, head drooping.

"Do it, you fucking cunt!" Damon snapped.

Toni was blocked for a moment as several figures moved into the frame. Three men in black.

She looked up.

Kane focused on were the tears streaming down her face.

"Fuck you!" Toni screamed as she sprung to her feet and lashed out, punching, scratching, fighting with all her might.

Her fingernails ripped the mask on the left side of the face of the largest man, Haggerty, leaving deep, bloody furrows.

In the background of the struggle was Damon's voice. "Me boyos love a woman with a bit of fight in her."

Haggerty sucker punched Toni. The sound of her nose breaking was clearly audible. Blood splattered and she slammed back against the bedpost, the rear of her head hitting the wood with a solid thump. She fell to the floor, dazed. She struggled to get to her feet, blood pouring from her face, as the three men closed in.

Kane turned the projector off. Rewound the film. Put it in the canister.

Looked at his watch. Noticed that his hand was shaking and ceased.

Kane sat down for several moments. Then he searched for two years ago. 1975. He found it. Tammy.

The machine whirred. The image was the room next door with the soundproofing. The plastic sheeting was stapled over the floor, walls and ceiling. A piece of plywood with the eyebolts was on the trestles.

A young woman wearing an evening gown was dragged in by two men dressed the same as in Toni's video. Haggerty and Dunne from their profiles. A brown sack covered her head. She was small, similar in build to Farrah. The men easily lifted her and put her on the plywood, face up. They chained her spread eagle, ankles and wrists.

The efficient way the two men worked in concert indicated it wasn't the first time they'd done the task.

She was begging, crying.

Once she was secured, the two men stepped out of frame. For over a minute the camera recorded her pleas and her desperate, futile, writhing attempts to free herself.

Kane forced himself to watch.

A masked figure entered the frame, a knife in hand. Short and portly it could have been Damon or more likely Dunne. He began to cut away her dress, very slowly. Then her bra and panties as she screamed and begged. He ran the knife over her body, pausing at certain places. He wasn't cutting. Yet. He was playing to an audience.

When the first blood was drawn, Kane turned it off.

He looked about.

There was much to do in the dark of night.

Wednesday Morning, 13 July 1977

PORT AUTHORITY BUS TERMINAL

A hooker wearing a short skirt and halter-top bladed by on roller skates, spinning artfully to give potentials a three-sixty of the wares, especially as she wore no underwear. Pimps enthroned on benches made no pretense at evaluating the girls disgorged by the buses from all points outside the city. People hustled to get in or get away.

Mostly away.

Dawn was a half hour away and the Port Authority was moving people.

Kane escorted Farrah to the numbered slot where her ride awaited. Not surprisingly, there were a handful of soldiers in Class-A's boarding the bus. Fayetteville, North Carolina bordered Fort Bragg, home of the 82nd Airborne and the Special Forces JFK Special Warfare Center and School along with the 5th and 7th Special Forces Groups.

Farrah didn't look like the ingénue in an expensive dress. Her face was pale, dotted with beads of sweat, and bore no make-up. Her hair was limp and pulled back in a scrunchie. She wore faded bell-bottoms and a loose, billowing top; underneath her back was swathed in bandages. Kane carried a small bag.

Kane indicated the bus parked on an angle. "This is it."

Farrah stared as if confused.

"You all right?" Kane asked.

"I'm not feeling well," Farrah said. "But that's to be expected. This is just. I don't know. No one has ever . . ." She shook her head.

Kane handed her the bag. "The money is in it along with some other stuff. Don't let anyone see it. You can trust Trun in

Fayetteville. His wife's name is Tam. Stay away from the soldiers."

"I know how to do that," Farrah said. "I know how to be a nothing."

"You're not a nothing," Kane said. He pulled a piece of paper out of his pocket. "This is their phone number, just in case, but they *will* be there at the bus terminal. And this guy—" he indicated another name and number—"He was with 5th Special Forces. Retired now. Call him if something bad happens. He knows Trun and Tam, too. He can help. He's your emergency rally point. But nothing bad is going to happen. I also put a knife in your bag. In case." He smiled. "It's bigger than the last one."

She looked him. Her eyes were red-rimmed. "Do you think of everything?"

"I wish I did."

She reached up. Her hand trembled as she touched the side of his face. "Why?"

Kane forced himself not to flinch as her fingers reached his skin. "You'll be safe in North Carolina. Don't come back or you'll really upset me."

"I don't think I'd want to see you upset." Her hand was still on the side of his face.

The driver shouted for everyone to board.

Kane reached up and gently removed her hand. "Good luck."

Farrah nodded and walked to the door. She looked over her shoulder. "My name is Sarah. I'll be seeing you, Will Kane."

Hydraulics hissed and the door shut.

Kane didn't move. The bus backed up with a rumble of diesel and choking exhaust. Brakes squealed. The bus lurched as the driver shifted into drive and it rolled from the darkness underneath the Port Authority into the burgeoning new day that already promised to be sweltering.

"Sarah," Kane said to himself. He reached for the moleskin notebook in his pocket, then stopped. "Sarah," he repeated.

MEATPACKING DISTRICT, MANHATTAN

Strong occupied Kane's spot, a cup of coffee in front and Morticia across the way. Kane didn't pause, going to the counter, reaching across and pouring from the warming pot. He took the cup to the booth.

"Do you mind if I join you?" he asked Morticia and Strong.

"You forgot your water and ice cubes," Morticia said. She made to slide out. "I'll get it."

Kane put a hand up. "I can do without."

"Living dangerously?" Morticia asked.

"Always." Kane sat next to her. She didn't move very far toward the wall. "Good morning, Detective."

"Good morning, Kane." Strong nodded at Morticia. "We were discussing poets. Did you know Morticia wrote a paper in college on Sylvia Plath?"

"I did not," Kane admitted. "Head in the oven chick?"

"Funny guy," Morticia said. "We were talking about the time Plath visited the city from college and was distraught to have missed seeing her hero, Dylan Thomas. She hung out at the White Horse Tavern over on Hudson and Eleventh, desperately hoping she could run into him, as he was known to frequent it. When that failed and she went back to school, she slashed her legs to see if she had the courage to kill herself."

Kane blinked. "How did *this* subject come up?"

"We were talking about the neighborhood," Strong said. "The White Horse is frequented by poets and writers. You know how conversations go."

"I'm not sure Kane does, Omar," Morticia said, easing the words with a smile. "Jack Kerouac hung out at the White Horse a lot since he lived across the street for a while."

"*On the Road,*" Kane said. "He died from drinking."

"Finding the gold in everything," Morticia said.

Kane was very aware of Morticia's closeness. "It's what happened. An interesting book but he really wasn't going anywhere, nor did he ever make it anywhere."

"Why did he have to?" Strong asked. "Maybe it's the journey?"

Kane shrugged. "I haven't figured it out."

"'It'?" Morticia asked.

"Life," Kane said.

"Perhaps there's nothing to figure out?" Morticia suggested.

"Getting a bit deep to start the day," Kane said.

"Is he always like this?" Strong asked Morticia.

"From the short time I've known him," Morticia said, "yes. But I'm working on him."

"Lucky man," Strong said to Kane. "This is what happens when my brain meanders and brushes up against another intriguing brain meandering." Something occurred to him. He shifted toward Morticia. "Were you aware that Melville worked in this area on Gansevoort?"

Morticia nodded. "When he was in the Customs Office."

Strong looked at Kane. "Did you know that?"

"Yes. After he wrote Moby Dick and couldn't make a go of it as a writer."

Strong raised his hands in a helpless gesture. He smiled his thanks at Morticia and returned his attention to Kane. "I was waiting for you."

Morticia pressed a hand against Kane's side. "I think that's my signal to leave."

Kane got out of her way and she went to tend to a pair of lingering ladies-of-the-early-morning.

"I'll watch the door for you," Strong said as Kane sat back down. "I know it makes you twitchy."

Kane nodded his appreciation. "Whose body did you find now?"

"I'll give you one guess."

"Alfonso Delgado."

"Yeah. He'd been dying for a while, so he probably got picked up by Cappucci's people shortly after he beat his wife."

"What do you mean a while?"

"He was given a concrete enema, his asshole sealed with superglue, and then chained to a pipe where he wouldn't be found right away."

Kane winced. "Someone was making a point. Where?"

"Pier 42," Strong said. "It's the last working dock on the lower west side, so he was discovered earlier this morning. He was alive when he was found, but you can't do much with someone whose bowels are full of concrete. He expired on the way to the hospital."

"Definitely making a point," Kane said. "Cappucci was acting as much on the photos as his daughter getting beat up."

Strong nodded. "Yeah. Thought you'd want to stay up to date on the body count."

"Is that all?" Kane asked.

"I don't know," Strong said. "Is that all? Are you done with the Cappucci crew?"

"I hope so," Kane said. "As long as they're done with me."

"Did you get your Jeep?"

"I will right after this."

"Let me ask you something," Strong said. "I read the hospital reports on those Delgado soldiers you beat up the other night. I saw what you did to Cibosky the day before he was killed. Why the hell do you even need a gun, Kane?"

"Other people have them," Kane said. "That negates what I can do with my body."

Strong nodded. "Makes sense."

"'Only dumb guys fight'," Kane quoted.

"What about it?"

Kane indicated Strong's massive hands. "The scars. You boxed."

"I did. I was dumb." Strong changed the subject. "Heard you were out at the 109 over the weekend."

"Nathan invited me."

"Heard the meeting didn't go well."

"You cops are as bad as old women," Kane said.

"Nathan wasn't far off base asking you for help," Strong said.

"No," Kane admitted, "he wasn't. He went about it the wrong way."

"Is there a right way with you?" Strong asked.

"What's that mean?"

Strong ignored the question. "What *do* you think of Son of Sam?" he asked. "We've both seen some rough shit. I've caught all sorts of killers, but he's different."

"Crazy."

Strong nodded. "Yeah. But the letters and the taunting. I don't get it."

"There are people who don't feel a thing when they kill," Kane said. "You must have had a few in the One Nine."

"Yeah," Strong said. "But that was war. I doubt they returned stateside and kept on killing."

"Take someone like that," Kane said, "and add in that they get a sort of high from doing it? Ever see anyone like that?"

Strong thought for a second. "A high? Maybe someone who didn't feel alive unless they were on the edge?"

"I'm talking about getting a charge from killing."

"I don't know," Strong said. He was quiet for a few moments. "Not sure this is what you mean but we had a guy who put a starlight scope on a fifty-caliber machinegun mounted on a tripod. Zeroed it in exactly at range to the NVA lines. He'd sit there at night and squeeze off a single round whenever he had a target. He could tag someone out to a mile and a half. He must have killed thirty or forty. Problem was he seemed to get into it a little too much."

"Think he fit back into society?"

"One night a mortar round landed in his hole while he was looking through the scope," Strong said. "But I get your point. Do you think Son of Sam is having fun?"

"'Fun' might be the wrong word," Kane said. "He's fulfilling a need."

"So he's found it," Strong said. "His purpose in life."

"It would appear so."

"You didn't tell your uncle this?" Strong asked.

"He pissed me off first. You tell him. But I don't think it will make much difference. It's what you said: details. Some detail will be the key to catching him."

Strong nodded. "You listened to me."

"I did. As a matter of fact, why aren't you on the Task Force?"

"No one's asked me," Strong said.

"Do you want to be?"

"I don't want to be," Strong said, "but I'd be of help."

"I'll call my Uncle Nathan. Hell, he offered Conner a spot."

"That would be a joke," Strong said.

"What happened between the two of you?"

"That would be for him to say."

"All right. I'll talk to Nathan. He owes me." Kane leaned over his coffee. "Let me ask you something, Strong. You've seen the worst of people on the job, right?"

"Yeah."

"Do you believe some people are evil? Pure evil?"

Strong' nostrils flared as he took a deep breath and slowly let it out. "Yes."

"And what if the law can't do anything about it?"

"Whom are you talking about?" Strong asked. "Not Son of Sam?"

"No, no, no. We're having a theoretical discussion," Kane said. "Making conversation like you were with Morticia. Brains meandering and brushing up against each other. Just on a different topic."

"Morticia's right. You're not good at it."

"You didn't answer the question."

"That's what the law is for," Strong said. "To stop the bad people."

"I'm not talking bad," Kane said. "I'm talking evil. Everyone they touch they destroy. They enjoy hurting and killing. What do you do?"

Strong puts his large hands flat on the table. "You follow your convictions. But remember you have a disadvantage with an evil person."

"What's that?"

"Your conscience," Strong said. He slid out of the booth. A broad wall of man facing Kane. "Whatever you do, Kane, remember you have to live with it the rest of your life. And I think your conscience is already pretty crowded." He stuck out his hand. "Good luck."

Kane shook it and switched sides as Strong left.

"More comfortable?" Morticia asked, gliding by.

"More secure."

"I like him," she said, nodding toward the closing door.

"You like everyone," Kane said.

"That's not true," Morticia protested. "I didn't like you for a long time."

"Now you do?"

"You're warming on me." She headed away to deal with new customers.

The Kid came in looking exhausted. Jeans, construction boots, red t-shirt.

Kane belatedly put the five on the table. "Tough night?"

The Kid nodded. "Yeah. Long one. And it's hot. Going to be a burner today."

"But sunny," Kane said.

The Kid smiled and he was momentarily transformed. "Yeah. You got it." He reached in a pocket and pulled out a wad of cash. "For the Cadillac."

"Told you. Keep it. Find a safe place to crash for as long as it lasts. The car's gone, right?"

The money returned to the pocket. "It's in pieces and parts that can't be traced."

"Good. What do you know about the old Nabisco Factory? By the High Line?"

The wary Kid shook his head. "There're monsters there, man."

"Monsters?"

"The toughest tricks in town. Drug dealers. And worse. You don't want to go around that place. People disappear."

"Okay," Kane said. "You want a job?"

The Kid's guard came further up. "Doing what?"

"Here." Kane indicated the diner. "Work for Thao in the kitchen. Bus tables. Maybe wait on some. I don't know. Thao would tell you what needs to be done. Stuff."

"'Stuff'?" The Kid sat down. "How can you offer a job? You got pull with the owner?"

"We own it," Kane said. "Thao and I."

"Who's Vic, then?"

"The guy we bought it from."

"Why didn't you change the name?"

"To what? Thao's? People will think it's an Oriental joint. Vic's is fine. It's been here for years. We'd have to change the signs and the phone number and all that shit if we screwed with the name. Plus, the locals consider it an institution. We don't want to mess with the locals, right? You gonna ask forty questions or you gonna answer my offer?"

"Can I think on it?"

"Sure," Kane said. "Let Thao know."

The Kid frowned. "Why don't I let *you* know?"

"My future is uncertain," Kane said.

"What?"

Kane waved it off. "Nothing. It's safe here, the work would be steady, and the pay, I don't know, Thao will figure it out. But he's a good guy. Generous."

The Kid laughed. "You're as good at being a boss as you are negotiating."

"Yeah, a man of many talents."

The Kid got up. "I'll let you guys know."

"Hey," Kane said.

"Yeah?"

"It would be safe here."

The Kid slowly nodded. "Yeah. It would." He headed for the door, but paused halfway there and turned. "Thanks."

Before the door shut behind him, Morticia glided over. "You *own* the place?"

"Thao and I," Kane said. "He hired you, didn't he?"

"Jesus, Kane. You're just full of secrets. I thought Thao was the shift manager and Vic was like most of the landlords. Absent. I didn't know you were my boss."

"I'm not the boss, okay? It's Thao's place. He does all the work. Forget I said anything."

"Yeah, like Darth Vader gets away at the end of the movie. You know, you guys could class the place up a little."

Kane sighed and closed his eyes. "Talk to Thao. Like you have about the seat covers already."

"That was just talk," Morticia said. "I didn't know he could do anything about it. I got some ideas. And seriously. *Good food!?*"

"It's true isn't it?"

"We can do better with the sign."

"'We'?"

"And you've got company." She glided away.

Kane opened his eyes. Toni approached, dressed for business.

Kane stood as she arrived and waited until she was seated.

"What's with the sudden gentleman act?" Toni asked. "Remembering your cadetiquette classes?"

"Delgado is dead."

"And good morning to you too," Toni said. "I heard."

"From Mrs. Delgado?"

"I heard. Let's leave it there."

"Okay."

"It's not your fault," Kane said.

Toni lifted a dark eyebrow. "Expand?"

"Ted." Kane tapped the scar on the side of his head. "A quarter inch and I'd be with Ted in Section Thirty-Four. Just would have taken six more months and happened on Hill 875 instead of 1338. That's war. It's random."

Toni was shaking her head before he finished the second sentence. "He wouldn't have gone to—"

"You're not remembering rightly," Kane said. "Did you invite Ted to visit West Point or did Ted ask to go with you? That visit was at the end of his junior year in prep school. Ted had to have already started his paperwork for the Academy by then. We all did. Takes a long time and you gotta get the congressional nomination in early. I thought about it the other night going through some old photos and remembered. We did talk about it in Beast. He asked me why I was there. And I told him. To get away from my dad. No way I wanted my old man to pay for my college, not that he was planning on it. Ted laughed and said 'ditto'. We were both escaping our fathers. He was trying to get away from the life your father had planned. He was going to West Point regardless of you or the guy you dated or that trip he took with you."

"Bullshit." But she said it with uncertainty. Her voice firmed up. "There's more to it than that. More that's my fault."

"The company swap in the 2/503rd? Because Charlie company commander was the guy you dated and didn't want Ted in his unit? Shit, Toni, Ted talked me into going with him to the 173rd. He wanted to be in the paratroopers; the best Infantry. I didn't care. I just said sure. I don't think Ted knew that guy was there. He never mentioned it. Just more bad luck. And it could have been Charlie Company on the ridge that day as easily as Alpha, in which case the swap would have saved his life. Trust me. I've pondered it a lot over the years and there's no answer."

"You've known about that?" Toni asked. "All this time?"

"Yeah," Kane said. "So as someone once told me, get off your weepy wagon."

Morticia came up and put coffee and orange juice in front of Toni. "Anything to eat, darling?"

Toni was staring at Kane, but she shook her head. "No, thanks."

Morticia slid away.

"What are you going to do with the Westway info?" Toni asked. "Your pictures of the maps?"

"What you asked me to do," Kane said. "Nothing. Delgado is dead and I'm done with it. Are you?"

"I'm working my way out."

"Work faster," Kane said.

Toni nodded. "I am. I've already rented office space for my new firm."

Kane raised an eyebrow. "No shit?"

"No shit."

"Tell you father yet?"

She grimaced. "That won't be fun."

"But as necessary as a new office."

"Yeah. I'll do it."

"Good."

"Thanks," Toni said.

"For what? Deep-sixing the pictures?"

"For telling me about Ted."

Kane reached across the table and took her hand. "That's what friends do."

Toni smiled and for a moment the worry fell from her face. "Yeah, Will. It is." She squeezed his hand.

Kane let go and she slid out of the booth. "I'll see you later? I want to show you the new digs when I've got the office set up."

"Sure."

Kane impressed her face from that momentary smile into his memory. He watched as she walked to the door.

Morticia slapped him on the back, a little too hard. "Sending 'em away smiling, Kane. You're getting better."

"Right."

Morticia moved on to serve a new table.

Kane grabbed his map case and went into the kitchen where Thao worked the stove and studied his textbook.

"Dai-Yu."

"Sergeant." Kane pulled a thick, legal size manila envelope out of the map case. "You should have this."

Thao didn't make a move to accept the envelope. "What is it?"

"Papers for the diner. Some other information."

"Why should I have it?" Thao asked as he put a plate onto the counter.

"Prairie Fire," Kane said.

Thao turned from the stove and book and gave Kane his full attention. "What are we going to do?"

"There's no we," Kane said. "I have to take care of something this evening."

"I hear you five by five, Dai Yu," Thao said. "What are we going to do?"

"Already told you. This is mine."

"Do you remember Cambodia?" Thao asked.

"I've never forgotten it," Kane said.

Thao glanced at the counter and lowered his voice. "Countersign?"

"We'll never forget that. Or the other missions. That's why you're *not* involved now." Kane placed the envelope on the counter next to Thao's medical book, took a step to the cook, put his hands on Thao's shoulders and leaned down, touching his forehead to the top of the shorter man's head. "This is personal, my old friend," he whispered.

Thao reached up and gripped the back of Kane's neck. His voice was low. "You helped me bury my wife. You lay with me a night on the grave as I asked. Van Van were very mad with you for that and slowing us down. You promised you would place my ashes with my wife when it is my time. And if your time is before mine, I will do as promised and place you with your son. I will hold you to that promise, Dai Yu." He let go of Kane.

Kane lifted his head and stepped back.

Thao held up his wrist with the bracelet on it and put it next to Kane's, tapping them lightly together.

Kane nodded. Then walked away. As he exited onto Gansevoort and the door shut behind him, he dropped into a squat and put a tremoring hand to his eyes. "Fuck. Fuck. Fuck."

Then he stood up straight and his hand was steady and his eyes were clear.

CIVIC CENTER, MANHATTAN

Kane sensed Mrs. Ruiz's glare as he stepped off the elevator. He gave her a little wave and a smile. "No one expects the Spanish Inquisition," he called out.

She folded her arms over her chest.

Kane marched in the opposite direction. Thomas Marcelle's secretary didn't have a chance to protest as Kane brushed past and opened the door. He invaded the inner sanctum of the firm's head, shutting the door.

"Mister Marcelle," Kane said.

Thomas Marcelle was reading a file, narrow glasses perched on his nose. He looked up, frowned.

The door opened behind Kane.

"You can't just come in here!" the secretary protested.

"But I did," Kane said.

"What do you want?" Marcelle demanded.

"I want you to get a message to Sean Damon," Kane said.

"Get Toni and Frank." Marcelle dismissed the secretary then focused on Kane. "Why don't you talk to him yourself?"

"I think he'll take it seriously coming from you," Kane said. "He barely knows I exist, although he was looking for something with my name on it recently."

Marcelle put the folder down and removed the glasses. "I tolerated Toni hiring you, Kane. Barely. A charity case. And because of Ted. But I'm done with you. Get out. You're fired."

"You're saying all the wrong things," Kane said. He half turned as the door opened and Frank entered, the same bodyguard who'd been with Toni at Studio 54.

"Get him out of here," Marcelle ordered.

Kane smiled and spread his hands slightly. "I don't want to leave yet, Frank."

Frank, a simple but not a stupid man, hesitated.

"At gun point if necessary," Marcelle added.

Kane looked over at Marcelle. "It's my limited understanding of the law that if a man shoots someone who pulls a gun on them, it's considered self-defense. Don't you have a client who just got away with that?" He focused back at the guard. "I'll be leaving in a few moments, Frank. After I finish telling Mister Marcelle some things he really wants to hear. Why don't you wait outside? I promise I won't do a thing to Mister Marcelle. Physically, at least."

Frank was on the horns of a dilemma but the door opened and Toni walked in. She took in the situation and put a hand on Frank's shoulder. "Wait in the hall, please."

Frank took the out.

"What's going on, Will?" Toni asked.

Kane pulled off the backpack. Reached in and pulled out a film case. "I visited Damon's shit hole last night." He waggled the case at Thomas Marcelle. "You can tell Damon he's missing several of his collection."

Toni had gone pale, at least as pale as her olive skin could manage. She walked to the wet bar and poured herself a drink.

Kane approached Marcelle's desk. "Do I have your attention?"

Marcelle was staring at the film case as if Kane had brought the plague into the office. "Yes."

"Do you know about the place where he keeps these?" Kane asked.

Marcelle shook his head. "What the hell are you talking about?"

"Not sure I believe you," Kane said. "It wasn't on your map in the board room so I'll allow you slack on that."

"How did you—" Marcelle sputtered.

Kane cut him off. "I hope for everyone's sake you have no idea what was going on there. Because if you do, you're damned." He returned the tape into the backpack with the others. "To get these back, tell Damon I want five hundred thousand dollars. Cash, nothing bigger than a fifty. I know he has it because he's been skimming those Noraid jars all over the country and we Irish tend to be fucking cheap. It will fit in a single duffle bag."

"You're crazy," Marcelle said.

Toni took her drink and slumped into a chair at the small conference table.

"Probably," Kane said. "You don't have to fire me. I quit."

"You don't know what you're doing," Marcelle said.

"I know what *I'm* doing," Kane said. "I haven't been up to speed on what everyone else has been doing. And I'm still probably a few steps behind. That's why I want out of this." He glanced at Toni. "That was your suggestion, wasn't it? For me to get out?"

Toni took a deep swallow of her drink and nodded. "Yes. But not like this. Damon will—"

Kane cut her off. "You going to let Damon know?" he asked Marcelle. "Tell him I'll bring the films to the same place I got them from. Tonight. Seven PM, sharp. Him alone. Nobody else. Not his Unholy Trinity. Tell him I have insurance if he double-crosses me."

"What insurance?" Marcelle demanded.

"It wouldn't be very good insurance if I told you, would it? Let me put it this way. I know more about what he's up to than these films. What both of you are up to. And there's solid evidence. Half-a-million is chump change compared to that, isn't it?"

Marcelle stood, face flushed. "Get the hell out of here."

"Something else," Kane said to the Marcelle patriarch. "Your daughter is done here. She's opening her own firm."

Toni stood and her mouth opened as if she was about to protest, but she said nothing.

"Bullshit," Thomas Marcelle said.

Kane turned and faced Toni, waiting.

Toni addressed her father. "No. It's not. I'm done here, too."

Thomas Marcelle was hanging at a loss for a response perhaps for the first time in his life. Except for when Damon confronted him to make a deal years ago.

Kane graced Toni with a smile. "Ted would be proud of you." He went to the footlocker. Spun the combination and opened it. He removed Ted's medals and the CIB. Placed them on the table next to Toni's drink. "I think you should have these. Not your father. That's what Ted would have wanted."

Then he removed Ted's sabre from the wall.

"You don't deserve this," he said to Thomas Marcelle. He handed it to Toni. "For your new office. Use it to cut off the dick of the next asshole who whips it out."

He left.

Wednesday Afternoon, 13 July 1977

BAYCHESTER, THE BRONX

A battered metal garbage can held domain in the street along the curb in front of the garbageman's house. It was a small, one-story house on Bruner Avenue in the northeast Bronx. Kane paused the Jeep. Three tiny bedrooms, one bath, a kitchen, a living room and a screened in front porch. There was a gravel driveway to a separate garage his father had built over the course of a year on his few days off. Despite the driveway and the garage, the can marked the possible parking spot for Kane's father who felt that patch of curb was his, whether he used it or not. Kane's mother had never driven a car, never mind owned one. Kane noted the new air conditioner sticking out of the side of the house where the master bedroom was located adjacent to the kitchen.

Kane drove the Jeep past, searching. Many cars had signs in the windshield, ripped off pieces of cardboard with NO RADIO written in marker. That was a more accurate indicator of crime in the neighborhood than any police statistic. There was finally an opening a block away, where Arnow Avenue dead-ended in a lot covered with rotting furniture, broken TVs and other debris among the weeds and dying trees and bushes.

The Jeep didn't have a radio, or much else, including a keyed ignition. Kane wrapped a chain around the steering wheel and stretched it to the eyebolt in front of the driver's seat. Put a heavy lock on it and pocketed the key.

Beyond the makeshift dump, a couple of blocks to the north on the far side of I-95 and bounded by the Hutchinson River Parkway and the river, was Coop City, which boasted of being the largest cooperative housing development in the world. Kane remembered when that area used to be swampland and another informal wasteland that he and other neighborhood kids spent their day in, which even the parents called the Dump, as if formalizing it made it into a playground.

With high hopes, a section of that swampland had been developed in 1960 into Freedomland, an amusement park that was to be New York City's challenge to Disneyland. Like the city itself, that high-minded goal had fallen far short and the park bankrupted in 1964 while Kane was at West Point. Then construction had begun on Coop City the year he graduated. Two years ago, the 'cooperative' had also gone bankrupt due to corruption and malfeasance, another sad tale among many in the city. Failure and despair lay over the area as heavy as the heat wave.

And this was the 'nice' part of the Bronx.

Kane was sweating by the time he walked to his childhood home. Four steps went to a level spot where a concrete walk cornered left around the house. Six more steps straight to the front door inside the screened in porch. That door was rarely used from some reason that Kane still didn't know and had never questioned.

Kane walked along the side of the house to the rear. His sister was on the back stoop, clothes-pinning wet laundry to a rope line that stretched to a pulley screwed into the single tree on the other side of matchbook sized yard, near the fence separating them from their rear neighbor. Kane remembered the tree as being much bigger.

"The prodigal brother returns," Mary said. "All hail." She was tall and slight of build, dark hair pulled back. She wore a formless, functional dress. Her face was pale and lacked makeup.

"Dad still hasn't bought Mom a dryer?"

"The air works," Mary said.

"Yeah. I see he got himself an air conditioner."

"For mom."

"Doesn't he sleep in the same room?" Kane asked. "Where is mom, by the way?"

"Uncle Nathan took her to the A&P a while ago. They should be back soon."

"How's our younger sister?"

"Doing her thing like you do your thing."

"She still playing the guitar? Doing gigs?"

"I imagine she is."

"She still drinking?"

"Why do you care?"

"And our brother?"

"Semper Fi like dad always says." She nodded toward the small dining room. "You can check the wall of honor in there for his latest pictures and awards and what-all." She looked at him. "You know, you can take your stuff any time you want. I put 'em in a box for you once dad took 'em down."

"Where is he?"

"I think he's at Camp Lejeune; if he's not at sea. Or on embassy duty."

"You don't know?"

"He's somewhere," Mary said. "Sort of like you were somewhere on the planet for almost five years when you disappeared." Mary pulled open the screen door and led the way into the tiny kitchen. The house was stifling, although a window fan was trying to move air.

"You should open the fridge," Kane suggested. "Cool things off."

"Sure, and you should come home more often now that you live in the city."

Kane noted the door to the master bedroom was closed and he could hear the AC running. "How about opening that? Not like the house is that big. Could cool half the place."

"Papa Bear wants it shut."

"Right. But he'll never know. When's he get home from work? Six? Seven?"

"You've been gone too long. He'll know."

"Right."

"What's up, Willy?"

Kane opened the fridge. Pretty bare, which explained the A&P trip. Some Black Label. "Dad still buys the cheapest beer, eh?"

"I wouldn't know," Mary said. "I don't drink it."

"Right." Kane checked the coffee pot. It was unplugged and cleaned, ready for the next morning brewing to start their father's day. He grabbed a glass and ran some tap water. "Can I use some ice cubes?"

"Only if you replace them," his sister said.

He reached for the freezer handle but Mary beat him to it.

"Mom still got that vodka in there?" Kane asked.

"Screw you." Mary cracked the tray and dropped a handful into the glass. Then she poured water into the empty slots and put it back in the freezer.

"How's it been going?" Kane asked as he sat at the small table with three chairs.

Before she could answer or he could take a sip, Nathan's car crunched up the short driveway. Kane glanced out, then back at his sister and spoke quickly. "Have you heard from Taryn at all? Anything?"

Mary was surprised. "No. Why?"

"Do you know how I can contact her? It's important."

"*No*," she said with 'end the conversation' emphasis. "Mom needs help with the bags."

Kane stared at his sister for a moment, then went out to help unload the groceries.

"Hey mom," he called out. "Uncle Nathan."

"William!" his mother straightened from her perpetual stoop, a woman broken before she had a chance to become a person, her drawn face lightening with a bright smile. She opened her arms wide and he stepped into her hug. She was short and stout, physically solid.

He wrapped his arms around her, pulling her head to his chest. "Hey, mom." She smelled of cigarettes, home and pain.

Nathan held out two paper bags of groceries and Kane released his mother and took them into the house. It didn't take long to unload as his mother only bought enough to fit in the two wheeled wire cart she'd roll up the hill the quarter mile to the A&P on Eastchester Road and back home. Having a ride didn't change that long-standing routine and cause her to exceed her weekly grocery allowance. Kane and Nathan sat at the kitchen table as his mother and sister quickly stored the food.

Mrs. Kane didn't pause, shifting from storing into preparing dinner. "Are you staying for supper, William?" she asked.

"I gotta work tonight, mom," Kane said. He tried to remember what the dinner was on Wednesday. All he could recall was fish on Friday.

"Doing what?" Nathan asked.

"Working," Kane snapped.

"Hey, I apologized for the other day," Nathan said.

"You did? To me?"

"Boys!" Mrs. Kane smacked a ladle on the countertop.

"Sorry, mom/sis," Kane and Nathan said in unison.

Mrs. Kane put a hand on Kane's head, running her fingers through his thick hair, avoiding the scar. "What if I make something just for you right now, Will? If I'd have known you were coming, I'd have made some lasagna, just for you."

"Need an empty stomach for what I've got to do," Kane said.

"And what's that?" Nathan demanded.

"All the cross border ops I went on," Kane said, "I rarely ever took a shit. They say some people get scared shitless in combat, and that was my version. I could go a week without."

Three pairs of eyes stared at him with varying degrees of shock and disapproval.

"William," his mother finally managed to say.

"I learned not to eat before an op," Kane said. "Just explaining."

"You going on an 'op' tonight?" Nathan asked.

"I'm taking care of business," Kane said.

"Will!" Mrs. Kane said, still stuck on the profanity.

"Sorry, mom. Didn't mean to be rude. Thanks for the offer, but I gotta pass for today. Maybe next time?"

Mrs. Kane shook her head and returned to preparing supper.

"What business?" Nathan asked.

Kane faced his uncle. "I'm glad you're here, Uncle Nathan. I gotta ask you something."

"What?"

"But first. Put Omar Strong on the Task Force."

"What?"

"You're repeating yourself," Kane said. "You said details will be the key. Strong's a detail guy. Uncle Conner said no to your offer. Get Strong on it. Then I'll accept your apology. You know he'd be a good addition."

Nathan twitched a nod. "I'll talk to the Captain."

"All right. Now. What I really want to ask you. The accident."

Mrs. Kane's ladle paused over the large pot. Mary crossed herself. Nathan's face shifted from uncle/brother to cop. Several seconds of silence ticked off.

"I realized something the other day," Kane said. "It's strange the things I never thought of before. Why was Taryn in that intersection? She was staying at her parent's house. It's out of the way for her to be on Gun Hill Road getting from her parents to LaGuardia."

"She was here." Nathan tapped the table. "Helping set up the welcome home party."

"Really?" Kane asked, watching his mother's back and Mary's face. "She wasn't here to talk about something?"

"She was excited you were finally coming home," Nathan said. "We all were."

"She didn't like being here," Kane said. "Dad didn't make her feel welcome."

"You were coming home from the war," Nathan said.

"From jail," Kane said.

"What's up your ass?" Nathan asked.

"Nate!" Kane's mother said. She threw drown the ladle and walked onto the back stoop, taking her purse with her, the screen door creaking shut behind her. She extracted a pack of cigarettes and lit one. She stared at the limp laundry, separated from the conversation, but could hear everything through the screen door.

"Conner says you were at the accident before him," Kane said to Nathan. "That you covered Joseph with your coat."

Nathan didn't respond.

"Was there paperwork in her car?" Kane asked. "A legal envelope? You know, one of those big ones. Might have had the

Marcelle Law Firm logo on it. In fact, it's something she might have brought in here and discussed with all of you."

Nathan returned Kane's gaze, thousands of interrogations having steeled the face and trained the eyes to look at the worst of humanity without blinking. "No."

"You sound pretty definite," Kane said. "Conner wasn't sure about the accident scene. And he was at work, not here, beforehand. You got there before him. What's weird is that the other day I saw a copy of a divorce decree in Toni's files. Dated the day before the accident. Toni said Taryn had the original with her that day."

"I didn't see nothing."

"You sound like Conner now," Kane said, "when Aileen asks him how many drinks he'd had as soon as he walks in the door. The thing is, Uncle Nathan, Taryn wasn't excited I was coming home. She was going to the airport to serve me a divorce and take full custody of Joseph. You all knew that. Everyone knew. And no one told me. All these years."

"You saw Taryn in the hospital after—" Nathan began.

Kane cut him off. "She was unconscious. Had a skull fracture. Remember? Since you were at the accident and helped load her on the ambulance. They put her out in the hospital because they were worried about her brain swelling and had to drill into it. I lay there all night, at the foot of her bed. Like a loyal dog. Then her parents came in. They knew too. Fuck. *Now* I know why they did what they did. They kicked me out. I didn't even get to tell her Joseph was dead. They took that from me."

"She knew," Nathan said.

Kane stopped. "What?"

"Taryn was conscious when they put her on the gurney for the ambulance," Nathan said. "I'm pretty sure she knew."

"More fucking news," Kane said, gripping the edge of the table, knuckles white.

"They coulda waited on the funeral for the kid," Nathan complained.

"His name was Joseph," Kane said. "And no, they couldn't. According to Islam a person should be buried within twenty-four hours."

"That's another thing—" Nathan started, but Kane cut him off once more.

"I don't want to hear about fucking religion." Out of the corner of his eye, Kane could see his mother stiffen, but she remained turned away. "Dad's still a protestant, isn't he? He doesn't go to church, but he didn't convert to Catholicism. Not that he practices, what is it? Lutheran? I didn't convert to Islam."

"Then you ran away," Nathan said.

Mary turned from the stove. "Why *did* you leave, Will?"

Kane looked at his sister. "I was angry."

"At Taryn for the accident?" Mary asked.

"I was mad at the world. At everyone and everything. And it was a mistake, sis, okay? I shouldn't have. But at the time it seemed the best option. I was afraid what would happen if I didn't go away. What I would do." He turned back to his uncle. "When Taryn regained consciousness, she told her family to keep me out. Then filed, re-filed I now know, for divorce except she no longer needed the custody part. I signed it and left the country. What was I going to do?"

"Will?" Mary's eyes were glistening. "That's the past. We all gotta let the past be. No sense dwelling on the terrible."

"Terrible is all I have. I've been mourning all these years for something that wasn't even there." Kane stood. He put a hand on his sister's shoulder. "If you do happen to see Taryn or talk to her, tell her I apologize. Truly. From the bottom of my heart. For everything." He walked outside. He leaned over his mother and kissed her on the top of her head. "I love you, mom," he whispered so only she could hear. "I'm sorry for having let you and dad down."

He left.

GREENWICH VILLAGE, MANHATTAN

The heat was unbearable, rising in shimmering waves from the asphalt and concrete. The sidewalks were almost deserted. The approaching evening offered little in the way of relief. It wasn't just the sun, it was the air itself. Cloying, humid, oppressive, perfectly still without the slightest hint of a breeze.

A summer day that Mother Nature delivered every so often to humble the paved island of Manhattan, the kings of Wall Street, the stars of Broadway, the movers and the shakers, to demonstrate who truly ruled.

The 'note' was pinned to Kane's door with a flourish of overkill: a cleaver in the center of a sheet of meat wrapping paper. The writing was in marker and childish, but the message was simple:

NORTH CORNR JACKSON SQ PK.
BRING WHAT YOU GOT

Kane pried the cleaver out of the wood and placed it and the note inside. There was no 'Don't Bring the Cops' as that was implied.

Kane shut the door and went through the apartment to the back. Pope sat on a bench in the shade, an extension cord running to a fan futilely spinning hot air over him.

"I may have misspoken about England's climate," Pope said. "One should not challenge the Gods of weather."

Kane joined him. "I remember lying in bed as a kid, soaked in sweat, the window open, listening to the jets taking off from LaGuardia. We were underneath the flight path. Couldn't hear the TV every three minutes for about ten seconds as they passed overhead. My dad would be pissed, which was pretty much the norm anyway. I'd hear the planes and think there are people coming and going places. Doing things. Not lying around sweating."

"They were moving and sweating," Pope said.

"Not on the planes."

"True."

They both lapsed into baked silence.

Kane finally broke it. "You might want to stay away for a few days."

"More visitors expected?" Pope asked.

"Probably not," Kane said, "but just to be on the safe side. I talked to the concierge at the Washington Square Hotel. Tell him I sent you and he's got a nice suite ready."

"All right. I appreciate it."

Another minute passed.

"Going prowling tonight?" Pope asked.

Kane checked his watch. "In a sense."

"Watch out for that Son of Sam," Pope said as Kane stood.

"He's a coward who ambushes unsuspecting people in the dark," Kane said. "He'd never come after someone he'd consider a threat. They'll catch him. Sooner rather than later. They've got people like my Uncle Nathan working on it. And they'll have a new guy. Very detail oriented. They'll find some little thread and pull on it and find whatever hole he's hiding in."

"Your confidence is reassuring," Pope said.

"The problem," Kane said, "is that there are other monsters out there, wolves among the sheep." He shook hands with Pope. "By the way, Patience is on the left. Fortitude on the right as you face the library. I'm all out of the former, but I've got the second in spades."

Pope stood, still holding Kane's hand. "Stay safe, son."

Wednesday Evening, 13 July 1977

GREENWICH VILLAGE, MANHATTAN

Kane exchanged a sympathetic glance with the sweating hooker who stalked by, pleading at the traffic, trying to find a paying customer, preferably with air conditioning in their car. A street vendor sweltered under his umbrella farther down the sidewalk on the northern pinnacle of the park formed by the intersection of Greenwich and Eighth Avenue. Both streets were one way heading north and merged at that point. Sizzling air reflected from the ground. Grates emitted rumblings from the subway line below and released even more hot air along with the peculiar odor from the underground tunnels of standing foul water, masses of people crowded together, trash, rats, dead things and electrified air.

Kane felt exposed as cars rolled by on both sides, but this was Damon's attempt to regain command of a bad situation. Along Horatio Street to the south, a dozen or so trees struggled to grow, back-dropped by apartment buildings. Their leaves drooped in the heat, the sap retreating into the branches and core. Kane wore his usual attire, with the map case looped over his left shoulder.

At precisely seven the long, gold limousine with darkened windows and Mercedes emblem on the front of the hood pulled up along Greenwich. The hooker took a tentative step forward but it went past her, so close she had to jump back to avoid having her feet crushed under the wheels. A rear door swung open toward Kane. He accepted the invite and the glare from the streetwalker as he entered.

The interior was dark and cool as air conditioning pulsed out of vents. It took a moment for Kane's eyes to adjust. He was seated in the left rear, facing forward. Another seat row faced rearward in the spacious passenger compartment. Sean Damon was on the right side. He wore a gray suit with a green tie indicating he might be color-blind.

Directly facing Kane was a slender, white-haired man with a Thompson submachinegun on his lap tracking Kane and fixing on him. The gunman, according to the press clipping and Pope's finger, was Winters, garbed in black trousers and turtleneck.

Damon had a bandage on the left side of his face, the only visible result of Farrah's slashes. "Glad to be out of the heat, lad?"

Kane nodded. "Not bad."

"Mercedes 600 Pullman," Damon said. "Only two hundred made so far."

"Right."

"V-8, single overhead camshafts and Bosch fuel injection," Damon continued. "Three hundred horsepower, although we lose fifty of that for the hydraulic system. But it's worth it."

"Sounds complicated."

"The Krauts are bastards about most things, but they can engineer. Got to give them that."

"They also make trains run on time," Kane said.

"Nothing wrong with that," Damon said.

"Depends where the train's going." Kane nodded toward Winters. "Got the twenty round box magazine. Smart. The drum tends to mis-feed."

"It does," Winters agreed.

Damon tapped the glass divider with a large ring on his right hand. It power opened. "Take us for a spin, Dunne, me boy."

The glass shut and the heavy car rolled.

"The reason I tell you this about the car," Damon said, "is that—oh, as a point of interest, Hugh Hefner has one. And the villains in two Bond movies were chauffeured in the same—I want you to understand something."

"You're a villain?"

"Look at your seat," Damon said, waving a hand.

The fine leather was in terrible shape. Dark stains and inadequate patch jobs speckled the surface, a stark contrast to where Winters and Damon sat.

"The trunk behind you," Damon said, "is steel lined. Serves two purposes. First, it's large and very secure for carrying important cargo, such as my luggage, and people whom I don't like and don't want to talk to. A person can scream all they want in there, but no one outside the car can hear. In here? The screams sound quite lovely given the acoustics."

"Good thing I'm in here then," Kane said.

"Don't be, you fuck. The second reason for the metal lining is if my friend here, Mister Winters, has to use his tommygun, he will riddle you, and the rounds, after they aerate your corpse, will rattle around in the trunk and be contained. And I don't concern myself with a spot of blood on the upholstery as you can tell."

"Maybe you could fit a guillotine in here?" Kane suggested.

"I'll think about it." Damon's dark glasses stared at him, face expressionless. "Are you armed?"

"Yes."

Damon pointed at a small table on the right side of the limo. "Put your weapons on that. Don't skimp. My associate in the front passenger seat will pat you down when we arrive at our destination and if he finds something deadly slipped your mind, it won't be pleasant."

"Otherwise it will be?" Kane reached for the .45.

Winters spoke up. "Two fingers, laddie. Thumb and forefinger only." His brogue was heavy for someone who'd grown up in Hell's Kitchen.

Kane did as ordered. Then he removed the knife from the sheath in the middle of his back.

"What's in the bag?" Winters said.

"Films."

Winters gestured with the muzzle, not enough to lose aim.

The map case joined the weapons. Damon leaned forward and snatched the case off the table. Looked inside. Checked the labels.

"They real, boss?" Winters asked.

"Unfortunately for this shit, they are." Damon put the film back in the map case. Laid it on the seat between him and Winters. "Where did you get them? Did that fucking cunt Farrah give them to you?"

"You know she didn't by the names and dates on them. Before her time. You know where I acquired them."

"Where is my sweet young lass?" Damon asked. "She was absent when we arrived to collect her from the hospital this morning."

"Not in the city any more. And she won't be coming back."

"I suspect not," Damon said. "But you'll be telling me where you sent her off to. And she'll die wherever that is. Slow and red like the cunt deserves for cutting me."

Winters chimed in. "Told you we should have killed the whore in the hospital yesterday, boss. No play time on her. Not worth it."

Damon emitted a spark of irritation. "We'll take care of it, Win. Too blatant and that spook copper might have gotten more interested."

"You owe her six thousand, four hundred and thirty-two dollars," Kane said.

"I do?" Damon was bemused. "What for?"

"The money you took from her."

"That was my money, lad. Everything she has is mine. Including her life."

"I'll be considerate though. I'll take it out of what you pay me," Kane said. "Is the money in the trunk? Safe and secure?"

Damon looked at his gunman. "He's ballsy, isn't he, Win?"

Winters nodded. "Stupid to boot. Bad combination, Mister Damon. You're spitting into the eye of a hurricane."

"And there's the matter of the man in the wheelchair you killed," Kane said.

"The legless spook?" Damon laughed. "Tried to be a hero."

"He *was* a hero," Kane said.

"Now, what's this insurance you boasted to Marcelle about?" Damon asked. "Certainly not your two police uncles."

"Where's my money?" Kane asked. It was hard to see out the tinted windows and stay oriented.

One hand on the pistol grip of the Thompson, Winters tossed a set of handcuffs to Damon. "Put 'em on."

Kane clicked the cuffs on his wrists.

The Mercedes rumbled through lower Manhattan, making several random turns.

"How did you find my place?" Damon asked.

"Which place? You've bought a lot of properties in Manhattan."

"Don't play stupid, you fuck, I'm too old for that," Damon said. He indicated the map case. "The place you stole these films from."

"Research," Kane said.

"I'm going to need more of an answer than that," Damon said. He stared at Kane, at least his dark glasses did, as if evaluating a side of beef. "I don't think you're a fucking eejit, are ya? From what Marcelle told me, you're a mite dangerous. Enough to get him in a panic and I'll grant he doesn't do that lightly. Everything I'm asking now, if you answer truthfully, saves you pain on the back end. But you're gonna answer eventually, lad. Easy or hard."

"Trinity Holdings," Kane said.

"How did you find out about that?" Damon asked.

"It's in city records."

"The fellow he rents from on Jane Street," Winters said to Damon. "He used to work for the Post."

"Did he find it?" Damon asked Kane.

Kane didn't respond.

"We'll deal with him later," Damon said. "The list gets longer. I'm tending to believe the cunt you work for has passed her expiration date."

"You already hurt her," Kane said.

"Nah," Damon said with a smile. "She wasn't hurt, was she, Win? Not too badly. Just taught a lesson. She was lucky it wasn't permanent. Haggerty was none too happy with her; took a while for those scratches to heal. So, you went to my factory."

"That's what you call it?" Kane asked as the Mercedes took a hard turn. "A factory?"

"As good a name as any."

"How about kill house?"

"How'd you avoid getting blown to pieces?" Winters asked.

"I was careful."

"You were careful." Damon said. "So why aren't you careful now? But perhaps you are. What's this insurance? Did you take more than these three films? Stash them somewhere?"

"No."

"You better not be lying to me, you fuck. You'll hurt for every lie. I think you squirrelled away some film as your insurance. But we'll find out." Damon rapped on the dark divider. It slid to the side a few inches. "Factory."

The glass shut. The Mercedes accelerated.

"How many people have you told about the factory?" Damon asked.

"No one."

"We'll learn the truth on that one too," Damon said. "You've stepped into very deep water here, boyo. Well over your head. You have no idea."

"You could enlighten me," Kane said.

"You'll see the light soon enough," Damon muttered as he turned and looked out the window on his side of the car.

Several turns. Then the limo bumped up on a sidewalk and descended into the darkness of the loading bay at 85 Tenth Avenue. The limo halted.

The front passenger door opened and shut with a solid thud.

The door next to Kane swung out and a large hand reached in, snatched him by the hair, and tumbled him onto the concrete. Before he could scramble to his knees, a flurry of kicks propelled him to a spot in front of the Mercedes, spotlighted by the headlights.

Kane remained on his back and looked up at the perpetrator. Haggerty, six foot eight, solidly built, and standing straight despite being in his late 70s. He was a former boxer and his flattened nose and cauliflower ears indicated he'd taken more than a few hits. He was dressed in the Trinity uniform of black slacks and black turtleneck. Several faint scars marked the left side of his face—Toni's nails.

Winters stood next to Haggerty, the tommygun at the ready. "Frisk him," he ordered the big man.

Haggerty knelt with a knee in Kane's chest, forcing all the air out of his lungs and accentuating the pain from the kicks.

Roughly searched. Rolled him over, knee into back. Finished the frisk. Stood.

"He's clean," Haggerty said in a surprisingly soft, raspy voice, indicating he'd taken some shots to the throat and consumed quantities of hard liquor.

"Get up," Winters ordered.

Kane rolled over, sat, and then stood.

Winters nodded for Haggerty to move. The former boxer climbed the steps to the loading dock and opened the doors to the freight elevator. The light from the single bulb cast a weak glow into the garage.

The rumble of the limo engine ceased and the headlights cut out.

The driver's door opened. The last of the Trinity, Dunne, was similar in appearance to Damon, just below medium height, whiskey belly, balding, and red-veined face. He sported a sawed-off double-barreled shotgun. Damon exited from the rear, carrying the map case.

"Get moving," Winters ordered Kane.

Haggerty came down from the loading dock, opened the trunk, and retrieved two duffle bags, hoisting one over each shoulder. Damon led the way up the stairs to the elevator. Dunne stood next to Haggerty inside the freight elevator.

"Far corner," Winters ordered Kane.

Damon put a key into the panel and turned it.

The doors scissored shut and the elevator rose. Winters had his finger on the trigger.

"That my money?" Kane asked, nodding toward the bulging duffle bags.

"Shut up," Winters said.

It halted and Haggerty opened the doors. Dunne stepped over the fishing line, disappeared for a second, then returned, spooling the line. He glanced at Kane.

"Vietnam vet, eh?"

Kane nodded.

"You know booby-traps eh?"

"I've seen a few," Kane said.

"Told you, boss," Dunne said to Damon.

"You still fucked up," Damon snapped and Dunne hung his head, a scolded dog. He walked to the plank and lifted it, removed the mine, and replaced the board.

"Clear, boss," Dunne called out.

Haggerty carried the duffle bags to the weapons cases and dropped them with a solid thud. Damon tossed Haggerty a keyring. The big man unlocked the room with the trestles and lined with soundproofing. He brought the keys back to Damon. Haggerty pushed the door open, then grabbed a piece of eye-bolted plywood with one large paw and carried it inside.

The sound of hammering, then stapling echoed out of the room.

Winters kept the machinegun trained on Kane from a safe distance as he positioned him in the center of the open space. Dunne had the shotgun resting on his shoulder, one-handed. Damon unlocked the film room. Glanced over his shoulder. "What are you doing, Dunne?"

Dunne was startled. "What, boss?"

"Point that scattergun at the bastard," Damon ordered. "He's not to be under-estimated."

"Yeah, boss."

Dunne brought the gun level in both hands. Damon disappeared into the film room.

"Mind if I sit down?" Kane asked, holding up his cuffed hands and indicating a wooden crate.

"Yeah, I fucking mind," Winters said. "Stay right where you are."

Kane indicated the weapons cases. "That's a lot of firepower."

"Shut up," Winters said.

"How are you getting it to the old country?" Kane asked.

"Not our problem," Dunne said.

"Shut up," Winters said to his cohort.

"He's gonna be—" Dunne started, but Winters interjected. "Give it a rest."

After several minutes, Damon came out of the film room. "All accounted for." He looked at Kane and shook his head. "What's your insurance, Kane?"

"Can I have my money?" Kane replied, nodding toward the duffle bags. "You can keep the guns."

"You're cheeky," Damon said. "I'll grant you that. Not your money and not mine either. Them and the guns be passing in the night. As you will be."

"I know where the guns are going," Kane said. "Surprised someone gave you them on the promise of payment."

"You don't know shit," Damon said. "I'm done fucking around with you."

"There are lines we cross," Kane said, "that can't be undone no matter how much we try. I finally accept that."

"What the fuck?" Dunne muttered.

"No time for philosophy or theology now," Damon said. "You can spout that shit with the devil when you meet him. See what he thinks of it."

Kane looked at Damon. "It's comforting to know all of us are past that line. We made the decisions that brought us to this place well before now."

The sound of stapling ceased.

"Take him in," Damon ordered Winters. "Put him on the board. I'll join you in a moment with the camera." He headed to the film room.

Winters indicated the other room with the muzzle of the Thompson. "Go."

Dunne tried to contribute macho by pulling back the hammers on the shotgun.

Kane reached the doorway to the torture chamber. He paused in the entrance. Haggerty waited by the plywood kill table, chains and shackles in hand.

Kane looked over his shoulder at Dunne and Winters. *"Life is for the living. Death for the dead. Let life be like music. And death a note unsaid'."*

"Keep praying," Dunne said. "Fat lot of good it will do you."

"Move," Winters gestured with the tommygun.

Kane reached out with handcuffed hands and grabbed a line of fishing wire he'd emplaced vertically just under the soundproofing opposite the door hinge. He dove that way, taking the line with him. He landed inside the room, next to the brick wall as the line pulled the clacker hidden under the soundproofing, firing the Claymore mine he'd wedged in the shadowed angle above the outside of the door. It also pulled the pins on two smoke grenades, one inside the room and one outside.

The Claymore detonated and shredded Dunne and Winters, seven hundred steel ball bearings ripping through flesh and bone. Red smoke billowed in all directions from the inside smoke grenade. Outside the door, a yellow grenade spewed forth, mingling with the residue smoke from the Claymore

Kane continued his dive, rolled, and came to his knees, head ringing from the danger close explosion on the other side of the bricks.

Haggerty blinked, waving one hand, shackles still in it, trying to clear away the red smoke. Someone screamed in agony outside, the sound echoing in the open space.

Kane shuffled toward Haggerty on the balls of his feet, right leg forward, cuffed hands up. Haggerty reverted to form, assuming a boxing stance. Then the big man belatedly remembered he had an advantage: the gun in his waistband. He reached for the revolver.

Kane slid in low with a sidekick directly into the front of Haggerty's locked left knee. The edge of the boot hit exactly and the knee buckled back, tearing ligaments and tendons. As big as Haggerty was, all that weight added to the negative pressure on the joint. The boxer went down in a spiral anchored on the broken leg, emitting a surprised gasp of pain. The fall added to the damage, but that was the least of Haggerty's problems as Kane was on him. A front snap kick toward Haggerty's face. Kane had been aiming for the forehead, but the tip of the boot went into the right eye socket, shattering the bones around that soft organ and rupturing the orb with a dull squish none of them heard as they were deafened from the Claymore.

Haggerty screamed as he fell onto his back.

Kane snatched the Dirty Harry revolver out of the boxer's waistband, cocking it as he stood. He fired the .44 Magnum once, the large bullet putting a decent sized black hole in Haggerty's

forehead and blowing out the back of the skull with a splatter of
blood, bone and brains onto the plastic he'd just laid out.

Kane wheeled to face the door, revolver in both hands. The
exit wasn't visible through the smoke. He moved to the right,
along the brick wall, gun at the ready.

The screaming outside descended to a desperate moaning.
Then a voice pleading in Latin.

Damon's voice cut through the smoke and the prayer. "Win?
Haggerty? Dunne?"

Kane estimated from sound that Damon was just inside the
door of the adjacent film room, smartly not venturing out into
the yellow smoke. Kane knelt and stiffened the fingers of his
right hand, holding the gun in the left. Jabbed down, punching
through the plastic sheeting. Into the soundproofing. Found
another line he'd emplaced the previous evening along the base
of the wall, hidden under the material. Pulled it.

The flash-bang grenade went off inside the film room with a
concussive explosion magnified by the small, brick-enclosed
space. Kane kept one shoulder on the wall for orientation and
rushed to the door of the torture chamber, out, to the left, along
the brick wall and into the film room.

Damon had a pistol in hand, but was disoriented, unable to
see or hear. With his free hand, Kane snatched the gun out of
the old man's hand and tossed it aside. Grabbed him by the
throat and dragged him outside. Threw him to the ground.

The yellow smoke dissipated slowly in the humid, hot air.
Dunne was dead, cut in half, his legs in tatters, his guts spilled all
over his corpse. Winters was alive, barely, hands wrapped around
his lacerated stomach, trying to hold his organs in. Most of his
clothes had been blown off, revealing pale, liver spotted, bloody,
old man flesh. He moaned and continued to whisper something
in Latin. Keeping an eye on Damon, Kane knelt next to the
gunman.

Winters repeated the first line of a prayer over and over. *"Ave
Maria, gratia plena. Ave Maria, gratia plena. Ave Maria, gratia plena."*

Winters turned his head toward Kane. His eyes were red and
bloody around the edges. He paused the prayer to a higher power
for a plea to a mortal one. "Finish me, lad. For the sweet love of

God." Then he resumed. *"Ave Maria, gratia plena. Ave Maria, gratia plena. Ave Maria, gratia plena."*

Kane was certain Winters had never answered the prayers or dispensed the 'love of God' to any of the uncounted who'd ended up on the plywood and then fed into the oven, incinerated into the smog of the city.

"Ave Maria, gratia plena. Ave Maria, gratia--."

Kane shot Winters in the side of the head.

Kane walked to Damon, who was slowly regaining his sight and hearing. The old man crawled on his stomach toward the elevator. Kane shot him in the back of the left calf, almost amputating the leg with the big .44 caliber slug.

Damon screamed and rolled over onto his back. "You fucking cunt! You fucking cunt!"

Kane stood at Damon's feet and aimed the big gun at his face.

Damon stopped screaming, taking deep, harsh, shivering breaths. Blinked several times and tried to focus flashed eyes. "Money. I got money. I can give it to you."

Kane didn't respond.

"Two million!" Damon hissed as his face spasmed in pain. "Cash, lad." He scooted backward on his good leg.

"Six thousand, four hundred and thirty-two dollars," Kane said.

Damon's face twisted in agony and confusion. "What?" His back reached the brick wall next to the elevator. "What?"

Kane aimed the muzzle of the big gun at Damon's head and his finger curled over the trigger.

A prick in Kane's neck. He reached up and pulled a six-inch long wooden dart with a feather on the end out of his skin. The gun dropped from his other hand.

He lost control of his muscles and fell to the floor.

Wednesday Evening, 13 July 1977

MEATPACKING DISTRICT, MANHATTAN

Breathing was a vain struggle as Kane's diaphragm refused to function. That horrid feeling of inhabiting a terrible nightmare and needing to run away, to fight back, to do something, anything, just wake up, but unable to make the muscles respond.

Except this was no dream.

Eyes fixed, lying on his back, Kane distantly saw dissipating yellow smoke and the ceiling. His ears rang from the Claymore, the flash-bang and firing the big revolver. He couldn't get his eyeballs to respond to his will. Nor his eyelids. He focused all his effort on breathing.

A voice managed to faintly penetrate the ringing in his ears. "Well, mate, you made a bloody fine mess here, didn't you?"

A tall figure loomed in Kane's peripheral vision and the voice clearly identified the speaker: Quinn. The Kiwi kicked the gun away from Kane's cuffed hands.

"I know what you're thinking," Quinn said. He was circling. "I'm too late to save these pikers. Damon's plan. Westway. The contracts and the Cappucci cut. That's a crack up." Quinn paused by Damon. "Ah. Still amongst us, old fella?"

Black spots appeared in Kane's eyes as his oxygen level depleted.

"I'll pay you," Damon begged Quinn.

"I'm sure you will," Quinn said. "Just not in the currency you expect."

Kane's diaphragm twitched a partial breath. Not enough.

Quinn straddled Kane. "You were too nice to him. Too good to the entire lot. Filthy pigs, these Irish. You're probably wondering if you're dying, ay, Kane? How's the breathing? The mixture is a touchy thing." Quinn disappeared from Kane's vision as he walked away, but his voice reached him. "You're not dying. It wears off. The headhunters use a certain mix to paralyze their prey. A different concoction to kill immediately. Big tribal secret. I didn't want to send you off to Valhalla. Not right away."

Kane took a slightly deeper breath. The black spots wavered.

Quinn approached from the right and waved a four-foot long tube of wood over Kane's face. "Quieter than your little gun, isn't it? This simple contraption took me a week to fashion in Malaysia. Went into the jungle with one of the elders who knew the traditional ways to find the exact right piece of wood. Not any will work, naturally. No, indeed. Another secret of their tribe. Then I had to drill it by hand and, I'll tell you mate, between you and me, that was a harsh piece of work. Could have bored it in a few minutes in a proper machine shop, but the trick is there wasn't any shop for a couple hundred kilometers. Lots of twisting and turning that old bore rod with my hands. Took me three days. Me palms was bleeding. Then you chip away the outside of the wood to narrow it down and—oh, fuck it, mate, you don't really give a shit about that, do you?"

Quinn was dressed in black leather pants and a long sleeve black shirt and green sneakers. He, and his blowgun, disappeared from Kane's limited view. Another partial breath. The black spots in his eyes were fading.

Quinn returned, rope in his hands. He slid an end under the handcuff chain, and made sure the cuffs were ratcheted tight on the wrists. Then he gathered slack and tossed both ends over the truss.

Quinn walked out of sight with the free ends of the rope. There was a ratcheting noise, indicating Quinn was using mechanical assistance. Kane's wrists were jerked upward by the cuffs, the steel cutting into flesh, but he couldn't feel it. He was elevated, an inert mass, until his hands were stretched over his head, his toes touching the floor. His head hung listlessly on his chest.

Quinn threw another rope over the truss. Expertly tied a noose. Kane could barely feel it as Quinn slipped the rope over his head and around his neck. Quinn disappeared from view with the free end of that rope. It was pulled taut but not tight, the noose snug around his neck.

"Comfy?" Quinn asked. "Don't worry. I won't forget about you." He knelt next to Damon, checking the leg. "You're bleeding pretty bad, mate."

"Help me," Damon pled. "I'll give you two million dollars. Get me to a hospital."

"You'll live a bit longer, old fella." Quinn pulled off Damon's belt and cinched it tight around the old man's thigh.

Kane's body began to come alive, but it was accompanied by an overwhelming itch. He blinked, a major accomplishment.

Quinn walked into the film room.

Kane's breathing was normalizing.

Quinn came out and went to Damon, once more kneeling next to the old man. "Where are your Noraid files?"

"What the fuck?" Damon sputtered. "I know you. You work for Cappucci. I'll give him more of the contracts. Get me to a fucking hospital. And kill that shitbird." He indicated Kane.

"In due time," Quinn said. "There is a proper order to things. First. Noraid."

"Behind the film processor," Damon said. "Leather-bound book. What in Bloody Jesus do you want that for?"

Quinn disappeared.

Kane was able to lift his head, relieving some of the pressure on his neck. His skin felt as if it were burning. A horrible itching he couldn't scratch, almost worse than the nothingness. Almost but not quite. He looked about. Quinn's blowgun was leaning against the wall next to the elevator. There was a large green canvas kit bag. The ropes were new and tied off securely, the up ropes angled about six feet away, the handcuff one wrapped through a winch and the other end tied off. The neck one was also tied to the pipe to which the winch was secured.

Do something, Ranger!

Quinn returned with a ledger.

"What the fuck you gonna do with that?" Damon demanded.

Quinn shrugged. "Me? Nothing. People I work for? Up to them."

Damon was confused. "What's Cappucci give a shit about that?"

Quinn laughed as he shoved the ledger in the canvas bag. "Cappucci? You've no clue, old fella." He glanced over at Kane. "You don't either, do you Captain Hero?" He nodded toward Damon as he rummaged in the bag. "He was my objective all along. Well, primary objective, let's say. Been working months to get to him and this book and set everything up for a smooth operation and you walk in and blow it all up in a few days. Got here just in the nick of time before you completely screwed the mission.

"I tried to stop you, Kane. Warned you. Pushed Delgado, then sent his fools after you. Finally had to kill the idiot. Not 'cause Cappucci ordered it, although he did, but because he was a liability. Plus, I need the daughter to be a widow before I wed her. Propriety and all that nonsense."

Kane swallowed, his throat muscles responding.

Quinn produced a whip in one hand and a blowtorch in the other. He walked over to Kane holding both. He held up the whip so Kane could see. "Do you feel sort of stupid now, mate? How do you think Delgado even knew about the piers?" He put the whip next to Kane's feet. "There's going to be a load of pain soon. Reflect on that."

Kane tried to speak, but all he could manage was an inarticulate rasp.

"Feeling better?" Quinn asked. "Don't worry, it won't last. Because I want you to experience every precious moment, we'll allow a few more minutes to pass."

"What the fuck are you doing?" Damon yelled. He sat with his back against the brick wall, the foot on his shot leg canted unnaturally, the bones shattered. "*Who* do you work for?"

Quinn went into the torture room. Came back out with the drill and an extension cord. He plugged it in, tested the drill. It whined with potential.

"The people you buy the guns for," Quinn said to Damon, "after you cheat them, of course, enjoy the persuasiveness of this jobber. A couple of the Brits I worked with in Oman told me what they saw in Northern Ireland." He strolled to the old man, the extension cord trailing. "I prefer other tools, but let's see how this works. I'm always open to new experiences. Part of the joy of living." He placed the bit above the kneecap of the wounded leg. "This how they do it, eh?" He reached out with his free hand and ripped the dark glasses off Damon's face. The old man's eyes were wide with fear.

"But, of course," Quinn said, "you're thinking you'll give Cappucci all the contracts if I save you, eh?"

Damon squirmed, trying to get away with one good leg. "Sure. Sure."

"But," Quinn said, "I'd be a fool to trust you. Without your Unholy Trinity, there's going to be lots of young eager fellows snapping at your heels. You've made a lot of enemies over the years. Methinks, I'll be better off working with whomever replaces you."

The drill powered and Quinn pressed the bit down, boring into the kneecap.

Damon screamed, the sound bouncing off the surrounding brick.

Quinn maintained pressure on the drill for several seconds, rotating his hand, expanding the hole in flesh and kneecap.

Then he jerked it out, dripping blood.

Damon's scream subsided to a whimper.

Kane flexed his arms, regaining more muscle control.

"Now, old man," Quinn said, "if you'd appreciate release from the pain, begin reciting the names of your Noraid, IRA and gun suppliers. Who'll be picking these weapons and money up?" He leaned forward, turning his head, making a show of putting his ear near Damon's mouth. "Whisper sweet nothings in my ear."

Damon began babbling something that Kane couldn't hear. As Damon was doing so, Quinn glanced at Kane and smiled.

Damon stopped and Quinn stood. "I'll be back to help you," he promised Damon. He walked in front of Kane.

"Moving," Quinn said. "Good."

"Why?" Kane managed to get out.

"'Why'?" Quinn acted puzzled. "Why what? Damon? A mission tasking. You? You're a threat. Nothing personal. You're a do-gooder, aren't you, mate? Getting that harlot out of town. She didn't know about this place when I asked her. She didn't know much of anything. Should have killed her but I'm running a smooth operation that's going to last years. I don't make messes like this cock-up of yours.

"Are you fighting the bad guys, Kane? But we're all bad guys, aren't we? Or are we all good guys? I can't remember sometimes. Still, I've got to maintain my cover and you've gotten a glimpse under it. You know how the dark world works. Not acceptable." He stared at Kane and remained silent for several seconds. Then blinked as if he'd lost his place in his own narrative.

"Who?" Kane asked.

"We playing the five W's now?" Quinn laughed, but there was no humor in it. "We both got the royal fucking over by our countries, didn't we? Except we're rare, useful tools. MI-6 approached me after I was cashiered. Said Her Majesty very much appreciated my actions in saving their ass in Oman and sincerely regretted that the New Zealand government separated me from the service and wouldn't let me come home, but there was a little job they thought I might help her with. As if I didn't know they'd ordered my government to cashier me and exile me." Quinn shook his head. "And you waltz in and blow the whole fucking thing up in less than a week. Truly remarkable. You should get a medal. Of course, they put me in for the VC and I end up here. With you. Isn't life intriguing?" Quinn blinked rapidly, a confused look passing over his face. "Yeah. Yeah. Quite wonderful."

Quinn walked to the film room. "Back in a sec, fellows." He returned, rolling the projector cart minus the device to Kane. Then went to the winch. Kane was lifted higher by the rope through the handcuff's chain, his feet leaving the floor. He was elevated far enough so that Quinn could push the cart underneath his feet, toes resting on it. The rope to the noose was now slack. Quinn went to where he'd tied that off on the pipe and removed the slack, securing it with a knot.

"Better?" Quinn asked. He went to Damon. Picked up the drill. Knelt next to the whining old man. "There, there, let's not be getting hysterical." Quinn grabbed Damon's shirt as the Irish fixer tried to get away.

"Two million!" Damon said. "In the duffels over there. Just take it."

"I can do that," Quinn acknowledged. "Don't really need your permission, do I?"

"You're fucking with the wrong people," Damon gasped. "The Provos will chase you to hell itself, you fucking cunt."

"You gave me names," Quinn said. "They're going to have their own problems soon. Besides they don't know I exist."

"I got insurance too," Damon sputtered. "If something happens to me. Someone knows that I'm here at this meeting."

"Something's *already* happened to you," Quinn pointed out. "And whoever this un-named entity who knows you're here and meeting the fellow with the noose around his neck? They don't know a thing about me. And, let's be honest, you're lying. Desperate people do that."

"It aint just the Provos," Damon babbled.

"Yes, yes, I'm sure." Quinn placed the drill on the other kneecap.

Kane put his energy into his arms and pulled. He was able to lift halfway up, toes leaving the cart, before the muscles couldn't do more. He lowered himself, his legs giving some support through his toes on the cart, but most of his weight hanging by his arms. The cuffs were dug deep into the skin and he was starting to feel the pain. Blood seeped over the metal.

The drill purred and Damon screamed.

Kane pulled up, all the way, his cuffed wrists in front of his face along with the rope to the noose. He lowered himself.

Quinn glanced over his shoulder. "I'll be with you shortly. Don't get ahead of things." He put the drill down and picked up the blowtorch. Flicked a lighter, igniting the flame. "This is where it gets interesting, old fella," he said to Damon.

Kane performed another pull up, eyeing the ropes angling down. The higher he went, the closer he was to them. Angles. Flashes of engineering and drawing classes at West Point.

Damon's screech wasn't human as Damon ran the blowtorch across his face, searing his eyes and burning skin to the bone.

Kane lowered himself, the cart rolling slightly as his toes touched down.

Damon next scream was cut off as Quinn blowtorched him from cheek to cheek, skin burning, peeling away, exposing teeth, the gums burning away, the tongue burnt to a stub.

"Eh, mate!" Quinn stood and faced Kane, the torch hissing in his hand. "What are you trying to do?" Behind him, Damon's face was a burned mess, a mirror of those five severed heads on the board in the 109 precinct. The old man was still breathing somehow as he slowly curled over onto his side, legs pulling up into the fetal.

"Now's when it gets interesting," Quinn said. He pulled a knife and cut the rope to Kane's hands. His weight jerked down on the rope around his neck, pulling the noose tighter. His feet kept it from cutting off his airway and Kane scrambled, grabbing the neck rope over his head, keeping the noose from tightening further.

Quinn pulled the cuff rope free, coiling it and putting it in the canvas bag. "Don't want to waste good rope." He kicked the cart from beneath Kane's feet and all his weight was through his hands on the noose rope.

"Hang on, mate, will you now?" Quinn said to Kane with a laugh as he turned back to Damon with the blowtorch.

The flame ran over Damon once more but there was no further noise as the old man died.

"Well." Quinn turned off the torch and faced Kane. "That's that. He went too fast. Doing all right?" he asked Kane.

As Quinn took a step toward Kane, the lights flickered, then went out.

Kane wasted no time, kicking out with his legs, swinging on the rope, hands keeping a steady grip despite the blood seeping from ripped skin. He swung back and then put all his body into penduluming forward once more, using the momentum. Working on the last mental image before the darkness, he lashed out with his left leg.

The tip of his boot hooked over the upward noose rope. His foot quivered on the line. Kane hung in a precarious balance, then twisted that ankle, getting the rest of his foot over the rope, leveraging with all the strength in that leg. He swung over the upward rope. It slid up his leg, into his crotch, anchoring him with a painful halt.

"What the bloody hell?" Quinn's voice echoed in the absolute darkness.

Kane cinched the rope tight between his legs, leaning his belly and chest on the upward angled rope. He opened his mouth and clamped down with his teeth on the rope. Dared to take his hands off the down rope and reached for his boot as he released with his legs, bringing that foot up. Snatched the short dagger out of his boot.

The lighter clicked and Quinn's face was highlighted in the tiny flickering flame ten feet away.

Kane cut the up-angled rope next to his feet. He fell, hitting the edge of the cart, then tumbled to the floor, a solid thud, and lost his grip on the knife. The noose was still around his neck, the severed rope over the truss.

Quinn had the lighter in one hand, the blowtorch in the other. Quinn brought one to the other, but the lighter flamed out before he could light the torch. Complete darkness once more.

Do something, Ranger!

Kane stood. Training kicked in and Kane grabbed the cut end of the rope dangling in front of him. His cuffed hands operated on muscle memory, loop, turn, through, tying an easy slipknot.

The lighter ignited, illuminating Quinn's face in a halo five feet away. The blowtorch lit with a purring hiss. Kane jumped onto the cart, gaining slack in the rope. Balanced himself on the cart.

Quinn laughed as he came forward with the blowtorch and swept it at Kane's closest leg. Intense pain exploded on the front of his calf but his focus was on the New Zealander. He tossed the expedient noose and it settled over Quinn's neck.

Kane kicked the cart out from under his own feet, pulling his legs up, grabbing hold of the rope connected to his neck as high as he could reach above his head.

The rope went taut and Quinn was snatched off his feet, dropping the blowtorch, the slipknot tightening around his neck. Quinn's hands scrambled, managing to keep the knot from cutting off his airway by getting a grip similar to Kane's.

The rope creaked on the truss as the two men hung in the air from the same rope on opposite sides of the truss, a foot from each other. The blowtorch was sputtering on the floor, casting a cone of light, just enough so they could see the shadows of the other's face.

Quinn's feet scrambled but they were ten inches off the ground. The same distance as Kane's with his knees pulled up.

They both had their hands on the rope, struggling to keep from losing air, passing out, then dying. Kane kept his legs tucked.

Quinn was blinking, trying to focus, to understand this sudden change. "Stand," he gasped as he realized Kane could put his feet on the ground and release the tension in the rope.

Kane smiled.

A spasm of rage passed over Quinn's face, then it displayed nothing for a moment. Quinn returned the smile.

Both men swayed very slightly on the rope, in perfect balance.

Five seconds passed.

Ten.

The blood from Kane's torn palms was soaking the rope, making it slippery. The pain from the burn on his calf was distant, something Charlie Beckwith would have laughed at.

Twenty seconds.

Thirty.

Quinn was still smiling. Kane was breathing, deep and slow.

A minute.

There were sirens in the distance. Someone responding to the explosions? Kane doubted it, given the neighborhood and the muffling of the brick walls and being on the top floor. This was an abandoned building. This was New York City. There were always sirens in the distance.

A minute and a half. The burn in Kane's arm muscles overtook any feeling from the real burn on his calf.

Kane stared into the lack of humanity in Quinn's eyes. The snake. The former SAS soldier, MI-6 spy, mafia hitman, serial killer, sadist, was still smiling. But it was incrementally shifting from smile to grimace.

A refrain chanted in Kane's mind: *'Another minute, Ted. Just one more.'*

"Stand," Quinn harshly whispered. One of his hands slipped and he had to quickly clamber to regain his grip.

'Another minute, Ted. Just one more.'

There was no longer a smile on Quinn's face. Not even a grimace. Confusion was spreading. He dropped an inch of his grip. The slipknot tightened a fraction.

'A New York minute, Ted. Just one more.'

Quinn kicked at Kane, striking a blow, but that dropped him slightly. The slipknot closed that tiny bit.

Kane's vision was fading, black specks floating in his field of vision. His lungs burned. His arm muscles quivered.

'Another minute, Ted. Just one more.'

Quinn's mouth moved, he was trying to say something, but all that came out was akin to a squeal.

Quinn's hands slipped and he scrambled to get a solid hold of the rope, but the noose sank into the skin, cutting off his airway. His eyes went wide. His feet flailed, trying to find purchase but ten inches is forever.

'Another minute, Ted. Just one more.'

Quinn's hands dropped away from the rope and his eyes became vacant as the snake departed.

'We're there, Ted.'

Kane stood.

Wednesday Night, 13 July 1977

MEATPACKING DISTRICT, MANHATTAN

Kane leaned against a light pole and numbly watched a ripple of small explosions punch out the plywood inside the windows on the top floor of the Nabisco building. Flames poured forth through the iron bars but the structure remained intact. His rucksack was on his back although he couldn't quite remember retrieving it or what he'd stashed inside before igniting the thermal charges and escaping. The Swedish K was slung over his shoulder, recovered from the crate he'd hidden it with the ruck under and tried to get to as one of his contingencies.

For the first time since he left the building, he realized the streetlight above him was dark. Not unusual, bulbs burned out. But up and down the street every streetlight was dark. Every building was dark. He wondered if perhaps he'd died and this was part of the process?

Was hell New York City in the dark?

A group of people ran by, yelling and screaming, drinking from liquor bottles. They paused, stared up at the fire, cheered and toasted it.

Kane looked south. The twin towers were two dark fingers except for the red aircraft warning lights at the top. In the far distance, the Statue of Liberty was a black silhouette against the lights of New Jersey except for the torch, which still glowed.

This wasn't the real hell. This was New York City.

Blackout.

What now, Ranger?

"I don't know," Kane mumbled. His legs gave out and he went to his knees, one arm looped around the dirty pole. Pain pulsed from the burn on his calf. Quinn's drug was still in his system, his brain foggy.

"Dai-Yu?"

Hands were on Kane's shoulder, a dark face looking down at him. A gold tooth. There were others with him. Two thin figures flanked the Montagnard.

"Help me," Thao said to his comrades as he slapped a syringe of morphine into Kane's thigh. He fixed the needle through the lapel of Kane's shirt, bending it to remain in place, combat habit intact.

Hands lifted Kane. A man on either side held him as they followed Thao, who had his crossbow at the ready and his machete strapped to his narrow waist. Kane's toes dragged on the street.

Kane glanced left. Wile-E. To the other side: the Kid.

They crossed 15th and went one block south to 14th then turned east toward Washington. They passed under the High Line

Ahead were the sounds of rioting, partying, looting. Sirens in all directions. A city going insane.

"Three more blocks," Thao said as they made a right and headed south on Washington.

"I can walk," Kane murmured, but his feet weren't responding.

"We got you," the Kid said.

"What the hell were you up to, Cap'n?" Wile-E asked.

Glass shattered and looters poured into a bodega to the left.

The small group reached the bend in Washington with the High Line just to the right.

"One more block," Thao said.

A dozen dark figures loomed out of the darker shadows underneath the elevated rail line.

"He's got a fucking crossbow!" One called, laughing,

Thao fired, the bolt hitting the man a glancing strike in the thigh, carving out a furrow of flesh.

"Fuck!" the guy cried out.

Thao reloaded.

Wile-E snatched Kane's .45 out of the holster and fired a round into the air. He leveled the gun at the group.

"We just scare them," Thao said to Wile-E. "No killing. I only wounded."

"Yeah, yeah, okay," Wile-E said.

The group scattered, the man with the wound limping after his comrades in crime.

"Hey," Kane weakly protested.

"Relax, Cap'n." Wile-E slid the pistol into the holster.

The diner was ahead. Standing on the corner of Gansevoort and Washington, torches in one hand, Mac-10 submachineguns in the other, were Van Van, dressed in matching dark suits. Their large car was pulled up on the sidewalk, headlights on, cutting across the front of the diner.

Potential looters were making a wide berth around that corner.

There were candles on the tables in Vic's. The Kid and Wile-E carried Kane inside and followed Thao's directions to put him on the counter. A tall woman floated into his field of vision, vaguely familiar, wearing bell-bottom jeans and a t-shirt, pale skin, short red hair.

She looked down at him "You're a real piece of work, Kane."

"Morticia?" Out of the corner of his eye he saw the Kid and Wile-E go out the door and join Van Van in the street, torches in hand.

"How many people are you going to hire?" she asked as she handed a black bag to Thao. "Do I get a raise? Run the shift?"

"You'll be fine, Dai Yu," Thao said, opening the bag and removing supplies. He handed a pair of blunted medical scissors to Morticia. "Cut away the pants around the injury. Do not pull off cloth that is burned into the skin, please."

"I really have no desire to get into your pants, Kane," Morticia said as she started to cut. "I do this under protest."

Thao checked Kane's body for other damage.

Morticia spoke as she worked. "Ryan was worried about you and—"

"'Ryan'?" Kane managed to ask.

"What happened to your throat?" Morticia was shocked as Thao shone a penlight on the bright red line of torn flesh around it. "Someone hang you?"

"Who. Is. Ryan?"

"The Kid." Morticia tossed a piece of jungle fatigue pants to the side. "He showed up at the end of shift late this morning and said you were asking about the old Nabisco Factory and acting kind of a downer. I told him the last part was normal, but he said more down than usual." Morticia was talking fast. "Then this Wile-E guy showed up looking for a job. He said you'd asked him about the factory too. Going to cut into my tips, by the way, so I want a raise. But we had them start redoing the booths. I'd already picked out the material with Thao. You'll like it."

"Right," Kane managed.

"I bet you don't even remember what color the booths were," Morticia said. "But then the power goes out and I got kinda worried." She grabbed a candle and peered at his leg. Despite her banter, her hands were shaking. "And Thao was kinda vibrating in place, which is hard to tell with him, but he was talking to me more than a sentence at a time, which isn't usual. I figured that meant he was upset. And it wasn't about the blackout. So when those two, what-do-you-call-'em, Yungs? show up, Thao takes Ryan and Wile-E to find you."

"Right," Kane said.

"Still the great conversationalist," Morticia noted as she pulled off the rest of the pant leg.

"What's your real name?" Kane asked, the morphine clouding his brain on top of Quinn's drug.

Morticia smiled. "Ha! Nice try."

"You'll be fine, Dai Yu," Thao repeated. "What happened?"

Kane had a moment of clarity. He sat up. His ruck was on a stool to the side. He pulled open the top. The leather ledger, the camera, and several film cases were inside. "Hide this, Thao."

"Yes, Dai Yu."

Kane shut the ruck. "I killed four wolves and a snake."

Kane laid his head back on the counter. Allowed the exhaustion and morphine to descend.

Friday, 15 July 1977

THEATER DISTRICT, MANHATTAN

"Stop that," Morticia hissed as Kane looked over his shoulder once more, checking the back of the theater. "Enjoy the movie."

"I bet Darth Vader escapes," Kane whispered to Morticia as the theater rumbled with the Star Wars sound track and spaceships firing at each other. Luke Skywalker made his epic run along the canyon on the surface of the Death Star.

Sitting to his left, Morticia punched him, hard, in the arm "Shut up!" she said, but it was loud enough for the Kid, on Kane's right, a bag of popcorn in his lap, to hear. On his other side was Thao.

"Sorry 'bout that," the Kid said.

Darth Vader's companion Tai fighter was hit by Hans Solo's Millennium Falcon and bounced into Darth Vader's advanced Tai fighter, which was sent spinning away from the Death Star.

Morticia leaned forward and across Kane. "Don't worry, sweetie. I love the movie." She slugged Kane's arm. "And you do too, don't you?"

"It's pretty good," Kane admitted and glanced over his shoulder.

Morticia rolled her eyes in the dark.

As the credits eventually scrolled, Kane fidgeted, anxious to be out the theater. The burn on his leg throbbed but it was the feeling of being trapped that prevailed. His hands were wrapped in bandages. When the Kid finally stood, after the screen went black, the three others joined him, the last ones to head for the doors of the theater.

"I hate it when the bad guy gets away," the Kid said.

"Don't worry," Kane said. "Sometimes they don't."

Thao gave him a glance, but said nothing.

They came out into Midtown Manhattan, blinking in the smog filtered sunlight. The city was still in the midst of recovering from the Blackout. The NY Post's headline the previous day had trumpeted *'24 HOURS OF TERROR'*, which, for once, had not been an exaggeration. As they walked toward the entrance for the subway, stretches of sidewalk were still littered with broken glass. Looted and burned out stores were clustered on certain blocks, with no pattern to the violence.

"How is the leg, Dai Yu?" Thao asked.

"Hurts, but works," Kane said. "Pain is weakness leaving the body."

"Tough guy," Morticia said. "You ever gonna tell us what happened?"

"Nope," Kane said.

She shook her head. "You're a piece of work, Kane."

"Do you mean that in a good or bad way?"

"I don't know any more," Morticia said. "Kinda depends on which day of the week it is."

They diverted into the street around a shop owner dumping bags of spoiled food onto the curb.

"And I've been thinking about it," the Kid said, still on the movie. "The chief bad cat was the Emperor, who Vader worked for. He's also out there with his fleet and storm troopers."

"Ah, yes," Thao said, "but the rebels destroyed the Death Star and won the battle."

"Yeah, that's true," the Kid said.

Thao nodded. "They fought the good fight. And there are times when winning and losing isn't as important as fighting for the right reasons."

They reached the dark mouth descending to the subway.

Kane paused and turned to the Kid. "Don't worry. There'll be a sequel where Luke beats Darth Vader. And eventually the Emperor."

"Really?" the Kid said. "You think so?"

"Absolutely," Kane said. "Because we can't let the bad guys win." He looked up. "Hey, it is a sunny day, isn't it?"

The Kid smiled. "Sure is."

They descended into the arteries of New York City, the shadows swallowing them up.

THE END

The next book in the Will Kane series is
Lawyer's, Guns and Money.
It will be published on 16 September. The first two chapters
follow the author's note.

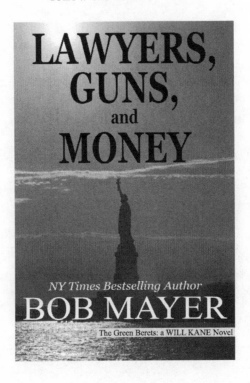

Author's Note:

This story is framed around historical events, but the people and details have been changed, except for significant historical figures.

The West Point class of 1966 lost 30 members, the most of any West Point class, in Vietnam. Four of the eight assigned to the 173rd Airborne were KIA.

Charlie Beckwith did run the Florida phase of Ranger School among his many assignments. He eventually formed Delta Force and led the Eagle Claw mission.

The 173rd Airborne was involved in numerous engagements in Vietnam including the battles of Hill 1338 and Hill 875.

There was a Green Beret Affair in 1969 where a double agent was executed. Colonel Rheault, the commander of the Fifth Special Forces at the time, was the basis for Colonel Kurtz in *Apocalypse Now*.

The Battle of Mirbat on 19 July 1972 was the tipping point in the defeat of the Dhofar Rebellion in Oman and one of the greatest victories in SAS history.

Son of Sam began his reign of terror on 29 July 1976. By July 1977 he had killed five and wounded six.

The New York City Blackout on the night of 13 July 1977 started at 8:37 PM and ended the next day with full restoration at 10:39 PM.

The old Nabisco Factory complex is now known as The Chelsea Market and is the most expensive piece of real estate in New York City.

The High Line is now a park and the 8th most visited tourist attraction in New York City.

Thanks to beta readers Laurie Turner and Ken Kendall.

Book two in the Will Kane series will be:

Lawyers, Guns and Money

Who protects the sheep from the wolves?
Another wolf.
Ex-Green Beret William Kane has crossed the line he vowed never to:
killing. But for every action there is a reaction and now there are forces
after him for revenge, chief among them the IRA. The CIA hasn't
forgotten about him either.
As the long hot summer of 1977 drags on and the Bronx burns,
Kane does some burning of his own, unraveling secrets from his past and
helping those who need his particular brand of justice.
His problem: where is his new line?
Who can he really trust?

Book three will be: **Walk On The Wild Side**. It will be
out in early 2020.

Present day Dave Riley, hero of the *Green Beret* series which
begins after the events of this book, will be back in his next
book on 9 December 2019 in **Old Soldiers**.

LAWYERS, GUNS AND MONEY

By

BOB MAYER

Send lawyers, guns and money
The shit has hit the fan
Lawyers, Guns and Money: Warren Zevon

Thursday Night, 4 August 1977

NEW YORK HARBOR

The Statue of Liberty's torch, flickering in the dark and shrouded by rain above New York harbor, could be an invitation or, more realistically, a warning. Since he was on the water, William Kane, who was fond of maps, likened it to those serpents drawn on the blank spaces of ancient maps with the dire warning: *Here there be monsters!* The city had been savaged by massive rioting during the nightlong Blackout three weeks earlier on the 13th of July, an explosion on top of what many considered two decades of a slowly filling cesspool of blight and decay. There were many who felt New York would never recover and that the Blackout had been the death knell.

Kane was rather ambivalent about the projections. New York had survived many trepidations and would plod into the future in one form or another. He used glimpses of Lady Liberty's torch to the southwest to fix the yacht's position in the rotten weather, drawing a mental line from it to the muted glow of the Twin Towers of the World Trade Center to the northeast. He twitched the dual throttles to keep the forty-two-footer in position, close to Ellis Island.

"That's the subway," Kane nodded his head, indicating the barely visible dark mass in the harbor three quarters of a mile to the north of the Statue.

"Excuse me?" The man Kane had labeled Money, since he wasn't big on remembering names, had been a pain ever since boarding, ordering him about as if Kane were a servant, which technically was true, given he was on the job.

Money was seated in a plush captain's chair to Kane's left rear. The Actress was in the chair next to him. Money was from Texas, a point he'd made within the first minute. He wore tailored jeans, a starched white shirt under an expensive sports jacket, alligator skin boots and a black Stetson crowning silver hair.

Kane's attire wasn't in the same income bracket, or fashion consciousness, with his dyed black jungle fatigue pants, grey t-shirt and denim shirt, sleeves rolled. He wore scuffed jungle boots, black leather, green canvas uppers, bloused inside the cuff of the pants with boot bands. A forty-five-caliber pistol rested in a supple leather holster under the denim shirt on his left hip, two spare magazines behind it on the belt, a commando knife in the small of his back and more assorted weapons here and there.

"Ellis Island," Kane explained his comment as he let go of one of the throttles and pointed. "Most of it is built on debris from subway excavation. Originally, it was only three acres, but landfill expanded that to over twenty-seven. On top of old oyster beds. The island wouldn't exist without the subway and vice versa."

"Doesn't look like much of anything," Money said. "My waste yard on the ranch has more acreage. My people were here long before Ellis Island let in the riff-raff." He checked his watch as if he had an important date, beyond the beautiful woman seated next to him who'd been vaguely pitching him a movie concept since they pulled away from Manhattan. "This is bullshit," he muttered.

The Actress reached out and put a hand on the Money's arm. "See? History. That interests people. That's our film's motif and—"

Money cut her off. "You know what the blackout did to *Superman*? How far over-budget that is?"

"That's because of Brando, not the city," the Actress countered. "They only shot a couple of weeks at the Daily News as a stand in for the Daily Planet. *Saturday Night Fever* is under budget."

"A dancing movie with that disco bongo drum crap. It's buying a stud-bull that can't get it up. It'll disappear without anyone noticing when it comes out." Money waved a dismissive hand. "The city's a pigsty." He indicated Kane. "We need a man with a gun just to go out on a boat. Are there pirates out here?"

Kane wasn't sure if the question was addressed to him, the Actress or rhetorical. His default mode was silence although he found the concept of pirates in New York Harbor intriguing. He vaguely remembered Brother Michael mentioning something about it in the city's history. Captain William Kidd had used the harbor as his base and had something to do with Trinity Church, which still stood

"And there's that loony, Son of Sam, shooting people," Money continued his New York City tirade, interrupting Kane's musings on Captain Kidd. "You know how much securing a set for three months in all the locations in that script would cost?"

The Actress, a voluptuous blonde wearing a low-cut dress that displayed her assets, and whose name Kane also couldn't remember although it rhymed with something, which he also couldn't remember, made a tactical shift in her pitch. "Perhaps if I show you the storyboards? They're in the aft cabin."

Money showed more interest in the possibilities below than above deck. The two descended via the hatch to Kane's left, Money leading. The Actress gave Kane a wan smile and rolled her eyes which earned her some points with the former Green Beret. She slid shut the teak door.

Kane checked his watch. Adjusted the engines and wheel, pointing the yacht north into the outgoing tide combined with the flow of the Hudson. He considered dropping anchor, since he had no idea how long 'going over the storyboards' would take and he was to the west of the shipping channel.

He stared at the faint silhouette of the Statue of Liberty to the port side, dredging up all sorts of history about it and the island upon which it was perched. To the south, the arc of lights on the Verrazano Narrows Bridge occasionally came into view five miles away, the separating line between the Upper and Lower Bay.

Kane cocked his head when he heard a muffled yelp for help. He sighed and headed below. Turned at the bottom of the steps toward the aft cabin. He passed through the Actress's scream as he slid open the door to the cabin. The Actress was on her back on the bed, scrambling to free herself, naked from the waist up. Money lay on top of her, also with his shirt removed.

"Okay, sir, leave the lady—" Kane began, but sensed movement to his right and brought that arm up in a reflexive high block partly deflecting the sap aimed at his head. The lead-filled leather weapon hit him a glancing blow on the side of his head and he staggered back.

Kane dropped to the deck, sweeping the attacker's legs with his left leg. As the man went down, Kane was on top of him, smashing his elbow into the attacker's face at close range. The man scrambled to get away from the furious assault.

Kane let him, getting to one knee and drawing the forty-five, thumbing off the ambidextrous safety as he brought it level.

A muzzle flashed in the open aft hatch and a bullet snapped by Kane's head accompanied by the sound of the gun firing. The shooter was behind and below the sap-man, standing in a small boat bobbing next to the narrow dive deck which helped explain the miss. Kane fired, but the sap-man got in the way and the round hit him in the shoulder, abruptly spinning him out of the hatch and into the small boat.

An outboard engine roared to life.

Two flashes and the crack of shots from the boat and bullets hit the ceiling above Kane. He sidled left, weapon at the ready.

The engine accelerated.

Kane crouched to the hatch on an angle. Peered around, muzzle leading. A zodiac rubber boat was accelerating to the west, a dark figure at the driver's console, a wounded man in the back, and a third figure kneeling and aiming a gun this way, but not firing.

Kane brought the forty-five up, but spun about as he sensed someone behind him.

His finger twitched but he didn't fire at the Actress. He turned back, but the boat disappeared between the Statue of

Liberty and Ellis Island in the rain and dark smudge of the Jersey shoreline.

"Fuck New Jersey," Kane muttered.

"Help him," the Actress said. She'd pulled her top up but that seemed to be the extent of her recovery.

"What happened?" Kane checked Money. It was obvious that Sap Man had hit him. Kane also noted the not inconsiderable pile of white powder on the small table next to the oval bed.

"I saw that guy coming up from behind and tried to warn Mister Crawford," the Actress said. "Did you shoot him?"

She was several lines behind in the script, but at least Crawford was stirring.

"I shot one of them." Kane felt along the wound. "His skull isn't busted. He's lucky."

"You really shot someone?" the Actress asked. "That was *really* loud! Really!"

Kane pulled off his denim shirt and used it to staunch the blood from the wound. "There's a first aid kit in the cockpit. Get it."

"Did you kill them?"

"First aid kit. Now!" Head wounds could be bad bleeders, a fact Kane had first-hand knowledge of given the old scar just above his right temple and extending underneath his thick, dark hair.

Crawford's eyelids flickered. "What the tarnation? Who slugged me?" He tried to sit.

Kane noted an old wicked scar on Crawford's abdomen, just below the rib cage. There was also an eagle, globe and anchor tattoo on the right shoulder.

"Easy," Kane said. "Stay down for a minute."

The Actress returned holding out the kit. "Here."

Kane took it and ripped open a gauze pack.

"I think I'm going to be sick," the Actress said.

"Head's over there," Kane said.

"What?" she was confused.

"Bathroom," Kane amplified. He turned to the older man and replaced the shirt with the gauze. The blood was mostly staunched. "You have a thick skull, Mister Crawford. You'll be okay. What day of the week is it?"

"What?"

"Day of the week," Kane repeated.

"Friday."

"Date?"

"Five August.

"Year?"

"Nineteen-seventy-seven. What in tarnation is going on?"

Kane didn't stop him from sitting up. "You don't have a concussion. You're probably gonna have a bad headache for a bit." Kane walked to the hatch. Some blood spatter on the dive deck. The attackers must have rowed up in the dark from directly behind since he hadn't heard the engine. "You got enemies?" he asked Crawford.

"Sure, I have enemies. No one worth their salt doesn't have enemies." He tried to get his shirt from the deck, but couldn't make it. "A man who doesn't have enemies isn't a man."

Kane picked it up and handed it to the older man. "Enemy enough to want to kill you?"

"What happened?" Crawford demanded as he buttoned the shirt.

"I've got to radio the cops," Kane said.

"Whoa, buckaroo, hold your horses!" Crawford tried to stand, leaned right, and fell back onto the bed. He held up a hand. "Just give me a sec, hombre." He slowly sat up once more, one hand on the bulkhead. "*What happened?*" he demanded in a voice used to being obeyed.

Kane gave a brief summary of recent events.

Crawford didn't interrupt. It took Kane under twenty seconds.

"No body?" Crawford asked.

"One of them is wounded," Kane said. "There's three bullet holes in here."

"They can be patched," Crawford said, but it was obvious his mind was moving on to larger issues.

"Get to the point, please," Kane said to Crawford.

"I'm not going to get stuck in this hell's half acre over a little blood on a boat and some bullet holes," Crawford said. "I've got important business to attend to this morning before I fly home."

"I just shot someone," Kane said.

"Not well enough. He's still breathing."

Kane didn't respond.

"They came at us," Crawford pointed out. "I doubt they'll be going to the police. Let sleeping doggies lie." He reached down and was able to pick up his Stetson without falling over. "Besides, you want to get involved in all this?"

Kane remained still, waiting for the inevitable.

Crawford felt his head, grimaced in pain. His hand came away sticky with blood. "Guess I won't be wearing my hat for a bit." He smiled crookedly at Kane. "Oh yeah, cowboy, we're all in this together."

"You were a Marine," Kane said.

"And you were Army," Crawford said. "Green Beret, right?"

"Your scar?"

"Jap bayonet on Makin Island."

"You were a Raider," Kane said.

For the first time Crawford seemed impressed. "You know a bit of history, eh?" He pointed at Kane with the hat in hand. "You got at least one scar I can see, compadre. And some fresh ones on your wrists and neck. I don't know what you got into recently but it wasn't pretty." Crawford shook his head, but stopped and winced. "Let it go. They'll be a tidy bonus in this for you. Take this boat back to the marina."

"You know who it was," Kane said.

"I don't have a blessed clue who it was," Crawford said. "But don't worry. My people will find out. Let them take care of it. New York cops couldn't find their behinds with both hands. All they're worried about right now is that Son of Sam bastard."

The Actress came out of the head and stood close to Crawford. "Are you all right?" she asked him.

"Fine, darling."

Kane indicated the cocaine. "Is that why?"

"It doesn't put a pretty shine on things," Crawford admitted. "But there's nothing to prove you didn't supply it."

"Please," the Actress pleaded. "I can't get in trouble."

"I shot someone," Kane said, but as he spoke the words, he knew they meant nothing and he was the one behind the script now.

"It's a done deed, cowboy," Crawford said. "And remember. We're the witnesses. We can remember it one way or the other." He looked at the Actress. "You on board, darling?" It was more a threat than a question.

She gave Kane an apologetic look, but nodded assent.

"Right," Kane said. "The marina." He headed for the bridge.

*****

It was still a dark and stormy night, which was a cliché, but clichés are truisms and Kane didn't have many of those in his life so he took it at face value. The rain made the current job easier as he scrubbed the blood off the dive deck. A positive was that the drizzle was warm.

He'd docked at the boatyard from which they'd departed and where Crawford's limousine had been waiting this entire time. Crawford had thrust five thousand in crisp, new hundreds, still bank banded, into Kane's hands without comment, before heading to the limo. The Actress, whose name he still couldn't recall, had scurried after him, barely getting inside before the door was slammed shut and rubber burned as it peeled away.

He considered calling Toni, his boss for this job, and telling her about the evening's events, but he wasn't certain what to make of it, so tomorrow would be soon enough. He pulled out a flashlight and shined it on the deck to check his work. Clean of blood.

There were scuffmarks in the decking that no amount of scrubbing was going to fix. The yacht was a rental, via Toni, and he figured he'd gone above and beyond this evening. She could deal with the boatyard owner and the bullet holes and the marks. It was likely the boat had seen worse damage from partiers.

He sat down, feet dangling over the edge, just above the polluted water of the Hudson River, not exactly feeling like

Huckleberry Finn on the Mississippi. Unconsciously he ran his hand along the scar on the side of his head.

It didn't make sense. One of the intruders had a gun, but the one who'd come in first had used a sap to attack Crawford. If the goal had been killing, the gun should have been first. Or both should have had guns. Unless a kidnapping? Crawford? The Actress? Or had Crawford and the Actress interrupted something?

Kane glanced over his shoulder. Went inside to where the initial attacker had come from the side of the cabin's hatch. There was another hatch there which led to the ladder descending to the engine room. It was unlatched. Kane pushed it open. He flipped on the light.

The bomb lay just inside, on the top rung of the ladder. A red light was flickering on top of the bundle of C-4, then it turned to green.

Wednesday, 19 November 1967

HILL 875, DAK TO, VIETNAM

"Benedicat vos omnipotens Deus, Pater, et Filius, et Spiritus Sanctus."

"Amen," Kane whispers under his breath while he studies the topographic map spread on top of his rucksack with his platoon sergeant.

"Finding God in the foxhole, L.T.?" Sergeant Carter asks.

"He's omnipotent," Kane says. *"He can find me if He wants to. Even here."*

Forty feet away, Father Watters finishes the abbreviated service, holding his hands over the cluster of paratroopers kneeling on the jungle floor around him. "Ite, missa est. Go forth. And be safe, my sons."

The most important aspect of the mass in the midst of the jungle, as far as Kane is concerned, beyond the comfort it gives those who believe, and those who don't, is the large number of soldiers in the cluster. More than ever before. An indicator everyone fears it isn't going to be a good day.

"Hey diddle, diddle, right up the fucking middle," Sergeant Carter complains about the operations order in a low voice only Kane can hear. *"They teach that at West Point?"* Carter is from Detroit, made his rank in Germany and this is his first tour in Vietnam. But he gets some experience points for his tough childhood.

"They taught us Caesar, Napoleon, Grant and MacArthur, to name a few," Kane says. *"They all did right up the middle one time or another."* And Kane remembers from his lessons that Grant in his memoirs regretted only one order out of all the carnage he commanded in the war—the final, frontal assault at Cold Harbor; right up the middle.

Kane looks at the objective; he can see as far as the dense surge of green that marks the base of Hill 875. "Not much choice."

"Why are we taking the hill, sir?" Carter asks.

"Because it's there." Kane tires of the questions to which there are no answers. After five months Kane is a veteran. He has more time in-country than Carter and most of the men in the reconstituted company of mostly replacements.

Kane looks at the trail that runs through the position. They'd marched up it this morning and the attack is going to follow it up the hill. *"I want an OP with an M60 behind us,"* he orders Carter.

Carter frowns and Kane knows he's thinking his platoon leader is putting a valuable machinegun pointing in the wrong direction. But memories of Beckwith and Ranger School always hover in Kane's brain. *'Don't be stupid!'*

"Get the OP out with a 60 and check the men, sergeant."

Kane was moved to Alpha company after the disaster at Hill 1338 in June. He's the senior platoon leader. It's disconcerting that he's commanding Ted's old platoon but there's no one in it who remembers Ted.

As Carter heads one way, Kane goes to the other end of the platoon. He kneels between two men. *"Canteens full?"*

Both young soldiers nervously nod, eyes wide.

Kane looks over their gear. Both are FNG. Kane doubts either of them even shaves yet. He inspects their weapons. *"Listen to your squad leader. Do what he says."*

The FNGs nod.

Kane moves down the line dispensing advice and as much encouragement as he can muster which is almost nonexistent.

Why are *they taking this fucking hill?*

Because it's where the enemy is.

*****

Fierce fighting ahead has been going on for almost an hour. But now?

Bugles behind them.

It's a trap.

The sound of the firing intensifies. Jets are screaming overhead, dropping heavy bombs on Hill 875. Artillery fills the gaps between air strikes.

Kane fires his M-16 on semi-automatic, actually aiming. He sees the enemy occasionally, a rarity. Khaki figures flit among the undergrowth and broken jungle. He implicitly understands they can also see him, but he's *always known they could see him. It is usually their advantage having the Americans blundering into them. But now they're attacking.*

He knows he's wounded and killed some of those figures, but it's not something to spend a moment on in the heat of battle.

He glances left and right, checking his men. Two soldiers are fetaled in their hole, not firing. "Carter!" Kane yells, getting his platoon sergeant's attention. He points at the two.

Carter slithers through the mud and undergrowth to the hole.

Kane can barely hear the radio over the sound of battle; the new company commander is calling in fire. Danger close. 'Grab them by the belt buckle'. That's the NVA's tactic to reduce the American's artillery and air power superiority. Get so close it can't be used.

Except in the direst of circumstances.

Delta and Charlie companies are in the lead and made contact earlier, attacking up hill. But now Alpha is being hit from behind. NVA pouring out of tunnels, coming through the jungle.

They're surrounded.

This isn't the Sky Soldier plan.

This is the NVA plan, long prepared, waiting for the Americans to blunder into the trap. They're in the midst of tunnels and bunkers and long-planned fields of fire.

The NVA are charging, some of them screaming insanely, some laughing, firing their AKs. To the left, a platoon CP, command post, is overrun, all the Americans killed at close range.

The company commander is standing, firing his pistol into the air to keep men from running; to prevent a complete rout.

Kane drops the magazine, slams another home. The perimeter is dissolving, men fading uphill toward Charlie and Delta.

"Hold the line!" Kane screams, but his voice withers beneath the screaming of bullets, artillery and jets.

There are too many NVA.

An M60 machinegun is firing nonstop thirty yards away, further down the trail at the location of the OP. It's the only thing saving Alpha from being completely overrun. Someone is making a stand.

For the moment.

"Hold the line!" Kane yells.

The handset jerks out of Kane's hand. He turns to see the cause. Blood is still pumping from the wound in the center of what used to be the RTO's face.

The RTO's death saves Kane's life as a round snaps underneath the front lip of his helmet and plows along the right side of his head and punches a hole through the rear of the helmet.

Stars explode in Kane's brain and he's knocked off his feet, steel pot flying.

Kane falls on top of his RTO. He's barely conscious, his head ringing. Although his ear is only inches from the soldier's mouth, he can't hear the man's desperate, whispered prayers. He does feel the RTO's final breath.

Kane's blood mixes with the RTO's.

Kane looks up. Jungle, a tiny patch of sky, the canopy shredded by the artillery. Blue sky. A bird flies past. Kane envies it.

The sky is blocked by a brown face leaning over him. Strangely, the Vietnamese smiles, revealing a gold tooth in the center. The Vietnamese says something but Kane can't hear him. He can only see the lips moving.

Bullets snap overhead. Artillery thunders. Kane hears that distantly, on another stage. The M-60 is still burning rounds, a last stand. Kane's head rings.

He's going to die. He knows it. The Vietnamese staring at him is going to kill him, just like Ted. He reaches across his body and pulls his West Point ring off. Shoves it into the blood and piss-soaked mud.

The brown face disappears and Kane feels a tug on his LBE. He's being dragged. Uphill.

He realizes the Vietnamese is a Montagnard CIDG. Kane tries to help, to push with his feet, but his body isn't responding.

The M-60 goes silent.

"Friendly!" the Vietnamese is calling out and Kane finally hears the word.

They're passing bodies. American corpses litter the trail that runs uphill toward Charlie and Delta.

"You heavy," his savior says, pauses, smiles once more. He raises his voice. "Friendly!"

Bullets crack past Americans running, retreating. Alpha has fallen apart.

Kane wants to stand, to issue orders, save his men. He can't get to his feet.

He's pulled once more. Through the mud, broken vegetation. Over an eviscerated body smearing blood and gore.

"Friendly!"

They pass between two wide-eyed, frightened paratroopers. They're pointing their M-16s downhill. The perimeter of Charlie and Delta.

Another five meters. Stops. The brown face is in front of him again. Grabs him by the shoulders and sits him against a tree. Fingers probe the side of his head. He can barely feel them.

"My arm! My arm!" someone is screaming close by. "Where's my arm?"

Artillery. Bombs explodes, the earth shakes.

What circle of hell is this?

"Mom. Mom. Mom." The voice is insistent. Kane wishes it would stop.

Kane's right eye is full of blood. He can barely see out his left. The casualty collection point is thirty feet away, near a CP. Too many bodies. Too many.

Father Watters pulls a paratrooper to the collection point. Someone tries to get him to stop, to make him get down, but Watters shrugs him off and heads back to the perimeter.

"Dai Yu?"

Kane focuses on the CIDG.

The man taps his chest. "I'm Thao."

"Thao," Kane whispers.

Thao points at the wound. "Lot of blood, but skull intact. You be okay."

"'Okay'?" Kane repeats.

A chopper flits overhead, cases of ammo and medical supplies tossed out, and its away fast, bullets following, tattooing the metal.

Kane puts one hand against the tree. Tries to get to his feet, collapses.

Thao points to the casualty collection point. "I get bandages. You stay. Okay?"

"Right." Kane's not sure he actually says the word. Everything is echoing.

Thao scampers off, dodging wounded, empty ammo cases, the dead, broken tree trunks, discarded helmets and other debris of war.

His men need him. Kane has to get back in the fight. He tries to wipe the blood out of his right eye but his hand has little strength.

Thao is back. "Easy, Dai Yu." He wets a piece of cloth and wipes Kane's face, surprisingly gentle amidst all the violence.

Thao has a syringe of morphine.

"No," Kane tries to say. He has to stay alert. Lead his men.

He doesn't feel it when Thao hits him his thigh with the morphine.

Thao gently clears Kane's right eye of blood. Father Watters is on his knees fifteen meters away, cradling a dying soldier in his arms, his head next to the man's ear, whispering Extreme Unction.

A jet screams by, angled across the axis of the hill, drops its bomb. Danger close.

The ground convulses. More screams.

"Weapon," Kane says to Thao. "My weapon."

Thao smiles. "Many weapons here. Wait, Dai Yu." He doesn't have to go far. He returns with a blood smeared M-16.

Thao points toward the sound of the bugles and the AKs and the screams. "I go get more wounded."

How can anyone be alive there?

How can anyone be alive here?

Kane grasps the M-16, uses it as a crutch to get to his feet. He sees officers gathering near the casualty collection point, coordinating the defense. He takes a step in that direction. Feels a whisper of something. Stops and looks up.

A jet is inbound. But it's coming from the wrong direction, along the axis of the ridge instead of across like the others.

The last thing Kane sees, silhouetted against the flash of the exploding bomb, is Father Watters making the sign of the cross over a dying soldier.

About the author: Bob Mayer grew up in the Bronx, New York,
City, graduated West Point, served in the Infantry,
including time as a recon platoon leader in the First Cav
Division, and in Special Forces (Green Berets) including
commanding an A-Team. After leaving active duty he
studied martial arts in the Orient and also was recalled to
Special Operations numerous times for Active Duty
Special Work.
He is the New York Times bestselling author of over 75 books.

His web site is
www.bobmayer.com

Thanks for the read!
If you enjoyed the book, please leave a review. Cool Gus
likes them as much as he likes squirrels!

For free eBooks, short stories and audio short stories,
please go to http://bobmayer.com/freebies/
The page includes free and discounted book constantly
updated.
There are also free shorts stories and free audiobook
stories.

There are over 220 free, downloadable Powerpoint presentations via Slideshare on a wide range of topics from history, to survival, to writing, to book trailers. This page and slideshows are constantly updated at:
http://bobmayer.com/workshops/

Questions, comments, suggestions: Bob@BobMayer.com
Blog: http://bobmayer.com/blog/
Twitter: https://twitter.com/Bob_Mayer
Facebook: https://www.facebook.com/authorbobmayer
Instagram: https://www.instagram.com/sifiauthor/
Youtube:
https://www.youtube.com/user/IWhoDaresWins
Subscribe to his newsletter for the latest news, free eBooks, audio, etc.

ALL BOOKS

THE GREEN BERETS
Eyes of the Hammer   Dragon Sim-13   Cut Out
Synbat   Eternity Base   Z: The Final Option
Chasing the Ghost   Chasing the Lost   Chasing the Son
New York Minute (June 2019)
Lawyers, Guns and Money (Sept 2019)
Old Soldiers (9 December 2019)
Walk on the Wild Side (early 2020)

THE DUTY, HONOR, COUNTRY SERIES
Duty   Honor   Country

AREA 51
Area 51   Area 51 The Reply   Area 51 The Mission

Area 51 The Sphinx   Area 51 The Grail   Area 51
Excalibur
Area 51 The Truth   Area 51 Nosferatu   Area 51 Legend
Area 51 Redemption   Area 51 Invasion   Area 51
Interstellar

ATLANTIS
Atlantis   Atlantis Bermuda Triangle   Atlantis Devils Sea
Atlantis Gate   Assault on Atlantis   Battle for Atlantis

THE CELLAR
Bodyguard of Lies   Lost Girls

NIGHSTALKERS
Nightstalkers   Book of Truths   The Rift
Time Patrol
This fourth book in the Nightstalker book is the team
becoming the Time Patrol, thus it's labeled book 4 in that
series but it's actually book 1 in the Time Patrol series.

TIME PATROL
Black Tuesday   Ides of March   D-Day   Independence
Day
Fifth Floor   Nine-Eleven   Valentines Day   Hallows Eve

SHADOW WARRIORS
(these books are all stand-alone and don't need to be read
in order)
The Line   The Gate   Omega Missile   Omega Sanction
Section Eight

PRESIDENTIAL SERIES
The Jefferson Allegiance   The Kennedy Endeavor

BURNERS SERIES
Burners   Prime

PSYCHIC WARRIOR SERIES
Psychic Warrior   Psychic Warrior: Project Aura

STAND ALONE BOOKS:
THE ROCK   I, JUDAS THE 5TH GOSPEL

BUNDLES (Discounted 2 for 1 and 3 for 1):
Check web site, books, fiction and nonfiction.

COLLABORATIONS WITH JENNIFER CRUSIE
Don't Look Down   Agnes and The Hitman   Wild Ride

NON-FICTION:
The Procrastinator's Survival Guide: A Common Sense, Step-by-Step Handbook to Prepare for and Survive Any Emergency.
Survive Now-Thrive Later. The Pocket-Sized Survival Manual You Must Have
Stuff Doesn't Just Happen I: The Gift of Failure
Stuff Doesn't Just Happen II: The Gift of Failure
The Novel Writers Toolkit
Write It Forward: From Writer to Bestselling Author
Who Dares Wins: Special Operations Tactics for Success

All fiction is here: **Bob Mayer's Fiction**
All nonfiction is here: **Bob Mayer's Nonfiction**